Kiss and Tell

By the same author

Waiting in the Wings

Kiss and Tell

DONNA HAY

ORION

First published in Great Britain in 2001 by Orion,
an imprint of the Orion Publishing Group Ltd.

Copyright © 2001 Donna Hay

The moral right of Donna Hay to be identified as the author
of this work has been asserted in accordance with
the Copyright, Designs and Patents Act of 1988.

A CIP catalogue record for this book is
available from the British Library.

Typeset by Deltatype Ltd, Birkenhead, Merseyside
Printed in Great Britain by
Clays Ltd, St Ives plc

All the characters in this book are fictitious, and any resemblance
to actual persons, living or dead is purely coincidental.

The Orion Publishing Group Ltd
Orion House
5 Upper Saint Martin's Lane
London, WC2H 9EA

Dedicated to the memory of Marjorie Riche

Acknowledgements

I couldn't have written this novel without the inside knowledge of a few people in the business. But since discretion is everything in TV soaps, I can't really name them without wrecking their careers. All I can say is a big thank you to J.S., the most indiscreet soap PR in the world, for the behind the scenes stories. Much of it was too libellous to use, but I enjoyed the gossip. Also thanks to M.S. for the inside information on celebrity weddings. Sorry if I've stretched the facts a bit to suit the story.

To all the soap stars who, wittingly or unwittingly, have given me ideas for this book and made my life so interesting over the past few years. And no, before you ask, you're not in it . . .

To Justine Holman at *TV Times*, Hellen Gardner at *Soaplife*, Jonathan Bowman at *Inside Soap* and all at *What's On TV* for helping to pay the mortgage and giving me access to the fascinating world of TV soaps.

To my friend Maureen Clark for passing on some of the valuable lessons she learned at university. So that's what they mean by 'higher' education . . .

To my agent Sarah Molloy and all at Orion, especially Jane Wood and Rachel Leyshon for their editing skills, Laura Wolverson for her help in publicity and the art department for doing great things with the cover. Also a special thanks to

Selina Walker, even though she took one look at the manuscript and promptly resigned.

Last but not least, thanks again to my husband Ken and daughter Harriet for being incredibly patient and supportive, for living on takeaways and for putting up with more artistic tantrums than anyone should ever have to tolerate.

Chapter 1

'You may kiss the bride.'

Jo smiled up at her new husband as he lifted her veil and lowered his head to kiss her. As their lips touched, a hush fell over the congregation, broken only by the sound of her mother's sobbing.

Then, suddenly, the doors at the back of the church creaked open and a woman stood there, silhouetted against a shaft of light. All heads turned to follow the elegant blonde as she stalked up the aisle towards them, her high heels clicking on the flagstones, her face hidden by her sweeping Philip Treacy brim.

'What the – who is she?' Jo glanced at the man at her side. He looked as if he'd been turned to stone. 'Steve?'

'Well, Steve? Aren't you going to tell her who I am?' The woman turned to Jo, her smile mocking. 'Perhaps I'd better introduce myself? I'm –'

'Cut. Sorry everyone, the boom was in shot. Can we go again?'

A groan went up from the congregation. All eyes turned accusingly to the man on the other end of the long pole holding the furry boom mike, who looked sheepish.

'Shit,' the blonde muttered. 'That's the first time I remembered my lines.' She turned and stalked back up the aisle, slamming the heavy door behind her.

'Right, if we could just go back to the kiss?' The first assistant director was silent for a moment, listening to the director's instructions on his headphones.

'And . . . action.'

This time it went without a hitch. As the first assistant called cut, there was a collective sigh of relief and everyone started talking at once. The vicar disappeared behind the choir stalls for a cigarette, a make-up girl arrived to touch up the mystery woman's lipstick, and the actress playing Jo's mother retrieved her copy of the *Guardian* from under the pew. As the grips moved in to position the heavy grey camera for the next shot, Jo turned to her husband of just three minutes.

'If you ever,' she hissed, '*ever* try to stick your tongue down my throat again I'll knee you so hard in the balls you'll be singing soprano. Is that clear?'

Brett Michaels leered. 'Go on, you loved it really. I know you single mums are desperate for it.'

'The day I get that desperate I'll shoot myself.'

'You don't know what you're missing, love. I've never had any complaints before.' Brett's muscles bulged inside his morning suit. As macho Steve Stagg, he was *Westfield*'s resident sex symbol. Several million women tuned in twice a week just to see him looking sweaty and wearing a vest. He was square-jawed, brutishly handsome and the most obnoxious man on TV, with the possible exception of Jeremy Paxman.

'Really?' Jo smiled sweetly. 'That's not what I read in the *News of the World*.'

That got him. He was still recovering from the Sunday tabloid revelations of his latest conquest, a wannabe glamour model called Linzi he'd picked up during a personal appearance in a Leeds nightclub. According to her, his ego was the only enormous thing about him.

His mean eyes narrowed. 'That little scrubber! She was just a scalp hunter.'

'Why was she wasting her time with you, then?' Jo stroked his cropped head. The charge hand, who was crawling around at their feet chalking their positions on the floor, gave a muffled snort. Everyone knew Brett was hypersensitive about his premature hair loss.

'At least I can always find someone to go to bed with!'

'Even if she does come in a box with a puncture repair kit.'

His brow was still furrowing over that one when she walked away, picking her way over the snaking electrical cables. 'Nice frock, by the way,' he called after her. 'Make the most of it, won't you darling? From what I hear it could be your only chance to wear one!'

Bastard, Jo thought. A readers' poll in *Inside Soap* magazine had just proclaimed him the Sexiest Man on TV. Whoever voted for him had obviously never been close enough to smell his breath.

There was a break while the cameraman set up the next scene. Jo wandered outside. It was a muggy July day and she could feel her gravity-defying hairdo wilting under her veil in the damp heat. The crew swarmed amid the crumbling, moss-covered gravestones of the churchyard, their t-shirts and jeans mingling incongruously with the smart suits and pastel hats of the wedding guests, clutching scripts, checking light levels and discussing camera angles.

Over by the beech tree, the unit manager squinted up at the dense yellow clouds gathering overhead. Jo could guess what he was thinking. They'd already done some outside shots in bright sunshine earlier that morning. A sudden downpour could mess up the continuity and wreck the whole shoot.

The real vicar was watching in bewilderment from the steps of the vicarage. Jo greeted him with a wave. 'Nice day,' she called.

'Is it?' He raised his eyes gloomily. 'I've just caught one of

3

your lot trying to move the font. He reckoned it didn't look right where it was.'

'Oh dear.'

'I told him, it's looked all right there since 1856.' He shook his head. 'I don't know what the PCC are going to say about all this. I only agreed to do it because I thought it might help our organ restoration fund. I didn't realise you were going to take the place over.' He nodded towards the string of dark blue Talbot TV lorries parked outside the lych-gate. 'You do realise I've got a funeral at four o'clock?'

'Sorry.' Jo hurried away guiltily. What else could she say? It was always the same with TV crews. When the *Westfield* circus rolled into town, everyone was expected to make way for it.

She pulled at her frilly neckline to cool herself down. She'd been sweltering inside her wedding dress for nearly six hours and her feet had swollen inside her white stilettos. She'd been fantasising about slipping them off but now she wasn't sure she'd manage it without surgery.

It had been a long day, and not a very easy one. Jo disliked location filming at the best of times, and this certainly wasn't one of the best. They'd arrived at seven that morning to find the unit manager arguing with a man from the council about parking arrangements. A lorry full of lighting equipment was stuck in traffic somewhere on the York outer ring road, and worst of all, the catering van hadn't turned up. Deprived of mood-enhancing coffee, the crew had started bickering and even Madge, the usually even-tempered make-up artist, was chucking blushers around in the wardrobe van. Everything had got hopelessly delayed, which meant hours of sitting around interspersed with bursts of frantic activity.

Tempers might have been fraying on set, but at least the fans were enjoying it. 'Coo-ee! Stacey love! You look gorgeous!' A small crowd of onlookers waved and cheered from the other side of the wall. Jo raised her hand in greeting. After four years in *Westfield*, she'd got used to people calling her by her character's name.

But the public's devotion never ceased to amaze her. *Westfield* would never be as big as *EastEnders* or *Coronation Street*, but the twice-weekly soap set in a York housing estate was still cult viewing. It basically told the story of two women – the formidable Ma Stagg and her extended family of thugs and delinquents, and tart-with-a-heart Maggie Evans. Maggie's countless failed marriages and relationships had left her with two grown-up daughters. Jo played the eldest, Stacey, a kind-hearted but not too bright girl who ran the local hairdressing salon with her younger sister Winona.

Today was a huge day for her character and for *Westfield*. It was the day when Stacey married Ma Stagg's eldest, macho minicab-driver Steve. For the first time, *Westfield*'s two great dynasties would be joined – unless you counted Maggie's one-night stand with Ma Stagg's husband Leonard after a drunken party in the Red Lion.

No wonder the public had turned up to watch. For the past year they'd followed the on-screen courtship, with all its ups and downs and inevitable dramas. Now they huddled under the watchful eyes of the Talbot TV security guards, clutching banners with 'STACEY 4 STEVE' on them. It amazed Jo that they could still believe it was all real, in spite of the cameras, the microphones and the fact that the wedding guests were milling around eating bacon sand-wiches.

Gravel crunched under her shoes as she picked her way down the path towards the catering van, which had finally turned up. Some of the wedding guests gathered around the hatch in their morning coats and elaborate hats, clutching styrofoam cups of coffee. Jo joined the queue behind a couple of extras, or background artists, as they were officially known.

'I was at that *Coronation Street* funeral last week,' one of them was saying. 'You know, you really can't beat Granada's catering arrangements.' She took a sip from her cup and grimaced.

'I know, they just can't seem to manage it here, can they?' They blocked the hatch, ignoring Jo as she bobbed impatiently behind them. 'So you were at the funeral, were you? They asked me, but I was a road accident in *Peak Practice* that day.'

'Excuse me,' Jo butted in finally. 'Do you think I could just get served? Only they'll be calling me for my next scene in a minute.'

The women stood aside. Jo could feel them looking her up and down as she ordered her coffee and doughnut. As she walked away one of them muttered something about 'pushy stars'.

'Looking down on the rest of us, just because her name's in the credits. I've been there too, you know. I was one of the first guests at Crossroads Motel.'

'Bet she's only been in the business five minutes,' the other agreed. 'Wait until she's been doing this as long as I have.'

'If she lasts that long. Between you and me, I've heard *Westfield*'s going down the ratings like a stone.'

Jo took her coffee and doughnut back to her trailer. On the way, she passed another, bigger caravan with blacked-out windows. This belonged to Eva Lawrence, *Westfield*'s oldest and biggest star. She'd been playing bossy matriarch Ma Stagg ever since the show started, and she never let anyone forget it. Her outrageous demands and starry tantrums had earned her a fearsome reputation on the *Westfield* set, along with the nickname Eva the Diva.

She never mixed with the rest of the cast, emerging from her trailer only when she was summoned for a take. The only one who was allowed anywhere near was her simpering personal assistant Desmond, a middle-aged man with all the backbone of a jellyfish. Jo could see him standing under a yew tree, limply holding three leads while Eva's fluffy, yapping little Bichon Frises did their doggy business around his feet. She used to feel sorry for Desmond, until she realised he actually enjoyed being downtrodden by Eva the Diva.

As with everything else at *Westfield*, there was a pecking order in the accommodation. Eva and Brett had trailers to themselves, closest to the set. Jo's was furthest away, and shared with the rest of her screen family. They were already there as she wrestled her crinoline through the narrow doorway, trying not to drip coffee down her cleavage. Lara Lamont, who played her younger sister Winona, was slumped in the only comfortable chair, a Gucci biker's jacket over her cerise bridesmaid's frock. She acknowledged Jo's arrival with a brief glance while yapping into the mobile phone she kept glued to her ear between takes.

'What do you mean, they won't let me choose my own stylist? Don't they know I'm doing them a big favour, posing for their crappy fashion shoot?' She shifted her long legs fractionally to let Jo struggle past. 'I don't care where they're flying me on location. I'm telling you Bernie, if I don't get my own stylist I ain't even leaving the airport.'

At the far end of the trailer, Viola Washington, who played their mother Maggie, took off her blonde wig and shook her henna-ed curls free. They spilled over her shoulders, clashing with her tight yellow suit. 'That's better. I thought my scalp was going to melt with that thing on.' She fanned herself with her wig. 'God, it's like an oven in here. You'd think they'd have air conditioning in these trailers, wouldn't you? I bet Eva the Diva's got air conditioning.'

'I bet Eva the Diva's got Desmond fanning her with a palm leaf.' Jo manoeuvred herself into the narrowest of chairs, her skirt billowing around her ears.

'Yeah right, Bernie, and what do I get out of it?' Lara's shrill voice filled the trailer. 'Some poxy holiday in Antigua. Did you tell them *OK!* has offered me a fortnight on the QE2? Did you?'

'Who's she talking to?'

'God knows. Another deal she's cooking up, I suppose.' Viola rubbed her eyes wearily. Away from the cameras, she abandoned Maggie's broad Yorkshire accent for her usual RADA drawl. She was a cultured, intelligent woman in her fifties, and about as far away from brash man-eater Maggie as it was possible to get. 'So how did it go with Steve the Stud? I notice he had you in his oily clutches.'

Jo shuddered. 'Don't remind me. Being kissed by Brett Michaels is like snogging a bicycle inner tube, only not quite so arousing.'

'Tell me about it, darling. I had an unfortunate little love scene with him last Christmas, remember?' Viola pulled a face at the memory.

'Doesn't sound like the lovely Linzi was too impressed either, judging by that *News of the Screws* story.'

'I know, wasn't it fabulous?' Viola smiled wickedly. 'You know, I hate those kiss and tell stories, but if anyone ever deserved it, it's that creep.' She put on the granny specs that hung from a chain around her neck and picked up her *Guardian* crossword. 'By the way, the press office dropped off a note for you. I stuck it in your mirror.'

Jo plucked out the envelope. Meanwhile, in the background, Lara was rapidly reaching diva pitch.

'No, you listen to me, Bernie. You tell them if I don't pick the stylist the deal's off. Understand? Off!' She jabbed the button on the tiny phone and flung it down on the counter top. 'Who the hell do they think they are?' she hissed. 'It's not as if I even need the stupid bloody publicity.' She swept her trademark long black hair off her shoulders. 'Christ, I'm doing them a favour. They're lucky to get me, you know. I turned down *Hello!*' She frowned. 'What's that you've got?'

'Just an interview request.' Jo stuffed the note into her bag. 'I'll give them a ring when we finish filming.'

'You're not going to do it, are you?' Lara stared at her in

8

horror. 'Why don't you just get the press office to give them some quotes? They do all mine.'

Only because they're afraid you're going to say something thick. Jo still remembered the press officer's exasperation when Lara had been asked for her views on European Monetary Union, and had somehow got the idea that she was discussing the Emu that had once lived on the end of Rod Hull's arm.

'Next you'll be telling me you answer all your fan mail!' Lara sneered.

Jo blushed. She didn't actually reply to all of them. She'd stopped answering the ones in green ink postmarked 'Maximum Security Wing' since that unpleasant incident with the underwear. 'So what do you do with yours?'

'The press office deals with it.' Lara gave a bored shrug. 'They handle all that kind of stuff.'

'Unless there's money in it,' Viola observed from behind her newspaper.

'And why not?' Lara's jaw jutted defiantly. 'The press give us a hard enough time, using our private lives to sell their papers. Why shouldn't we exploit them too?'

Before either of them could answer, Lara's phone trilled again and she snatched it up.

Jo and Viola exchanged glances. Lara Lamont was twenty years old and exotically beautiful, with all the youthful arrogance of someone who had never had to sit by a silent phone waiting for work. Until three years ago her biggest claim to fame had been a walk-on part in a Burger King ad. Then a *Westfield* casting scout had plucked her from the obscurity of a Leeds youth theatre and catapulted her into the limelight. From a Saturday job in Miss Selfridge, she now spent her nights out in trendy clubs, dated boy bands and – if the press rumours were to be believed – had an expensive cocaine habit. Most dangerously of all, she had started to confuse fame with talent.

Jo finished her cake and brushed the crumbs off her frock.

9

She took a quick look at herself in the mirror and winced. It was very Stacey – shiny white satin with a ruched-up skirt, puffy sleeves and a low-cut bodice scattered with handfuls of rhinestones. Her dark blonde hair was caught up in a mass of ringlets under a sparkly tiara. Dolly Parton meets Bo Peep with a touch of Ivana Trump thrown in, she decided.

'My mother would love me in this,' she said wistfully.

Viola looked sympathetic. 'Still putting pressure on you to get married, is she?'

'Pressure? My mother would make the Moonies look positively laid back.'

She tweaked her veil over her face. What her mother failed to understand was that finding the right man wasn't that easy. She was thirty-three years old, with two children and a job that put her in the public eye. She'd had more than her fair share of men who wanted to date her because she was famous, men who resented her because she was famous, and men who couldn't wait to become famous themselves by telling the world what she was like in bed. Experience had made her cautious.

Besides, she already had one failed marriage behind her. She was in no hurry to rush into another one.

'Maybe you should give up on men?' Viola suggested. 'Stick to women. I could fix you up, if you like?'

Jo smiled. Viola played a nymphomaniac on screen, but away from the cameras she ran an animal sanctuary in the Yorkshire Dales with her lifelong partner Marion. The newspapers had tried to do a few shock-horror lesbian exposés on her, but given up when they realised her life was neither shocking nor horrific, but actually rather dull.

'Thanks, but I don't think my mother would ever forgive me,' Jo said. 'It's bad enough having an actress for a daughter. If I turned out to be gay as well she'd never be able to hold up her head at the Nether Yeadon Ladies Bridge Club again –'

'Fucking hell!' Lara's shriek interrupted them. She switched off her phone. 'You'll never guess what!'

'Don't tell me.' Jo adjusted her tiara. '*Hello!* has offered you ten grand and a week at Butlins?'

'Huh?' Lara frowned. 'Oh, I get it. A joke, right? Very funny.' She looked around at them. 'Trevor Malone's been sacked.'

'You must have got it wrong,' Viola said. 'Trevor Malone's fireproof.'

'Apparently not.' Lara waggled the phone at them. 'Not from what I've just heard, anyway.'

The stunned silence was broken by a rap at the door and the production assistant calling out, 'They're ready for your next scene.'

As usual, they were filming the scenes out of order, starting with the wedding ceremony inside the church. For the rest of the afternoon they were doing outside shots of Jo arriving with her mother and sister, who were still trying to talk her out of going through with the wedding.

Unlike in the studio, they only had one camera on location, which meant every scene had to be shot several times from different angles. It was slow going. Then, just when Jo thought it was all over, the production assistant pointed out that Lara had her hair tucked behind her ear for one take and not the other, which meant redoing the whole thing all over again.

Jo lost count of the number of times she ran up and down the church steps. All she knew was that she had blisters the size of satellite dishes.

'Remember it's your big day. You're supposed to be radiant with happiness,' the first assistant director reminded her. He acted as go-between on set, taking orders from the unseen director, who lurked in one of the string of dark blue lorries, hunched over a bank of monitors with the vision mixer and production assistant.

'You try being bloody radiant in these shoes,' Jo muttered. The air was still oppressively hot, the putty-coloured clouds so low they seemed to be pressing down on her as she leaned against a gravestone, fanning herself with a script. She could feel herself getting a headache, which wasn't helped by the scratchiness of her veil or the steady thrum of the generator in the background.

Added to which there was all the muttering going on between takes. It seemed to get louder as the afternoon wore on.

'Apparently he was called into a meeting with the Head of Drama this morning.'

'Nigel in post-production saw him clearing out his desk about an hour ago.'

'The press office has denied it, so it must be true.'

Poor old Trevor, Jo thought. As far as everyone was concerned, Executive Producer Trevor Malone was *Westfield*. He'd come up with the original idea fifteen years before. He'd created the York housing estate and all the characters who lived there. He decided who was to be born, and who was to die. It was like telling God he wasn't up to the job any more.

By the time filming finished for the day, the press office had given up trying to deny the rumours.

'Why did they get rid of him, do you think?' Jo wondered as she and Viola took off their make-up in their trailer. Lara had already rushed off for a crisis meeting with her agent.

'I don't know. Falling ratings, I expect. *Westfield* hasn't been doing too well lately. I suppose they think they should get someone new in.'

'Yes, but to sack Trevor —' They all owed him so much. He was like a father-figure to the cast, firm but fair, and always very good about people taking time off for the odd panto or extended holiday in the rehab clinic. 'I feel so sorry for him.'

'It's us I feel sorry for.' Viola fluffed up her curls. 'You don't know what it's like when a new Executive Producer takes over. They want fresh talent. New blood. Sexier characters. You wait and see. In six months this place will be crawling with the likes of Lara Lamont.' She drew a sharply-nailed finger across her throat. 'It's not just Trevor's head that will roll.'

'Oh God.' Jo slumped in her chair, her wedding veil in her hand. *Westfield* was her security. And with two children to bring up, the last thing she needed now was to be on the dole and looking for acting jobs.

'You'll be all right.' Viola noticed her dismayed expression. 'You're young and pretty, and the viewers like you. It's the oldies like me they'll want to get rid of.' She leaned forward, examining her neck. 'I wonder if I should have my face lifted?' she mused.

But Jo wasn't listening. In spite of what Viola had said, she wasn't reassured. She'd heard about this happening time and time again. Ratings were falling, so it was out with the old and in with the new.

And if they could get rid of Trevor Malone, surely no one was safe?

Chapter 2

She was looking forward to a peaceful hour or two to reflect on the problem when she got home, as it was Duncan's turn to look after the children. But as soon as she put her key in the door and heard squabbling from upstairs she knew it wasn't to be.

Ignoring the thuds and crashes from overhead, she went into the sitting room, where Roxanne the resident but very part-time nanny was curled up on the sofa, getting stuck into some juicy phone gossip.

'He never! The cheeky bastard. I hope she told him where to go?' She frowned as Jo entered the room. 'Look, I've got to go,' she said grudgingly. 'Yeah, that's right. She's come home.'

She put the phone down with a martyred sigh. 'What are the girls doing here?' Jo asked.

'*He* dropped them off about half an hour ago. Said he had some work to do.'

'Again? But that's the second time this week.'

'Yeah, I know. And he said he can't have them this weekend either.'

'You're kidding?'

'I'm not. I'd say something about it if I were you.' Roxanne picked moodily at her split ends. She was a lanky twenty-year-old with an unfortunate complexion and all the infectious enthusiasm of a slow worm.

Bugger. Jo's heart sank as her fragile domestic arrangements crumbled around her. Why was her ex-husband always doing this to her?

She dumped her bag and fleece jacket on the hall stand, pulled off her trainers and went into the kitchen. As she flicked the switch on the kettle there was a crash from upstairs that rattled all the mugs on the draining board. Jo leaned against the worktop and braced herself. Sure enough, a moment later she heard feet thundering down the stairs.

'Mummy, tell her!'

'You tell her to keep her hands off my things.'

'I wasn't touching your things. I wouldn't want your stupid, stinking things.'

Jo switched the kettle off and reached into the fridge for a bottle of wine instead. So much for slowly unwinding from the day. She'd only been in the house five minutes and already she felt like a coiled spring.

'What's for tea?' Chloe changed the subject abruptly. She was six years old and alarmingly like her father, with her fair curls, blue eyes and absolute certainty that she was always right.

'Give me a chance, I haven't thought about it yet.' Another domestic obstacle reared up before her. She hadn't planned on cooking anything. Besides, the children's tea was another of Roxanne's largely neglected duties.

'But we're hungry.'

'I'll think of something.'

'Daddy's got a new car.' Chloe changed the subject again.

'Has he indeed?'

'It's a Landrover Discovery,' Grace added. She picked a handful of grapes from the fruit bowl and stuffed them in her mouth. 'You should see it, it's really cool. Why can't we have a car like that?'

'Because we can't afford it.' And neither could Duncan. At least, that's what he always told her whenever she asked for some money for the children. 'Anyway, it's far too pretentious,' she added. 'Why does he need a Landrover in York? The most rugged terrain he ever encounters is Tesco's car park.'

She topped up her glass and decided she owed Duncan a furious phone call when she felt up to it.

'Did you have a good day at school?' she asked.

'Not really.' Grace picked off more grapes. 'Don't forget I'm going to Sophie's bowling party tomorrow.'

'Tomorrow?' Jo stared at her, appalled. 'Why didn't you tell me?'

'I put the invitation on the noticeboard, like you said.'

Jo looked at the pinboard, groaning under the weight of funny cards, family photos, Chloe's drawings and, buried deep underneath, important letters. When did she ever have time to wade through that?

'You should have reminded me.'

'I'm reminding you now.'

'I mean a couple of days ago, not now! Where the hell am I going to conjure up a present from?' She looked wildly around the kitchen, wondering how Sophie would feel about a gift-wrapped packet of salt and vinegar crisps.

'We could make something?' Chloe suggested. 'Like a Barbie house. They did it on *Blue Peter* yesterday. You just get a box, and cut out some little holes —'

'Yeah, right!' Grace snorted. 'I'm really going to turn up at a party with a stupid box, aren't I? Besides, no one takes presents to parties these days. It's so — babyish.' She gave Jo a withering look. Grace was eleven going on nineteen. She bristled with cool, from her braided hair to her oversized trainers. But underneath she was as shy as her sister was outgoing.

'I like presents on my birthday,' Chloe protested.

'That's because you're a baby, isn't it?'

And then they were off again, bickering and sniping at each other. Jo sipped her wine, closed her eyes and tried hard to think beautiful thoughts. But they all came back to how much she wanted to strangle Duncan.

'Right, that's it.' She put down her glass. 'I'm going to phone your father.'

An awed hush fell. 'I hope you're not going to start swearing?' Grace said reprovingly.

'I don't swear.'

'Yes, you do!' Chloe pointed out. 'We heard you. The last time you had a row, you called Daddy a —'

'Well, this time I'm going to stay perfectly calm,' Jo cut her off. 'But you'd better go upstairs just in case,' she added as an afterthought.

The phone was answered by a very young, foreign-sounding girl. Jo was still struggling to make herself understood when Duncan came on the line.

'So much for working,' she said tartly. 'No wonder you couldn't have the girls.'

'As a matter of fact, Thea is helping me research my next chapter.'

'I bet she is.'

Duncan sighed. 'Is that why you called, to interrogate me about my love life? I thought all that finished when we split up?'

'I couldn't care less who you sleep with,' Jo snapped. 'Why did you send the girls home?'

'I thought I explained to that half-witted nanny of yours, I have to work.'

'And what do you think I do all day? Knit? You know I have a script to learn —'

'Oh come on, darling, it's hardly the same thing is it? How long will it take you to learn a few lines? Especially when most of them are only one syllable.'

Jo gripped the phone tighter, imagining it was Duncan's smug little neck. 'We can't all produce works of art all day. Some of us have to earn money, real money, instead of contemplating our navels.'

'And some of us would rather not compromise our artistic integrity.'

'Integrity doesn't pay the bills, Duncan. And it doesn't put shoes on your children's feet. Or buy big cars,' she added waspishly.

To her annoyance, Duncan just laughed. 'Oh dear, here we go again. Why do I feel another lecture coming on? How poor hard-done-by Jo has had to sacrifice her promising theatre career to feed her children because bad old Duncan refuses to churn out commercial trash.'

'I'd be amazed if you churned out anything,' Jo retorted. 'One novel in three years is hardly prolific, is it? When are we going to see this next masterpiece of yours?'

'When it's finished. Which won't be very soon if you keep disturbing me.'

'So about this weekend –'

But he'd already hung up. Jo slammed down the phone, wondering how she'd ever married someone so self-centred.

But she'd been just the same, once upon a time.

They'd met at university. She was studying English and drama, he was one of her lecturers. Despite the ten-year age gap, they'd shared the same dreams. He was going to write the definitive modern novel. She was going to take the acting world by storm.

But then real life intervened. A year after leaving college Jo found herself pregnant. By the time she'd got over the shock, she and Duncan were married.

Grace's birth might have been an accident, but it changed her life. Suddenly playing all the major Shakespeare heroines by the time she was thirty didn't seem as important as taking care of her precious baby daughter. Duncan was surprised at her loss of ambition, but grudgingly agreed to stay in his college job to support them. The plan was that when Grace was older Jo would go back to work so he could concentrate on his writing.

Which she did, for two years. And then Chloe came along.

If getting pregnant with Grace was a surprise, Chloe was a disaster. This time Duncan wasn't so understanding. He resented being forced to take over as breadwinner again. He wanted Jo to have an abortion, but she refused. Frustration and arguments followed, and within a year of Chloe's birth they'd split up.

Jo listened to Chloe's imperative tones ringing out from the sitting room. How ironic that the child Duncan hadn't wanted to be born should turn out so much like him. But unlike Duncan, Jo had adored her from the moment she was born.

Her script lay on the work surface. She put it guiltily to one side and started to prepare supper. Perhaps if she could keep Roxanne off the phone long enough, she might be able to snatch half an hour to go through the next day's scenes.

But no such luck. She was draining pasta over the sink when Roxanne appeared in the doorway. 'Right, I'm off now,' she announced.

'Off? Where? Oh bugger!' Jo missed the colander and scalded her hand.

'Out with my friend Wendy. You said I could go, remember?'

Jo racked her brains. No, she couldn't remember. But with her chaotic life it wasn't surprising. 'It's not your night off, is it?'

'No, but you said I could switch them because *he* was having the girls. You said I wouldn't be needed.' Roxanne stuck out her chin, sensing opposition. 'You *promised*.'

'Did I?' Jo put on her best wheedling face. 'Look, I don't suppose –'

'No.' Roxanne shook her head. 'I can't cancel. Wendy's waiting for me. We're going down Micklegate. I can't let her down, can I?'

'No, I suppose not.' Jo's shoulders slumped. 'Off you go, then. Have a nice time.'

'I will. Don't wait up.' Roxanne tugged her cropped top over her non-existent bosom. Jo looked at the length of leg appearing from her bottom-skimming skirt and wondered if she should say anything. Would her parents in Thirsk approve of her going out like that? But by the time she'd opened her mouth, Roxanne had already gone.

'Yuk, what's this?' Grace made a face as Jo put her plate in front of her.

'Spag bol, what does it look like?'

'That's got meat in it, hasn't it? Vicky Carling says meat is murder.'

'Vicky Carling doesn't have to eat it, does she?'

Grace pushed her plate away. 'I'm a vegetarian.'

'What's a vegetarian?' Chloe piped up.

'Someone who doesn't eat meat.' Grace thrust her face towards her sister. 'You know what you've got on your plate, don't you?' she said ghoulishly. 'Little chopped up bits of baby calf. And do you know how they kill them? They –'

'That's enough, Grace!' Thankfully the phone rang, saving them from more grisly details. Chloe raced to it first.

'Hello, Grandma.' Jo put down her fork. Just what she needed. 'Yes, I'm fine. Yes, Grace is fine too. Mummy?' She ignored Jo's frantic head shaking. 'Yes, she's here. Do you want to speak to her?' She handed the phone over. Jo took it reluctantly.

'I'll deal with you later,' she threatened. 'No, not you Mum.' She leaned back, closed her eyes and prepared herself. Audrey only ever rang for two reasons. One, so she could berate her for being a working mother and neglecting her children, and the other –

'You'll never guess who I had coffee with this morning? Marjorie Redman. You remember Marjorie? Very big in the WI. You and her daughter Susan used to go to Brownies together?' While Jo was still racking her brains, she went on,

20

'She was telling me Susan's just got herself engaged. To a merchant banker.'

'Lucky old Susan.'

'I know. And she's such an unfortunate-looking girl, too. All that hair on her upper lip. And that squint. I don't know how she managed it.'

Jo could hear the naked envy in her voice. Competition for eligible men was fierce among the mothers of Nether Yeadon. After five years as a divorcee Jo sensed she was becoming a social embarrassment, harder to place than a dysfunctional dog at the RSPCA.

'Well, you know what they say, Mum. Love is blind.'

'Of course, Marjorie's delighted,' Audrey went on, not listening. 'I mean, the poor woman was beginning to give up hope. But it just goes to show, it's never too late.'

Even for me, Jo thought. 'Mum, she's only thirty-three. She's hardly on the shelf.'

'Yes, I know. But by the time a woman gets to your age most of the men are either divorced or − you know, the other way.'

'So Susan's tracked down the last single, straight man in North Yorkshire. Good for her.'

'There's no need to take that tone, Joanne,' Audrey sniffed. 'I just thought you'd be interested. After all, Susan is a friend of yours.'

The last time she'd seen Susan was when she'd put a live frog in her sleeping bag on Brownie pack holiday. She hardly counted as a bosom buddy. But Jo could imagine her mother's panic as she ticked off yet another name on her list of her friends' unmarried daughters. Soon she would be the only one left.

'Of course, I suppose it helps that she has such a good job,' Audrey went on. 'She probably meets lots of nice men that way. She's an accountant, you know. Such an interesting line of work.'

'I meet plenty of men too,' Jo pointed out.

'Yes, darling. But they're actors.'

Jo could feel her shoulders hunching around her ears. Grace and Chloe had abandoned their supper and disappeared off to watch *EastEnders*. She wished she could join them. 'Was there something else you wanted, Mum? Only I've got a lot of work to catch up on this evening.'

Oh God, why had she said it? Cue Audrey's second favourite subject. 'You work too hard, you know. If only you had someone to share the burden with –'

'I have a nanny.'

'You know what I mean.'

Jo sighed wearily. 'Yes, Mum, I know. But I don't have to wash the nanny's socks or worry about who she's sleeping with behind my back.'

'Well, if you're going to take that tone –' The phone went down with a crash, leaving her holding a buzzing receiver. She knew she would have to ring Audrey back and apologise. But not yet. First she was going to load up the dishwasher, run herself a long, hot bath and tackle that script.

Most of her scenes for the following day were with Viola. Jo sank under the bubbles and concentrated on the lines. At least her screen character Stacey didn't have too much trouble with her mum. But with three broken marriages, countless disastrous lovers and a reputation as *Westfield*'s resident slapper, Maggie Evans was the last person to hand out advice on her daughter's love life.

She'd barely been in the bath five minutes when the door burst open and Chloe and Grace fell through it.

'Will you help me with my maths homework?' Grace demanded.

'It's hardly my strong point.'

'Doesn't matter. If I get it wrong I can just tell Mrs Carter it's your fault.'

As Grace dashed off to fetch her books, Chloe took off her clothes and climbed into the tub. Jo sighed and put down her

22

script. It looked as if, yet again, Stacey and her emotional dramas would have to wait.

By nine o'clock, she'd finally talked the girls into bed and poured herself another glass of wine. Huddled in her tatty towelling bathrobe, she sat at her dressing table and stared up at an alarming crack in the ceiling. The house, like the rest of her life, was threatening to fall down around her ears.

Her mother was right. It would be nice to have someone to share things with. Someone to come home to at the end of a long day. Much as she adored the girls, it would be wonderful sometimes to have a conversation that didn't revolve around Beanie Babies or boy bands.

But what did she have to offer anyone, except two stroppy children, a chaotic home and a private life that occasionally featured in the *Daily Mirror*?

She picked up a brush and tried to pull it through her hair. Even after three washes it was still tangled with sticky lacquer. No wonder she was fighting a losing battle against the split ends.

For a moment she toyed with the mad idea of having it all chopped short. She'd be hauled up for a major telling-off – it was written into her contract that she couldn't alter her appearance without consulting the producer – but it might be worth it just to watch the production team having a collective coronary.

God knows she needed to do something. She scowled at her reflection in the dressing-table mirror. She might not have Susan Redman's squint or hairy lip problem, but she was no Kate Moss either. Her nose was too short, her mouth too wide. Her hair was just about blonde, thanks to a few fading summer highlights, and cut in a thick, layered bob. Her eyes were large and expressive, but the colour of dirty pond water with permanent shadows of exhaustion.

Yes, it would be nice to find a man, she thought. But men were terribly high maintenance. If she had a man she might have to do something about herself. She might have to go to the gym. She might have to remember to have her legs waxed before they started to look like a Greek taxi driver's. She might have to be vivacious and alluring when all she really wanted to do was slouch around the house in her faded old bathrobe and fall asleep in front of *Newsnight*. On second thoughts, perhaps she was better off on her own.

She was just picking up her script yet again when the phone rang. Jo took a deep breath, hoping it wouldn't be Audrey calling for round two of their mother-daughter ding-dong.

But it was Viola. 'I just thought you ought to know, I've been doing some digging and I've found out who our new Executive Producer is going to be,' she announced breathlessly.

Jo steeled herself. 'How bad is it?'

'The worst,' Viola said. 'It's the Grim Reaper.'

Chapter 3

She sounded so grave Jo nearly laughed. 'Who?'

'Richard Black. The Grim Reaper. Don't tell me you've never heard of him?'

'Well, no –'

'Darling, the man's an absolute monster! How do you think he got his nickname? His appearance means instant death,' Viola said, not waiting for an answer. 'You remember *A Country Village*? That sweet little afternoon soap? Who do you think sent the bulldozers in and turned it into an out-of-town shopping centre?'

'No!'

'And he was the one who put the legionnaires' disease into the central heating ducts at *Willington General*. Wiped out the whole staff in one go. The man makes Stalin look compassionate. You must have heard what happened to poor old Eithne Pollock?'

'Wasn't she in *Coachman's Way*? The one who had the nervous breakdown?'

'That's right. She lived for that programme. It was all that kept her going after her husband left her for a chiropodist. But Black sacked her. Even her therapist begged him to keep her on, but he wouldn't hear of it. A pointless drain on the ratings, he called her. I think it was the last straw for poor Eithne.'

'What happened to her?'

'You might well ask,' Viola said darkly. 'The last I heard, she was demonstrating electric sanders on the Home Shopping Channel. I tell you, the man is death. The question is – which of us will be next?'

With that troubling thought on her mind, Jo fell into bed with her script. She'd just finished reading and turned out the light when she heard feet pattering across the landing. A moment later Chloe's warm little body was snuggling up to hers.

'Mummy,' she whispered. 'Can we have a hamster?'

'I don't think so, darling.'

There was a pause. 'Mummy?'

'Hmm?'

'Have we got millions of pounds in the bank?'

Jo pulled away and looked down at her. 'What makes you ask that?'

'Simon Beckett says we have. His mum reckons because you're on telly we must be filthy rich.'

'Simon Beckett's mum shouldn't believe everything she reads in the papers.'

'And she says that's why you never help out at school. She says you'd probably expect a few thousand to turn up at the summer fête. That's not true, is it?' Chloe frowned.

'Of course it isn't.' Jo cuddled her closer. It hurt when the girls got teased or picked on because of who she was. The only reason she didn't help out at the school was because, like most working mums, she simply didn't have time. Would Simon Beckett's mother be so quick to criticise if she worked in a bank? she wondered. But just because she happened to be an actress and on TV, for some reason everyone thought she was fair game.

'So we don't have millions in the bank?' Chloe interrupted her angry thoughts.

'I'm afraid not.'

'But have we got enough to buy a hamster?'

'We'll see.' A moment later Chloe was asleep. Jo lay awake, listening to her soft breathing.

If only they did have millions in the bank, she wouldn't be worrying now. It hadn't occurred to her just how much she needed *Westfield*. The job might have its drawbacks, but it had given her financial security. After she split up with Duncan, Jo had suddenly found herself alone with two small children and no money. She was too proud to ask her parents for help, especially as Audrey made it clear she blamed Jo for the break-up. For months they'd struggled along on virtually nothing in a dingy, damp flat while she searched for work. She'd done all kind of odd jobs, from waitressing to selling fitted kitchens over the phone, just to make ends meet.

In the meantime, she'd tried to find acting work. But she'd lost count of the auditions she had to turn down because she couldn't find anyone to look after the children, or because the job would involve touring, or filming away from home.

And then, just as she was beginning to give up hope, along came *Westfield*. Trevor Malone's offer was like a dream come true. Suddenly they had enough to live on. It was regular work, and she didn't have to travel. It might not be the challenging career she'd dreamed of when she was at college, but at least it meant she could buy a house, and build a life for herself and the girls.

And now she was in danger of losing it all. Jo stared into the darkness. 'Which of us will be next?' Viola had said.

Guilty and selfish as it made her feel, Jo just prayed it wouldn't be her.

By the following day, news of the Grim Reaper's imminent arrival had spread around the *Westfield* studios. As Jo drove through the security gates, she spotted a removal van parked outside the doors of the main building, which housed all the production offices. Slowing down, she recognised Trevor's battered old desk being loaded on to the back.

Jo felt a twinge of sadness. She remembered standing in front of that desk, the day Trevor offered her the job. He'd seemed so all-powerful then, it was hard to believe he could be pushed aside so easily.

'The king is dead. Long live the king.' Rob Fletcher, who played her screen brother-in-law Tony Stagg, drew up alongside her on his bicycle. He might be a wife-beating womaniser on screen, but away from the cameras he was quiet, bespectacled and a paid-up member of Greenpeace. 'How long before the rest of us are being bundled out like that, I wonder?'

The *Westfield* set, with its outdoor lot, indoor studio sets and annexe of dressing rooms and wardrobe department, stood away from the main production building, separated by a tree-lined courtyard. Jo parked her yellow Cinquecento in its usual spot in the artists' car park, but instead of heading straight for her dressing room, she took a detour into the studio building. Rob's comment had unsettled her. With all the comings and goings around her, she needed to be reassured that at least somewhere it was business as usual.

It was a vast, barn-like building, its high roof criss-crossed by a complex lighting gantry. Inside it was like a little world within a world, cut off from the outside by dense sound-proofing, an odd jumble of little rooms and shops, all with plywood walls, and doors and stairs that led nowhere.

Ahead of her the set dressers were busy in the café set, laying the tables and filling the chiller cabinet with pre-packed sandwiches. They'd done it a million times before so they worked with quick, silent precision, rarely having to consult the memory-jogging Polaroids that showed where all the props should go in each room. These were the regular sets, which featured in every episode. From over on the far side of the building came the sound of hammering and a tinny radio as the other temporary sets were put up for the episode they were due to film the following day.

When Jo had first arrived at *Westfield* it had seemed strange to see the sets, looking much smaller and shabbier than on screen, arranged side by side amid camera equipment, lighting and props. Now it all seemed as familiar as her own home. But for how much longer, she wondered.

She wasn't the only one who was feeling apprehensive. Everywhere Jo went, there were pinched, anxious faces. People were snapping at each other. Every snippet of gossip was seized upon and dissected.

'I wonder when he's coming?' mused Viola, as they gathered in the green room later that morning. It reminded Jo of a student common room, with its fug of cigarette smoke and clutter of coats, bags and scripts on every armchair. The walls were lined with tattered call sheets reminding the artists when they were due in the studio, and pigeon holes stuffed with unanswered mail. A monitor in the corner showed what was happening on the studio floor. Which at that moment was very little, since most of the actors were huddled around exchanging ciggies and information. Besides Jo and Viola, there were Rob Fletcher and another actress, Judy Pearce. Brett was in a corner, playing with his Gameboy in a great show of indifference.

'No idea. They're keeping it very hush-hush.'

'I just hope we get another pay day before we all get the boot.'

'Well, I think it's outrageous,' declared Judy, who played Ma Stagg's downtrodden daughter-in-law Andrea. In real life no one would have dared tread on her. 'We should talk to the union about it. They can't treat us like this.'

'I think you'll find they can, darling,' Viola said. 'You can complain all you like, but if you've got any sense you'll just keep your head down and hope for the best like the rest of us.'

'But what about our contracts?' Judy insisted. 'I'm signed up until the end of the year.'

Viola sent her a pitying look. 'Do you really think that

matters to the Grim Reaper? If he wants you out, he'll find a way to do it. He enjoys undermining people, so I've heard.'

They puffed on their cigarettes in brooding silence. In the background, a couple of bemused technicians wandered on to the monitor screen and off again. Jo hadn't even met Richard Black and she already hated him.

'Well, I think they've made the right choice,' Brett looked up from zapping aliens. 'I've always said we needed some changes on *Westfield*. It's about time we got rid of some dead wood.'

'I take it that doesn't include you?' Jo asked.

'Of course not.' Brett's lip curled. 'They wouldn't dare get rid of Steve. He's the only reason women watch this show.'

Jo fought the urge to slap the smirk off his face. The worst of it was, he was probably right.

'I'm not so sure about you, though,' Brett added. 'Personally, I think it was a mistake to marry Steve off. The viewers preferred him young, free and single. I can't see you lasting much longer.'

'At least it means I won't have to put up with you and your wandering hands,' Jo snapped back to hide her panic.

'If only we knew when he was coming,' Viola said.

'Maybe he's already here?' Rob's eyes darted around the room. 'Maybe he's watching us all now, listening to what we're saying?'

'Don't talk rubbish!' Viola retorted. But they all clammed up instantly.

'This is ridiculous. They can't just keep us all in the dark like this,' Jo declared. 'I think we should go up and find out what's going on.'

'You don't mean – the top floor?'

'Why not? What's to stop us going up there? After all, we have a right to know.'

Everyone stared at her. The top floor was the Mount Olympus of *Westfield*, where all the heads of department lived. Artists were only ever summoned there when they were in trouble, or about to get a big new storyline. No one, but no one, went up there of their own accord.

'Maybe you're right,' Viola agreed slowly. 'Maybe someone should go up and find out what's going on.'

Jo nodded. She was still nodding when she felt all eyes turn in her direction. 'What – me? Oh no, I couldn't.'

'It was your idea,' Judy pointed out.

'Yes, but I wasn't volunteering!'

She was still wondering how she'd been pushed into the job as she stepped through the whispering doors of the executive lift out on to the top floor.

Her footsteps were silenced by acres of flawless cream carpet as she crept down to the end of the long corridor to what had once been Trevor Malone's office. She felt distinctly out of place in her combat trousers, t-shirt and battered old Reeboks, her hair pulled back with one of Grace's pink plastic bulldog clips. Fortunately there was no one around, although she could hear muffled voices from behind closed doors as she passed them. Meetings were in progress. Was Richard Black in one of them? she wondered. Was he already here, stalking the corridors like the shadow of death?

If he was, he hadn't moved into his office yet. Jo found Trevor's door and gingerly pushed it open. A vast, empty space roughly the size of a football pitch greeted her. Ahead, through a wall of glass, the *Westfield* set lay like a toy town. From here she could see everything – the tiny streets, with their shops and house fronts propped up by huge timber struts, and the studios beyond, which housed all the interior sets. How often had Trevor stood at this window, she wondered, looking down over his creation?

She turned away, and nearly fell over a battered old cardboard box sitting forlornly in the middle of the floor, bearing the words, 'RUBBISH FOR DISPOSAL'.

Jo felt a pang. That just about summed it up for Trevor. Perhaps for all of them.

Then something caught her eye. A glint from under the flap of the box. Jo knelt down to look, and her breath caught in her throat.

There, stuffed into the box with all Trevor's old papers, some books and the battered name plaque from his door, was a small glass statuette. Jo lifted it out carefully. His National TV Award. She remembered the night he'd collected it, how they'd all crowded on to the stage, tears in their eyes, hugging each other, the applause ringing in their ears. Trevor had stood in the middle of it all, too choked with pride to speak, just gazing down at it. His award.

She felt her eyes blurring. And now someone had just dumped it in a box to throw away. They'd got rid of the man, and now they wanted to get rid of his memories too.

'What do you think you're doing?'

The voice startled her so much she nearly dropped the award. Her eyes travelled from the Bruno Magli slingbacks, up the slim legs, past the sharply-cut black suit to meet a pair of hostile grey eyes.

She stood up until she was level with them. 'I'm Jo Porter.' She stuck out her hand, but the woman ignored it.

'I suppose you've been sent by Maintenance at last?' she snapped.

'I —'

'You should have been here half an hour ago. I want this rubbish cleared before Mr Black's furniture arrives.'

Jo was about to point out her mistake, then thought better of it. At least if she took Trevor's box she could save it from the garbage chute.

But first she had to make sure. 'Are you — er — certain you want to get rid of all this stuff?' she said. 'Some of it looks quite valuable —'

'Of course I want to get rid of it. Why do you think it says rubbish on it?' The woman's finely plucked brows arched. 'Oh, I see. You think you might be able to make a few quid, do you? Well frankly, I don't care what you do with it, as long as it doesn't stay here.'

She stalked out of the office, leaving Jo boiling with indignation. High-handed bitch! She could only be Richard Black's secretary. She wondered what had happened to that nice Mrs Hoskins. Probably gone the same way as poor old Trevor.

As she staggered down the corridor, her legs buckling under the weight of the box, she met the woman by the lift doors. She was flicking through some post, ignoring Jo as she struggled, puffing and panting, to balance the box on one knee while trying to reach the lift buttons.

In the awkward silence that followed, she tried again to make conversation. 'So – er – have you worked for Richard Black long, then?'

The woman looked her up and down. With her sleek dark hair, knuckle-duster cheekbones and a voice that could etch glass, she oozed superiority from every well-groomed pore. 'I've been *Mr* Black's PA for nearly two years.'

'You must know him quite well, then?'

'Well enough.' Was that the faintest trace of a smirk?

'What's he like?'

Her well-bred nostrils flared. She looked as if she would rather be making small talk with the box. 'We get on extremely well.'

As if that's any recommendation, Jo thought, as the lift doors whispered open. She hauled the box inside, wedging the doors open with her backside, then turned back to face the woman. 'So – um – any idea when he's arriving?' she panted.

'Oh, you'll meet him soon enough.' Her tight little smile was the last thing Jo saw before the lift doors closed on her.

Trevor Malone lived on the top floor of a converted Victorian house in a once sought-after but now seedy part of Harrogate. Jo still wasn't sure if she was doing the right thing as she parked her Cinquecento under the watchful eye of some teenagers hanging around the kebab house opposite. After all, she'd only known Trevor through work. They weren't exactly close friends. Not close enough for her to drop round unexpectedly, anyway.

She opened the boot and dragged the box out on to the kerb. What if he didn't want to see her? What if he didn't want to see this box? What if he'd deliberately left it all behind because the memories were too painful? He'd really thank her for turning up on his doorstep with them, wouldn't he?

Traffic streamed past her as she dithered on the pavement. Across the road, a couple of men were arguing outside a minicab office. Well, she couldn't just pack up and go home now. It wouldn't feel right. Squaring her shoulders, she hauled the box up the stone steps towards the battered front door.

No one answered when she rang the bell. Jo was just about to give up when the door suddenly opened and a frail, elderly man stood there.

'Oh, I'm sorry,' she began to apologise. 'I was looking for –'

'Jo?'

She peered closer. 'Trevor?'

'What a wonderful surprise.' His smile lit up his lined, tired face. 'What are you doing here?'

'I – er –' She tried not to stare. Crikey, what had happened to him? He looked as if he'd aged thirty years overnight. 'I came to bring you this,' she pulled herself together enough to reply. 'You left it at the office.'

'Ah.' He looked down at the box. 'So I did. I wondered if it would turn up.' He crouched down, lifted the flaps and took out the award. For a long time he just stared at it, not moving. Jo's heart sank.

Then Trevor looked up and she saw the shimmer of tears in his eyes. 'Thank you,' he said. 'You don't know how much these things mean to me.' He gazed reverently at the statuette. 'I wanted to collect them myself, but I couldn't bring myself to go back.' He was fighting to hold back his emotions. 'I was half afraid they might have dumped them.'

He was so overcome she felt tears pricking herself. 'I'll help you carry them upstairs, if you like?'

'Thank you, my dear. You're very kind.' He placed the award carefully back in the box and straightened up. 'Perhaps you'd like to stay for a cup of tea?'

'Well, I –' Jo was about to refuse, until she saw the desperate loneliness in his eyes. 'That would be very nice,' she agreed.

She followed him into the dark passageway, which smelt of overcooked cabbage, cat's pee and damp, and up several flights of narrow stairs. The sound of shouting and blaring television sets came from behind closed doors on every landing.

'Go through to the living room,' he said, when she finally gasped her way to the top-floor landing. 'I'll put the kettle on.'

His flat was sparsely furnished and very eighties, with black ash and smoked glass everywhere. Jo sank into the deep embrace of a black leather sofa, and looked around her. One wall was lined with photos of Trevor and various celebrities, including most of the *Westfield* cast. There were no family photos, she noticed. It was rumoured that Trevor was gay. Others reckoned he was just married to *Westfield*. Looking at the photos made her feel even more sad and angry.

How could everyone have forgotten him so quickly? He'd only been gone three days, and already it was as if he'd never existed. It had become bad luck even to whisper his name.

'Looking at my rogues' gallery?' Trevor shuffled back in with a tray. 'Some people have certainly changed, haven't they?'

Especially you, Jo thought. He seemed to have shrunk physically since he'd left *Westfield*. His frail shoulders were hunched beneath his shabby cardigan. Grey whiskers sprouted from his chin. Was this really the man who'd wielded so much power over them all?

'It was so kind of you to come.' His hands shook slightly as he poured her tea. 'You're the first person who's spoken to me since – you know.'

'The others send their love. They keep meaning to call, but you know what filming schedules are like.' Jo couldn't meet his eye.

'Of course.' He knew she was lying, which made it worse. 'So, how are things at *Westfield*? Did the wedding go okay?'

Jo tried to cheer him up with some gossip, which he seemed to appreciate. He talked about *Westfield* as fondly as other people discussed their grandchildren.

'I really miss the place,' he sighed. 'Silly, isn't it? I still can't get used to getting up in the morning and not having anywhere to go.'

His forlorn face brought a lump to her throat. 'You'll be back, you'll see. They won't be able to run the place without you.'

'I doubt it, my dear. I wouldn't want to come back, anyway. Not once Richard Black gets his hands on it. I shouldn't think I'll recognise the place in six months.'

Jo shivered. Why did people keep saying that? 'Do you know him?'

'You could say that.' He lifted his cup slowly to his lips. 'As a matter of fact, I gave him his first job, nearly fifteen years ago, as a production assistant on *Westfield*. He just turned up at the studios one day, out of the blue, and demanded I take him on. Couldn't have been more than seventeen at the time. He was an arrogant sod even then.'

'So what's he like?'

'Totally ruthless. If Richard wants something, he won't let anyone or anything stand in his way.' His mouth thinned. 'I remember at that very first interview I asked him what kind of job he wanted. He looked me straight in the eye and said,

"Yours." And he's been after it ever since.' His face grew bleak. 'I handed him the knife, and now he's stabbed me in the back with it.'

'What do you mean?'

'Oh, you know how these things work in television. A whisper here, a few rumours there. He's been spreading dirt about me for years, telling everyone I'm not up to the job. He's got some friends in high places these days. People listen to him.'

'But surely they listen to you, too? After all, you created *Westfield*!'

'Once upon a time, maybe. But things change.' Trevor looked wistful. 'TV companies don't want good drama any more. They want sensationalism, something to push up the ratings. And that's what he's promised them.'

He looked so old and defeated, Jo reached out impulsively and touched his hand. It was stone cold. 'Things will work out. You'll find another job.'

'I doubt it, my dear. Who'd want an old fool like me? No, at least I've got enough sense to know when I've been put out to grass.'

They chatted for a while about the old days, until it was time for her to leave. As he saw her to the door, Trevor suddenly clutched her arm.

'Be careful, won't you?' he said. 'Don't trust him. I did once, and look where it got me.'

Jo smiled ruefully. 'I aim to stay out of his way if I can.'

'I'm serious!' As he thrust his face close to hers, she caught a whiff of stale whisky. 'Watch out for him. Because he'll certainly be watching you.'

'Thanks for the warning.' Jo edged out of his grasp.

They reached the front step, and she planted a kiss on his thin, bristly cheek. 'Take care of yourself, Trevor,' she said. 'And don't forget to come and see us if you're passing.'

He shook his head. 'Thank you my dear, but somehow I don't think I'll be seeing *Westfield* again.'

Chapter 4

The sun stopped shining on the day of the funeral three weeks later. The sky was steel grey and a damp mist clung to them as they lined the graveside.

It could have been a scene from *Westfield*. Brett, Rob and Eva Lawrence huddled together on one side of the grave. On the other was Viola, flanked by Jo and Lara Lamont, all dressed in sombre black.

Except this wasn't make-believe. This was all too horribly real.

Jo gripped her red rose so hard the thorns dug deep into her fingers, but she barely noticed the pain. She was too numb with shock to notice anything.

It had all happened so suddenly. A stroke, according to the coroner's report. Trevor died quickly and painlessly in his sleep. He wouldn't have known anything about it, so they said. But Jo knew, and so did everyone else, that it was a broken heart that killed him.

There were no relatives or friends at the funeral. The cast and crew of *Westfield* were his only family. Burly cameramen shouldered his coffin from the church in grim silence. On the other side of the grave, Eva Lawrence stood motionless, her face white against her sable coat, supported by her loyal assistant Desmond.

As the coffin was lowered, Lara stepped forward, a rose in her hand. She was wearing a new Dolce and Gabbana frock coat, and as she paused dramatically beside the grave, Jo heard the click of a camera.

'I don't believe it,' Viola hissed through her tears. 'She's brought a bloody photographer!'

'Probably another exclusive deal.' Jo could just imagine the headline in *OK!*: 'Soap Tragedy – Lara Lamont Invites Us To The Funeral And Shares Her Grief'.

Sickened, she turned away – and then she saw him. A tall, dark figure, standing under a yew tree on the other side of the churchyard, the collar of his raincoat turned up against the clinging mist.

As the service ended and the mourners began to disperse, Jo picked her way across the grass to where he'd been standing. But he was gone. She reached the trees just in time to see a dark green Audi disappearing up the road.

'Come to make sure old Trev's dead and buried, I suppose.' Jo swung round and found herself facing the smiling, oleaginous features of Charlie Beasley, showbiz reporter and chief muckraker of the *Globe*. He was thirtyish and deceptively harmless-looking, in his spectacles and shiny grey suit.

'Don't you vultures have any respect?' she snapped.

'You know who that was, don't you?' Charlie ignored the question. 'Richard Black. The Grim Reaper himself. Might have known he'd be hanging round in a graveyard with a name like that.'

Jo stared down the road. So that was him.

'Bet he's going home to crack open the champagne,' Charlie went on. 'This couldn't have worked out better for him if he'd planned it.'

Jo opened her mouth, then shut it again. Thrusting her hands in her pockets, she started to walk away. Charlie fell into step beside her.

'Now he hasn't got Trevor looking over his shoulder, he can do as he likes. 'Course, it's not such good news for you lot. Rumour is he's got some big changes planned. Must be a bit worrying, eh?'

Jo bit her lip. After four years on *Westfield*, she knew when a tabloid journalist was trying to trap her.

'Still, I suppose it's time for a change. That's why they got rid of Trevor, after all. And he won't be the last, from what I hear.' Charlie panted to keep up with her. 'I've heard the Grim Reaper's already sharpening his scythe. But I suppose you know all about that, don't you?

'I don't listen to gossip. That's your job.'

'Oh, this isn't gossip, love. It's fact. He's drawn up his hit list. And guess who's at the top of it?'

Jo gritted her teeth. 'I don't know and I don't care.'

'Maybe you don't. But I wonder how poor old Viola will manage when she's out of work? It's no joke, is it, being on the dole at her age?'

That did it. She stopped dead. 'What did you say?'

'You mean you haven't heard?' Charlie blinked in mock surprise. 'Your co-star's for the chop. And so are a few of the others. They say he's getting rid of anyone over fifty. Sad really, isn't it?'

It was more than sad. It was heartbreaking. Jo looked across the graveyard to where Viola was comforting Lara. If it was true, she would be utterly devastated.

If it was true. Charlie and his tabloid pals weren't above spreading a few lies to goad a reaction out of their victims.

'No comment.' She started to walk off again, but Charlie caught up with her.

'Still, I don't suppose it bothers you, does it? I expect you'll be all right. It's just the old ones who don't stand a chance. And let's face it, they were all getting a bit past it, weren't they? Just like Trevor Malone.'

Jo reached her car and fumbled in her bag for her key.

'Besides, it's got to be good news for you, hasn't it? All those sexy new storylines to get your teeth into? With Viola and that lot out of the way, you could end up one of

Westfield's biggest stars. I reckon you've got a lot to thank Richard Black for.'

'I've got nothing to thank him for. If it wasn't for him, Trevor Malone might still be alive!'

She could have bitten off her tongue. Charlie's brows shot up. 'Are you saying you think he's responsible for Trevor's death?'

'No, I –'

'So what are you saying, then?'

'Nothing. Nothing at all,' she backtracked wildly.

'You sounded pretty sure just then. Are you saying Trevor died because he was sacked from *Westfield*?'

'No –'

'You think he died of a broken heart, is that it?' Charlie's eyes gleamed behind his spectacles. 'And as it was Black who got him sacked, he's the one who caused his death. He virtually murdered him, is that what you're saying?'

'I'm not saying anything –' She found her key, unlocked the car and dived in. As she started the engine, Charlie bent down and grinned through the window.

'Thanks, Jo,' he said. 'Your comments have been most helpful.'

'GRIM REAPER CLAIMS HIS FIRST VICTIM', declared the headline on the *Globe*'s front page the following morning. Under it were the words, 'He killed Trevor, says soap star Stacey.'

Jo spotted it on a rack outside a newsagent's as she was driving the girls to school. She jammed her foot on the brake, nearly causing a multiple pile-up behind her.

'Mum!' Grace, who was trying to finish off her homework in the back, yelled in outrage. 'You've made me put a big scrawl right through my map!'

'Sorry.' Jo moved off again, oblivious to the blaring horns behind her. It was a mistake. It had to be.

But it wasn't. She bought a newspaper after dropping the

girls off. She was still sitting behind the wheel of her car, staring in horror at the words on the page, when her mobile went off.

It was Louise, *Westfield*'s press officer. 'Have you seen the *Globe*?'

'I'm looking at it now.'

'You didn't really say all that, did you? Please tell me you didn't.'

'Of course I didn't. Well, not all of it, anyway. I might have said something. Oh God, I don't remember!' She certainly didn't remember saying that Richard Black was a murderer, or that he had an innocent man's blood on his hands. But it was there, in black and white.

'Why on earth didn't you talk to me first?' Louise raged. 'You know what reporters are like. They're sharks, sniffing around for blood.'

It's my blood everyone will be after, Jo thought. 'I only said what I felt,' she defended herself lamely.

'Yes, but it wasn't true, was it?'

'How do you know? I saw Trevor just before he died. He was heartbroken at being sacked –'

'But he wasn't –' There was a silence at the other end of the line.

Jo gripped the phone. 'What did you say?'

'Nothing.'

'Louise!'

She heard her sigh on the other end of the line. 'Look, let's just say there's more to this story than meets the eye, okay? You should have checked your facts with me first.'

'I know. I'm sorry.' Jo bit her lip. 'Perhaps I could apologise –'

'No!' Louise bellowed. 'Don't say a word. You've already done enough damage.'

'But surely –'

'Not a word. No retractions, no apologies. Not a single word. To anyone. Do you understand?'

'Yes,' Jo agreed meekly.

'I'll tell them you were unhinged by grief,' Louise went on, thinking aloud. 'Yes, that might work. I'll tell them you were temporarily insane and didn't know what you were saying. Of course, it would have to happen today,' she said. 'You do realise it's Richard Black's first day? What do you suppose he's going to say when this lands on his desk?'

'Perhaps he won't see it?' Jo suggested optimistically.

It was hardly a realistic hope. As she slunk into the *Westfield* studios half an hour later, it felt as if the whole world had got hold of a copy.

Typically, the first person she met was Brett Michaels. As he swaggered past her in the corridor, he leered and drew a finger across his throat. Her empty stomach churned.

And there was worse to come. Someone had stuck the Sits Vac page from *The Stage* on her dressing room door.

'Very bloody funny!' she snarled, slamming the door.

'My God, I'm amazed you dared show your face this morning.' Viola was examining the bags under her eyes in the mirror, her red curls pinned back off her face with a big silver clip. 'I thought you would have left the country.'

Jo slumped down in her chair. 'I take it you've seen it too?'

'Darling, hasn't everyone? Someone's enlarged it on the photocopier and stuck it up in the green room. You are daring!' She peered closely at her face. 'Do you think I should have my lips pumped?'

'No.' Jo stared despairingly at her own reflection. She could have her entire face pumped and it wouldn't do her employment prospects any good. Not now she'd put her foot in it so comprehensively. 'So has anyone spotted our new boss yet?'

'Not so far. We've seen his poisonous PA though. Kate, I think her name is. She came stalking through here about an hour ago.'

'Probably looking for me.' Jo bit her lip. 'Oh Vi, I should have kept my mouth shut, shouldn't I?'

'It might not have been the best career move you've ever made,' Viola agreed. 'But personally, I think you did the right thing.'

'You do?'

'Absolutely.' Viola nodded. 'Suicidal, but definitely the right thing. Someone needed to speak up. I'm just glad it wasn't me, that's all.' She went back to counting her crow's feet.

Jo buried her face in her hands. It was too much to hope her little gaffe would pass unnoticed. But at least she hadn't been summoned up to the top floor. She could only pray Richard Black was too busy sacking people to read the papers.

And for a while, it seemed as if her prayers had been answered. The morning's filming went by with only the occasional snigger and sideways remark for her to contend with. By lunchtime Jo was beginning to breathe again. Perhaps she was worrying over nothing? After all, Richard Black must be a pretty astute kind of man. Surely he wouldn't allow himself to be swayed by idle tabloid gossip . . .

She finished her scenes, changed back into her jeans and sweater and was on her way out of the building when she met Kate coming towards her.

'There you are,' she said. 'I've been looking for you. Mr Black would like to see you in the top floor conference room. Immediately.'

Chapter 5

'Any idea why he wants to see me?'

'I should have thought that was obvious.' Kate sent her a withering look.

Jo glanced at her little car, sitting tantalisingly across the car park, and thought about making a run for it. But it was no good. She could run, but she couldn't hide. She wasn't too sure she could run either, since her legs had turned to jelly the moment she saw Kate's minxy little face coming towards her.

They made their way up to the top floor in silence. Jo passed the time plucking invisible fluff off her sweater. Someone should have warned her this was going to happen. If she was going to get a roasting at least she could have been better dressed, instead of looking scruffy in jeans and trainers.

'Haven't I seen you somewhere before?'

'Er – I don't think so.' Jo squirmed as Kate studied her. The lift suddenly felt small and stifling.

'No, I'm sure I've seen you on the top floor –'

'Here we are.' The lift doors opened and Jo rushed out. Kate glanced at her watch.

'Five minutes late. Everyone will be waiting.'

'Who's everyone –?' She never finished the question, as Kate pushed open the door marked Conference Room. Suddenly she found herself confronted by a sea of faces. Everyone, from the cast, the crew and the production team, to the girls in admin and accounts, was there. Even Eva the Diva, who normally didn't mix with the plebs, was sitting in a far corner, her heavily made-up face frozen under her improbable jet-black wig.

The room fell silent and all eyes swivelled in her direction as she made her humiliatingly public entrance. Had the Grim Reaper called them all in to witness her public disembowelment?

Jo tried to slink in at the back but unfortunately Viola had saved her a seat so she was forced to shuffle her way to the front row. She could feel Brett's smirk following her all the way.

And then she was face to face with the Grim Reaper himself.

He was younger than she'd imagined, no more than mid-thirties, although his severely-tailored suit made him look older. He stood at the front of the room, flanked by Kate and Louise the press officer, surveying them all with narrowed eyes.

So this was the famous Richard Black. No wonder everyone was so in awe of him. He seemed to tower over them all, and not just because of his commanding height.

'Now we're all finally here, perhaps we could make a start?' He didn't raise his voice, but the room instantly fell silent. 'As you all know, my name is the Grim Reaper. But I prefer to be called Richard.' Everyone laughed politely. Jo was too terrified to crack a smile.

He wasn't smiling either. She studied him covertly, taking in the strong face, the short dark hair with just a hint of curl, the hard, cynical mouth. He wasn't exactly handsome, but there was an aura of power about him that was disturbing.

'I won't beat about the bush. *Westfield* is in trouble. Big trouble. I wouldn't be here if it wasn't.' He would have made a fantastic poker player, Jo decided. It was impossible to tell what was going on behind those dark, expressionless eyes. 'I've been brought in to put it right. Now I realise I might not be the most popular choice for the job –' This time no one dared to laugh. 'But whether you like it or not I'm the best chance you have of saving your jobs. If the ratings keep falling the way they are, in six months' time this whole show could be axed.'

There were murmurings among the audience. No one had realised the situation was this bad.

Or was it? Jo watched him closely. 'Don't trust him,' Trevor had said. She was beginning to see what he meant.

'I have to tell you now, I intend to do anything necessary to put *Westfield* back where it belongs,' Richard went on. 'And that includes changing storylines and getting rid of characters who have outlived their usefulness. I'm not here to give you any false promises. Some of you will have to go.' Jo swallowed hard. Was he looking at her? 'I shall be looking at the situation closely over the next month or so before I make any long-term decisions. But before any of you start getting too complacent, I should remind you that no one is indispensable. This show is bigger than any of the characters in it.' Jo noticed Brett's smile slip a fraction. 'Now, having said all that, I hope we can all work together. But if anyone thinks they may have a problem with the way I do things, perhaps it would be best if they left now.'

There was a long silence. Jo shrank in her seat as all eyes turned to her.

'And one more thing,' he added. 'Some of you may have read certain reports in the gutter press this morning.' Oh God, here it comes. Jo stared at her shoes and willed herself to disappear. 'Now I realise emotions may be running high following the recent – tragic events.' He cleared his throat. 'Which is why I'm taking no action on this occasion. But I can't allow this constant bleating to the press to continue. It's bad for *Westfield*, and I won't tolerate it.' His gaze swept over them like an Arctic breeze. 'From now on, all comments must be directed through the press office. If anyone gives any unauthorised interviews, I won't hesitate to sack them. Is that understood?'

There was a general murmur of agreement. Jo forced herself to lift her eyes from the scuffed toe of her trainers and realised with a shock that he was looking straight at her, piercing and direct. Heat flooded into her face as she dropped her gaze back to the floor.

'Good,' he said quietly. 'In future, if you have any complaints about the way things are done around here, please bring them to me, not Charlie Beasley.'

'Well, I reckon you got off lightly there,' Viola said as they emerged from the lifts into the production centre reception ten minutes later.

'You think so?' Jo could still feel her face burning.

'God yes,' agreed Lara, flicking back her long dark hair. 'I thought you were in for a right bollocking.'

She couldn't have been more mortified if he'd dragged her up to the front and flogged her in front of everyone. And he knew it too. 'I still think he's a bastard,' she muttered.

'Well, I wouldn't want to get on the wrong side of him,' Lara said. 'Although he's dead sexy, isn't he?'

'He put me in mind of Mr Darcy,' Viola nodded. 'You know, very aloof on the surface, but loads of simmering passion underneath.'

'I've always liked powerful men. I wonder what he'd be like in bed?' Lara mused. Jo stared at them both.

'I don't believe you two! Didn't you hear a word he was saying? He was threatening to sack us all.'

'Not necessarily,' Viola pointed out. 'Only if we cause trouble.'

'And you're prepared to suck up to him so you can keep your jobs?'

They looked at each other. 'Obviously,' Lara shrugged.

'And so should you, if you want to keep yours,' Viola reminded her.

'But have you forgotten what he did to Trevor?'

'Not that again!' Viola raised her eyes heavenwards. 'My God, Jo, haven't you dropped yourself in it enough?'

'Besides, Trevor can't have been up to the job, or *Westfield* wouldn't be in so much trouble, would it?' Lara added.

'So that makes it all right, does it?' Jo turned on her. 'Don't you understand, it's not what they did, it's the way they did it? Just throwing him out like – like an old Hoover bag. And we all know who was behind *that* –'

'Can I have a word?' She'd been so busy sounding off she hadn't noticed Louise the press officer approaching. 'In private,' she added, grabbing her arm and steering her towards the press office. Jo just had time to see Viola and Lara's dismayed faces before the door slammed.

Louise crossed the room to her cluttered desk and began sorting through the toppling mountain of papers. 'About what you were saying –' she began.

'I know, I know,' Jo held up her hands. 'It's okay, I'm not going to start shouting to the press again. It was a stupid thing to do. But you can't stop me having an opinion.' She lifted her chin defiantly. 'Or do our thoughts have to be censored too? Don't tell me, we're living in some kind of police state. Any minute now big posters of Richard Black are going to appear all over the place, with "The Grim Reaper Is Watching –"'

'Trevor Malone wasn't sacked,' Louise cut her off. She was in her thirties, a plump, dark-haired girl with a permanently harassed expression from keeping tabloid hacks at bay. 'He could have stayed at *Westfield* if he'd wanted. It was his decision to leave.'

'But I don't understand,' Jo faltered. 'Everyone knows they brought Richard Black in to replace him.' Then the truth dawned. 'Oh, I get it. You mean he was offered some kind of poncey, made-up job, like Associate Executive Consultant in charge of paper clips –'

'He could have stayed in his old job, with his old salary.

All he had to do was share some of the day-to-day responsibility with Richard.'

'Let him make all the decisions, you mean? Well, I'm not surprised he left. It doesn't sound as if they gave him much choice, does it? God, can you imagine working with someone like that? Knowing he's watching you, just waiting for the chance to get you booted out –'

'It wasn't like that.' Louise rescued a piece of paper from the slipping avalanche on her desk. 'Look, I'm not supposed to be telling you any of this. But I thought you should know, in case you start spreading any more stupid lies.' She handed Jo the paper. 'This is the press release I prepared on the day Trevor Malone left *Westfield*. To set the record straight. Go on, read it. It's all there.'

Jo perched on the edge of the desk and skimmed through the two-page document. But it still didn't add up. 'I don't understand. It says here –'

'It says the Head of Drama at Talbot TV planned to sack Trevor because he really wasn't up to the job any more. He *wasn't*,' she insisted, as Jo opened her mouth to protest. 'Anyway, Talbot wanted to bring in Richard Black. But he said he'd only come here on condition that he could work alongside Trevor. Apparently they go back a long way, or something.'

'Trevor gave him his first job,' Jo murmured.

'Well, Trevor wasn't having any of it,' Louise went on. 'His pride couldn't take the idea of sharing *Westfield* with anyone. So he packed up his stuff and left. But he made sure everyone believed he'd been sacked.'

'That's the bit I don't get. Why would he want people to think that?'

'Aiming for the sympathy vote, I suppose,' Louise shrugged. 'You know, poor old man gets kicked out by thrusting young executive? He wanted to make sure Richard got the worst possible welcome when he arrived. And it worked, didn't it?'

Jo looked down at the press release, a curtain of hair hiding her flushed face. Trevor had deliberately used her, and she'd fallen for it. 'So why didn't you send this out?'

'Richard wouldn't let me. He said he didn't want to get embroiled in a war of words. But if you ask me, it was out of loyalty to Trevor. It's just a shame the old man didn't feel the same way, isn't it?' She took the paper out of Jo's hand and pushed it back to the bottom of the pile. 'Promise me you won't breathe a word of this to anyone? My job would be on the line if he found out.'

Jo stood up, her brow furrowed. She was too confused to tell anyone anything. 'But you can't deny it did kill Trevor, leaving *Westfield*? I mean, he must have that on his conscience?'

Louise shook her head. 'It was his liver. Trevor had a serious drink problem towards the end. Another little fact Richard made sure we hushed up.'

Jo thought back to the last time she'd seen him. Those shaking hands, the smell of stale alcohol on his breath. No wonder he'd been losing his grip over the last few months.

She left the press office, still dazed. As she made her way from the production centre across the tree-lined courtyard back towards the studios, she suddenly spotted the towering figure of Richard Black striding towards her.

She froze. All the terrible things she'd said rose up to haunt her. Oh God, what must he think of her? He was coming nearer. Maybe it wasn't too late to apologise? As he drew level, Jo gave him a big smile.

'I just wanted to say –'

But she never got a chance to say it. He whisked straight past her. He didn't spare her the briefest glance, but Jo knew he'd deliberately ignored her.

She watched him go, feeling crushed. So much for staying out of his way. She had the bad feeling she'd just put herself right in his firing line . . .

Chapter 6

'Do we have to go?' Chloe and Grace sat side by side on the sofa, their expressions pained.

'Yes, we do. School starts next week.'

'But we hate shopping!'

'Especially for school uniform. Yuk!'

'Believe it or not, it's hardly my idea of a great time, either.' Jo gritted her teeth. 'Look, I'll tell you what. We'll get it done quickly and then treat ourselves, shall we?'

That got them. 'What kind of treat?' Grace wanted to know.

'Can I have a hamster?' Chloe piped up.

'Well, I was thinking more of tea in Bettys,' Jo admitted. 'But we'll see, shall we?'

By the time she'd spent three hours buying skirts, blouses and PE kits, and arguing with Grace about why kitten-heeled mules did not constitute sensible school shoes, she felt exhausted enough to agree to anything.

Chloe bore her new pet exultantly into Bettys tea room, followed by a grumpy-looking Grace.

'It's not fair,' she grumbled. 'She's got that and I haven't got anything.'

'You can share the hamster.'

'No she can't!' Chloe's eyes were wide with outrage.

'I don't want your stupid old hamster.' Grace snatched up

the menu. 'Anyway, I'm going to save up and buy a python. They eat hamsters.'

'They don't!'

'Do!'

'Tell her, Mummy. Tell her she can't have a python.'

'You can't have a python. And stop playing with that thing, Chloe. I'm sure you're not supposed to bring animals in here.' Jo gazed mournfully at the No Smoking sign on the table. She'd given up before the children were born, but in moments of stress the occasional desperate need for a ciggie still overcame her.

Fortunately they forgot their squabble and concentrated on choosing the biggest cake on the trolley. Jo poured herself a cup of tea from the silver pot and closed her eyes, wallowing in the momentary peace. This place was so civilised. The tinkling of cups and saucers and the murmur of conversation mingled with the pianist playing soothing Gershwin numbers. Waitresses in frilly aprons glided between the marble-topped tables carrying silver tiered dishes of scones and sandwiches. On the other side of the big plate-glass windows it had started to rain. Office workers and late shoppers were hurrying home, their coats turned up against the sudden downpour. Jo nibbled a sliver of ham sandwich and felt glad that she wasn't one of them.

But her happiness evaporated when she glanced around and spotted Richard Black standing at the 'Please Wait Here to be Seated' sign. And he wasn't alone. Jo barely had time to digest this fact before her instincts slid into automatic.

'Mummy, why are you under the table?' Chloe's head appeared upside down.

'I'm hiding.'

'Who from?'

'My boss.'

'Where?' Jo grabbed her just as she was climbing on to her chair for a better look.

'Sit down! I don't want him to see me.'

'Why not?'

'Because he's mean and he hates me.'

If she was in any doubt about that when he first arrived, the past four weeks had helped put her mind at rest. It wasn't just the fact that he ignored her. He seemed to ignore everyone. But it was the way he ignored her. He had an unnerving habit of turning up in the middle of filming and hanging around behind the cameras, watching but not watching, managing to be hostile and unaware of her presence at the same time. It was quite a gift.

Jo peered out from under the table. 'Can you see where he's sitting?'

'Over in the corner, I think. Is he the cross-looking one?'

She edged her way back into her seat. 'That's him.'

'Who's that woman with him?'

'That's his PA, Kate. She's a sort of secretary.'

'Why does he need a secretary on a Saturday afternoon?' Grace asked.

Why indeed? Jo watched them as they sat in the corner, studying their menus, surrounded by designer carrier bags from the posh shops in Petergate. They'd obviously been shopping together, which could only mean one thing: Kate and Richard Black were an item. It didn't surprise her.

'So what are you going to call that thing?' Grace asked Chloe.

'Pudding.'

'What kind of a stupid name is that? You should give it a cool name, like Fatboy Slim.'

'I'm not going to call it Fatboy, am I? That's a horrible name, isn't it, Mummy?'

'If you say so, darling. Now please close that box up before we get thrown out.' Jo couldn't take her eyes off Richard. He was wearing a suit, for heaven's sake. On his day off.

Or perhaps he never took a day off? His Audi was in the car park every morning when she arrived and his light always seemed to be shining from the top floor every night when she left.

Thanks heavens the café was crowded so they managed to get through their tea without being spotted. Jo paid the bill, grateful to escape. She was just gathering up her shopping when Chloe let out a scream.

'Where's Pudding?'

They all stared at the empty box. 'It must have escaped.' Grace stated the blindingly obvious. 'I bet you didn't shut the box up properly.'

It wasn't the most helpful remark. Chloe immediately started howling. 'Pudding! I want Pudding!'

Her voice rose above the muted clink of cups and cutlery. Waitresses were sending them odd looks from across the busy restaurant. From a neighbouring table, Jo heard one middle-aged man hiss to his wife, 'Listen to that! If she was my grandchild, I'd give her bloody pudding!'

'Let's just look for it, shall we? It must be somewhere.' Jo and Grace got down on the floor, while Chloe screeched her head off above them.

'Can I help?'

She lifted her eyes from the carpet to the hand-made brogues of Richard Black. Great. Just what she needed. 'We're fine, thank you,' she said with as much dignity as she could muster.

The shoes didn't move. 'Have you lost something?'

No, I just didn't feel enough people were staring at me, so I thought I'd really try and make a spectacle of myself. She started to answer but Chloe beat her to it.

'I've lost Pudding!' she shrieked. Richard looked unnerved. He'd obviously never been this close to a child before, let alone an hysterical one.

'Her hamster,' Jo said. 'It's escaped.' She only wished she could do the same.

'I see.' He considered this for a moment. 'And what exactly were you doing with a hamster in here?'

55

'Well, you see, he gets so lonely in his cage, I just thought I'd bring him for a browse around Debenhams —' Jo gritted her teeth. 'What do you think I'm doing with it?'

'We've just bought it,' Grace explained.

'Ah.' He nodded wisely. 'In that case, may I make a small suggestion?'

'Yes?'

'I don't think you'll find it like that. If you keep flailing your arms around you'll just frighten it even further away.'

So now he was an expert on rodent psychology, was he? Jo stared up the length of his immaculately pressed trousers. 'And what do you suggest?'

'You should offer it some encouragement.' He handed Jo's plate, with the remains of her sandwich, to Chloe. 'Here, break this up into crumbs. It's not the most suitable food in the world, but perhaps we can lay a trail to entice it back.'

Chloe stopped howling and obediently got to work. She seemed reassured now Richard was on the case, as if he alone would be equal to the task of tracking down her missing hamster. Jo fought down feelings of annoyance. She just wished he'd bugger off and leave her to deal with this crisis in her own haphazard way.

As if things weren't bad enough, suddenly Kate was standing over them too, her Jimmy Choo slingbacks tapping impatiently.

'Richard, what — oh, it's you.'

'Watch where you're putting your feet,' Jo warned. All she needed now was for Pudding to come out of hiding and be impaled on those vicious spiked heels.

Kate ignored her. 'Are you coming, Richard?'

'In a minute.' He took the crumbs from Chloe's sticky hands and knelt down beside Jo. She watched him scatter them on the carpet under the table, painfully conscious that he wasn't doing his expensive Italian tailoring any good. 'Right,' he said. 'Now all we've got to do is wait.'

Jo glanced up at Kate, who towered over them. 'Look, you really don't have to do this –'

'Shh.'

It felt as if they were kneeling there for hours. The whole room seemed to be holding its breath. The piano fell silent and every teaspoon in the place stopped tinkling as everyone stopped to watch.

Jo cringed. This was a nightmare. It was also positively the last time she would ever set foot inside this place. Not that she'd have any choice. They'd probably have armed guards watching out for her next time.

'Look, I don't think this is going to –' she began, but suddenly Chloe was pointing excitedly.

'It's Pudding! He's come back!' Sure enough, a sandy ball of fluff came snuffling out from the shadowy recesses of a corner table, blissfully hoovering up the crumbs in his expanding cheeks. Richard scooped him up gently as the whole café erupted in spontaneous applause.

'Safe and sound,' he said.

'Thanks.' Jo took the hamster from him.

'No problem.' He stroked the hamster with his finger. He had long, artistic fingers, she noticed. 'Pudding, eh? Perhaps you should call him Houdini?'

For a brief moment she thought she saw the shadow of a smile. Then it was gone.

He stood up, brushing the crumbs off his knees. Chloe blinked up at him in awe. 'Are you the man Mummy was hiding from?'

'Don't be silly, darling. I wasn't hiding from him!' Jo covered her scalding embarrassment with a forced laugh.

'Yes you were. You said he was mean and he hated you!' Her voice suddenly seemed to echo off the bronze mirrored walls.

Kate snorted. Jo couldn't meet Richard's eye. She couldn't imagine what he must be thinking. Or rather, she could. Only too well, in fact. 'Come on, I think we'd better get this little one home, don't you? Before he does another disappearing act.'

Just her luck, they all left at the same time. They made an awkward group, sheltering under the awning from the rain.

'Well – er – thanks again.'

'Where are you parked?'

Why did he have to ask that? 'We haven't –' Chloe piped up, but Jo clamped her hand over her mouth.

'It's just around the corner,' she pointed vaguely. 'About a minute away. Less than a minute, in fact. So – um – we'll be going. Come on, girls.' She shepherded them out into the rain.

'Why did you say that?' Grace demanded, as they ran across the wet street. 'You know we left the car at home.'

'Yes, but I didn't want him to know that, did I?' Jo pulled up the hood of Chloe's anorak.

'Why not?'

'Because then he might offer us a lift home, that's why.'

'So? What's wrong with that? At least we wouldn't get soaked!'

What indeed? Jo couldn't answer. She just had the vague feeling that the less time she spent in Richard's company, the less chance he'd have to disapprove of her.

They took a detour down the narrow, cobbled street of Stonegate, stopping every few seconds to look in the windows of shops selling teddy bears, toys and various touristy knick-knacks. There seemed no point in hurrying. Jo was already as drenched as she could possibly get. Her trainers squelched and her hair hung in rats' tails around her face, dripping cold water down the back of her neck.

They came out of Stonegate and were just crossing Duncombe Place when Chloe suddenly cried out, 'Look, it's your boss again!'

There was no escape this time. Richard's Audi was already slowing down beside them. The window glided down and he leaned across.

'Where did you say your car was parked?'

'Um —'

'It isn't,' Chloe broke in cheerfully. 'Mummy just said it was so you wouldn't give us a lift.'

Oh bugger. Jo closed her eyes, mortification washing over her. She could feel herself blushing to the unhighlighted roots of her hair.

'Really, there's no need,' she tried to laugh it off. 'We only live off Clifton Green. We can easily walk it in ten minutes —'

'And we have a dinner reservation in Leeds for eight,' Kate pointed out quickly. 'I'll never have time to shower and change.'

For a second it looked as though that was the end of it, until Chloe wailed, 'But Pudding's box is getting soggy. What if he escapes again?'

'And I've never been in an Audi convertible before.' Grace ran an admiring hand over the gleaming paintwork.

'Looks like you're outvoted, doesn't it?' Richard leaned across and opened the back door.

Outmanoeuvred, more like. The children had caused her some embarrassment in her time, but this was definitely the worst, Jo decided, as they squeezed into the back seat, dripping all over the flawless upholstery. She nursed Pudding's newly acquired cage on her lap and prayed Chloe wouldn't throw up her chocolate éclair. In front of her Kate's shoulders were rigid. She could feel the weight of her hatred bearing down on her.

'This is a cool car,' Grace announced, as they headed out of the city past the looming stone gateway of Bootham Bar. 'Why can't we have one like this?'

'Because we don't need one.' She looked out of the window, trying not to listen to Richard and Kate's whispered conversation. It didn't take a genius to work out they were having a domestic. Or that she was the cause of it.

Then suddenly, the car stopped, flinging them all forward

so sharply Jo's earring got caught in the bars of the cage. Kate got out, slamming the passenger door. Without a backward glance, she strode back off in the direction of the river, her head down against the rain, her high heels clicking on the wet pavement.

'Have you two had a row?' As usual, Chloe's timing was impeccable.

'You could say that.'

'What about?'

'Leave Mr Black alone,' Jo said hastily. 'Let him concentrate on his driving.' But Chloe hadn't finished with him.

'Is that your wife?' she asked.

'No.'

'So you're not married, then?'

'No.'

Jo slunk down in her seat. All Chloe needed was a twinset and she could have been Grandma Audrey. 'Darling, I don't think –'

'Mummy isn't married either,' Chloe said. 'She was, but she and Daddy split up.' Richard didn't answer. Jo wondered if he was even listening. 'Daddy's got a new girlfriend. Her name's Thea and she doesn't speak English. But Mummy hasn't had a boyfriend for ages, have you Mummy?'

'I'm sure Mr Black isn't interested in hearing about my personal life.'

'Daddy says he's not surprised,' Chloe went on. 'He says Mummy's impossible to live with. He reckons a man would have to be a saint to –'

'Oh look! A cow!' Jo shouted, pointing out of the window.

'Where?' Chloe clamoured to have a look.

'Sorry, I could have sworn I saw one.'

'A cow, in the middle of York? How lame can you get?' Grace said scornfully.

Jo stared at the back of Richard's head. She had the horrible feeling he was secretly laughing at her.

'Turn right here,' she said in a clipped voice.

They pulled into their road of tall, grey-stone Edwardian terraced houses. She was out of the car before he'd put on the brake.

'Thanks for the lift,' she said.

'Not at all.' Richard glanced at the girls, who were fighting over the doorkey. 'It's been most – entertaining.'

'His car's nice,' Grace commented, as they watched him drive away.

'He's not mean at all,' Chloe added.

Jo watched the car until it turned the corner. 'I'm not so sure,' she muttered.

Chapter 7

'STACEY TO FACE AXE – OFFICIAL', the headline in the *Globe* proclaimed. Underneath was a *Westfield* still of her looking suitably mournful, with the subhead, 'Charlie Beasley's Tips For The Chop'.

Jo tried to stop herself buying a copy on her way to work, but she couldn't. It was like probing an aching tooth.

'The stars of *Westfield* will have even less to smile about today, as they gather in the office of new Executive Producer Richard Black to learn their fate,' she read, as she waited at the traffic lights. 'Black, known in the business as the Grim Reaper, was brought in by Talbot TV bosses to halt the show's drop in the ratings. After six weeks in the job he's now ready to make some drastic changes, including axing some familiar faces. Black refused to comment on the rumours today, but as one insider told us, "There are a lot of very nervous people around here at the moment."'

Jo tossed the newspaper on to the passenger seat in disgust. What did Charlie Beasley know, anyway?

But he wasn't the only one who'd got hold of the story. All week, the tabloids had been speculating about the forthcoming changes at *Westfield*. It had become a running gag between them, to see who could come up with the most bizarre and outrageous soap deaths. So far she'd been mown down by her husband's runaway minicab, caught in the crossfire of a gangland killing and electrocuted by a set of heated rollers. It would have been funny if it wasn't so worrying.

And then on Friday they'd all received notes with their usual scripts, telling them Richard Black would meet them the following Monday 'to discuss their future'. Suddenly the rumours seemed harder to dismiss.

Luckily Jo didn't have too many scenes that morning, because her concentration was in tatters. In between takes, Richard Black had been summoning the cast one by one. Some emerged looking relieved, others in tears. While the rest waited, the atmosphere was leaden with expectation.

'I've got a brain tumour,' was Viola's doleful pronouncement as they met on the café set. She was sitting at one of the tables, scratching a pattern in the checked plastic cloth with a scarlet-tipped nail while the cameras arranged themselves around her. Her gloomy face was reflected on monitors all around the set.

'No!' Jo sank carefully into the seat opposite. Her character Stacey's sprayed-on jeans were so tight she couldn't sit down without dislocating her pelvis. 'How do you know that? You haven't been summoned already, have you?'

'No, but it's got to be, hasn't it? You know all those headaches my character's been having lately? It's going to be something serious, I know it.' Viola glanced around at the background artists silently reading their newspapers at the surrounding tables as they waited for the next take. 'Besides, the *People* said so yesterday.'

'You can't believe everything you read.'

'Why not? Those bastards know everything before we do.'

'Yes, but the press office denied it, didn't they?'

'Which means it must be true.' Viola's face looked lined and tired under the harsh studio lights. The strain was obviously getting to her. 'Look what happened to Reggie Allthwaite. They were still denying he was going to cop it the day that bus ran him down. You wait and see. Any day now they'll be tagging my toe and carting me off to the morgue!'

'You won't be the only one,' Jo sighed. 'I suppose you've read Charlie Beasley?'

'That reptile! Take no notice of him, darling. It's all speculation.'

'Yes, but Richard Black's got every reason to sack me, hasn't he? I'm the one who talked to the press. I'm already down as a troublemaker, remember?'

'I'm sure that's not true.' Viola grimaced as one of the set dressers slid a bacon sandwich in front of her. 'Oh God, do I have to? You know I'm a vegetarian.'

'You're supposed to be an actress, aren't you? Pretend it's a veggie burger,' Brett sneered from the sidelines. He was hanging around waiting for his cue, still wearing the smug grin he'd had since the day Richard Black arrived. 'Heard the news?' he said. 'Judy Pearce has got the push.'

'You're kidding!' Viola's cerise painted mouth fell open. 'I don't believe you.'

'Suit yourself. But when I left the green room she was on her third box of Kleenex.'

'Can we have some quiet on the set, please?' Aidan, the first assistant director, called out. There was a moment's pause while he listened intently on his headphones to the director's instructions coming from the gallery. 'Positions please.' The background artists put down their newspapers. Jo got up and took her place behind the café door, ready for her entrance. Behind her, a crudely painted diorama showed part of the outside street from which she'd supposedly just come.

'And . . . action.' The two background artists launched into an animated mime of conversation. As Jo opened the door, she deliberately emptied her mind of what was going on and tried to concentrate on her scene.

It wasn't easy. Ironically enough, Stacey and Viola's character Maggie were supposed to be discussing rumours that a property developer was going to send the bulldozers in and flatten the whole of Westfield to create an enormous Park and Ride site.

'I suppose you've heard the news?' Jo caught the rasp of emotion in Viola's voice and knew she wasn't acting.

'It's only rumours, Mum, we don't know anything for sure yet.' She eased herself into the chair, wary of her hip-crushing jeans.

'That's what you think. You don't know what they're all saying. They know the truth, even if we don't.'

'They don't know anything! You of all people should know what the gossips are like. They wouldn't know the truth if it came up and bit them on the backside. It's just stupid stories put about by people who want to feel like they've got one up on the rest of us, that's all.' Jo shot a glance at Brett, who was still hanging around behind the cameras.

'You might think it's only stories, but you wait.' Tears clustered dangerously in Viola's eyes. 'Next thing we know there'll be bulldozers at our doors and Westfield as we know it will be history –'

She broke off, too choked to speak. Fortunately at that moment one of the background artists' mobile went off, distracting everyone and giving Viola a chance to collect herself.

'I'm so sorry.' She fumbled in the pocket of her nylon overall for a tissue. 'It was terribly unprofessional of me to lose it like that. I don't know what came over me.'

'I do.' Jo reached across the table for her hand. 'You're desperately worried, just like the rest of us. But there's nothing we can do, except sit and wait.'

'You're right.' Viola sniffed back her tears and dabbed her eyes with her tissue. 'God, I wish I could be as calm as you.'

'Calm? Me? Don't you believe it,' Jo pulled a face. 'You'd be amazed what three years of drama training and a handful of St John's Wort can do.'

With the background artist suitably chastised and everyone back in their places, they managed to get through the scene fairly quickly. Viola then went off to the green room to find out the latest news while Jo was left with the terminally awful Brett Michaels.

He oozed on to the set, looking tough in his trademark vest and stone-washed jeans. As he sat down beside her, Jo was nearly choked by the overpowering effect of his cologne. 'God, what are you wearing?'

'Like it?' he leered. 'One of my fans sent it to me. She said it summed up my character.'

'You mean it gets right up people's noses?' Jo shuffled her chair away.

'Very funny. I wonder if you'll still be laughing when the Grim Reaper's finished with you?'

'I could say the same thing. You haven't been summoned to the top floor yet, I notice.'

'No need.' Brett reached across and helped himself from the plate of sausage rolls the set dresser had placed on the table. 'I know exactly what's going to happen to me.'

A slow, painful death, I hope. Jo's empty stomach churned as she watched him cram the sausage roll into his mouth. 'And what's that?'

'Nothing. I told you, I'm bullet-proof.' He sprayed crumbs across the table. 'My character is the most popular in this show, and Black knows it. That's why he wouldn't dare get rid of me.' He grinned, revealing a mouthful of half-eaten sausage. 'And I bet Steve will be even more popular when he's a grieving widower. I wonder how they'll kill you off?'

'They won't need to,' Jo said. 'I'll probably kill myself at the thought of a lifetime with you!'

Just then the props girl rushed over. 'You weren't supposed to eat those!' She pointed at the crumbs Brett was hoovering off his plate.

'So?' Brett leaned back in his chair and gave her one of his sexiest smiles. 'You can run off and fetch some more, can't you darling?'

'But you don't understand. They were old stock from the canteen. We cut the green bits off —'

Maybe there is a God after all, Jo thought as she watched Brett rush off set, looking sick.

They took a break for lunch, but no one really felt like eating. Instead Jo headed for the green room to join the others. Lara had just emerged unscathed from her interview with the Grim Reaper, and was all smiles.

'You know, he's not that bad,' she was telling Viola. 'Although he asked all these stupid questions about how I saw my character developing. I told him, look, I'm only there to say the lines, right, I don't get paid for thinking.' She twisted her long dark hair thoughtfully. 'He smiled a bit when I said that. I think he quite fancied me, actually.'

Meanwhile, in the opposite corner of the room poor Judy Pearce was hunched beside the coffee machine, doing a phone interview with *Inside Soap*, explaining how glad she was her contract hadn't been extended.

'No honestly, I'm relieved,' she insisted. 'It's given me the push I needed. It's so easy to get too comfortable in a place like this. You forget why you became an actress in the first place.'

'To be on the dole?' Viola took a long drag on her cigarette. Her scenes were over for the day, so she'd changed out of her overall and wig, back into her own baggy purple shirt, black leggings and boots. Her dyed red curls were caught up in a multicoloured chiffon scarf.

'This isn't the end, it's a new beginning,' Judy was saying. Jo and Viola exchanged wry looks. 'A fresh start. A challenge. There's so much to look forward to. No more typecasting. No more being creatively straitjacketed —'

'— No more regular pay cheques.' Jo could understand what Judy was saying, but she would happily go on wearing a creative straitjacket if it meant she could pay the bills and feed her children. But she had a terrible feeling it wasn't going to work out like that. She was certain Richard Black had it in for her. Her fate had been sealed the day she crossed his path.

Judy put the phone down and collapsed back in her chair. 'Thank God that's over,' she said. 'I need a gin. Lying through my teeth always makes me thirsty.'

'So have they said what's going to happen to you?'

'Apparently I'm going off to help run an orphanage in Romania.' She shook her head in disbelief. 'Can you imagine? My character hasn't had a selfless thought in five years and suddenly she's turned into Mother Teresa.'

While she went off in search of alcohol, Jo stared at the clock. Richard Black had promised to see everyone by six o'clock. That could mean another four hours of waiting and wondering.

The green room phone rang, and everyone jumped. Jo and Viola looked at each other.

'That'll be him,' Viola whispered. 'I wonder who he wants next?'

God, I hope it's me, Jo thought. If she had to wait any longer they'd be scraping her off the walls by six o'clock.

But it wasn't. 'Oh well, here goes.' Viola gave her a brave smile as she headed for the door. 'Wish me luck.'

'You won't need it,' Jo smiled back. If anyone needed luck, it was her.

After a quick break she was called back on set. This time she was in the hairdresser's where Stacey worked with Lara's character Winona. The set, with its pink fittings, floral wallpaper and rows of shampoo bottles, was as familiar as her own home. Yet somehow today she couldn't seem to find her way around. She bumped into the hairdryers and tripped over cables. She'd given the poor mute background artist five backwashes by the time the scene was finally finished.

'What's got into you?' Lara demanded irritably. With her own future at *Westfield* now settled, it didn't occur to her that anyone else could still be feeling the strain.

Meanwhile, the gossip flew thick and fast around the set as more and more people emerged from their ordeal. Apparently Eva Lawrence had summoned her Rolls and gone straight home, despite the fact she still had scenes to do. It was left to her assistant, Desmond, to explain that Miss Lawrence was 'indisposed'.

'Don't tell me he's sacked her too?' Aidan, the first assistant, looked shocked.

'No, but she was really shaken. Apparently that awful man reduced her to tears.'

Lara's lip curled. 'Good for him. She's done it to enough people in her time.'

Jo listened to them all, her stomach churning. Even when Viola appeared and gave her an excited thumbs-up from behind the cameras it did nothing to ease her flutterings of apprehension.

Why was he leaving it so long? she wondered. If it was good news, surely he would have seen her by now?

Then, just when she thought she couldn't stand it any longer, Brett suddenly appeared on set and said, 'It's your turn.'

'My turn for what?' Jo blinked stupidly at him, her mind suddenly blank.

'To see the Grim Reaper, of course. His PA just called the green room. He's ready for you.'

'But he can't be!' Having waited all day for the call, Jo was thrown into a complete panic. 'I can't go and see him like this. I need to get changed first –'

'That's up to you,' Brett said casually. 'But if I were you I wouldn't keep him waiting too long. He might not like it.'

Brett was probably right, Jo reflected, as she crossed the courtyard to the production building. All the same, she felt at a distinct disadvantage in her sprayed-on jeans and bright pink clingy Lycra top with lips and nails to match. How could Richard Black ever take her seriously looking like this?

She hadn't even had time to do anything to her hair. It was still a fluffy sticky mess, thanks to the make-up department and a can of industrial-strength hairspray. Jo nervously tried to smooth it down as the lift doors hissed open and she found herself on the top floor.

There was no one to meet her at the lift. What was she thinking of? Did she really expect Kate to be standing there with a red carpet and a glass of champagne?

Unlike the rest of the building, which was always alive with activity, the top floor was strangely silent. Jo teetered along on her white stilettos towards Richard Black's office at the end of the corridor, her footsteps muffled by the thick cream carpet. In half an hour her ordeal would all be over. As would her career, probably.

Kate's desk in the outer office was empty. Jo hesitated for a moment. Should she go straight through and knock on Richard Black's door? But as she took a step towards it, a sound from inside stopped her in her tracks. There was a lot of whispering going on, followed by some husky laughter. Then she heard Richard say, in a slightly annoyed voice, 'Kate, I'm working.'

'You're always working.'

'I don't have time for this –'

'But you're so tense. Come on, let me try and relax you.'

Jo edged closer. Surely they weren't – they couldn't be –

'God, that feels good.' They were! Shocked, Jo went into sharp reverse – and backed straight into a towering rubber plant.

The next few seconds seemed to pass in slow motion. In the silent office, the toppling plant sounded like a giant redwood crashing to the ground. Jo made a last frantic grab at it, but lost her balance and fell on top of it, taking a pile of files from Kate's desk with her.

As she struggled to release herself from the dense foliage, the door was flung open and there were Richard and Kate.

'What are you doing with those files? They're confidential.' Kate stormed over and began gathering them up, ignoring Jo as she grappled free of the rubber plant.

'It was an accident.'

'And what are you doing up here anyway? No one sent for you.'

'Yes, you did.'

'I certainly didn't. And I think I would have remembered, don't you?'

'But I got a message –' Colour drained from her face as the truth dawned on her. Bloody Brett Michaels! This must be his idea of a sick joke. She could imagine him down in the green room now, laughing his rapidly receding head off.

'I – I'm sorry,' she stammered. 'I must have got my wires crossed –'

'It doesn't matter,' Richard came to her rescue. 'You're here now, so we might as well get on with our meeting. Come into my office, would you?' He stood aside to let her enter. Jo strutted past him with as much dignity as she could muster while still picking bits of leaf out of her top. 'Perhaps we could have some coffee, Kate?' he added.

'As soon as I've finished tidying up this mess.' Jo caught Kate's look of suppressed fury as Richard closed the door on her.

The office had changed a lot since Trevor's day. Gone was the cluttered chaos of spilling filing cabinets and overflowing desk. In its place was a vast, clean space with white walls, flawless cream carpet and gently curving pale wood furniture. A small laptop computer was the only thing that marred an otherwise empty desk. The general ambience was calm, controlled, giving nothing away. It suited him, Jo decided.

Surprisingly, in the corner was a narrow fish tank. 'I didn't know you were an animal lover?' she said, then realised what a stupid remark it was. She didn't know anything about him.

Richard smiled slightly. 'Kate had them put in. They're supposed to be good feng shui or something. Apparently if one of them dies it's because they've absorbed the bad energies intended for the owner.'

I'm surprised any of them are still living, Jo thought. With the amount of bad energy being directed towards Richard Black this afternoon, it was a wonder they hadn't all gone fins up by now.

'Please take a seat.' He directed her to one of the strange bendy-looking chairs. In her nervous state she forgot all about her tight jeans and sat down too quickly. She bit back the yelp of pain as she felt her pelvis dislocate. Fortunately Richard didn't seem to notice as he sat down on the other side of the desk, picked up some papers and shuffled through them.

'As you know, I'm meeting everyone today to discuss their future at *Westfield*. I've spent the last few weeks exploring the dynamics of the show, and how everyone fits into it.'

He glanced up at her. Jo fixed him with an unblinking stare. Think cool, think aloof, she warned herself. The jeans had cut off her circulation and she could feel her legs starting to go numb. 'I think you'll agree, we've taken quite a few wrong turnings with your character over the past few months. According to the demographic profiles, Stacey isn't popular. She's perceived as being too bland, too boring.'

He looked up at her again. Waiting for me to cry, Jo thought. She wouldn't give him the satisfaction. He might be able to send Eva the Diva home sobbing, but Jo Porter was made of sterner stuff.

'Her marriage was a mistake, too,' he went on. 'The focus group reports all state that people would prefer –'

'Look, you don't have to go on with this,' she interrupted him. 'I'm being sacked, right?'

Surprise flickered in his dark eyes. 'What makes you say that?'

'I don't need a focus group to tell me you don't like me.' She lifted her chin. 'I don't blame you. We didn't exactly get off to a good start, did we?' She stood up. 'Let's face it, Mr Black, whatever your research had come up with you were never going to keep me on, were you?'

She had the brief satisfaction of seeing him lost for words. Making the most of it, she walked to the door, willing herself not to trip up and spoil her exit.

'Ms Porter? Jo?' She was halfway out when he spoke.

Jo hesitated. She wanted to finish off with a spot of huffy door-slamming but her curiosity got the better of her. 'Yes?'

'How would you like to have an affair?'

She stared at him. It was impossible to tell what was going on behind those eyes. 'Is this some kind of joke?'

'I'm not laughing.' He didn't look as if he ever did. 'I believe we could pull your character around. The way I see it, your main problem is that you've been allowed to become a cipher to Brett Michaels. It's time we tried you with your own storyline. That's what made me think of an affair.'

It all seemed too good to be true. 'But my character's only just got married!'

'I know. That's what would make it so interesting. Everyone knows Stacey's a devoted wife. No one would expect her to fall passionately in love with another man. Imagine the tension that would create.'

'So who would I have an affair with?' She just prayed it wouldn't be sleazy building society manager Harry Parnell. He'd already slept with most of the female characters in *Westfield*, including Lara and Viola's characters. It was a standing joke who would be next.

'I haven't decided that yet.' Richard put down his papers and steepled his fingers in front of his face. 'I think we'll bring in someone new.'

Someone new. No more fighting off Brett's wandering hands or his curry breath.

'So? What do you think?'

She was too dazed to think anything, except that she

73

would like to rush across the room and kiss him. 'I thought you didn't like me?'

'I never let my personal feelings interfere with my work. You're a very talented actress, but you've been underused. I mean to change that.'

She realised he hadn't answered her question. Or perhaps he had.

'So does Brett know about this yet?'

Richard shook his head. 'I'm not seeing him until tomorrow morning. Apparently he has some ideas of his own about how his character should develop in the future.'

'I bet he has.' No doubt they included him becoming mayor of *Westfield* and having sex with as many women as possible.

He sent her a shrewd look. 'Do I take it there's a certain amount of tension between you and Brett?'

Jo bit her lip. She didn't want him to think she was difficult. 'He's – um – very popular with the viewers –'

'I'm sure he is, but that's not what I asked.'

'I never let my personal feelings interfere with my work,' she parroted his own words back at him.

'I'm very glad to hear it.' Was that the shadow of a smile? He closed his file and stood up, dismissing her. As she headed for the door, he suddenly said, 'Wait a moment.'

She held her breath as he came around the desk to her. He reached out his hand and for one insane moment she thought he was going to pull her towards him for a kiss.

'I couldn't help noticing – there.' He plucked something from her hair and held it out to her. 'You had a bit of leaf in your hair.'

Jo cringed. So much for being cool and aloof. No wonder he was smiling at her. He probably couldn't wait for her to leave the office so he could tell Kate and they could both laugh their designer socks off.

'Thanks,' she said, plucking it from his fingers with as much aplomb as she could muster. To distract from her withering embarrassment, she added, 'So what's going to happen to Brett, if I get a new love interest?'

There was an unmistakable twinkle in Richard's eyes. 'Oh, I have something in mind for Mr Michaels. Something that will really challenge him . . .'

'Gay? Fucking *gay*?'

Brett stormed around the sweetshop set, knocking props flying. He kicked the door so hard his foot went straight through the plywood.

'Temper, temper.' Jo and Viola exchanged wry looks over the counter.

'Does that man know what he's doing? Does he? How can my character be gay? It's fucking impossible. The man drives a *cab*, for God's sake. He's got testosterone pouring out of him!'

'So did Rock Hudson, and look at him.'

'Well, I think it's a terrific idea,' Rob Fletcher said earnestly. 'It's such a brave thing to do, to take a character like Steve and fearlessly redefine the accepted gender parameters —'

'Why don't you let them redefine *your* fucking parameters, if you're so keen?' Brett growled. Jo giggled, and he swung round to face her. 'This is your fault! You put Black up to this, didn't you?'

'Don't blame me. You were the one who kept saying you wanted to take your character in a new direction, remember?'

'I didn't mean I wanted him to become a fucking shirt-lifter!'

'Ooh, very politically correct,' Viola tutted.

'Come on, Brett, it's only a soap,' Jo reasoned. 'No one's going to take it seriously.'

'*I* take it seriously. And so will my fans.' Brett jabbed his finger inches from her nose. 'Let's face it, ninety per cent of women only watch this crap show because of me. How will they feel when they find out my character's gay? I'll tell you how they'll feel. Let down. They'll probably organise a bloody lynch-mob!'

Your fans couldn't organise a piss-up in a beer tent, Jo wanted to say. But Brett's balding head was beginning to glow red under the hot studio lights. If she said anything he'd probably spontaneously combust.

'Maybe you'll start to appeal to the men instead?' Viola suggested sweetly.

His jaw muscles twitched. 'It's all right for you, you're a bloody lesbian. You don't care what anyone thinks of you. Well, I'm not going to stand for it!' He thumped his fist on the counter, making the pick'n'mix display rattle. 'I'm not going to stand by and watch that moron assassinate my character. Who gave him the fucking job, anyway? This would never have happened if Trevor Malone had been in charge!'

He stalked off the set, scattering technicians as he went.

'Where's he off to?' Aidan asked.

'Gone in search of his feminine side, I think,' Viola replied.

Jo smiled. Maybe Richard Black did have a sense of humour after all.

Chapter 8

'Ow! That hurts.'

'It wouldn't if you kept still – oh, I give up. I don't have time to fight with you this morning.' Jo dropped the hairbrush as Chloe wriggled away yet again. She winced up at the ceiling, where Roxanne's thumping techno-garage music was clashing with Grace's latest boy-band CD. 'Hurry up, Grace. I'm late as it is!'

'Why do you have to work today?' Chloe pushed her toast crusts through the bars of Pudding's cage. 'It's Sunday. You never go to work on a Sunday.'

'I told you, we have some special filming to do in a hospital, and they'll only let us do it today – damn!' She rescued a blackened slice of bread from the toaster. Today wasn't going to be a good day.

She was trying to put on her make-up and cram down her breakfast when Grace came clumping down the stairs.

'I hate this dress. Why do I have to wear it?' she demanded.

'It's lovely, darling.' Jo didn't look up from applying her mascara.

'I look like a freak.'

Jo raised her eyes and felt immediate sympathy. She certainly didn't look like Grace. Her skinny legs stuck out from the flouncy, daisy-edged hem. It didn't help that she insisted on wearing huge trainers with it.

'Just wear it for today,' she pleaded. 'Grandma keeps asking why you never wear anything she buys you.'

'That's because she never buys me anything decent,' Grace grumbled. 'I wish we didn't have to go to Grandma's. She's always moaning at us. "Wash your hands, wipe your feet, you surely don't expect me to walk the streets with you looking like that –"'

Jo hid a smile. Given the choice, she wouldn't go either. But it was yet another of Roxanne's days off, Duncan claimed to be working again and so her mother had graciously agreed to step in and look after the kids.

A little too graciously, in fact. 'No trouble at all,' she'd chirped, when Jo plucked up the courage to call. 'Stay for supper when you pick them up. Your father and I hardly ever see you these days.'

No martyred sighs, no disapproving remarks about working mothers. Not even the merest hint that her children would end up on drugs or running away with their physics teacher searching for the love they never got at home. Jo felt wary. Either Grandma Audrey had discovered Prozac, or she was Up To Something.

She was just making another assault on Chloe's untidy curls and trying to find her script when Roxanne swanned in wearing her dressing gown, the *Sunday Times* under her arm and a plastic bag on her head.

'Why are you wearing that?' Chloe was transfixed.

'I'm deep conditioning my hair. I've got a date tonight.' She flicked the switch on the kettle, flopped down at the kitchen table and reached for the *Style* section.

Jo suppressed a surge of envy. 'Has anyone seen my script?'

'I forgot to tell you, I'm playing an angel in the infants' Nativity,' Chloe said.

'That's wonderful, darling.' Jo tipped her bag out on to the table, scattering keys, pens, ancient parking tickets – but no script.

'And you've got to make me a costume. There's a letter about it in my school bag.'

'Me?' Jo looked up, as Grace snorted into her cornflakes. 'Don't they have teachers for that sort of thing?'

'All the other mummies are making them.'

All the other mummies stay at home having tennis lessons and Tupperware parties, Jo wanted to retort.

'Anyway, it's not for ages yet,' Chloe said reassuringly. 'Nearly three weeks. I know you can do it, Mummy.'

Jo looked apprehensive. 'I suppose I'll have to.'

'Is that what you're looking for?' Roxanne nodded towards Pudding's cage.

'Oh my God!' Jo stared in horror. 'Right, who did it?' She whirled round to face them. 'Who used my script to line the hamster's cage?'

'Someone with excellent taste, I should imagine.'

'Daddy!' The girls scrambled from the table to greet Duncan as he stood in the doorway, looking irritatingly calm and unruffled. She'd almost forgotten he'd promised to take the girls down to her mother's for her.

'You really should learn to calm down, darling.' He winked at Roxanne, who blushed to the roots of her plastic bag. 'Why don't you try meditating?'

'Good idea.' Jo extracted her script and shook the crumbs off. It was damp and smelt suspicious. 'And would that be before or after I've helped the girls with their homework, done the ironing, been to the supermarket —'

'Okay, okay, no need to go on. You're not my wife now, remember.' Duncan turned to the girls. 'Right, who's for a trip to sunny Nether Yeadon?'

'Me!' Chloe and Grace rushed to get their coats. Jo followed them.

'Now don't forget to say please and thank you, will you?' she warned. 'Grace, try not to bite your nails. And Chloe —'

She was still nagging when the front door closed on her. Jo felt a pang of jealousy as she peered through the glass. The

79

girls were climbing into Duncan's gleaming Discovery without a backward glance. No wonder, she thought. Their father was always laughing and joking, and never behaved like a miserable trout. If only she wasn't so short-tempered all the time.

Roxanne paused on her way up the stairs. 'You know, your ex is quite nice really,' she commented.

Jo watched the car drive away. 'He can afford to be,' she muttered.

They'd been given permission to film in an outpatients section of the local hospital that wasn't open on a Sunday. The location team had obviously been hard at work, trying to make it look as much as possible like a busy casualty department. Signs had been changed and new ones put up, and the place was crowded with background artists, all nursing various injuries while reading the Sunday papers and talking into their mobiles.

According to the storyline, Eva's character Ma Stagg had been beaten up by her new man friend, a former Catholic priest who, unknown to Ma, was a bigamist and part-time drug dealer. She'd been rushed to hospital and now her dutiful daughter-in-law Stacey was anxiously waiting for news. Her mother Maggie was with her, although why she'd bothered to come when she was Ma Stagg's sworn enemy no one could quite explain.

'Vi, when Jo asks you how you're feeling, I believe your line is "Fine." Not "Why, what have you heard?"' Aidan pointed out for the fifth time.

'Sorry darling, I wasn't thinking.'

'Yes, you were,' Jo accused her. 'You were thinking about that wretched brain tumour again, weren't you?'

'I can't help it. I know Richard said I had nothing to worry about, but that was two months ago. How do I know he hasn't changed his mind?'

'He won't.' Although Jo was beginning to wonder that

herself. Eight weeks on and her new love interest still hadn't materialised. Every time she asked anyone in the casting department about it, she was fobbed off with vague talk of shortlists and checking availability. Meanwhile, she was still in Brett's clutches. Although, after visiting a couple of gay clubs with Viola and getting a rapturous response, he was getting used to the idea of becoming a gay icon.

The scene was wrapped up quickly, and Jo moved on to her next, which unfortunately was with Eva the Diva. She was proving to be a difficult patient, propped up on a trolley in a curtained-off cubicle, puffing away on a Silk Cut while a tearful make-up artist pleaded with her.

'But you've just been beaten up!' she was saying. 'Couldn't I just give you a teeny little black eye –'

'You're not touching this make-up and that's final.' Eva's tiny eyes narrowed under their sooty coating of mascara.

Meanwhile, behind the cameras Aidan was going frantic. 'Look at her,' he muttered. 'She's supposed to have been beaten unconscious and she's done up like she's going to a fucking wedding!'

'It does seem a bit strange,' Jo agreed. 'But you know how touchy she is about looking good on screen.'

'Touchy? You're telling me. Some poor sod tried to put a bandage round her head and she nearly broke their arm.'

Jo eyed the unnaturally glossy black wig perched on top of Eva's head. No one had ever seen her natural hair underneath. Some people speculated she didn't have any. The only one who knew the truth was her personal on-set make-up artist, who was sworn to secrecy. But Eva was paranoid about looking her best on screen, come what may. Her character was the only charlady in existence who turned up to scrub offices in full make-up and a diamond big enough to sink the *Titanic*.

'It's no good,' Aidan sighed, after another twenty minutes of pointless wrangling. He listened carefully to the voice coming over his headphones. 'The director says we've got to go for a take, make-up or no make-up.'

'Thank God.' Jo glanced at her watch. She'd promised her mother she'd be there at six, and it was nearly five already. And the cameras hadn't even started rolling yet.

Luckily Eva seemed in a good mood since she'd won her battle over the make-up, and the scene moved quite fast. But just as they were wrapping up and she was lighting up her third Silk Cut, a serious-looking woman in a white coat appeared.

'There's no smoking, except in the day room,' she pointed out severely. Eva ignored her. 'What's wrong, can't you read the signs? I said –'

Jo cringed as Eva turned her head slowly, fixing the woman with a withering gaze. 'Do you have any idea who you're talking to?' Every word was etched in acid. 'I am the star of this fucking show.'

'And I'm a doctor in this fucking hospital.' The woman didn't flinch. She walked across the room, plucked the cigarette from Eva's lips and stubbed it out. 'You're quite welcome to smoke in the day room, but if you light up in here again I will have you removed. Understood?'

Eva was still frozen with disbelief as Jo hustled the woman out of the cubicle. 'We'd better stand clear,' she whispered. 'I don't think anyone's ever stood up to Eva like that. There's no telling what she might do.'

'I'm not afraid of her.' She smiled for the first time. It made her look younger, less frosty. 'Actually, it's you I came to see. It's Jo Porter, isn't it? I'm Ursula Meredith, a consultant paediatrician here. I'm afraid I've come to ask you a huge favour.'

Jo frowned. 'Me?'

'One of my young patients is a big fan of yours. It was all I could do to stop her coming down here herself when she heard you were filming here today. I wondered – I know it's

82

a lot to ask, but do you think you could spare a moment to go up and say hello? It would mean so much to her.'

'Well, I –' Jo glanced at her watch. Ten to six. Her mother would have a seizure if she was any later than half past.

'I wouldn't ask, but she's been going through such a bad time lately. She was due for a kidney transplant last week, but at the last minute it didn't happen. Now she's back on dialysis and she's really down about it. Poor love, she was pinning all her hopes on that operation. Her biggest dream is to be like any other eleven-year-old.'

'She's eleven?'

Dr Meredith nodded. 'Her birthday was last week. The day of the operation, would you believe? She's spent so much of her life hooked up to those machines, and she's always been really good about it. But now –'

Jo wasn't listening. Grace was eleven, and she never seemed to stand still. How must it be for a child not to have that freedom? 'Of course I'll come up and see her,' she said.

'Are you sure?' Dr Meredith looked hopeful. 'I don't want to keep you, if you've got to rush off somewhere –?'

Jo thought of her mother. Audrey would be fuming anyway, another half an hour wouldn't make much difference. 'Nowhere as important as this,' she said.

As it turned out, it was nearly seven when Jo finally got on her way. The Sunday traffic was terrible. Jo tapped her fingers on the wheel and cursed expressively. She couldn't even phone to say she'd be late because she'd just realised that she'd left her mobile on the kitchen table when she'd tipped out her bag. This could well trigger another Cold War with her mother.

And if her lateness didn't do it, her appearance certainly would. Jo sneaked a cautious look in the rear-view mirror, and winced. Her face still bore traces of Stacey's tarty screen make-up, and she had a large spot brewing on her chin. And she could only imagine what her mother would make of her scruffy jeans, sweater and trainers. Audrey wore a Country Casuals two-piece to do the gardening.

She pulled into the sweeping gravel drive of The Pines and felt the familiar urge to scream. Audrey was waiting on the steps for her. 'There you are, I – what have you done to yourself?' She looked horrorstruck. 'You could have changed!'

'Yes, Mum, I could.' Jo fumbled with the lock of her Cinquecento. 'If I'd had an afternoon to spare I daresay I could have had a manicure and a bikini wax too. But I've been working.'

Audrey tutted. 'That's the trouble with you working mothers, you never have time for anything, do you? It was different in my day. I would never have dreamed of going out to work when you were small. Call me old-fashioned, but I always thought my place was at home with you –'

Jo glanced at her watch. Thirty seconds. That had to be some kind of a record. She smiled sweetly and went past her into the house, her trainers squeaking on the polished parquet. 'Where are the girls?'

'Helping your father with the compost heap. Don't you want to go upstairs and freshen up?' She blocked Jo's way.

'Not really. I'll just collect the girls and go home, if you don't mind.'

'But you're staying for supper, aren't you?'

'I'd love to, but I can't. It's been a long day and I want to get the girls to bed, as it's school in the morning –' Then she noticed her mother's expression. 'Oh no, Mum. Not another one!' she groaned. 'Who is it this time?'

'I don't know what you mean,' Audrey sniffed.

'You're trying to fix me up again, aren't you?'

'I may have invited Rosemary Warrender around for supper.' Her mother couldn't meet her eye.

'And Rosemary Warrender wouldn't by any chance have a son who's single?'

'Actually he's divorced. And don't look at me like that, I

84

know you'll like him. He's a dentist,' she said in an awed whisper, as if oral hygiene was some kind of matrimonial Holy Grail.

'I don't care if he's a brain surgeon! I've told you, Mum, I can find my own men.'

'Well, you don't seem to be having much success so far,' Audrey pointed out unkindly. 'Anyway, it won't hurt to meet Simon, will it? I've told him all about you. Rosemary and I are sure you'll hit it off.'

'Really?' Just like she'd been sure she'd hit it off with Timothy, the computer engineer who'd spent two hours describing how to re-install a hard drive. Or Will, the embittered divorcee who thought all women were money-grabbing bitches.

'He's bound to be snapped up soon. He's already taken Joyce Prentice's daughter to the Dentists' Dinner Dance,' Audrey went on. 'I know you think I'm interfering, but I'm only doing it for you.'

'I realise that, Mum, but I'm not interested.'

'How can you not be interested? For heaven's sake, Jo, you've been divorced longer than you were married. I'm beginning to think no man will ever be good enough for you.'

'Maybe you're right. Maybe I just don't want to get married again. Maybe I enjoy being on my own.'

'And what about those girls? Don't you think they need a father?'

'They've got a father.'

'I mean a proper, permanent father, not one who turns up when it suits him. You broke up their family, Jo. You owe it to them to find someone else.'

Before she had a chance to respond, the door flew open and the girls tumbled through. Chloe was howling.

'Mummy, she smacked me!'

'No, I didn't.'

'You did! Tell her, Mummy.'

Jo caught her mother's eye. Audrey was shaking her head in a definite 'If only they had two parents none of this would happen' way. 'Get your coats, girls. We're going home.'

Instantly the howling stopped. 'But I thought we were staying for supper?' Grace protested.

'Grandma's made chicken pie. A real one, not out of the freezer like we have.'

Jo couldn't bring herself to look at her mother. 'It sounds lovely darling, but we'll have to come back another time.' She guided them towards the door.

'It's not fair!' Chloe was outraged. 'I don't want to go home. I want to stay with Grandma and Grandad!'

'She wants to be part of a proper family,' Audrey murmured. Jo clenched her teeth together so tightly she could hardly breathe, let alone reply.

She herded the children quickly into the car. Knowing her luck, Simon Warrender could be closing in right now, popping Tic-Tacs in anticipation of his big night.

'But I don't understand,' Chloe protested as she swung the car out of the drive. 'Why couldn't we stay at Grandma's?'

'Because she and Mummy had an argument, stupid,' Grace cut in. 'Grandma wants Mummy to get married, and she doesn't want to. Isn't that right, Mummy?'

'Something like that.' Oh Lord, she'd have to learn to keep her voice down.

'You're not going to get married, are you Mummy?' Chloe's eyes were huge with concern in the rear-view mirror.

'Of course she isn't,' Grace scoffed. 'She's far too old to get married. And she'd never choose anyone we didn't like, would you, Mummy?'

'No, darling.' Chance would be a fine thing.

In spite of what she had told her mother, she didn't enjoy being alone. Of course she wanted someone to share her life with. But she had a bad feeling she'd left it too late. As Grace pointed out none too kindly, she wasn't just on the shelf, she was past her sell-by date.

'I wouldn't mind if you married Richard,' Chloe said. 'I liked him.'

'I'll bear that in mind,' Jo said, and laughed all the way home.

Her argument with her mother, plus rampaging pre-menstrual hormones, meant she slept badly and woke up the following morning with a pounding headache and a foul temper. By the time she'd packed the girls' lunch boxes, found various lost items of PE kit and listened to Roxanne waxing lyrical about her wonderful new boyfriend, she was just about ready to kill. It didn't help that the spot on her chin now threatened to engulf her entire face. It lurked there, huge, red and shiny, defying all her attempts to mask it with concealer.

And just to make her happiness complete, when she reached the *Westfield* studios she found some idiot had parked a battered old pick-up truck in her parking space.

Jo slammed her car door and stalked towards it. But as she approached, a huge grey shaggy head suddenly appeared at the window and a volley of deep-throated barking sent her into sharp retreat.

Furious, she sought out the security guard. 'Do you know who's parked in my space?'

He dragged his eyes away from the *Sun* and peered out of the window. 'Looks like some sort of van.'

'I can see that! Who does it belong to?'

'Search me.'

Jo fumed. And these were supposed to be security guards? Some maniac could park a lorryload of Semtex right under their noses and they wouldn't even blink.

'But it's in my space. What am I supposed to do?'

The guard wrestled with the problem for a moment. 'Park somewhere else?' he suggested finally.

'Fine. Thanks for your help!'

She finally found a parking space around the other side of the building. By the time she'd trudged all the way back to the studio block, she felt she could quite possibly murder the next man she met.

'Sorry I'm late.' She stormed into Make-up and flung herself into the nearest chair, beside Viola. 'You won't believe it, but some selfish bastard has just dumped his van and his scruffy mongrel right in my space.'

'Do you mind? You can call my parentage into question if you like, but Murphy's is as pure as the driven snow,' said a voice behind her.

Jo looked up. There, reflected in the mirror, was the most beautiful man she had ever seen.

Chapter 9

'Irish wolfhound,' he drawled. He had a voice like Hugh Grant.

'Sorry?'

'Murphy. My dog. He can trace his bloodline back to the last century.'

'Ah. Right.' She willed herself to say something intelligent, but her tongue was welded to the roof of her mouth.

'Sorry about your space.' He pushed his flopping blond hair out of his eyes. He was tall, narrow-hipped and totally gorgeous, in faded Levis and an old leather jacket. 'I was late myself. I'm supposed to be here for a photo session. I wasn't thinking when I dumped the truck.'

'It doesn't matter.' She'd already forgotten about it, mesmerised by his intense turquoise eyes.

'We haven't been properly introduced, have we?' He held out his hand. 'I'm Marcus Finn.'

'Jo Porter.'

'So you're Jo?' A slow smile lit up his face. 'I understand we're going to be lovers?'

If he hadn't been holding on to her hand she would have slipped out of her chair in shock. As it was, she could only whimper.

'Marcus is your new love interest,' Viola explained with a knowing smile.

'What? You mean you −? Since when?'

'I was cast last week.' He frowned. 'You look a bit upset. Is there a problem?'

'N-no, not at all. It's just no one told me.' No one told her he would be so young, either. Or so incredibly sexy. She took in the cheekbones, the sulky mouth, and the thickly-lashed, melting aquamarine eyes.

'I hope you're not disappointed?'

Jo's mind reeled. Stunned, yes. Alarmed, definitely. But disappointed . . .?

'No,' she said. 'I'm not disappointed.'

'Good.' He looked her up and down with leisurely interest. 'Neither am I, as it happens.'

'You lucky bitch!' Lara hissed, as they gathered outside on the freezing set later that morning, waiting for the next camera angle to be set up.

'I don't know what you mean.' Jo huddled inside her *Westfield* anorak as the icy November wind whipped around her ears. Any minute now someone would shout 'Action' and one of the wardrobe girls would come and wrestle it off her. She wanted to enjoy the warmth while she could.

'Like hell you don't! Why didn't they cast him for me? He's far too young for you,' Lara pointed out with her usual tact. 'Imagine snogging him all day and getting paid for it.'

'I'm a professional. It makes no difference to me.' She pulled up her collar, hoping Lara wouldn't notice her blushing furiously.

'Yeah, right. So you don't mind if you kiss him or Brett Michaels?'

'I'd rather kiss a baboon's bum than – oh, hi Brett.' Jo beamed as her screen husband loomed into view. Despite the bitter weather he was still wearing a vest to show off his bulging biceps. He scowled back.

'Have you met Marcus?' Lara asked.

Brett grunted. 'Can't see what all the fuss is about. Looks like a complete tosser to me.'

'Takes one to know one,' Jo grinned, as he stomped off to argue his lines with the director. 'He's not his usual cheery self this morning.'

'Are you surprised?' Viola drifted up to join them. She too, was huddled inside a *Westfield* coat. 'He's got some competition, hasn't he? He's frightened he won't be the Number One hunk when our Mr Finn hits the screen. You should have seen him in Make-up this morning. The girls were all drawing lots to see who got him, and who got Marcus.'

'Don't tell me,' Jo said. 'Brett got the loser?'

'Worse than that. He got Daphne.'

'Blimey, no wonder he's pissed off.' Brett always liked to limber up every morning with a little light flirting with the make-up girls. Daphne Mansfield was a sour-faced old boot who wielded a blusher brush like a Gurkha knife. Up until now, Brett had never had to subject himself to her services.

'So where's the lovely Marcus now, then?' Viola looked around.

'No idea. Louise from the press office whisked him off about half an hour ago. I think he had some publicity shots to do.'

'Lucky Louise,' Viola sighed. 'He really is rather gorgeous, isn't he? I tell you, if I wasn't a lesbian and twice his age I'd definitely be interested . . .'

Brett's evil mood lasted all morning, and he seemed determined to take out all his frustration on Jo. All they had to do was walk down the street having an argument. But every time she did the scene well, Brett would either corpse or deliberately fluff his lines so they had to do it again. Then he started tinkering with his watch, trying to break her concentration.

While he held up filming for what seemed like the fiftieth time, Jo flopped down on the step outside the pub and looked around, hugging her knees to keep out the bitter wind. Her breath rose in misty coils into the frozen air. The sky was steel grey and threatening overhead. She fantasised about wrapping her fingers around a steaming mug of hot coffee.

But she was lucky compared to some. The actors who played the *Westfield* market traders, for instance, never had the luxury of working inside. You could spot them easily in the canteen. They were either blue with cold or half cut from the hip flasks they kept in their pockets.

Christmas might still be five weeks away, but in *Westfield* the trees and the decorations had already come down. Across the street, the props people were busily planting plastic snowdrops in Ma Stagg's front garden. By the time the real Christmas finally came, these would be replaced by plastic daffodils.

As she flicked through her script, she felt someone watching her. She looked up. There was Marcus, loitering behind one of the cameras. As their eyes met, he winked and hit her with the most lethally sexy smile she had ever seen. Jo jerked her gaze back to her script, blushing like a schoolgirl.

She wasn't the only one who'd noticed. 'Looks like you've got an admirer,' Viola said, as she patiently succumbed to the make-up girl's comb.

'I don't know what you mean.'

'Come off it. You must have noticed the new boy's been hanging around that monitor for the past twenty minutes.'

'He's probably just trying to familiarise himself with the filming schedule.'

'So why hasn't he taken his eyes off you?'

Jo laughed it off, but she couldn't help feeling secretly pleased. She also couldn't help wishing she was wearing something more flattering than Stacey's tacky acrylic sweater and leggings.

She didn't allow herself to look up again until the first assistant called a break in the filming. By then, Marcus had gone.

Complaining bitterly about the cold, they all made their way down to the canteen to thaw out. Louise the press officer met them in the doorway, looking frantic.

'Have you seen Marcus?'

'Have we?' Lara rolled her eyes. 'God, he's gorgeous!'

'He's also meant to be doing an interview. I've been plying the woman from *TV Times* with doughnuts for the past half hour, but I think she's beginning to suspect something.' She turned to Jo. 'If the worst comes to the worst I may have to offer you as a substitute.'

'How nice to feel needed.' Jo picked up a tray and went to the counter, where Joyce the canteen assistant was waiting for her, arms folded across her massive bosom.

'Only cold stuff now,' she announced flatly. 'I've turned off the fryer.'

'You're kidding!' Jo's jaw dropped. 'But I've been looking forward to a fry-up for the past two hours. It's the only thing that's kept me going.'

'You should have come in earlier then, shouldn't you?' Joyce's narrowed eyes disappeared into the fleshy folds of her cheeks. 'The fryer goes off at half past one, you should know that by now.'

So what was I supposed to do, walk off the set? Jo stared in impotent fury across the counter. It was no use arguing with Joyce. One wrong word and she'd have those metal shutters down before you could say 'Welsh rarebit'.

'How about a jacket potato?' she pleaded.

'Oven went off at one.'

'But I'm starving!'

'There's sandwiches. And it's no good you looking at me like that,' she added. 'I don't run this place for your convenience, you know.'

Obviously, Jo thought.

No sooner had she sat down with a limp-looking tuna and cucumber on brown when there was a commotion outside and a shaggy, slobbering monster hurtled through the door, followed a second later by Marcus clinging on to the other end of a rope lead. Jo recognised the monster from Marcus's truck.

They skidded to a halt at the counter, and the dog reared up, putting his huge paws on top of the till, his tongue lolling. 'Take no notice of Murphy, he's just a bit peckish.' Marcus grinned around apologetically. 'He'll be all right when he's had his bacon and sausage fix, won't you boy?' He patted the grizzled head, which was practically level with his own.

He'll be lucky. Jo glanced at Joyce's twitching face. 'You can't bring that – that thing in here!' She pointed a shaking finger at Murphy.

'Why not?'

'Because – it's against health and safety regulations!'

'But he gets so upset if I leave him on his own.' Marcus fixed her with a sorrowful look. 'He was abandoned as a puppy, you see. Tied to a railway line by a heartless owner. He was only seconds away from death when they found him. Ever since then he's had this terror of being left anywhere.' He reached across the counter and stroked Joyce's fat wrist. 'Can't he stay, please? He won't be any trouble. And neither of us has had a decent meal in two days.'

Jo chewed her leathery sandwich crust and watched, fascinated, as Joyce's mouth disappeared into her pouchy face. Her cheeks grew redder and she looked as if she was about to combust, until –

'I'll put the fryer on,' she grunted. 'Sausage and bacon, did you say?'

'And eggs and fried bread, if it's not too much trouble?'

'Did you see that?' Viola whispered, as Joyce waddled off. 'She's never done that before.'

She's never met Marcus Finn before. Jo watched him stroll across the canteen to where Louise and the woman from *TV Times* were waiting, both looking hacked off. Within minutes they were all smiling, the journalist was feeding

Murphy the remains of her doughnut and Louise was blushing like a schoolgirl. Wherever he went, he seemed to leave a trail of fizzing female hormones in his wake.

It wasn't hard to see why. With that blond hair and those wicked turquoise eyes, he looked like a fallen angel. He had a wonderful body too, broad-shouldered and lean-hipped, his long faded-denim legs stretched out in front of him, his white shirt carelessly unbuttoned to offer a glimpse of smooth, tanned skin.

'He's totally gorgeous,' Lara sighed. 'I wonder if he's attached?'

'Only to his dog, by the look of it.' Jo pushed the remains of her sandwich away. It was too disgusting to persevere with.

'He's charming the pants off that journalist. Why doesn't she ask him if he's got a girlfriend?'

'You know they're not allowed to ask about our personal lives!'

'So? That's never stopped them before.' They watched in envy as Joyce shuffled over with a huge, sizzling plate of fry-up. This in itself was unheard of – Joyce rarely emerged from behind her counter, except to lock the doors in someone's face. As she pushed the plate in front of Marcus, he looked up and gave her a dazzling grin which sent her reversing awkwardly into the chilled cabinet.

'Even she's got the hots for him,' Lara whispered.

Viola shook her head. 'He looks like trouble to me.'

'I know. That's what's so sexy about him. Besides, you say that about every man.'

'Yes, and aren't I always right?'

'So how did you get into acting?' the journalist was asking.

'By accident, I suppose.' Marcus took a piece of bacon off his plate and fed it to Murphy. 'I didn't seem to be much good at anything else. After I was expelled from boarding school –'

'You were expelled?' The woman's notebook twitched. 'What for?'

'Oh, various things.' Marcus shrugged. 'I suppose what really did it was when the headmaster caught me smoking dope in the girls' locker rooms –'

'If we could just go back to *Westfield*.' Louise looked panic-stricken. 'As you know, Marcus plays Steve Stagg's long-lost cousin Vic. He arrives mysteriously in the middle of Steve's birthday party. Stacey doesn't know who he is but she fancies him immediately.'

I know how she feels, Jo thought. Not that it would do her any good. Marcus was a good ten years younger than her, and far too sexy.

'So what attracted you to *Westfield*?' The journalist asked.

'The money mostly.'

'You mean you weren't a fan of the show before you started?'

'To be quite honest with you, I've never seen it before in my life. I don't even have a television.' Jo could see Louise's fixed smile growing steelier by the second. 'But now I'm here and I've had a chance to meet my co-stars' – he looked directly at Jo, who choked on her coffee – 'I must say I can't believe my luck.'

'Told you he had the hots for you,' Viola whispered.

'Don't be ridiculous,' Jo and Lara snapped back in unison.

The interview was wrapped up soon afterwards. As the journalist put away her notebook and tape recorder, Marcus came over to their table.

'Thank God that's over!' He sat down in the chair beside Lara and picked up her cup. 'Can I have a swig of your coffee? I've got a monster hangover.'

'Would you like a paracetamol?' Jo offered.

'Thanks. I knew you were an angel the moment I set eyes on you. Although to tell the truth, I'd be better off with a hair of the dog. Not you, Murphy,' he added, patting the enormous grey head that had wedged itself firmly across his denim-clad thighs.

'I suppose you were out celebrating your new job last night?' Viola said.

'So they tell me,' Marcus winced. 'Although I can't remember a thing about it, until I woke up in someone's back garden this morning.'

'Sounds wild.' Lara tossed back her dark hair.

Sounds awful. Jo suddenly felt very old indeed.

As Lara and Marcus discussed their worst hangover experiences, she found herself pinned to her seat by Murphy. She distracted him with the remains of her sandwich. His eyes were brown and gentle, but he still looked as if he could swallow her head whole.

Just then the others were called back for their next scene. Lara went reluctantly, with a last longing look at Marcus. Normally Jo would have headed straight for the green room, but with Murphy's head now firmly across her knees she was stuck to her chair.

'Well?' said Marcus. 'Did I do okay?'

She looked up, straight into those melting aqua eyes. 'Sorry?'

'The interview. You were watching me the whole time. I assumed you were making sure I didn't make an idiot of myself?'

Jo felt a warm tinge in her cheeks. 'Actually, I wasn't listening.'

'Weren't you?' He smiled. 'That's a pity. I need someone to keep an eye on me.'

Louise came over before she could reply. 'Well done Marcus, I think you made a good impression there,' she beamed. 'Now, would you like me to show you around the studios?'

'Thanks, but Jo's already offered.'

'Oh. I see.' Louise looked crestfallen. 'Well, if there's anything you need, you know where to find me, don't you?'

'What was all that about?' Jo asked, the moment Louise had gone.

'I'd much rather you showed me around. You don't mind, do you? Only I think we should spend some time getting to know each other.' He tilted his head beguilingly. Viola was right, she thought. Marcus was definitely Trouble.

They walked from the canteen out of the main production building across the tree-lined courtyard towards the studios. Jo pointed out the long, low row of Portakabins that housed the green room, the dressing rooms and the make-up and costume departments, aware all the time that Marcus was watching her and not paying the slightest bit of attention to anything she was saying.

'And these are the studios.' She flicked on the switch, flooding the vast, barn-like building with light.

'So where is everybody?' Marcus looked around.

'They don't shoot in here on a Monday. That's when they do all the scenes on the outside lot. I – um – noticed you were there this morning.'

'I just fancied a look around. I hope I didn't put you off?' He suddenly seemed very close. Jo tripped over a snaking electrical cable in her haste to get away.

She distracted him by pointing out the interiors for the pub, the shops, café and various houses. 'We rehearse in here on a Tuesday and Wednesday, and film all three episodes on Thursday and Friday,' she explained, aware that her voice was going up and down like a choirboy on the verge of a career change.

'A five-day week?' Marcus stepped behind the pub bar and ran his hand thoughtfully over the beer pumps. 'I don't think I've ever done one of those.'

'It doesn't always work like that. If you're in the middle of a big storyline you might be in every day, but otherwise it could be just two or three days a week. And you usually get a break afterwards. I think we might be busy over the next few weeks, though. Once we – er –'

'Start our affair?'

'I'm afraid there's no beer in those pumps,' Jo changed the subject abruptly. 'With the number of takes we do, we'd all be paralytic by ten o'clock.'

'I can think of worse things.' Marcus looked up at the optics. 'What about this lot?'

'All non-alcoholic. Only the fruit juices are real, the gin and vodka are straight water. But watch out for the whisky.' She was aware she was gabbling, but she couldn't stop herself. 'That's a mixture of burnt sugar and water, and it's absolutely disgusting.'

'I'll remember that.' He came back round to her side of the bar. 'Oh well, I thought it was too good to be true. Alcohol *and* a beautiful woman to sleep with. It's just a shame they're both an illusion, isn't it?'

As he moved closer, Jo took a step backwards and was immediately goosed by Murphy's cold wet nose.

'I'll show you the dressing rooms,' she squeaked.

She led the way, Marcus and Murphy close behind her, past the Make-up and Wardrobe departments. On the way they met a slight figure, huddled in a heavy mink coat, coming in the opposite direction. Between her turned-up collar, enormous sunglasses and black velvet turban there was little of her face to see as she scuttled past, her head down.

'Hi,' Marcus drawled. The woman hesitated for a fraction of a second. Jo could see her small, lashless eyes narrowing behind her tinted lenses. Then she rushed on without a word.

'Blimey, who was that?' Marcus stared down the corridor after her.

'That,' said Jo, as the make-up room door slammed, 'is Eva the Diva. She plays Ma Stagg.'

'Friendly soul, isn't she?'

'You should see her when she's in a bad mood.' Jo smiled. 'I wouldn't take it personally. She hates everybody. And no one's allowed to see her until she's been locked in Make-up for at least three hours. They have to rebuild her every morning – wig, eyelashes, teeth, the lot. Just like Franken-stein's monster.'

'Without the winning personality?'

'Eva's the star of *Westfield*. Just remember that and you should be okay.'

'I thought that big meathead with the muscles was the star?'

'Brett? No, he just thinks he is.' She stopped in front of a door. 'Here we are. God, you're lucky. Looks like you've got your own dressing room.'

'Is that a good sign?'

'Put it this way, only Brett and Eva get their own rooms. I still have to share with Viola and Lara.'

'Lara – is she the pretty one with the long dark hair?'

Jo pressed her lips together. 'That's her.'

Like all the other dressing rooms – apart from Eva's, of course – it was simply furnished, with just a dressing table and mirror, a wardrobe, and a couch. 'Well, here we are. It's pretty basic, but you can bring in your own stuff to make it more homely if you like. Apparently Eva's is like a palace, full of antique furniture and rugs and things. Not that I've ever been in there, of course.' She was gabbling again.

'It's brilliant.' Marcus flung himself down on the couch, closely followed by Murphy. 'This is a lot comfier than some of the floors we've been sleeping on lately, isn't it Murph?' The dog thumped his thick, shaggy tail in agreement.

'Don't you have your own place?' Jo asked.

'You could say I'm kind of between addresses.'

'Since when?'

'Since my last girlfriend kicked me out.' He yawned. 'I've been dossing down with friends until I get myself sorted out.'

'So you're – er – single at the moment?'

'Apart from Murphy. He's my minder. He wakes me up in the morning, he reminds me to eat, and he finds our way home at night when I'm too legless.' He ruffled Murphy's head. 'And he's got great taste in women too. He soon sees off the unsuitable ones.'

Jo smiled nervously. 'Sounds ominous.'

'Oh no, he likes you, I can tell. Which is just as well, really.' Marcus pushed the fair hair off his face so she could see into the clear, ocean-green depths of his eyes. 'I think I should warn you, I have a terrible habit of falling in love with my co-stars.'

She was still struggling for a suitable reply as the door opened and Richard Black came in.

'Marcus, I – oh, I see you two have already met?' He frowned at Jo.

'I've just been telling Jo how much I'm looking forward to working with her.' Marcus's eyes twinkled.

'I see.'

Unfortunately Murphy chose that moment to get off the couch and trot over to investigate her groin with his nose.

'Yes well, if you'll excuse me, I'd better be getting back on set.' She pushed him off, deeply embarrassed. 'I'll – um – see you soon.'

'I hope so.' Marcus' grin sent her stomach plummeting down to her stilettos.

She'd barely reached the end of the corridor when Richard caught up with her.

'I'm sorry if it was a shock for you, finding out about Marcus like that,' he said. 'I wanted to tell you myself, but I've been in endless production meetings for the past few days –'

'It doesn't matter,' Jo said.

'So what do you think of your new love interest?'

She gazed back down the corridor towards Marcus's door. 'He looks perfect to me.'

Chapter 10

'You're very dressed up. Going somewhere nice?'

'Only work.' Jo feigned great interest in the contents of the toaster.

'Oh yeah? And since when have you started wearing skirts for work?' Roxanne scraped out the marmalade jar with her knife. 'And make-up. You never usually wear make-up –'

'Well, I'm wearing it today, aren't I?' Jo saw her blink of surprise, and felt contrite. 'More toast?' she offered.

Roxanne held out her plate. 'Anyone would think you had a fancy man.'

'And what's that supposed to mean?'

'It was a joke, no need to bite my head off. I mean, you wouldn't really have a fancy man, would you? Not at your –' She broke off.

'Not at my age?' Jo finished for her. Roxanne was right. She was behaving like a teenager, but she couldn't help it. After three weeks of working together, she had a fully-fledged crush on Marcus Finn.

It was the only way she could describe the way she felt. The way she blushed idiotically whenever he came near her. The way she giggled at his jokes. The way she fantasised about him. She hadn't been like this since Duran Duran were in the charts and she'd had a thing about Simon Le Bon.

She pounced on her script when the production assistant brought them round on a Friday afternoon, to find out how many scenes they would have together. She'd even started to look forward to Monday mornings.

According to the storyline, Stacey and Marcus's character Vic were supposed to fancy the pants off each other. They were desperately trying to keep their feelings under control, with Stacey being married to Vic's long-lost cousin Steve. But all that pent-up passion was there, just waiting to explode. For once, Jo knew just how Stacey felt.

She also knew it was ridiculous and pointless. Marcus was too young for her. He was wild and impulsive. The most reckless thing she'd done recently was buy luxury loo rolls instead of the environmentally-sound recycled variety. She wasn't actually old enough to be his mother, but there were times when she felt like it.

And yet . . . she was only thirty-three, just eight years older than him. Hardly menopausal, whatever Roxanne might think. And he did seem to spend a lot of time flirting with her. Perhaps he liked older women?

'Hello Mummy. You look funny.' Chloe's nose wrinkled as she came into the kitchen. 'You smell funny too. Is that perfume?'

'Look, what is this?' Jo slammed down her mug as Roxanne and Grace gathered closer to have a sniff. 'Can't I dress up once in a while without someone calling the fashion police? I just felt like looking nice for a change, okay? Is that such a crime?'

Roxanne slid diplomatically from the table. 'I think I'd better get you two ready for school. Mummy's obviously in one of her moods.'

'I am not in a mood.'

'Maybe she's having a period?' Grace suggested. 'We had a lesson about it in school.'

'Why does everyone keep talking about me as if I'm not here?'

'What's a period?' Chloe ignored her. 'Does it make you want to dress up and paint your face all funny?'

'Have you got your costume for the Nativity?' Jo changed the subject as the others giggled. 'It's the final rehearsal today, isn't it?'

Chloe nodded. 'But I don't want to go to school today. I don't feel well.'

'Nor would I, if I had to wear that stupid costume!' Grace sniggered into her Rice Krispies.

'It isn't a stupid costume!'

'No, it isn't.' Jo shot her eldest daughter a warning look. 'What's wrong, darling?'

'My tummy hurts and I feel sick.'

Jo felt her forehead. She was a bit clammy. 'I'm sure this tummy ache isn't too serious. Maybe it's just first-night nerves? All actors get them.'

'Really?'

'Of course. I know some professional actors who are actually sick before they go on stage.'

'Especially if they have to go on with an old pair of net curtains and a couple of coathangers strapped to their back,' Grace muttered.

It seemed to do the trick. Chloe went off to school with Roxanne, swinging her Nativity costume in a Sainsbury's carrier bag. Jo felt a pang of guilt. Grace was right, it was a pretty limp effort. She vowed next year she would get her act together. Either that, or hire one from the Theatre Royal.

When she got to work, the first person she ran into was Kate, looking sharply elegant as ever in a taupe Nicole Farhi suit, her dark hair slicked back in a perfect chignon.

'I've been asked to give you this,' she said.

Jo looked down at the thick, expensive-looking cream envelope. 'What is it?'

'It's called a letter.' Kate smiled. Clearly this was what passed for humour on her planet. 'It's an invitation, actually. To Mr Black's drinks party.'

'Mr Black is having a drinks party?'

'Didn't I just say that?' There was no doubt about it, she was on top form today. 'It's next week. I need your reply by tomorrow at the latest.'

'Is anyone else going?'

'Well, we're hardly likely to have invited just you, are we? Oh, and by the way, Richard's having a breakfast meeting for the cast and crew tomorrow at eight thirty, to discuss some proposed changes in the production schedule. He wants you to be there.'

'But I can't!'

Kate had started to walk away. Now she turned back, very slowly. 'What do you mean – you can't?'

'I've made other arrangements for tomorrow morning.'

'Well, you'll just have to cancel them, won't you?'

'But it's my daughter's Nativity play. I can't miss that, can I? Couldn't you just have this meeting without me?' she pleaded.

Kate gave her a look that could cut through steel. 'Richard is expecting you.'

High-handed cow. Jo watched her clicking down the corridor, and willed her to trip over.

Richard would just have to un-expect her, wouldn't he? There was no way she was missing Chloe's big moment.

She headed for the green room to find the others howling at an interview Brett Michaels had done with the *Radio Times*.

'Listen to this.' Viola gasped for breath. '"I reckon if Shakespeare and Dickens were alive today, they'd be turning out scripts for *EastEnders* and *Westfield*." What does he know, anyway? He'd find a *Carry On* film highbrow.'

Jo was hardly listening. She'd spotted Marcus in the corner with Lara, their heads close together as they practised their lines. Lara kept flicking back her long dark hair, a sure sign she was flirting.

Viola put down the magazine and looked at Jo. 'You look nice. Got a job interview?'

'Not you as well?' Jo sighed. 'Blimey, it's only a skirt. I didn't know it would cause such a fuss.'

'We just didn't realise you had legs, that's all.' Pete Hurst, who played sleazy Harry Parnell, leered. 'Quite nice ones too, from what I can see.' He ran his eyes up to her hemline. 'You should show them off more often, love.'

As Jo made a face and yanked down her hem, she glanced over to catch Marcus's reaction. He was too captivated by Lara to notice.

'They make a lovely couple, don't they?' Viola whispered.

Jo nodded, but a disappointed lump rose in her throat. So Marcus had found someone new to flirt with. Someone younger, sexier and with infinitely better legs, whatever that old lech Pete Hurst might say.

They were interrupted by Ros, the Organising Stage Manager, whose job it was to watch over the goings-on in the green room and make sure the artists were where they should be, whether it was in Make-up, on a photo shoot or on the studio floor for their next scene. Depending on what drama was going on inside the green room at the time, her job also included finding lost keys, passing on instructions to nannies and cleaners, and summoning taxis for tired and emotional stars.

'I've just had a call from Wardrobe,' she said. 'They said to tell you they're sorry, but they're running late so could you go down and collect your clothes for your first scene?'

'I should bloody well think not!' Viola tossed her red curls indignantly. 'You phone them back and tell them she wants her costume delivered to her dressing room as usual. They wouldn't dare do that to Eva Lawrence, so why should they expect us to –'

'It's okay,' Jo interrupted her. 'I might as well go myself.' Especially since no one has even noticed I'm here, she added silently, with a last look at Marcus's turned back.

It was easy to see why Wardrobe were under pressure. Jo could hear the rumble of the washing machines halfway up the corridor. She opened the door and found herself enveloped in the warm, damp fug of drying laundry. Somewhere in the middle of it, Bernice the costume designer was hard at work ironing, while her sidekick Gaby consulted the bulky diary into which was scribbled the various scenes and what each character was supposed to be wearing.

'So I said to her, "Look Eva, you might be the star of the show but that fur hat has got to come off,"' Gaby shouted over the noise of the washing machines. She flicked over the page and pinned in another Polaroid. Occasionally she got it wrong and someone emerged from the pub wearing a completely different jumper to the one they'd been wearing inside, but miraculously most of the time her system seemed to work. 'I told her, "For one thing it's not in character, and for another we'll have all those animal rights so-and-sos climbing over the walls trying to free the bloody thing. It's the plastic rain hood or nothing," I said.'

'You didn't!' Bernice looked disbelieving. 'And what did she say?'

'Not a lot she could say. She was having her teeth put in, for a start.'

They both fell about. 'Mind you,' Gaby went on, 'that Marcus Finn's gorgeous, isn't he? I had to go shopping with him the other week. I tell you, it's almost worth putting up with Eva the Diva, just to see him in his boxers −'

Jo coughed. Two blonde heads lifted.

'Well, look at you,' Bernice smiled. 'You're looking very −'

'Don't say it!' Jo held up her hand. 'Yes, I'm wearing a skirt. No, I don't have a job interview, or a fancy man. And I'm not having a period.'

'Ooh, get you!' Bernice and Gaby exchanged wide-eyed looks. 'Are you sure about that, dearie?' Gaby asked. 'Only you're crabby enough. And don't sit there,' she shouted, as Jo collapsed into a chair. 'You'll squash Keanu.'

Jo rescued the dummy baby from behind a cushion. Until

Judy Pearce left, he'd been her toddler's stand-in during rehearsals. She'd often said she preferred him to the real thing.

She sat down and cradled Keanu in her arms. 'So what am I wearing today?' she asked. Then she saw Gaby's sly smile. 'Oh no – please don't tell me it's the cerise angora?'

'Sorry. That's what it says in the book. You were wearing it in the last scene, so you've got to be wearing it in the next one.'

'I'm always wearing it.' Jo watched Gaby disappear through the doorway that led into the long, dark room beyond. The room was like a sartorial Aladdin's cave, lined with clothes rails. Each character's clothes hung in separate sections, with their shoes, hats and accessories piled up in boxes underneath. Her character's clothes seemed to stand out in the gloom, all skin-tight neon Lycra and fluffy jumpers, not to mention the spray-on jeans and tarty white heels. 'Why does all my stuff have to be so awful? Why can't I have something a bit more chic? More designer?'

'On our budget?' Gaby returned with an armful of clothes. 'Tell you what, you talk the scriptwriters into letting you win the lottery and we'll see what we can do. In the meantime –'

'It's the cerise angora. Yes, I know.' Jo snatched it out of her hands. It was just horrible. Too short, too fluffy, too garish, with a disgusting sequinned motif on the front that looked as if she'd just been sick down it. Which was exactly what she felt like doing whenever she wore it.

But she could have been wearing a strategically placed copy of *Sporting Life* and Marcus still wouldn't have noticed. He barely acknowledged her as she stepped on to the hairdresser's set. He was too busy larking around behind the reception desk with Lara.

'So Jo, you and Vic are lusting after each other, but you know you can't do anything about it because it wouldn't be fair on Steve,' Aidan reminded them. 'Now you've got to stand by and watch while he makes a play for your kid sister.

And Marcus, you're redirecting all your pent-up passion to Winona because you can't have Stacey.'

That's a joke. Jo scowled at them. Any pent-up passion certainly wasn't heading in her direction.

She folded towels and rearranged shampoo bottles feverishly. What had she done wrong? A few days ago she'd been the one getting all Marcus's attention. She knew it couldn't go any further, but it had been nice while it lasted.

The crew suddenly parted as Eva Lawrence stalked on set, followed by her ever-faithful assistant Desmond. She took her place at the basin with an air of wounded resignation, clutching a salon gown around her.

'Oops, looks like Eva's upset someone again!' Lara whispered. It was a standing joke on *Westfield* that whenever Eva the Diva became too demanding, the script department got their own back by writing in a scene at the hairdresser's, knowing how terrified she was about losing her wig.

In this particular scene, Jo's character Stacey was supposed to be chatting with Ma Stagg over the washbasins when Vic came in and started flirting with Lara's character Winona. Jo found she could play Stacey's simmering jealousy without even trying. Her only problem was keeping the evil look off her face between takes.

'So how come a beautiful girl like you doesn't have a boyfriend?' Vic asked, when the cameras started rolling.

'Maybe I'm just choosy?' Winona teased back.

Like hell, Jo thought bitterly. After a night hitting the tequila slammers in her favourite Leeds clubs, it was harder to pick up a minicab than Lara Lamont.

Vic leaned closer. 'So what does a man have to do to get your attention?'

Being a Premier Division footballer usually does the trick. Failing that, just wave a platinum credit card.

'Watch it!' Eva hissed as Jo squirted shampoo in her eye.

Winona smirked. 'What do you suggest?'

Jo watched, frozen with shock, as Marcus planted a kiss on

Lara's mouth. The next second a piercing shriek echoed around the studio. It was coming from Eva the Diva.

Jo looked down at what appeared to be a drowned black cat in her hands. Without thinking, she screamed and flung it across the studio. It sailed up into the air and landed with a flop high up on the lighting gantry overhead. It was only when she heard Eva's strangled cry and saw her wispy grey head that she realised what she'd done.

'Oh God, I'm so sorry!' She didn't know whether to laugh or scream.

'You stupid cow!' With great presence of mind Desmond leapt forward and flung a towel over Eva's head. 'There, Miss Lawrence, we'll get you a Valium,' he soothed. Shooting a final, furious look at Jo, he bundled Eva off the set in a head lock. From under the towel came the sound of incoherent whimpering.

There was a shocked silence, then the whole studio exploded.

'Christ, did you see that?'

'I thought she was going to die!'

'I thought *I* was going to die! I don't know how I kept a straight face.'

'We'd better take a break, give her time to calm down.' Aidan's voice rose authoritatively over the babble. 'And for God's sake, someone get that wig off the ceiling before she comes back.'

Mortified, Jo escaped to her dressing room. It wasn't long before Lara followed, bringing Marcus with her.

'Ooh look, it's the *Westfield* wig-lobbing champion!' Lara giggled. Jo retreated behind Viola's discarded *Guardian*. Why did she have to bring him in here? Dressing rooms were supposed to be private. They could have gone to the green room if they wanted to chat. Or to his dressing room. God knows, they certainly didn't seem to want to include her in their little *tête à tête*.

She tried not to listen to them gossiping about all the

people they knew on the club scene. How could she have ever hoped to keep up? Lara was lively, fun and spoke Marcus's language. Jo had never taken an illicit substance in her life, and was sick after two glasses of wine.

Lara was prattling on about some fabulous new members-only bar that had just opened in Leeds. 'You mean you haven't been there yet? You've got to go! How about tonight? They're having a party to launch Image Incorporated's new album. I'm on the guest list.'

'Sounds like fun,' Marcus drawled. 'How about you, Jo? Do you fancy a night out clubbing?'

Jo crushed the pages of the newspaper, her knuckles white with fury. As if ignoring her wasn't enough, now he was making fun of her too.

Lara leapt in before she could think up a suitably cutting reply. 'I really don't think it's Jo's scene, somehow.'

'Why not? You'd love to come, wouldn't you?'

She gave him her frostiest glare over the top of the newspaper. 'Actually, I couldn't think of anything worse.'

Marcus looked hurt. 'But it'll be fun.'

'Spending the evening with a bunch of hyperactive kids pretending to be cool? I don't think so.' She did her best to look supercilious. 'I think my tastes are a little more sophisticated than that.'

Sophisticated? Who was she kidding? She was destined for an evening cleaning out the hamster's cage.

She folded up her newspaper and stood up. Marcus watched her. 'Where are you going?'

'To the green room. I'm sure you two would prefer to be alone. I know I would.'

She swept out of the dressing room. But she hadn't gone very far when Marcus caught up with her.

'Was it something I said?' he asked.

'I don't know what you mean.'

'Oh come on, I can tell you're in a mood.'

'I'm surprised you even noticed.'

She started to walk away but he grabbed her arm, swinging her around to face him. 'What's that supposed to mean?'

She was about to tell him, then changed her mind. It was just too pathetic. 'Forget it.'

'Is this about me and Lara?'

Her eyes flashed. 'Why should I care what you two get up to?'

'It is, isn't it? You're jealous because you think I fancy her.'

'Don't flatter yourself!' She turned her face away. 'Anyway, it's obvious how you feel about her. You've been chatting her up all day.'

'Only because I had to. It's in the script, remember?'

'And is it in the script that you have to ignore me?' The words were out before she could stop them.

'Actually, it is.' He tilted her chin to look up at him. 'Look, we're supposed to be fighting our feelings, right? I chat her up and you get jealous.'

'Yes, but that doesn't mean you have to do it in real life!'

'Maybe not, but that's the way I work. I can't just switch my emotions on and off. I have to feel them here.' He took her hand and laid it over his heart. Jo felt the warm, hard muscles underneath his t-shirt and her knees turned to jelly.

'You mean to tell me,' she said slowly, 'that you've been ignoring me and deliberately flirting with Lara so it would look right in the *scene*?'

'And it worked, didn't it?' Marcus's aqua eyes sparkled. 'You really wanted to rip her hair out by the roots, didn't you?'

'Please don't mention hair.' Jo looked sheepish. Maybe she was a bit jealous. And Marcus was right, that afternoon's scenes had been some of the easiest she'd ever done. The emotions were all there, barely suppressed. But even so . . .

'I wish you'd told me this before,' she grumbled.

'But it wouldn't have worked then, would it?' Marcus

grinned. 'Although I have to say you made it pretty hard to ignore you this morning. You looked so sexy in that skirt –'

The sound of throat clearing made her turn round. Richard Black was at the other end of the corridor. How long had he been there?

Long enough, judging by the look he was giving them.

'Can you tell me where I'd find Eva's dressing room?' he said. 'I understand there's been some difficulty on the set.'

As Marcus gave him directions, Jo shuffled her feet and stared at the floor. She felt like a guilty schoolgirl who'd been caught snogging behind the bike sheds.

And she hadn't even done anything. Yet.

Chapter 11

She spent the whole journey home wishing she'd never given in to such a mad impulse. Why had she agreed to go clubbing with Marcus? What was she trying to prove? That she could compete with the likes of Lara? She wasn't even the night owl type. Her idea of a good night was a video and takeaway with the girls and in bed by ten.

She didn't know what to wear, either. Not a lot, if Lara's photos in the newspapers were anything to go by. She seemed to get by with little more than some strategic body piercing.

Jo frowned at her reflection in the rear-view mirror. Somehow she couldn't see herself sporting a belly-button ring and a couple of henna tattoos. The last time she set foot in a nightclub, it was all frilly shirts and Culture Club. She was so far out of fashion she was almost back in it. Perhaps she could dig out her old legwarmers and start a revival?

Or perhaps she should just play it safe in her little black dress? Or better still, not go at all? Lara wouldn't miss her. And as for Marcus – surely it was better not to turn up than to make a complete fool of herself?

As she drew up outside the house the front door flew open and Roxanne appeared on the step. 'Jo! Thank God you're home!' Her face was blanched with anxiety. 'It's Chloe. They sent her home from school –'

Jo didn't wait to hear any more. She pushed past Roxanne and headed for the sitting room.

Chloe was lying on the sofa, looking even whiter than the toy polar bear she clutched. Her round blue eyes were ringed with dark circles.

'Oh Mummy,' she wailed. 'I've got first-night nerves. I was sick on a shepherd.'

'Shh, darling. It's okay. Mummy's here.' Jo knelt down and touched her forehead. It was clammy with sweat.

'But it went in the manger and everything –'

'It doesn't matter.' She pushed a damp strand of hair off her face.

'She's been sick three times.' Grace was curled up in the armchair. She looked both disgusted and impressed. 'She vomited on the rug. And that cushion. And she was nearly sick on the hamster too.'

'I wasn't sure whether to ring you at work.' Roxanne hovered, holding a plastic seaside bucket. 'She seemed okay an hour ago. Then she suddenly got worse –' As if to prove it, Chloe suddenly jacknifed upright and retched. Jo grabbed the bucket just in time.

'It's probably a tummy bug,' she said. 'These things take hold so quickly. The important thing is to keep her cool. Can you bring me a damp flannel?' As Roxanne rushed off, Jo turned back to Chloe. 'Mummy will make you more comfortable.'

'Do you think I'll be well enough to be in the Nativity tomorrow?'

'I jolly well hope so. I'm looking forward to seeing this show of yours. You'll be fine in the morning, you'll see.'

But there was the evening to get through first. And Jo knew she wouldn't be spending it clubbing. Leaving Roxanne to mop Chloe's sweaty brow, she went into the hall and called Lara's mobile.

Lara answered immediately. From the deafening techno

beat in the background it sounded as if she was already getting stuck into some serious partying.

'Really? Oh, that's bad news.' Lara tried – and failed – to sound disappointed as Jo explained the situation. 'Still, never mind. I'm sure Marcus and I will have fun without you.'

I bet you will, Jo thought, putting down the phone.

Roxanne was standing in the doorway. 'You could have gone out,' she said. 'I would have coped.'

'I know, but I would have been worrying about her all night.' Jo glanced through to the living room. Grace was reading Chloe a story, being careful to stay out of vomiting range. 'Besides, it probably would have been awful.' She'd never know now, anyway.

It turned out to be a long night. Chloe clung to her all evening, stopping only to throw up every hour or so. At first Grace was fascinated, but after a couple of hours she pronounced it all too gross to bear and stomped off to her room for an early night. Roxanne had already retreated upstairs with the portable TV and Jo's copy of *Cosmo*.

Jo washed Chloe's face, changed her into fresh pyjamas and settled her down in her bed. She looked so small, snuggled up under the big double duvet.

'Do you think they'll let me be in the show tomorrow, Mummy?' she croaked.

'Of course they will, sweetheart. Why shouldn't they?'

'I was sick on Jamie Dunsford. And Mrs Parkin was very cross. What if they make someone else an angel instead of me?'

'Then they'll have me to deal with,' Jo said firmly. 'How are you feeling now?'

'A bit better.' Just to prove it, Chloe was suddenly and comprehensively sick all over Jo's lap. She then fell into a deep and peaceful sleep, leaving Jo to stagger bow-legged to the bathroom.

The perfect end to a perfect day, she thought. And what were Lara and Marcus doing now? Dirty dancing in a darkened nightclub? Playing some serious tonsil hockey, perhaps? Whatever it was, it was probably more fun than sponging sick off her jeans.

She pulled them off and tossed them into the washing basket and was just wiping down her shirt when the doorbell rang. Jo glanced at the clock. Who could be calling at half past eleven?

It was Marcus. He stood in the doorway, clutching a bottle of wine, looking devastatingly sexy in black jeans and his old leather jacket, his blond hair falling into his eyes.

'I came to see what changed your mind,' he said.

'Didn't Lara tell you? Chloe was sick.' She yanked her shirt down, conscious of his gaze lingering on her thighs.

'I know that's what she said. But I wasn't sure if it was just an excuse?'

Jo's eyes flashed in outrage. 'You seriously think I'd lie about my daughter being ill?'

'I suppose not.' He looked sheepish. 'How is she now?'

'Sleeping, thank God.' Jo glanced over his shoulder into the street. His pick-up truck was parked under a street lamp. 'Where's Lara?'

'Snogging with the DJ, the last time I saw her.' He tilted his head, fixing her with those incredible sea-green eyes. 'Well? Aren't you going to invite me in?'

Jo summed up the situation shrewdly. 'You mean Lara ditched you so you thought you'd come round here instead, is that it?'

'No!' He looked hurt. 'Actually, I'd decided to come round before Lara ditched me.' He smiled appealingly. In spite of herself, Jo couldn't help smiling back. 'So can I come in? Please? I've brought a bottle of wine.' He waved it at her.

It was tempting. But after the night she'd had she just couldn't face it. 'Sorry, I'm hardly in the mood for entertaining.'

'You're certainly dressed for it.' His eyes travelled up her bare legs again. Jo manoeuvred herself behind the front door.

'Some other time, maybe. I'm a bit tired.'

'You mean to say I blew my last five ninety-nine in Oddbins for nothing?' He turned down his mouth. He had a very sexy mouth. 'Oh, go on. One drink won't hurt, surely?' He stopped and sniffed the air. 'What's that smell?'

There was a nasty sour aroma coming from somewhere. In panic, Jo realised it was her shirt.

She had to get changed, and it seemed quicker just to give in than to stand and argue. 'Okay, one drink,' she agreed. 'The kitchen's through there. I've got to get dressed.'

'Not on my account, surely?'

She ignored him and hurried upstairs. She crept around her bedroom, tracking down jeans and a sweater in the darkness, resisting the mad urge to slip on the sexy silk dressing gown she'd bought in a moment of La Perla madness. Downstairs she could hear Marcus was clattering around in the kitchen, opening drawers and cupboards.

Jo tried to quell the absurd feeling of excitement that bubbled inside her. He was a friend, that's all. No, not even that. He was just someone she worked with. Practically a stranger. And he was staying for one drink. Nothing more to it than that, no matter what her torrid imagination might be coming up with.

He'd already made himself at home in the living room when she got back downstairs. Jo found him lounging on the sofa, a glass in his hand. Murphy, she noticed with dismay, was stretched out on the floor beside him.

'I couldn't leave him in the truck. He yells his head off.' Marcus handed her a glass. 'I hope you don't mind?'

'I suppose not.' Jo picked her way over the thrashing tail. 'So does he go everywhere with you?'

'More or less.'

'Even to bed?'

He gave her a slow, sexy smile that made her instantly wish she hadn't said it. 'Not always.'

She sat cross-legged on the floor and sipped her wine. The

118

silence lengthened awkwardly. What should she say? Jo wondered. She couldn't talk about the latest clubs like Lara. They had nothing in common, except work. 'So – er – what do you think of *Westfield*?'

'It seems great. But I can't see myself staying there for long.'

'No?' She tried to keep the disappointment out of her voice.

'Well, it's not really what you become an actor for, is it? Doing the same thing, day after day, year after year. If I wanted a job like that I'd work in a bank. At least then I'd get a pension.'

'That's true.' She'd felt like that herself once, before reality had intervened and made her rethink her ambitions. She wondered what he must think of her, stuck in the same job for the past four years. 'How did you get into acting?'

'It seemed like a good idea at the time. I kept being kicked out of school, and it was pretty clear I wasn't going to end up at university. Drama school seemed like an easy option.'

'Which college did you go to?'

'Most of them,' he grinned. 'I'm afraid I'm not very good at sticking to things. Especially rules. I think it's genetic. My family isn't known for its staying power. We get bored too easily.' He held out the bottle to her. 'More wine? You've hardly touched yours.'

'No thanks. I've got to be up early in the morning. I'm watching my daughter be an angel. And believe me, that doesn't happen very often.' She smiled at him. 'Tell me more about your family.'

'You wouldn't believe me if I did.' He slid on to the floor next to her, his long legs stretched out in front of him. He reminded her of a cat, with his lithe limbs and sleepy green eyes. 'Most people seem to find my family set-up a bit weird, to say the least.'

'Sounds intriguing.'

'Let's just say we're not what you'd call a traditional nuclear family.'

As he painted a picture of his chaotic home life, Jo was shocked. His parents, various brothers and sisters and assorted friends and hangers-on lived in a kind of commune deep in the Gloucestershire countryside. But it didn't end there. From what Marcus said, it sounded as if his father had repopulated the local community single-handed. Other women passed through the household more often than the local service bus. And each relationship seemed to have produced a little Finn. It might not be nuclear, but there was certainly a lot of fall-out.

'Doesn't your mother mind all this philandering?' she asked.

'Why should she? She's free to do the same. In fact, Felix and Freya aren't biologically my father's children, although of course they live with us. Anyway, it's hardly philandering if she knows all about it, is it?'

'I suppose not.' Jo had a sudden vision of numerous little blond children running around barefoot, watched over by a lecherous old beardie and his kaftan-wearing wife. It was like something out of the sixties. 'I can see why people find it strange, though.'

'That's their problem. But I wonder how many of them have lovers on the side? It's a funny old world, isn't it? It's okay to have an affair as long as you keep it secret. But if you try to be open and honest about it you're considered some kind of mad hippy.'

He leaned over, topping up her glass. This time she didn't stop him. He'd moved closer so their shoulders were touching and his thigh was brushing against hers. If she just turned her face a fraction he would be close enough to kiss . . .

Then, as if he could read her mind, he said, 'Can I stay the night?'

'What?'

'Can I stay? I'm in no fit state to drive.' He held up the empty bottle. 'And frankly, I've got nowhere else to go. I've sort of run out of friends' floors.' He looked downcast, like a little boy.

Jo thought about it. 'Well, I suppose you could have the sofa –'

'I'd rather sleep with you.'

She nearly dropped her glass in shock. Talk about direct!

'I'm afraid my daughter's beaten you to it,' she said, trying to sound light-hearted although her voice was wobbling all over the place. 'Besides, I hardly know you.'

'What's there to know? You don't need to see my CV to know you want me. And I want you.' He was so close they were almost breathing the same air.

Jo finished her wine with a gulp. 'You don't waste any time, do you?'

'What do you want me to do? Play games? Go through a big charade of asking you out, swopping phone numbers, going on a date?'

That would be nice, she thought. 'Isn't that how relationships usually start?'

'Who said anything about a relationship?'

It was like a bucket of icy water over her head. 'I see. So we're talking about a one-night stand, are we?'

'A night, a week, a lifetime – who knows?' Marcus shrugged. 'Why do we have to stick labels on everything? Why can't we just enjoy the moment, and see what happens?'

'I like labels.'

'Well, I don't. They frighten me.' He reached up and traced her jawline. 'I'm just trying to be honest with you. I like you. And I think you like me. Maybe we could have a relationship, I don't know. Like I said, I've never been very good at sticking to anything. But I know we could be very, very good together –'

He brushed her lips with his finger. The slightest touch,

121

but it sent electric shockwaves through her. Mesmerised, she watched his mouth coming closer. Another second and he would be kissing her –

Suddenly there was a loud yelp, followed by a tidal wave of furniture as Murphy shot to his feet. Jo dived to catch the glasses as his tail swept the coffee table.

'What happened?'

'I think I knelt on his paw. It's okay, Murph, don't be such a wuss.' Marcus ruffled the shaggy head. 'Now, where were we?'

'I think I was just about to make some coffee.' Jo scrambled to her feet as Marcus closed in again.

She escaped to the kitchen and leaned against the door, her heart doing a frantic salsa against her ribs. Oh God. Marcus Finn, gorgeous blond love god that he was, actually wanted to sleep with her.

And she wanted to sleep with him. She absent-mindedly emptied half the coffee jar into the cafetière at the thought. But it was all wrong. She might be old-fashioned, but she liked relationships. She liked talking, finding out about each other, the slow burn of sexual anticipation. Jumping into bed with someone, no matter how amazingly sexy, wasn't her style.

If Marcus cared anything about her, he'd respect that. And if he didn't . . .

She carried the tray back into the living room. 'Look Marcus, I hope you don't think I'm being –' she started to say, then stopped. He was stretched out on the sofa, snoring gently.

'Marcus?' She put down the tray and took the glass from his lolling hand. Murphy lifted his head from his huge paws long enough to give her a reproachful look.

Jo smiled wryly. So much for white-hot passion. With a sigh, she went off to the airing cupboard in search of a spare duvet.

Chapter 12

She had a highly erotic dream that night. She was covered in banana yoghurt and Marcus was licking it off. Her body became one huge quivering erogenous zone as his tongue delicately explored every inch of her. Her navel, her breasts, the hollows in her collarbone, her ears . . .

She stirred. Something *was* licking her ears. But there was nothing sensual about the rasping, slurping tongue, or the warm drool running down her neck.

She opened her eyes. Soulful brown eyes gazed back at her from under quizzical Denis Healey brows.

'Bloody hell!' She tried to move but she was pinned to the bed by twelve stone of hairy canine. 'Help!'

Murphy sensed her panic and started barking, giving her a faceful of stale doggy breath. He leapt off the bed and bolted for the door just as Chloe, Grace and Roxanne came through it.

'Mummy, why is there a strange man on our sofa?'

'He's – um – a friend.' Jo clutched her chest, checking for broken ribs.

'What sort of friend? A boyfriend?' Grace was suspicious. 'He's not moving in with us, is he?'

'Of course he isn't moving in.' She breathed in carefully. At least her lungs still worked. 'What time is it?'

'Ten past eight.'

'Ten past eight?' She flung off the duvet and tumbled out

of bed so quickly the blood shot straight to her feet. 'Why didn't anyone wake me?'

'We were too busy watching that man.' Chloe, thankfully, seemed none the worse for her night of throwing up.

Jo searched for her dressing gown. 'Go and get dressed, girls. I just need a quick shower.'

'But that man –'

'He won't bite you. Now hurry up!'

The girls shuffled off, but Roxanne lingered behind. 'So who is he?'

'His name's Marcus and he's just joined *Westfield*.' Jo delved under her bed. 'Have you seen my other slipper?'

'How old is he?'

'Twenty-five, I think.'

'So he's a lot younger than you, then?'

'Astounding, Einstein.' Jo threw on her dressing gown and one slipper, and headed for the door. But not before she'd caught the look Roxanne gave her. It was a look of envy mingled with disgust. *Toy boy*, it said.

'Jo.' She followed her across the landing. 'About this Marcus –'

'What about him?' She swung round. 'Look, I told you, he's just a friend, okay? There's nothing going on between us.'

'I know, but –'

'You think he's too young for me, is that it?'

'No, but I just wanted to tell you he's –'

Jo backed in through the bathroom door.

'– in the shower,' Roxanne said.

He was just stepping out of it, his fair hair dripping, water glistening on the golden, hard-muscled planes of his body.

'Come to join me?' he grinned.

'I – I –' She didn't know where to look. Or rather, she knew exactly where to look but was trying very hard not to. 'I'm sorry,' she blurted out.

'No problem.' He reached unhurriedly for a towel and

124

rubbed his hair. 'I'm sure you must have seen a naked man before?'

Not like you, I haven't. Jo risked a glance at his reflection in the mirror. He was like Michaelangelo's David, perfectly in proportion. Well, most of him anyway.

'I – I need a shower,' she stammered.

'I gathered that. Would you like me to scrub your back for you?'

'I think I can manage, thank you.'

'Call me if you change your mind.'

And then he was gone. Jo slammed the bolt across the door and showered quickly. After she'd washed, dressed and dried her hair she found Marcus at the kitchen table, calmly ploughing his way through a bowl of Rice Krispies. Chloe watched him like a scientist conducting a particularly fascinating lab experiment.

'Your dog doesn't look very friendly,' she said.

'Don't you believe it. He's a gentle giant.'

'What if he eats Pudding?' She glanced anxiously towards the hamster's cage.

'He won't. He never touches pudding, he's watching his figure.' He looked up at Jo and grinned. Her stomach did a backflip and ended up tangled around her lungs.

'So, who wants breakfast?' she said brightly. As Chloe reached for the Sugar Puffs, Jo noticed Grace hanging back in the doorway.

'I'm not hungry,' she muttered.

'You, not hungry? That's a first.' Jo flipped the switch on the kettle. 'Shall I make you some toast?'

'I told you, I don't want anything!' With a final scowl at Marcus, she slammed the door. Jo listened to her footsteps stomping up the stairs.

'I wonder what's wrong with her?'

'She doesn't like him.' Chloe, blunt as ever, nodded towards Marcus.

Jo felt a blush rising. 'I'm sure that's not true –'

125

'It is! She said he was horrible, and his dog was even worse, and she said if you marry him she's going to run away from home and live with Daddy.' She plunged her hand into the cereal packet, searching for the free gift.

Mortified, Jo forced herself to meet Marcus's eye. Luckily he was smiling.

'I suppose this means we'll have to cancel the register office?' he said.

He left soon afterwards. There was an awkward moment as they stood on the step.

'Are you sure I can't offer you a lift?' he asked. 'It might be a bit of a squash with you, me and Murphy in the truck but I'm sure we could manage it?'

Jo shook her head. 'It's Chloe's Nativity this morning.' She bit her lip. 'Look, Marcus, about last night –'

'Sorry I fell asleep just as things were beginning to get interesting.'

'That's just it, I don't think they were. It's not that I don't find you attractive or anything,' she said quickly. 'It's just – I take sex very seriously.'

'So do I.' His eyes glinted.

'That's not what I meant –'

'I know exactly what you mean.' He took her face in his hands and his lips brushed hers. 'But don't worry, I haven't given up on you yet.'

With a wink, he was gone, Murphy at his heels. Jo closed the front door, turned around – and bumped straight into Chloe.

'He kissed you!' she crowed. 'I saw him. He is your boyfriend, isn't he Mummy?'

'No, he isn't.' Jo looked up. Grace was on the stairs, watching her with silent reproach. Before Jo could say anything, she ran back up to her room and slammed the door.

With Grace cold-shouldering her, and Roxanne treating her

as if she was some kind of cradle-snatching pervert, it was a relief to get to work that afternoon.

Lara and Viola were already in the dressing room, having been working all morning. Lara was on her mobile as usual, while Viola was engrossed in an article on non-invasive cosmetic surgery in *She*.

She looked up as Jo entered. 'Have you heard the news? Lara's getting married.'

'You're kidding? But she hasn't even got a boyfriend!'

'She has now. Some DJ she met in that club last night.'

'Blimey.' Jo gaped at Lara. 'So what's she doing now? Breaking the news to her parents?'

'You must be joking! She's calling her agent to try and fix up a magazine deal for the wedding. Apparently this is too good a photo opportunity to miss.'

Jo shook her head. 'That girl doesn't buy a packet of Tampax without trying to sell the exclusive rights to someone.'

'That girl doesn't buy anything,' Viola pointed out. 'She lives on freebies. Free holidays, free cars, free clothes – people are falling over themselves to offer her stuff.'

'Why don't they ever offer us anything?'

'Because we're not glamorous enough, darling. They want someone young and beautiful, like Lara.'

Not everyone wants Lara, Jo thought. She remembered Marcus's kiss that morning, and a delicious shiver ran through her. He wanted her.

Although God knows why. She examined her reflection, bare of make-up, her blonde hair caught up on top of her head with a glittery plastic bulldog clip. She hadn't made the most alluring impression that morning, stomping around in her ratty old dressing gown and one slipper.

'Sorted!' Lara turned off her phone, smirking trium-phantly. 'Bernie reckons he can do a deal with *Goss* magazine for the wedding, if we get married on Valentine's

Day. And they might even cover the cost of the honey-moon.'

'What? You mean you'd even have a photographer following you around the bridal suite?'

'Why not?' Lara shrugged. 'I can't wait to tell Leon.'

'Leon? This is your new boyfriend, is it?'

'Fiancé. Although we haven't got the ring sorted out yet. We'll probably have to get *Goss* involved with that, too. It'll make a great spread, don't you think?'

Jo wondered if Lara saw her whole life in glossy full-colour photos. 'So what's he like, then?'

'Who? Oh, you mean Leon? He's really cool. He's a kind of entrepreneur. You know, nightclub promoter, DJ, pop video producer – all that kind of stuff. And he knows everyone in the music business.' She inspected her finger-nails. 'He thinks I should make a record. To cash in on my famous name, sort of thing.'

Viola and Jo exchanged horrified looks. This Leon character might know a lot about the music business, but he'd obviously never heard Lara sing.

'So what happened to Marcus?' Viola asked.

'God knows. He disappeared after we got to the club. Said he had to see someone. His dealer, probably.'

Jo's smile faded. 'You don't think – he does drugs?'

'Jo, everyone does drugs.'

'I don't.'

'Everyone who's anyone,' Lara said crushingly. 'Anyway, where do you think I should get married? I quite fancy somewhere exotic. Or maybe a stately home –'

'Won't your parents want you to be married at your local church?'

Lara stared at her as if she was mad. 'Yeah, right. I bet *Goss* will be dead chuffed with an eight-page pullout set in bloody Wakefield!' She narrowed her eyes. 'You've never done anything like this, have you?' Jo shook her head. Strangely, no glossy lifestyle mags had ever beaten a path to her scruffy

Edwardian terrace. 'You've got to play by the rules. Give them what they want. Do you really think all those posh homes they show are real?'

'Well –' She had to admit she'd always thought it suspicious that every actor except her lived in Conran-designed splendour.

'Of course they're not. It's all done up for the cameras, isn't it? Most of the time they're shot in hotels. Or they turf out the star's old tat and hire in some good stuff.'

'But why bother? Surely if the readers want to know how these people really live –'

'That's just it, they don't! Look, would you really want to buy a magazine to look at photos of people's houses if they were just like yours? No, you want to buy a dream. And this way everyone's happy. The celebrities get to look good, the magazine gets some nice pictures, and no one ever finds out that Dale Winton's got rotten taste in curtains. Simple, see?' She tucked her dark hair behind her ears and went off to film her next scene.

Viola and Jo stared at each other. 'It's a whole other world, isn't it?' Viola shook her head sadly.

They were interrupted by the dressing-room phone. Jo picked it up. 'Hello, Jo Porter speaking.'

'So you've finally turned up, have you?'

She recognised the voice on the other end of the line, and her blood ran like ice through her veins. 'Richard?'

Viola started dancing around in front of her, doing some kind of frantic flapping mime. Jo was still trying to figure it out when Richard said, 'So where were you this morning?'

Oh God. The breakfast meeting. 'Look, I can explain –'

'My office. Now.' He cut her off like a blade of steel. 'And this explanation had better be bloody good!'

'Oh God, I'm really sorry,' Viola said, as she put the phone down. 'With all the excitement about Lara, I forgot to warn you. Richard was absolutely spitting when you didn't show up this morning. You're in massive trouble.'

Jo stared at the phone. 'Thanks,' she said. 'I think I'd already worked that out for myself.'

By the time she reached the top floor she'd decided a grovelling apology would be in order. She was in the wrong, after all. She should have let him know personally that she couldn't make the meeting. She'd meant to, but with everything else going on yesterday she'd forgotten all about it.

Kate couldn't hide her malicious smile as she showed her into Richard's office. He was standing at the window with his back to her, but she could tell from the rigid set of his shoulders that he hadn't calmed down at all.

'Well? What have you got to say for yourself?' His voice was low and full of leashed anger.

'I –' Her carefully researched speech deserted her. 'Look, I'm really sorry about this morning. I realise I should have let you know personally, but –'

'But something came up, is that it?' He turned around slowly. His eyes blazed black in his hawk-like face. 'It's too late for apologies. Five hours too late. I expected you here at eight thirty this morning.'

'Yes, but –'

'I told you to be here. What's wrong? Couldn't you get out of bed?'

She gritted her teeth. He didn't want to hear her explanation, he just wanted to bully her. Well, it wouldn't work. 'I'd made other arrangements.'

'But I wanted you here. And since I'm the one who pays your vastly inflated salary I expected you to do as I ask!' He rested his hands on the desk and leaned towards her. 'Everyone else managed to fit this meeting into their extremely busy lives, so why not you? Or does your love life take precedence over your other commitments?'

'Love life?' She stared at him, confused. 'I don't know what you mean –'

'Then perhaps you're not aware of the latest gossip?' He

picked up a copy of the *Evening Press* and flung it across the desk at her. 'Imagine my surprise and delight when I pick up the first edition of the paper and find *that* little snippet staring at me. No wonder you couldn't drag yourself away!'

Jo read it over several times. It was just a tiny paragraph on the inside page, but it exploded in her brain like a Scud missile.

'*Westfield* Stars in Secret Love Tryst', it said. And underneath, 'They may have to fight their mutual attraction on screen but in real life it seems actress Jo Porter has already succumbed to the charms of her gorgeous *Westfield* co-star Marcus Finn. Marcus, soon to be seen on screen as her new love interest, was spotted leaving Ms Porter's Clifton home early this morning. Were they just rehearsing, or is it the real thing?'

Jo dropped the newspaper back on the desk. 'But – this is a load of rubbish!'

'Are you saying he didn't stay the night?'

'Well yes he did, but – it wasn't like that!' she protested, as Richard's eyes narrowed. 'He's just a friend, that's all.'

'A very close friend, if that story's anything to go by.'

'I –' She started to explain, then stopped herself. 'I don't think my private life has anything to do with you.'

'You're absolutely right.' His icy response took her aback. 'Frankly, Ms Porter, I couldn't care less if you entertained half the male population of North Yorkshire. But I do care when it starts to affect your work. I expect one hundred per cent commitment from you. And if you can't give that, then maybe it's time you starting redefining your priorities!'

Jo gasped. 'Now just a minute! When have I ever missed a day's filming? When have I ever been late on set? When have I ever refused to do an interview, or a photo shoot, or one of the other mindless publicity stunts the press office dream up? Just because I miss one meeting –'

They were interrupted by the arrival of Kate. 'Sorry to butt in, but I've got some hysterical teenager called Roxanne on the phone for you.' She looked disapprovingly at Jo. 'I've told her she'll have to call back but apparently it's a matter of life and death –'

Jo didn't wait to hear any more. She rushed to the phone on Richard's desk and snatched it up, hammering the buttons with trembling fingers until she picked up the right line. 'Roxanne, what it is? Is it the girls? Is it Chloe? Don't tell me she's been taken ill again –'

'No, everything's fine. I just thought you ought to know – Pudding's gone.'

It took a moment for her frantically pounding heart to slow down. 'What?'

'He wasn't in his cage when I came back from the shops at lunchtime. His door was open and he'd gone.' Roxanne gulped. 'I think – he felt neglected.'

As the adrenaline rush subsided, Jo didn't know whether to laugh or cry. 'So you phoned me to tell me the hamster's run away from home?' She glanced at Richard. He was standing at the window again, staring out. She could only imagine what he must be thinking.

'What do you think we should do?' Roxanne wailed. 'The girls will be so upset.'

Jo suppressed a sigh of irritation. 'Well, you could try looking for him. Although he's probably halfway to Siberia or wherever it is they come from by now.'

'But what if –?'

'Look, Roxanne, I really can't think about this now. You sort it out.' She put the phone down. When it came to a crisis, Roxanne had all the survival instincts of a lemming. She really should have held out for a Norland Nanny.

Richard turned around to face her. But before he could say anything Jo was ready for him. 'The hamster's left home. Yes, I know it's trivial as far as you're concerned, but it's important to the girls. Just like Chloe's Nativity was important to her. That's where I was this morning. I told Kate but you can check with the school if you don't believe me. The number's in the book.' Her chin lifted. 'Of course, if you'd rather believe the word of a gossip-monger who doesn't even know me and didn't bother to find out whether he'd got his facts right, that's entirely up to you.'

She saw his eyes flicker but her anger had taken over and it felt as if her mouth was on autopilot. 'And please don't try to lecture me about redefining my priorities, Mr Black. Because as far as I'm concerned my children come before anyone and everyone else. Even you. You might like to think you're some kind of omnipotent power up here in your big office, but in my list of priorities you feature precisely nowhere!'

She slammed out of his office before he had a chance to respond. As she stormed past Kate's desk, the PA lifted her head and said, 'I'll put you down as a "no" for the drinks party, shall I?'

Chapter 13

By the time the drinks party came around a week later, Jo still hadn't made up her mind if she should go. Especially as she was trying to stay out of Richard's way.

'But you must come!' Viola insisted. 'Look on it as a way of building bridges. It could give you the chance to apologise?'

'Me, apologise?' Jo was indignant. 'Why should I? I meant every word I said.'

'Yes, but it might have been more tactful not to say it. It doesn't pay to fall out with the man who pays your wages. Besides' – Viola sent her a sly look – 'you must admit it did look rather incriminating, Marcus leaving your house at the crack of dawn like that.'

Jo rolled her eyes. 'Not again! It was all just a –'

'– a misunderstanding. Yes, I know, you've told me a million times. But don't you think you should be telling that to Richard Black?'

'I don't see why.' She'd had enough trouble explaining it to everyone else. She might have got away with it if the *Globe* hadn't got hold of the story and blown it out of all proportion. Now it felt as if the whole world knew. Reactions had been mixed. Viola found the idea of Jo and Marcus hysterically funny, Lara was full of contempt, and her mother had been on the phone straight away, wanting to know if she should be thinking about caterers.

But maybe Viola was right? It didn't pay to fall out with the likes of the Grim Reaper, especially if she wanted to keep her job. 'All right, I'll go – but I'm not going to grovel to him,' she warned.

'No one's asking you to, darling.' Viola patted her shoulder. 'Just don't antagonise him either.'

Richard Black lived on the top floor of a smart warehouse conversion on the banks of the River Ouse, overlooking King's Staith.

'I've always wondered what these places were like,' Viola said as she, her partner Marion and Jo squeezed into the lift. 'I hear they cost a fortune, especially for a river view.'

'I'm sure Richard can afford it.' Jo flattened herself against the wall to make room for Marion's bulk. In her mannish suit and stout shoes, her brown hair cut in a severe bob, she was a complete contrast to Viola, whose floaty multicoloured dress made her look like a bird of paradise. It always amazed Jo how someone like Vi could have ended up with a woman who made Ann Widdecombe look feminine.

She wasn't looking forward to this. She'd managed to steer clear of Richard up until now, but this would be like walking into the lion's den. She was terrified he would bawl her out again in front of all the other guests. And although deep down she knew that wasn't really his style, it didn't stop her palms growing clammier as the lift moved slowly upwards.

The doors opened straight into an apartment roughly the size of a small football stadium. Most of the guests had already arrived. They huddled at one end of the cavernous space like nervous cattle who'd just spotted the abattoir lorry pulling up. A brace of waiters worked the room with trays of wine and canapés. As they entered, a woman in black appeared and silently helped them off with their coats.

Viola caught her breath. 'Oh my God, it's so – so –'

'Minimal?' Jo helped herself to a glass of wine from a passing tray.

The room was starkly bare apart from two enormous white sofas squaring up to each other across a huge expanse of polished pale wood floor. It almost made Jo weep to look at them. They spoke of a lifestyle unencumbered by people who weren't allowed to eat chocolate unsupervised. And as for that floor . . . she shuddered to think what it would look like once Grace had rollerbladed through the place a few times.

Two of the walls were almost entirely glass, offering a fabulous panoramic view of the river and over the rooftops of York to the dramatically beautiful Minster beyond, lit up against the night sky. Over in the corner, a halogen spotlight illuminated a single twisting hazel branch in a sculpted glass vase. Other than that, there was nothing. It was like the nuclear winter of interior design.

Jo looked around for Richard and found him, on the other side of the room, talking to a couple of *Westfield*'s regular directors. He wasn't difficult to spot. His impressive height and aura of power drew her gaze immediately.

He was dressed immaculately as usual, in an expensive-looking suit that matched his dark colouring. He really did have wonderful taste, Jo thought. But perhaps Kate did all his shopping for him? Although she couldn't imagine Richard Black being told what to do or what to wear . . .

As if he sensed he was being watched, he suddenly turned around. As their eyes met, the unexpected lurch of sensation in the pit of her stomach nearly made Jo drop her glass. Then, before she'd managed to regain enough control of her features to smile, he slowly and deliberately turned his back on her again.

'What do you think, Jo?'

'Sorry, what did you say?' She dragged her attention back to Viola and Marion, who were helping themselves to handfuls of nibbles from another passing tray.

'I was just saying, they haven't got a single Christmas decoration up. Do you suppose they're Jehovah's Witnesses or something?'

'Just incredibly trendy, I think. Christmas is probably too naff for them.' God knows what they'd make of her house. Every inch was covered with baubles and tinsel and the girls' dodgy home-made paper chains. It was like Santa's Grotto gone mad.

Jo glanced back at Richard. Even now, at a party, he seemed totally in control. His dark, hawk-like gaze scanned the room, missing nothing. Although for some reason it never strayed her way. She was surprised how much it piqued her.

Viola handed her canapés to Marion and took a cigarette from her bag. No sooner had she lit it than Kate appeared.

'Do you mind?' she said. 'I hate passive smoking.'

'Oh God, so do I. There's nothing worse than breathing in someone else's smoke when you're gasping for one yourself, is there?' Viola offered her the packet. 'Here, help yourself, darling.'

As Kate's narrow face twitched, Jo cut in quickly. 'I like your flat. It's so − um − large.'

'Do you think so? I find it rather cramped.'

'Cramped? I've played in theatres smaller than this.'

Kate gave her a supercilious smile. 'I'm sure you have.' She was wearing the sparest of designer dresses, a strapless sheath of beige Lycra which clung to her bird-like body, making her look understated and fabulously elegant at the same time. Next to her, Jo felt fat and dowdy in her faithful old black number. She could feel wisps of blonde hair escaping from her hastily-constructed chignon.

'I must say it's very sensible of you to put all your furniture away if you're having a party.' Viola took a long drag on her cigarette and blew a smoke ring into the air. Kate fanned it away, her nose wrinkling.

137

'Actually, this *is* all the furniture. I believe a few well-chosen pieces make more of a statement.'

'I wonder what statement she's making?' Jo mused, as they watched her push her way back into the party throng.

'"I'm a pretentious cow," probably.' Viola frowned at the dinky little canapés Marion was holding. 'I don't know about you, but I need some serious food. Shall we go and investigate the kitchen?'

'You go on ahead. I'll catch you up.'

They headed off to the kitchen, leaving her alone. Jo looked for Richard. The people he'd been talking to had drifted back to the group, leaving him on his own. She watched him apprehensively. She knew she couldn't leave it like this, with neither of them speaking. Viola was right, she had to rebuild some bridges, and it was now or never. She gulped down her wine, took a deep breath, and headed towards him.

She was halfway across the room when he looked up and saw her. Instantly he turned on his heel and headed in the opposite direction, leaving her standing there, glass in hand, her mouth frozen in a greeting she'd never had a chance to utter.

For a second she stood, stranded in the middle of the room, not knowing what to do next. Richard's exit had been so abrupt, so unexpected, so downright bloody *rude*, she didn't know how to react. She sneaked a glance around, certain that the whole room must have witnessed her public snubbing, but no one seemed to be looking her way. Except Kate, who had obviously seen the whole thing and was smirking into her Semillon Blanc.

Embarrassment gave way to outrage. *Bastard*, she thought. Here she was, trying to offer an olive branch, and he'd thrown it back in her face. Well, sod him. If he wanted to be like that, so could she.

She went into the kitchen, which was just as pristine as the rest of the apartment. It looked like an operating theatre,

138

with millions of tiny halogen bulbs reflecting pinpoints of brilliant light off the highly-polished aluminium work surfaces.

Viola and Marion were tucking into the buffet with Brett Michaels and his latest girlfriend, a pretty young thing with the longest of legs and the shortest of wispy slip dresses. With her blonde hair in girlish plaits, she looked like a schoolgirl.

'Where's your boyfriend Marcus tonight?' Brett sneered.

'I have no idea.' She hadn't seen him since that fateful morning at her house. They'd had no scenes together, so there was no reason for them to meet.

'You mean he's dumped you? Shame. Still, it's probably for the best.' Brett scooped up a handful of Thai noodles and crammed them into his mouth. 'He was too young for you, darling.'

'Of course, you'd know all about that, wouldn't you?' Jo glanced at the blonde by his side.

'Now, now, children,' Viola said as they squared up to each other across the polished steel table. 'It's Christmas, remember? The season of goodwill and all that?' She looked around her. 'This place is incredible, isn't it? Can you really imagine anyone living here?'

'That depends what you mean by living, doesn't it?' After the way he'd snubbed her Jo was in the mood to dish the dirt. 'People like Richard and Kate don't live like the rest of us. They have lifestyles. They spend their whole lives eating out at the right restaurants, buying the right clothes and pretending to understand half the stuff in the Saatchi Gallery. I mean, look at all this.' She swept her hand disdainfully around the kitchen. 'I don't suppose either of them actually uses any of it. They probably don't even know how half of it works. They only bought it because some smart Sunday supplement said it was the thing to have. It's all for show, just like everything else in this arty-farty flat.'

'Jo –' She heard Viola whisper her name but she was in no mood to stop.

'Take that bin,' she said. 'Have you ever seen anything so ridiculous? You couldn't get an After Eight wrapper in there without it overflowing. But I bet it cost more than my month's mortgage –'

She was suddenly aware of an ominous silence in the room, and a strange prickling on the back of her neck. Turning slowly, she found herself looking up into the Arctic gaze of Richard Black, standing in the doorway.

'Sorry to interrupt. I only came in to get some food.'

They all watched in silence as he picked up a plate and began to help himself from the buffet. Jo felt as if she'd been turned to stone. All except her face, which flooded with hot, humiliated colour.

'Wonderful – er – party.' Viola struggled to break the tense silence.

'Is it?' Richard shot Jo an icy glance and then left, slamming the door behind him.

They stared at each other in silence for a moment, then Viola stifled a scream with her fist. 'My God, did you see his face? I just wanted to die!'

'I think I just have.' Jo downed her glass of wine and poured herself another with shaking hands. Oh God, she'd really done it now.

I don't care, she told herself. He deserved every word. So why did she feel so wretched?

'GET THAT FUCKING DOG OFF MY SOFA!'

Kate's scream, echoing from the far end of the apartment, nearly made her drop the bottle. They all rushed for the door to see what was going on.

Murphy was stretched out on one of the pristine white sofas, his tail thumping happily against the cushions. Kate was standing over him, her face contorted in a reasonable impression of Munch's *The Scream* while Marcus looked mildly on.

'He's not doing any harm,' he said.

'Not doing any harm? Do you know how much these sofas cost? Do something with him!'

'What do you suggest?'

'I don't know, do I? Put him out on the roof terrace.' Kate pointed a shaking finger.

'But what if he gets lonely and tries to jump?'

'Then tell him to call the bloody Samaritans! Just get him out of here!'

Everyone started laughing, but Jo didn't join in. She was too busy staring at Marcus's hand, which in turn was fixed on the well-upholstered bottom of Louise, *Westfield*'s press officer.

Jo hardly recognised her. She'd swopped her usual sober suit for a sprayed-on pair of leather jeans and a black t-shirt, neither of which did her any favours.

'I'll take him.' Louise stepped forward and grabbed Murphy's collar, hauling him off the sofa. 'Come on, boy. Let's go walkies.'

Jo watched her drag the shaggy hearthrug towards the glass doors. She was obviously on good terms with Murphy and his master. And she'd thought *she* was too old for Marcus. Louise was a lot closer to forty than she was.

'Hi, angel. Long time no see.' She jumped as Marcus flung his arm around her shoulder, pulling her so close she could feel his warm breath on her neck. He smelt gorgeous, as if he'd just stepped out of the shower. He looked pretty gorgeous too, in a loose white shirt and faded jeans, his freshly-washed hair flopping in his eyes. 'Missed me?'

'Not really.'

'I was going to phone you, but there's been so much stuff happening I never got round to it. You wouldn't believe what's been going on this week.'

'I'm sure I wouldn't.' Louise was coming back towards them, pushing her way through the crowd like a heat-seeking missile. Jo quickly disentangled herself from Marcus's embrace. 'Hi, Louise.'

'Hello, Jo.' Her dark hair was brushed loose, and she was wearing a lot more make-up than usual. Somehow it didn't look quite right on her plump, kind face.

'Isn't she fabulous?' Marcus put his arm around her waist. Louise turned an unfetching shade of pink under her thick foundation. 'Lou's saved my life. She found out me and Murphy were sleeping in the truck and she's been letting us stay at her place. Isn't she an angel?'

'She must be.' Jo noticed the possessive way Louise slipped her hand into his, and felt a twinge of pity for her. She wondered if she knew Marcus was commitment-phobic. If not, she soon would.

That could have been me, she thought. If she'd let Marcus into her bed that night . . . She was surprised at how relieved she felt.

'We're going to have to move the car, Marcus. It's parked on a double yellow,' Louise said.

'Forget it. No one will notice.'

'But I might get a ticket.'

'So what?'

Louise chewed off her crimson lipstick anxiously. 'It's all very well for you to say that. You're not the one who'll have to pay it.'

'So move it, if you're that worried.'

'Come with me?' she pleaded.

'For heaven's sake, it's only round the corner! Besides, I'm talking to Jo.'

Jo caught Louise's worried look. So that was it. She was terrified of leaving Marcus alone with her. 'Don't mind me,' she said, 'I'm just off to the loo.'

She left them to it and went off in search of the bathroom. Poor Louise, she thought. Keeping Marcus Finn away from other women was like trying to keep a dog away from lamp-posts.

Needing the loo had just been an excuse to get away, so she lingered in the bathroom for a few minutes, poking around. Like everywhere else in the apartment, it was all very sleek, shiny and minimal, from the mirrored walls to the fluffy white towels and gleaming chrome and polished marble surfaces. There were his and hers washbasins, lined with precisely arranged toiletries – La Prairie for Kate, Creed aftershave for Richard. Jo sighed enviously. The closest she ever got to pampering was a quick slosh of Chloe's Super Matey.

She checked her reflection and reapplied her lipstick. All these mirrors did her no favours, she decided. Looking at herself from all angles first thing in the morning would probably be enough to send her straight back to bed for the rest of the day.

What am I doing here? she thought. She didn't want to be at this party, and Richard certainly didn't want her here. The best thing she could do was leave. If she was quick she might even get home before Roxanne put the girls to bed.

She emerged from the bathroom and started hunting for her coat. There must be a cloakroom somewhere around. She pushed open the first door she came to and found herself in Richard and Kate's bedroom. Blue moonlight flooded in from the window wall, illuminating the vast white expanse of bed, the only furniture in the bare room.

She was about to retreat when she suddenly realised she wasn't alone. On the other side of the room, outlined in moonlight from the window, was Richard.

Chapter 14

He had his back to her, and a slight breeze from the open window lifted his dark hair as he stared out at the river. Smoke coiled from a cigarette, apparently forgotten between his fingers. He'd taken off his jacket and his shirt gleamed blue-white in the moonlight.

For a split second she forgot who he was and where she was, and watched him. She'd never noticed what an amazing body he had. It was an athlete's body, his broad shoulders tapering to lean hips and long legs. She wondered when he found time to work out at the gym, since he always seemed to be behind his desk.

'Did you want something?' His voice startled her.

'I was – um – looking for my coat.'

'The cloakroom's back down the hall, turn left.'

'Thanks.'

She had turned to the door when he suddenly said, 'You're not leaving?'

'I think it's best, don't you?'

He turned slowly. His face, etched in moonlight, was unreadable. 'Why?'

'It's obvious, isn't it?'

'Don't tell me, my – what did you call it? – lifestyle offends you so much you can't bear to stay a moment longer, is that it?'

Jo squirmed. 'No, but –'

'But you don't approve of the way Kate and I live?'

'I didn't say that —'

'I believe you did. You were quite voluble on the subject, in fact. Even our bin offended you, as I recall.' He stubbed out his cigarette in an equally designer-like ashtray.

She could feel herself flushing hotly. 'Look, I'm sorry. I had no right to say those things. I was just angry at you — for ignoring me.' There. She'd said it.

Richard frowned. 'When did I ignore you?'

'Back there, when we first arrived. I was coming over to talk to you and you walked away.'

'My mobile went off. I went outside to answer it. I tried to find you afterwards. That's why I came into the kitchen. But you were busy talking to your friends at the time.'

Shame washed over her. 'Like I said, I'm sorry,' she mumbled. 'But I really think it would be best if I went —'

'Wait.' She was groping for the door handle when he spoke. His voice was so soft she barely heard it, yet it was enough to stop her in her tracks. 'Do you want a cigarette?'

She turned to face him. He'd moved from the window to sit on the bed, and was opening a packet of Marlboros. He clamped one between his lips and held out the rest out to her. 'Well? Do you want one, or don't you?'

Jo shook her head dazedly. 'No thanks.' She watched, fascinated, as the brief flare of his lighter illuminated his face. 'I thought Kate didn't approve of smoking?'

'She doesn't.' He took a long drag, his eyes meeting hers through the haze of smoke. 'By the way, you were right. It is an absurd bin. I've been telling Kate that ever since she bought it. But it didn't cost a month's mortgage.'

'Oh?'

'More like top of the range BMW. Joke,' he said, as Jo's face changed. 'Sit down if you like. I won't bite.'

There was no reason for her to stay, but she didn't want to leave, either. She moved cautiously to perch on the end of the bed. 'Don't you want to go back to the party?'

'To be quite honest, I can't stand parties. And I'm sure everyone will have a much better time if I'm not there.'

'What makes you say that?'

'Let's face it, half the people in that room only came because they were afraid I'd sack them if they didn't.'

'That's not true –'

'Isn't it?' His eyes were cynical. 'What is it they call me? The Grim Reaper. No one can look at me without seeing their P45s.'

Jo couldn't help smiling. 'Maybe it's your image?'

'My image? I didn't even know I had one.'

'Of course you have. Everyone has. It's what the world sees.'

'And what exactly does the world see?'

Perhaps she shouldn't have downed two glasses of wine in rapid succession. Jo tried to think tactful. 'Someone aloof and unapproachable.'

He blew a smoke ring and watched it rise to the ceiling. 'Maybe that's the way I like it?'

'Then maybe you shouldn't wonder why people are afraid of you?'

'Are you afraid of me, Ms Porter?'

She looked into his face. 'No,' she whispered. What she was afraid of was the strange sensation that suddenly hit the pit of her stomach.

'So what do you suggest?' he said softly.

'S-sorry?'

'How do you think I could make myself more – approachable?'

'Um – I'm not sure.' She tried to drag her mind back from the alarming track it had found itself on. 'Maybe you should lose the tie?'

'What's wrong with my tie?'

'There's nothing wrong with it. It's just you're always wearing one. It's hardly relaxed, is it? You make people feel as if they're here for a job interview.'

'I see. So what should I wear? A kaftan? A cardigan? If I walked around dressed like Val Doonican, would that be relaxed enough for you?'

Oh God, now she'd offended him again. She was just about to make a flustered apology when she caught it. The faintest twitch at the corner of his mouth. He was teasing her, she realised with a shock.

Her shoulders, which had been hunched around her ears, relaxed a little. He was quite human really. Alarmingly so, in fact. If she wasn't very careful, she might even find herself liking him.

But she shouldn't be doing this, sitting on a bed in the dark with the Grim Reaper. It was way too surreal, and far too dangerous . . .

'So, how's the prodigal hamster?' Richard aimed another smoke ring at the ceiling. 'Did he ever come home?'

She frowned. 'How did you know about –' Then it came back to her. She'd taken the call from Roxanne in his office. Fancy him remembering. 'No, I'm afraid poor Pudding may have ended up being the cat next door's main course.'

'Your daughters must have been very upset?'

'Inconsolable is the word, I think. Poor Chloe still insists on leaving the cage door open at night, just in case he decides to come back. She even leaves a trail of crumbs from the back door to encourage him. She's certainly attracting rodents, but not the hamster variety –' She broke off, seeing him yawn. 'I'm sorry, I shouldn't be boring you with my domestic dramas.'

'I don't find you remotely boring.' Their eyes met, and Jo felt a sudden, unexpected jolt. She looked away, confused. 'Actually, I'm a bit jet-lagged. I flew in from New York this morning.'

'Really? Business or pleasure?'

'Definitely business. Some American network bosses are interested in buying *Westfield*.' He rubbed his eyes. 'I've been out of the office for the past two days, otherwise I would have seen you sooner.'

'Me? Why?'

'To apologise. I was wrong to fly off the handle about you and Marcus. You were right, your personal life is none of my business.'

'But I don't have a personal life! I mean, there's nothing going on between me and Marcus. He just turned up on my doorstep late one night, that's all.'

'And now he's turned up on Louise's.' He searched her face. 'How do you feel about that?'

'Sorry for Louise, I think,' she shrugged. 'Marcus Finn isn't exactly ideal boyfriend material.'

'Don't you find him attractive?'

'Well, yes. But there's got to be more to it than that, hasn't there?'

'Like what?'

'I don't know – chemistry, I suppose.'

'Chemistry?'

'You know. When you look at someone and everything just feels totally right –' He turned his head to look at her and suddenly she found she couldn't say any more. The air between them seemed to be crackling.

Then from down the hall came a blast of Marvin Gaye, breaking the tension and releasing her from the spell.

'They'll be wondering where we are,' she said.

'Probably.'

'Maybe we should go back and join the party?'

'Good idea.' Neither of them moved. It was Jo who reluctantly dragged herself to her feet first. After a moment, Richard stubbed out his cigarette and followed her.

Several couples were already slow dancing when they rejoined the party. Among them, she noticed with surprise, were Marcus and Kate. Although they were hardly smooching. Kate was holding him at arm's length like a smelly dishrag.

As soon as she spotted Richard she came over to join them, Marcus trailing after her. 'He's drunk,' she hissed. 'And his wretched dog's eaten all the canapés.'

'Only because no one else was touching them.' Marcus leant over and planted a damp, wine-flavoured kiss on Jo's mouth.

'Where have you been, anyway?' Kate looked put out. 'I've had to entertain this lot all by myself.'

Jo glanced guiltily at Richard. Nothing remotely intimate had happened between them, so why did she feel as if it had?

'Well, now you're here the least you can do is go and circulate.' Kate stuck a glass of wine in his hand and pushed him towards the rest of the crowd.

'Come on, angel, let's dance.' Jo flinched as Marcus folded his arms around her waist. 'I've been longing to get you on the floor all night.'

'What happened to Louise?' she asked, as he pulled her into his arms to the sound of 'Sexual Healing'.

'No idea. Gone home, I think. She got in a bit of a strop earlier, just because I was talking to Brett Michaels's girlfriend.'

'I can imagine. Maybe you should have gone after her?'

'Why? I'm having a good time. Besides, she doesn't own me.'

'Obviously not.' Marcus was a very sexy dancer. He held her so close their bodies seemed to be moulded together. Jo felt his hands snaking up and down the length of her spine without a tingle of interest. She was right. There was definitely no chemistry there.

Then, over his shoulder, she caught a glimpse of Richard and Kate. They were working the crowd, smiling, chatting and laughing together, the perfect couple in every way. He wasn't even looking her way.

If there had been any chemistry between them five minutes ago, it had been soon forgotten.

Chapter 15

'No way, Duncan. You're not doing it.'

'Can't we just talk about this like reasonable adults?'

'There's nothing to talk about. You're not having them and that's that.'

'I might have known you'd overreact.'

'Overreact?' Her voice rose shrilly. 'What do you expect me to do when you drop something like this on me?'

'They're my kids too. And you always have them at Christmas. I've never complained, have I?'

'Yes, but I don't take them to the other side of the world, do I?'

'It's only for a couple of weeks.'

A couple of weeks? Only the most magical weeks in a child's life. And Duncan wanted to take the girls to Florida.

'Besides, they'll have a fantastic time. You wouldn't want to deny them that, would you?'

Trust him to hit below the belt with some good old emotional blackmail. 'No, but –'

'And I think I should be allowed to spend some quality time with my own children, don't you?'

Pity he didn't think that on a Friday night when she came home from work and found him revving that wretched juggernaut of his outside the house, impatient to drop the girls off.

'Couldn't you take them some other time?' she pleaded.

'I've already explained that. Some friends have rented a villa for Christmas and New Year and they've invited me and the girls along. Just think about it, Jo. They could be spending Christmas in Disney World.'

She felt herself wavering. He was right, the girls would have a terrific time. And she did have them to herself the rest of the year. But Christmas was special. The thought of not seeing their excited faces on Christmas morning tore her apart.

'Tell you what,' Duncan suggested. 'Why don't we let the girls decide? They're old enough to make up their own minds, don't you think?'

Jo agreed. But she should have known Duncan would get in first, wooing them with tales of spending Christmas Day with Mickey Mouse. It made her mince pies and reruns of *The Brave Little Toaster* look pretty dull by comparison.

'Dad says there'll be films all the way,' Grace told her excitedly.

'And he says we can keep the sick bags, even if we haven't used them,' Chloe added.

'Sounds wonderful.' Jo tried to hide her disappointment, but Grace noticed.

'We don't have to go, if you think you'll be lonely?' she said.

'Me, lonely? Heavens no! I'll have a lovely time.'

'But what will you do on Christmas Day?' Chloe picked up on her sister's concern. 'You'll have to eat a whole turkey by yourself!'

'I expect I'll go and share Grandma's,' Jo lied. 'Don't you worry about me, I'll be fine. We'll have our Christmas together when you come home.'

'With cards and presents?' Chloe asked.

'Everything. I'll even keep the tree up.'

'It'll be bald by then,' Grace said, but she looked slightly more cheered. 'You're sure you don't mind?'

'I think it's a lovely idea. Daddy deserves a turn to see you at Christmas, doesn't he? And it won't seem like a minute before we're together again.'

She was right, it didn't seem like a minute. It seemed more like years.

'Now you're sure you've got everything?' She followed Duncan's luggage-laden trolley at the airport the day before Christmas Eve, dodging through the excited holiday crowds. 'Have you got Chloe's teddy? And Grace's —'

'If you've packed it, I've got it.'

'What about those instructions I wrote down for you?'

'In my pocket. Although God knows why you think I need an instruction manual to look after my own kids!'

'Yes, but you've never looked after them for this long, have you?' An anxious thought stopped her in her tracks. 'Oh no, I nearly forgot — Grace's ears play her up on long flights. I'd better nip to Boots and get her something —'

'I already have. You see, I'm not as hopeless as you think.' Duncan's face softened. 'Look, they're going to be fine. They'll have a great time, and I promise I'll get them back to you in one piece by the first week in January.'

At Passport Control, Jo hugged them fiercely. She kept a smile plastered on her face as she watched them disappear through the security barrier. Half an hour later she was in the multi-storey, sobbing behind the wheel of her Cinquecento.

The house felt empty without them, especially as Roxanne had gone back to Thirsk to spend Christmas with her family. Jo never imagined she'd miss the blaring music or the squabbles until she realised how oppressive silence could be.

Christmas morning was even worse. After all those years when she'd woken up before dawn to the children jumping all over the bed, when she'd lain among the discarded wrapping paper and yearned to close her eyes for just an extra half-hour, she now found she couldn't sleep at all. She woke up before dawn and lay, staring into the darkness, imagining the girls asleep in their beds on the other side of the Atlantic. Missing them was like an ache inside her.

The day stretched ahead of her, long and empty. Jo sat at the bedroom window, watching the neighbours' kids careering up and down the street on their new bikes, oblivious to the cold, grey rain. Was this how lonely old people felt? she wondered. Like an outsider, looking in on other people's happiness?

It could have been worse. She could have gone to her mother's for Christmas. Audrey had invited her, although once she'd let it slip that she would also be inviting Rosemary Warrender and her still available son, Jo decided against it. Next to her mother's determined matchmaking, a solitary Lean Cuisine didn't seem so bad after all.

She'd promised the girls she'd save their gifts until they got home, but there were still a few to open. Some Clarins stuff from Viola. An Ibiza club remix CD from Roxanne. A book on DIY from her father, who had long since given up any hope of her finding a man. And some expensive underwear from her mother, who obviously hadn't.

There was also a card from Grace and Chloe, a rare collaboration between the two of them. It was obvious who had been in charge of the writing and who had done the decorating. Grace's neat 'To the Best mum in the World' was nearly obliterated by an untidy mass of glitter and feathers. Jo felt the hot sting of tears every time she looked at it.

The girls rang just after lunch. They sounded so happy and excited Jo could have gone on listening to them gabbling for ever, but then she heard Duncan's voice in the background warning them not to stay on the line too long.

'We've got to go,' Grace said. There was a long pause, then she added quietly, 'I miss you, Mum.'

'Me too, darling.' A lump rose in her throat. Grace was always the cool one, never wanting to be cuddled or fussed over. Jo ached to cuddle her now.

By eight o'clock she'd had a bath, changed into her old dressing gown and eaten roughly her own body weight in

Twiglets. She was curled up on the sofa watching the big movie and trying to decide whether she could be bothered to open another box when the doorbell rang. Jo rolled off the sofa to answer it.

'I hope you don't mind me calling?' Richard said.

She stared at him in the doorway, his overcoat turned up against the freezing wind, rain dripping off his dark hair. Frankly, it had never even occurred to her that he might. 'No, of course not. Would you – er – like to come in?'

He shook his head, scattering raindrops like a wet dog. 'I won't disturb you. I only came to give you this.' He pulled a small cardboard box from inside his coat. 'I just happened to be passing a shop yesterday, and I noticed it. I know it won't replace the one they lost, but I thought it might help?'

Mystified, she took the box, wondering what on earth could have brought him across York on Christmas night, and in such filthy weather. She nearly dropped it as she felt something scuffle inside.

'Oh God, it's not –' Cautiously she undid the end of the box. The yellow streetlight illuminated a pair of shining black eyes and twitching nose. 'A hamster!'

'It's all right, isn't it? I mean, I haven't squashed the poor little bugger or anything? He's been living in my sock drawer since last night.'

'No, he's fine. He's gorgeous. The girls will love him.' Except the girls were several thousand miles away. For the hundredth time that day her eyes swam with hot tears.

'Jo?' Richard looked uncertain. 'Look, I can always take it back if you don't think it's a good idea –'

She opened her mouth to speak, but no sound came out. Then, to her horror, she burst into tears.

He hesitated a fraction of a second. Then she felt his arms go round her, holding her stiffly. 'I take it this isn't to do with the hamster?' he said.

'I'm sorry.' His coat felt rough and damp against her cheek. 'I'm really, really sorry.'

Then it all came out, in a long, incoherent babble. About Duncan and the girls being in the States, and her being alone.

'I know I'm being selfish and pathetic, but I miss them so much.' She sniffed back a sob. 'I even have to keep their bedroom door closed because every time I walk past and see their empty beds I just start crying again –'

'It's okay.' Richard patted her shoulder. She could feel his unease in every rigid muscle of his body. Poor man. He'd only tried to do a good turn. He was probably wishing he hadn't bothered.

'I'm sorry.' She pulled away and wiped her face on the back of her hand. 'You must think I'm a complete idiot.'

'Of course not.' He didn't sound too convinced. 'You're upset, that's all. Anyone would be.'

Maybe, she thought. But would anyone be stupid enough to put out a mince pie and a glass of sherry for Santa, knowing he wasn't going to come?

'Thanks for the hamster. It was really kind of you to think of the girls. And to bring it all this way on Christmas night. You and Kate must have a thousand better things to do?'

'Actually, Kate's gone down to Sussex to spend Christmas with her family.'

She frowned up at him. 'And you didn't go with her?'

'I'm not really the type for big family get-togethers.'

'You mean you've been on your own all day?'

'So have you.'

'True.'

They both looked down at the hamster snuffling inside his box. Finally, Richard said, 'Well, I won't keep you –'

'Do you want to come in for a drink?' The words were out before she had time to think about them.

He hesitated. 'Are you sure? I don't want to impose.'

'You won't be. I was just thinking about cracking open a

bottle of wine. I won't feel so guilty if I share it with someone.'

She showed him into the sitting room, handed him the wine to open and left him depositing the new hamster in Pudding's old cage while she ran upstairs, splashed her blotchy face with cold water and changed into the first thing she could find, a pair of faded jeans and a grey cashmere cardigan. By the time she got downstairs Richard had taken off his overcoat, poured them each a glass of wine and was standing by the fire, dangerously close to the huge, lopsided Christmas tree.

'I wouldn't get too close to that if I were you,' Jo warned. 'It's like everything else in this house. Not exactly stable.'

'I've just been admiring your decorations. They're very – unusual.'

'Tacky, you mean?' She grinned. 'The girls did it. They insisted on doing half the tree each, which is why there's a bald strip around the middle.'

'A kind of demarcation zone?'

'Grace actually wanted to label her half, but I talked her out of it.'

'And did they make these – er – things too?' He examined a toilet roll tube lavishly plastered with glitter and cotton wool.

She nodded. 'I keep promising myself that one day I'm going to ditch it all and treat myself to something tasteful from Paperchase, but I just can't bear to throw them away. Each one's got its own memory.' She took a quick glug of wine to swallow the lump rising in her throat. Don't get all weepy again, she warned herself.

They sat down at opposite ends of the sofa. But despite the safe distance between them, Jo still felt wary. She kept sending him sidelong glances. There was something different about him. She just couldn't put her finger on what it was . . .

Then it dawned on her. 'The tie!'

'What?'

'You're not wearing a tie.'

'Oh, I see what you mean. I decided to take your advice.' He looked down at his chinos and blue chambray shirt. 'Although it takes a bit of getting used to –'

'It's a big improvement.'

'Thanks.' His grin was so unexpected, Jo nearly dropped her glass in shock. She'd never seen the Grim Reaper smile before. He should definitely do it more often, she decided. It transformed him. He looked younger, less forbidding – and infinitely more attractive.

As the evening went on, she was surprised how easily the conversation flowed. The wine helped, of course. As they finished off one bottle and worked their way steadily through another, they talked about everything from work to politics to how infinitely depressing Christmas could be when you had no one to share it with. Jo even found herself telling him all about the girls, and Duncan, and how their marriage finally broke up the day she came home and found him in bed with one of his students.

'I was hurt more than shocked,' she said. 'I'd always suspected Duncan had other women. I just never imagined he'd bring them home to our bed.' She sipped her wine. 'Maybe he wanted me to find out, to push me into leaving. Neither of us was really happy. We probably would never have married if I hadn't got pregnant.'

'Then maybe it's a good thing you split up when you did? There's nothing worse than growing up in a house full of misery and hate.'

Jo looked sidelong at him. The firelight flickered on his sombre face, highlighting the high cheekbones and long, straight nose. 'You sound as if you speak from experience?'

'Maybe.' There was a faraway look in his eyes. 'And you've never thought about getting married again?' He changed the subject.

'You sound just like my mother. She's desperate to see me find a man.'

'But you don't want to?'

'Well, you can't exactly pick one off the shelves at Men'R'Us, you know.' She finished her drink and reached for the bottle, topping up both their glasses. 'Most men my age are either married, or divorced, or so terrified of commitment they run a mile when they find out you're a single mum with two kids.'

'So I'm guessing there's no man on the scene at the moment?'

'Are you kidding? The last time I had a man in my bedroom was over a year ago. And that was only the BT engineer putting in an extension.' She stopped short. Did that make her sound too desperate? God forbid, she didn't want him to think she was making a pass at him or anything. 'I mean, I've had offers,' she went on quickly. 'But I have to be careful. I don't think it's good for the girls to be trailing loads of boyfriends through the house. They need stability.'

'I wish my mother had felt the same.' Richard stared broodingly into the fire. 'After my father walked out on us she brought in a succession of uncles and stepfathers, each more disastrous than the last. She said my brother and I needed a man about the house. But it was her who needed them, not us.'

He finished his drink. Jo silently refilled it, and waited for him to go on. 'She married twice. The first was a compulsive gambler who managed to lose our home and every penny we had, and the second –' His eyes narrowed, as if even the memory was too painful. 'Well, it doesn't matter now. It was all a long time ago.'

But not forgotten, judging from his expression. 'I'd like to hear about it.'

He hesitated, as if he was dredging up the memories from some deep, inner recess of his being. Then he said, 'Edward Sheppard. He was a doctor – well-respected, enough money to give us the life my mother wanted for us. He was supposed to be our salvation, after we lost everything.'

'But he wasn't?'

'No, he wasn't.' Richard's voice was flat. Only the twitching muscle in his jaw betrayed his tension. 'Everyone thought he was such a saint, taking on a woman with two kids, but my God, he made her pay. He never let her forget what he'd done for her – for all of us. She used to put a brave face on it for our sakes, but I knew what was going on. I saw the bruises.'

'He beat her up?'

'Only ever behind closed doors. He had his good name to consider, after all.' His face was bitter. 'My brother and I were at boarding school most of the time, so we didn't see the worst of it. He made sure we were out of the way. And he knew my mother would never tell anyone. She was too ashamed. Ashamed that it was her fault, that she'd let us all down again.'

'But why didn't she leave him?'

'How could she? She'd run out of options. She had no money of her own, nowhere to live. We depended on him for everything. She didn't feel she could put us through that again. Losing our home, our stability. Not after last time.'

'So she stayed with him?'

'Not exactly. When I was seventeen, she sent Jez and me back to boarding school. One morning she waited until Sheppard had gone to do his morning surgery, then she went into the garage, put a hosepipe on the exhaust and killed herself.' He recited the facts in a toneless voice. 'She knew if she walked out on him we'd be penniless. I suppose she thought if she was dead he'd have to look after us. At least we'd be all right. It was the only way out, as far as she could see.'

As he lifted his glass to his lips, Jo had to clench her hands together to fight the sudden, overwhelming urge to put her arms round him. She couldn't even begin to imagine the pain he must have gone through. Must still be going through, if his taut, bitter face was anything to go by.

'What happened then?'

'What do you think? It made me feel sick to watch him, playing the grieving widower, soaking up everyone's sympathy, when it was him who killed her. He let them all believe she did it because she was unbalanced – clinically depressed, he called it. But I knew the truth. And I made sure he knew it too.' He swallowed hard. 'I said I didn't want anything to do with him, or his money. I told him I'd look after myself, and Jez. The next day I left school and started looking for a job.'

'Which is how you met Trevor Malone?'

He frowned. 'How did you know that?'

'Trevor told me. He said you were an arrogant sod.'

'I was! To tell the truth, I was actually as scared as hell. I had no experience, no qualifications. The only thing I could do was bluff. I didn't even know the first thing about working in TV. As far as I was concerned, it was a job, and it paid well enough to find a place to live for Jez and me. That's all I was worried about. I could just as easily have ended up mending roads or driving a milk float.'

'You'd probably have ended up running the show whatever you did.'

Richard smiled. 'Maybe. But I was lucky. It just happened to be a job I enjoyed. And I was willing to work hard. I was only the gofer, but I put in more hours than anyone else, I asked questions, I volunteered for the jobs no one else wanted to do. In the end I made such a bloody nuisance of myself they had to promote me. Trevor Malone was great, too. He taught me a lot. He was more of a father to me than either of the men my mother married.'

'But he tried to make it sound as if you'd put him out of a job?' Jo felt a pang of pity. She realised now how much that must have hurt him.

160

Richard shrugged. 'He was an old, sick man, just trying to salvage what was left of his pride. I can't blame him for that.'

'But it can't have been easy for you, taking over at *Westfield*. And I made things worse with that stupid story in the *Globe*. I'm sorry,' she mumbled.

'You weren't to know. Besides, I'm the Grim Reaper, remember? I can take it.' His smile didn't reach his eyes. 'I didn't get that name for nothing, you know. I can be a ruthless bastard when I want to be. I've destroyed careers in the past. I demand perfection and total commitment from everyone I work with. I'm ambitious, arrogant and probably impossible to live with.'

'And those are just your good points?'

He grinned again, and Jo felt her stomach do an absurd backflip. She reached for the wine bottle just as Richard did the same, and their hands brushed briefly.

'I'm sorry.' He let go of the bottle as if it had been electrified.

'No, please, you have it.' She tucked her feet up under her. Was it her imagination, or were they sitting a lot closer than they had been?

She watched him refill her glass, then his own. The wine must definitely be going to her head, because she was seriously starting to fancy him. If she wasn't very careful she might be tempted to do something about it. And even with the best part of a bottle of Fitou inside her, she could tell that would be A Very Bad Idea.

'So why does Kate stay with you, if you're that impossible to live with?' Now why did she have to go and bring that woman's name into it? A chill wind seemed to blow through the room, taking some of Richard's warmth away with it.

'Kate understands me,' he said shortly. 'We're alike in a lot of ways. We both know what we want out of life – and what we don't.'

'And what don't you want?'

'Marriage. Kids. All the domestic stuff that goes with them.'

It was like a slap in the face. 'You mean you don't want children? Not ever?'

He smiled wryly. 'Don't look so shocked. Not everyone's desperate for that kind of commitment, you know.'

Of course she knew. Her ex-husband was one of them. 'I realise that, but –'

'It's not that I hate kids or anything,' Richard went on. 'It's just I don't think I'd be any good at all that messy, complicated family stuff. I'd rather concentrate on something I am good at, like my career. And I know Kate feels the same.'

She stared at him, amazed. 'Well, I suppose it's your choice. But I just couldn't imagine my life without Grace and Chloe.'

'Really? Even if it means making the kind of sacrifices you have?'

'I don't see that I've made any sacrifices –'

'There's your career, for a start. I've been going through your CV,' he said, as Jo's eyes widened. 'Most other actresses in your position would have moved on from *Westfield* by now, but you're still there. There must be a reason for that?'

Jo bristled defensively. 'Maybe I like it there?'

'Or maybe you like the fact that it's regular work and regular money?' Richard suggested. 'You're a talented actress. Too talented to stay in a downmarket soap for the rest of your life.'

'I wouldn't let Eva and the others hear you say that!'

'I'm serious.' Richard leaned towards her, his arm along the back of the sofa nearly touching her hair. 'You're wasted at *Westfield*, and you know it.'

'Is this your way of telling me I'm sacked?' Jo joked feebly.

'Of course it isn't. I'd never want to lose you.'

Their eyes met, and held. Jo gripped her glass with both hands to stop it sloshing everywhere.

162

'Well, I'm not going anywhere,' she said firmly. 'Perhaps you're right. Perhaps I could have had a meteoric career if I hadn't had my children to consider. But I wouldn't swop them for all the BAFTAs in the world. A career can't take the place of a family.'

'It can't let you down or screw you up, either.' Richard's eyes were hard. 'Let's just say my past experience had put me off the idea.' He finished his drink and put down his glass. 'I'd better be going. It's nearly midnight.'

'Is it?' Jo glanced at the clock. Had they really been talking for four hours? It didn't seem that long. She uncurled herself from the sofa.

'I'll have to leave my car and walk back. I've drunk too much to drive.'

'In this weather?' Jo listened to the rain lashing against the window. 'It sounds as if it's got worse.'

'Thanks for telling me.'

She watched him shrugging on his overcoat. 'You could – um – stay the night? I mean, you could sleep in Roxanne's room. She's away until tomorrow night –' She gabbled on, painfully conscious that every word sounded like a come-on.

'I don't think that's a very good idea, do you?' Richard smiled. 'I seem to remember your hospitality landed you in the *Globe*'s gossip column last time.'

'I doubt if even Charlie Beasley is so desperate for a story he'd hang around in the bushes on Christmas night. Especially not in filthy weather like this.' She followed him into the hall.

'All the same, I'd better be getting back. Kate will be home in the morning.' He turned up the collar of his overcoat. 'Thanks. I've really enjoyed this evening.'

'Me too.'

She watched him go, his broad shoulders hunched against the rain. It wasn't until he was halfway down the street she realised how badly she'd wanted him to stay.

Chapter 16

'Well, this is it, darling. Our big moment of passion. I hope you're ready for it?' Marcus winked over the rim of his coffee cup.

'I can hardly wait.' Jo ignored his hand, which strayed towards her knee. Marcus had been winding her up all morning about their first big love scene. He seemed remarkably cheerful considering it was their first day back at work after the New Year. He was looking pretty good too, his faded Levis and white t-shirt clinging to the sculpted planes of his body. There could be a lot worse jobs than being paid to make love to Marcus Finn, she decided. 'Don't get too excited. It's difficult to get passionate when you've got three cameras pointing at you.'

'Oh, I don't know. It sounds quite kinky to me.' Marcus took a box of Tic-Tacs out of his pocket and popped one. 'Besides, I'm practising for when it happens for real.'

'Don't hold your breath, will you?'

He grinned. 'Come on, you know you're just playing hard to get. You want me as much as I want you. And you might as well know, I've made a new year's resolution to get you into bed.'

Jo choked on her coffee. 'Marcus! How many more times do I have to tell you, I'm not interested?'

'And how many more times do I have to tell you, I never give up?' He stroked her thigh, the touch of his fingers warm and insistent through the sprayed-on denim. A couple of months ago Jo might have found it wildly exciting, but now it just irritated her. There was only one man on her mind at the moment, and unfortunately it wasn't Marcus.

No matter how much she tried to forget about Richard, the memory of Christmas night wouldn't go away. She hadn't felt that close to a man for a very long time. And she was sure he felt the same.

But how could he? He was still very much involved with Kate. And even if he wasn't, he'd made it clear Jo wasn't his type. She was everything he didn't want – a single mum with two kids and no ambition.

That was what she told herself in her gloomier moments. But then her wildly romantic, optimistic side took over and she'd start picturing them together. Just one big, happy family . . .

'So why don't you want me?' Marcus interrupted her fantasy.

'Sorry? Oh, I don't know. Where do I start? You're wild, irresponsible, monumentally unfaithful –'

'Yeah? And?'

'And I'm none of those things. Besides, you've already got a girlfriend. Louise, remember?'

'Oh, her.' Marcus shrugged, 'Actually, we've split up.'

'Since when?'

'Since I realised I couldn't get you out of my mind.' He gave her a look that would have melted the knicker elastic of half the women in Britain. 'Besides, I couldn't handle her stomping around in a permanent strop. It was worse than being in jail, having to tell her where I was going the whole time.' He squeezed her thigh. 'So what do you think? Can I come round tonight?'

'No!' His persistence made her laugh. 'I told you, I'm not interested in a one-night stand.'

'God, you women are all the same!' Marcus rolled his

eyes. 'Why can't you just enjoy the moment, instead of analysing where things are going the whole time?'

Jo carefully removed his hand from her leg. 'If you have to ask that, Marcus, then you and I aren't going anywhere.' He looked mournful, like a kicked puppy. 'Look, it's nothing personal. I'm really flattered, honestly. But it's just – well, the chemistry isn't there.'

Marcus's eyes gleamed with the light of challenge. 'You want chemistry? I'll give you chemistry.'

A few minutes later they took their places on set to rehearse the scene. According to the script, after weeks of steering clear of each other, Stacey and Vic's sexual tension finally exploded in a massive argument in the hairdresser's, followed quickly by a mammoth snogging session in the stockroom.

'Remember, this is the scene where all your pent-up feelings are about to blow,' Aidan instructed them. 'You know what you're doing is wrong, but you just can't help yourself. So really let rip with those emotions.'

Whether she was just fresh from her Christmas break or she had some pent-up feelings of her own she needed to unleash Jo wasn't sure, but as they did the scene she could feel real anger and frustration building up inside her head like a pressure cooker. Marcus picked up on her cue and soon they were yelling and screaming their lines at each other across the set. But when Jo forgot herself and slapped his face, everyone was startled. Especially Marcus.

'I'm sure that's not in the script,' he muttered, rubbing his cheek.

'Sorry.' She bit her lip. 'I got a bit carried away.'

'No problem. As long as you don't mind me doing the same?'

'That was brilliant.' Aidan listened to the director's instructions on his headphones, then gave them the thumbs up. 'He says to keep that in.'

'Do we have to?' Marcus scowled.

But the next time she slapped Marcus, instead of flinching away he came right back at her, trapping her face between his hands and pulling her towards him for a passionate kiss that stopped her mouth and nearly her heart and entire nervous system too.

He released her, his ocean-green eyes glittering. 'How's that for chemistry?' he whispered. Then he stalked off, leaving her to listen dazedly to the applause and cat-calls of the rest of the crew.

Stunned, Jo made her way back to her dressing room. But when she opened the door there was Marcus, leaning back in her chair, his feet up on the dressing table.

'Okay, we'll do it your way,' he said.

'What are you talking about? And how the hell did you get in here –'

'This – relationship thing. We can give it a go, if you want?'

'Not again!' Jo sighed. 'Look Marcus, I told you, it wouldn't work.'

'How do you know that, if you don't try? We could go out, if you like? A proper date. How about that?'

Jo looked at his eager face. 'You're very sweet and I'm terribly flattered, but really I'm not interested.'

He shook his head. 'You're a hard woman, Jo Porter. You're lucky I don't give up that easily.' He dragged his feet off the dressing table and stood up. As he left, he handed her a scrap of paper. 'Here's my mobile number. Call me when you change your mind.'

'Don't you mean "if"?'

Marcus grinned over his shoulder. 'I know what I mean.'

After a tiring day, she was looking forward to a long, hot soak in the bath, followed by a few mindless hours in front of the TV. But as she turned into her terrace of grey-stone Edwardian villas, she spotted her mother's beige Honda parked outside the house and remembered Audrey was paying one of her visits. She usually dropped in when she was up in town, meeting a friend in Browns. Fortunately for all of them, it didn't happen very often. Her visits could be very disruptive.

Sure enough, as she opened the front door she was greeted by a furious-looking Roxanne.

'If anyone wants me, I'm upstairs,' she snapped.

'What about the children's tea?'

'Ask her.' Roxanne shot a sullen glance towards the kitchen, whence came the sound of clattering pots and pans and Audrey's voice, rattling out instructions.

'Don't bite your nails, Grace dear. Chloe, do you have to spread your things all over the place like that? And watch your drink, you'll knock it with your elbow. Now, who wants to lay the table for me?'

Jo gritted her teeth and followed the sound. In the kitchen she found the girls slumped at the table looking as if they'd lost the will to live, while Audrey stood at the cooker, a flowery pinny over her smart box-pleated skirt and blouse, stirring something in a pan. As Jo opened the door Grace and Chloe rushed to greet her like a couple of castaways who'd just spotted the rescue ship.

She hugged them and went over to greet her mother. 'Hi, Mum. Something smells nice.' She sniffed the air appreciatively.

'Yes, well, I thought my grandchildren could do with some proper, home-cooked food for a change, instead of all that convenience rubbish.' Audrey offered a powdered cheek. 'I really don't know why you keep that girl on, Joanne. She's neither use nor ornament.'

Here we go again. Jo stifled a sigh. 'Roxanne's okay. And the girls adore her.'

'Yes, but she's not very experienced, is she? I asked her where you kept the *bain marie* and she looked at me as if I was talking absolute riddles.' She scraped her spatula noisily around the bottom of the pan. 'She obviously hasn't the first idea about nutrition. I mean, you only have to look at her to see that. So thin – and those spots! No, if she can't pull it out of the freezer or stick it in the microwave she just doesn't want to know. No wonder those girls always look so peaky –'

Jo left her ranting to herself and tiptoed back out of the kitchen. She met Roxanne coming down the stairs.

'I mean it,' she hissed. 'If she mentions carrots one more time I'm out of here.'

Jo glanced at the kitchen door. 'I think I'll come with you.'

She had a bath and tried not to think about the hostilities that were brewing downstairs. Just as she stepped out of the tub and tucked a towel around herself, the doorbell rang.

'Can someone get that?' she called. There was no answer. A moment later, it rang again, more insistently this time. 'Will someone please answer that bloody –'

As she came charging out of the bathroom, wearing a towel, her hair dripping, she was confronted by Richard in the hall below with her mother.

For a split second they stared at each other. Then Audrey cut in briskly. 'It's all right, dear, you get dressed. I'll look after your guest.' With a meaningful flash of her eyes, she led Richard into the sitting room.

Oh shit. Shit, shit, shit. Jo ran around the bedroom, throwing open drawers and cupboards and pulling out their contents. The last thing she needed was to leave Richard at the mercy of her mother. Audrey would make Torquemada the Grand Inquisitor look positively reticent.

She unearthed a pair of black trousers and a white Kookai top from the depths of her wardrobe. That would do. Casual but not too scruffy.

What did he want, anyway? She tried not to get her hopes up as she yanked a brush through her hair. It was probably something to do with work. But then wouldn't he have called her to his office? No, it had to be personal. Something

169

he couldn't talk about at work. Something he couldn't talk about in front of Kate. Jo's hand shook so much she sprayed a generous squirt of *Obsession* into her ear instead of behind it.

As she hurried downstairs Audrey came flying out of the sitting room.

'Why didn't you tell me you were expecting someone?' she hissed. 'I could have taken the girls out and let you have the place to yourselves.'

'But I wasn't expecting –'

'And look at you. You haven't made much effort, have you? Couldn't you have done something with your hair? Here, let me do it.'

'Mum! I'm not five years old.'

Jo snatched the comb back from her mother's hands and went into the sitting room. Richard was perched uncomfortably on the edge of the sofa while Chloe curled up beside him, messily eating a yoghurt. Grace was stretched out on the floor, watching *Neighbours* at full blast. Jo's heart sank. Welcome to family life, she thought.

But what her daughters lacked in finesse, Audrey more than made up for in fawning ability. 'Are you sure I can't offer you a drink?' she asked. 'Something to eat, maybe?'

Jo cringed. She'd be asking if she could lick his brogues clean for him next.

'I'm fine, thank you.' Richard was stiffly polite.

'I'll take the children into the kitchen so you two can be alone, shall I?' Jo listened to her manhandling the protesting girls down the hall. Subtlety wasn't her strong point.

'Sorry about my mother,' she said.

'Not at all. She's been taking very good care of me. So far I've been offered two cups of tea, three gin and tonics and a round of ham sandwiches.' His dark eyes twinkled.

'You're lucky she didn't ask for your bank account details.'

'I think we were just getting to that when you arrived.'

Jo looked apologetic. 'I'm afraid she sees every man as a potential son-in-law.' Oh God, why had she said that? Now he'd think she was fishing. 'Not that there's any chance of that happening with us. What I mean is –'

'I know what you mean.' He smiled. Not surprising, really, since she'd just dug herself a big hole and fallen, red-faced, right into it.

She sat down on the sofa. 'So what can I do for you?' she asked. 'This is getting to be quite a habit, isn't it? You dropping in.'

He nodded. 'Actually, I wanted to talk about the last time I came. I didn't know whether I should come round or not. I've been turning it over in my mind for days. But in the end I knew I had to see you again.'

Jo's heart did a mad tumble in her chest. So she hadn't imagined it. He fancied her, too. In spite of everything he'd said, the attraction between them was too strong. She forced herself to stay calm. 'Any particular reason?'

'We – er – both had a bit too much to drink that night.' He stood up and paced the room, choosing his words carefully. It touched her that he was so unsure of himself. 'I'm afraid I may have revealed a little more of my true feelings than I intended.' She was about to tell him not to worry, she felt the same way, but he went on, 'I told you some things I've never told anyone before. Things even Kate doesn't know. About my family and so on.'

'I see.' She eyed him warily. She was no expert, but this didn't sound like a declaration of love.

'The thing is, I don't want it to go any further. The press would have a field day if it was to get out. It's not just for my sake.' His words came out in a rush. 'There are other people to consider. My brother, for instance. I don't want anyone to get hurt.'

But Jo had stopped listening. 'Do you seriously think I'd go to the press with a story like that?' She shook her head in disbelief. 'What kind of person do you think I am?'

171

'I didn't mean it like that. I'm just asking you to be discreet, that's all. You talked to them before, didn't you?'

Was he ever going to let her forget that? 'That was different. I was tricked into giving that story.'

'Exactly. That's why I'm asking you to be extra careful this time.' He sat down beside her. 'I'm appealing to you as a friend,' he said softly.

A friend! She didn't know whether to laugh or cry. 'I think it's for the best if we forget that evening ever happened, don't you?' She glanced away so she wouldn't see the look of relief in his eyes. She was already hurting enough.

'You're probably right,' he agreed. There was a long pause. 'I hope I haven't offended you, coming round like this? I just thought it was important that we both knew where we stood.'

Oh, she knew where she stood, all right. On the outside looking in. 'Yes, well, I think we both know that now, don't we? So – was there anything else? Only I do have things to do this evening. You know, a life outside *Westfield*?'

'Of course. I'm sorry.' He stood up. 'Thanks again – for being so understanding.'

He opened the door and Audrey fell through it. 'Going already?' Her face was a picture of disappointment. 'Won't you stay for dinner?'

'No, thank you.' He glanced at Jo. 'I think I've already outstayed my welcome.'

'What did you say to him?' Audrey barely waited until the front door was closed before she launched into Jo.

'Why ask me? You probably heard it all through the door anyway.' Jo was too angry and disappointed to care if she sent her mother off into a sulk. Angry with Richard, and with herself for ever thinking she had a chance with him.

'It's such a pity.' Audrey watched wistfully through the window as Richard's Audi drove away. 'He seemed such a nice man.'

'Yes, he is, isn't he?' Jo couldn't keep the edge out of her voice. 'Unfortunately, he doesn't feel the same about me.'

'Well, it's about time you found yourself someone who did.'

'You know something? You're absolutely right.' Jo reached for her bag and started to rifle through it.

'What are you doing?'

'For the first time in my life, Mother, I'm taking your advice.' She found the scrap of paper she was looking for, picked up the phone and punched in Marcus's mobile number.

Chapter 17

Jo took another slug of her ice-cold designer beer and winced. God, it was horrible. Pretentious, overpriced and completely lacking in taste. Just like the rest of this place.

I'm having a great time, she told herself again. But after two hours of trailing from one packed, smoky pub to another, her conviction was beginning to wear thin.

It had been Marcus's idea to go on the infamous pub crawl known locally as the Micklegate Run. Jo had heard of it, of course, and she'd occasionally witnessed the streams of screeching, scantily-dressed clubbers making their way from Micklegate Bar down to Rougier Street, stopping at every pub and club on the way. But she'd never had any desire to join them. And now, squashed into a dark, sweaty corner of a packed nightclub, her beer bottle almost wedged up her nose, she realised why. She felt overdressed in her cream linen shift dress, her feet hurt like hell, and her temples were throbbing in time to the thumping techno dance music. Whatever happened to going for a quiet drink? she wondered.

The evening had got off to a bad start when she'd called for Marcus at the address he'd given her – the basement flat of a converted Victorian house in Holgate Road – and Louise had opened the door.

It took her a moment to recognise *Westfield*'s press officer beneath the puffed, blotchy face. She looked as if she'd been crying for days. She wore a faded pink dressing gown, her dark hair falling into her mascara-smudged eyes.

'Louise! I – er – didn't expect to see you here?'

'Why not? It's my flat.'

'Your flat? But I thought –' She was still groping for the right words when Marcus appeared, wearing just jeans and drying his hair on a towel.

'You're early,' he grinned. 'Come in, I won't be long.'

He disappeared to get ready, abandoning her in a desperately awkward silence with Louise.

'Would you like a cup of tea?' Louise offered.

'Thanks.' Jo followed her into the kitchen. She knew she had to say something. 'Look, Louise, I don't know what's going on here, but I would never have agreed to go out with Marcus if I'd known you two were still together.'

'We're not.' Louise banged the kettle down. 'He's just staying here until he gets a place of his own sorted out.' She wiped her nose with her sleeve and smiled. 'It's okay, we've talked and I'm fine about it. Honestly.'

She didn't look fine. Suddenly this date didn't seem like such a good idea after all.

'Ready?' Marcus appeared in the doorway, looking amazingly sexy in black jeans and t-shirt, his freshly washed hair flopping in his eyes. Louise, who had been rinsing mugs under the tap, suddenly dropped them and rushed out of the room.

Marcus watched her go. 'What's up with her, I wonder?'

'Isn't it obvious? God, Marcus, why didn't you tell me you were still living with her?'

'I didn't think it was important. I told you, we've split up.'

'Yes, but she's obviously not over you yet, is she?' Jo gnawed her lower lip. 'Maybe we'd better call it off tonight?'

'Why?'

Because you need to sort your life out, for a start. 'I think Louise needs more time to adjust to the – er – situation.'

'That's her problem, isn't it?' His green eyes were harder than she'd ever seen them.

Now, suffocated by a fug of cigarette smoke, sweat and cheap perfume, she was beginning to wish she'd walked out when she had the chance. She looked around for Marcus and spotted him over the crush of elongated, youthful bodies, caught up at the bar. As she watched, a group of girls pushed their way towards him. One of them, barely older than Roxanne and about fifty times as gorgeous, dressed – if that was the right word – in PVC hot pants and a bra top, tapped Marcus on the shoulder and handed him a pen. Then, to Jo's astonishment, she suddenly unzipped her shorts and wriggled out of them, exposing her pert, perfect bottom for him to sign. Grinning, Marcus obliged. But as he handed back the pen the girl suddenly wrapped her arms around his neck and practically sucked his face off, while her friends shrieked encouragement.

Jo waited for the jolt of jealousy. But to her surprise, she was more concerned that she would never again see the tenner she'd sent him to the bar with.

'Mineral water, as requested.' He appeared in front of her and pressed another ice cold bottle into her hand. Jo squinted at the Japanese label. She couldn't even drown herself in alcohol as she was driving.

'You hate this place, don't you?' Marcus read her thoughts.

'No, really, I –' What was the point of lying? Jo pulled a wry face. 'I just don't think I'm cut out for clubbing.'

'Why didn't you say so? We'll go.'

'Not to another pub!'

'Don't tell me you have something better in mind?' Marcus grinned and reached her hand. 'What are we waiting for?'

'Call me picky, but this wasn't quite what I had in mind,

either.' Jo pulled her cardigan around her shoulders and shivered.

'Why not? It's not hot, or smoky. And it's certainly not noisy.'

'That's because it's a bloody graveyard!' She looked warily around her. The tombstones looked like jagged teeth in the moonlight. Behind them, the black outline of the church rose starkly against the night sky. When Marcus suggested they found somewhere quiet where they could be alone, she hadn't expected it to be quite this quiet.

A damp chill seeped through her dress. 'I think I'm sitting on someone.'

'I don't suppose they'll mind.'

'No, but I do. Couldn't we go somewhere else?'

'We could always go back to your place?' His arm slid around her.

'With my mother and the girls? I don't think so.'

'What about mine, then?'

'And listen to Louise sobbing in the next room?'

'Look like we're stuck then, doesn't it?' He massaged her shoulders. 'God, you're so tense. Why don't you relax?'

'How can I? I feel like I'm in the middle of the *Thriller* video. I keep expecting the dead to rise from their graves and you to turn into a zombie.' Some date this was turning out to be. But it wasn't really Marcus's fault she was in the wrong place at the wrong time – and with the wrong man.

'I know what will relax you.' To her horror, he reached into his pocket and took out what looked like a thin, elongated cigarette with a twisted end.

Jo gawped. 'Tell me that's not what I think it is.'

'Depends what you think it is, doesn't it?'

He tugged out the cardboard end with his teeth and spat it on to the grass. As he lit it, Jo caught the sweet, sickly aroma and nearly gagged with terror. 'Oh my God! Supposing someone sees us?'

'I think this lot are past caring.' He took a leisurely drag on the joint and passed it to her. 'Go on, try some.'

'No thank you.' She primly tugged her dress over her frozen knees.

'You don't know what you're missing.'

'A stiff jail sentence, probably.'

'Haven't you ever felt like living dangerously? It's a lot of fun.'

'I'll take your word for it.' Right now she'd settle for being curled up with the girls and the latest Harry Potter.

She shivered and looked around. This is it, she thought. I am officially on the Date From Hell.

And the sooner she got away, the better.

Then it came to her. She slid across the tombstone towards him until their thighs were touching. 'I've been thinking . . . Maybe we should go back to my place after all?' she whispered.

His eyes gleamed through a haze of heavily scented smoke. 'Great.'

'The girls would love to meet you.' She smiled at him. 'After all, now we're having a *relationship* you're going to be playing a big part in their lives, so they should get to know you.'

Even in the darkness she could see he'd turned pale. 'It's so wonderful that you like kids,' she went on. 'You don't know how hard it is to find a man willing to take on a woman with children. Especially not as lively as my two.'

'T-take on? Lively?'

'Of course, they don't mean any harm. They're angelic really, as kids go. But they really need a man around. You know, a father-figure? Someone they can build a really good *relationship* with.' She reached across and laid her hand on his knee. 'You wouldn't mind if they called you Uncle Marcus, would you? At least for now . . .'

'Er – no, of course not.' Marcus stubbed out the joint and scrambled to his feet. 'But maybe we should make it another night? I'm – er – worried about Louise. You're right, she was upset when we left.'

'Surely that's her problem?' She repeated his words back at him.

'All the same, I shouldn't have walked out on her like that.' He backed into a gravestone in his haste to get away. 'We've – um – probably got things to discuss, don't you think?'

'Maybe you're right.' Jo hid her smile behind her hand. 'I'll drop you off, shall I?'

Chapter 18

Jo looked at herself in the mirror and nearly choked. Why Lara had ever asked her to be a bridesmaid she had no idea. Looking at the dress, she could only assume it was because of some long-held grudge.

It was like a tribute to bad taste. Everything about it was seriously abhorrent, from the eye-watering orange colour to the hacked-about neckline and ragged hem. It was supposed to be a cutting-edge designer classic, but it looked as if it had been slung together by a first-year fashion student after a heavy night in the Students' Union bar.

And what was this sticking in her head? No ordinary flowers for Lara. She had to have a circlet of designer barbed wire. Every time Jo moved, it was like DIY acupuncture.

'Ooh, must have a shot of that, love – hold it. Perfect!' She flinched as a flashbulb exploded in her face. *Goss* magazine had been there to capture every excruciating moment of the Valentine's Day extravaganza. They'd gone with the happy couple to choose the rings, to meet each other's parents, and on the carefully orchestrated hen night, for which Jo had been forced to undergo a major makeover with a bossy stylist. And afterwards the happy couple were flying off to Bora Bora, where no doubt a photographer would also be waiting to capture the conjugals on celluloid.

Meanwhile, elsewhere in the Bridal Suite, watched by

assorted make-up artists, stylists and photographers, the bride was having a slanging match with her mother.

'I told you, you're not wearing it!' She and her frock filled the doorway to the en suite bathroom. It was a vast, billowing creation made, apparently, from chicken wire and parachute silk. Alexander McQueen meets the Montgolfier brothers, Jo decided.

Lara's mother looked fetchingly normal by comparison, in a lilac two-piece and matching hat. 'But I bought it specially –'

'I told you the stylist would bring your outfit, but you didn't listen, did you? Oh no, you had to go and buy something like *that*!' She pointed a shaking finger.

'But what's wrong with it, dear?'

'What's wrong with it? This is supposed to be a stylish occasion, in case you hadn't noticed. There are celebrities here, people on the front line of taste and fashion. You'll show me up.'

'I think she looks lovely.' Jo noticed Mrs Lamont's trembling lip and stepped in quickly.

'Who asked you?' Lara turned on her. 'And where's Marcus? He's supposed to be giving me away.'

'Oh, surely not, dear. I thought your father –' Mrs Lamont flinched as Lara swung round again. She was a terrifying sight, her jacked-up bosom heaving, her eyes flashing malevolently underneath metallic false lashes.

'I hate you all!' she yelled. 'This is my big day and you're all going to spoil it!'

'Hold it there, love!' Somewhere behind Jo a flashbulb popped.

'Now, Dawn dear, don't get yourself all upset –'

'Don't call me that! I told you never to call me that! My name's Lara, can't you get that into your thick head? Lara, Lara, LARA!' With a tortured sob, she flung herself across the king-sized bed.

'She's overwrought. It's excitement, I expect,' Mrs

Lamont whispered to Jo. 'She was exactly the same when she was a little girl.'

It's a shame you didn't slap her legs while you had the chance, Jo thought. Even Chloe was beyond throwing tantrums like that.

She wondered if Lara's see-sawing mood had anything to do with her fiancé Leon's 'wedding gift' that had arrived in a small package that morning. While her mother had oohed and aahed over how romantic he was, Lara had disappeared into the bathroom and emerged some time later, bright-eyed, runny-nosed and hyperactive. Now she was rapidly descending into paranoia.

Jo couldn't stand much more. 'Maybe I should go downstairs and see what's happening?' she suggested, edging towards the door.

'If you see Marcus, tell him to get up here THIS MINUTE!' were the last words she heard as she closed the door on the hysterical bride.

The Leeds hotel where the wedding was being held was so drop-dead stylish there was a six-month waiting list to book a room there.

Jo gazed around the teeming reception area with awe. It looked like an invasion from Planet Celeb. A gaggle of supermodels towered over the latest cool boy band. A black American rap singer exuded attitude in the corner, surrounded by a posse of leather-clad homeboys armed with mobile phones.

Viola joined her just as a couple of trendy breakfast TV presenters wandered past, followed by a Booker prize-winning novelist.

'How the hell does Lara know him?' Jo said. 'I thought she only ever read the fashion pages of *Elle*?'

'You'd be surprised. Here, have one of these.' Viola slipped a glass into her hand. 'Freezer-chilled vodka. You may need several of them, if you're going to carry off that frock with any kind of conviction.'

'You don't exactly blend into the background yourself.' Jo smiled at her flowing tunic and trousers in swirly gold print that clashed spectacularly with her henna-ed curls.

'Well, you know, I thought I'd make the effort. Seeing as we're mixing with some real top-notch stars.'

'You can say that again.' Jo sipped her drink. 'I don't know anyone, do you?'

'Neither does the bride, so I've heard.' Viola lowered her voice. 'Apparently it was in her contract that she had to have certain celebrities here or she wouldn't get her money. They didn't want any old nameless riff-raff either, which is why we weren't allowed to bring our other halves.'

'Marion isn't here?'

Viola shook her head, her dangly earrings jangling. 'She doesn't mind, she's happier at home looking after the animals. But really, can you believe it?'

'Knowing Lara, I'm afraid I can.' Jo craned her neck. 'So which one's the bridegroom?'

'I think it's that one over there. In the white biker's jacket. With the ponytail.'

'Not the one who looks as if he's been upholstered at World of Leather? He's old enough to be her father.'

'He's also rich and well-connected enough to launch her pop career.' Viola looked around. 'Ooh, don't look now, but here comes Mr Darcy. Doesn't he look frighteningly sexy in that suit?'

Jo glanced over her shoulder, straight into the laser-beam eyes of Richard Black. She hadn't spoken to him since that night at her house, over six weeks ago. In that time she'd managed to convince herself that her fleeting attraction was over. But seeing him again was like a punch in the solar plexus. Oh bugger, I really do fancy him, she thought weakly.

'That horrible bitch Kate isn't with him. Shall we go over and say hello?'

'No! I don't –' But it was too late. Viola already had hold of her elbow and was steering her across the room towards him.

'Richard! Thank God, another familiar face. We were beginning to think we were at the wrong party, weren't we darling?' Viola beamed at Jo, who was too tongue-tied by Richard's penetrating stare to reply. Why didn't he say something?

Then, finally, he did. 'What,' he said slowly, 'are you wearing?'

In spite of her nerves, Jo couldn't help laughing. 'You should see the bride.'

'That bad?'

'Worse. Stick a couple of gas burners up her skirt and she could take Richard Branson round the world.'

His slow smile lit up his smoky grey eyes. Jo felt her heart kindling in response.

Then Kate appeared. She was dressed in a brilliant scarlet Dolce and Gabbana suit and matching Philip Treacy hat that looked sensational with her dark colouring but did nothing for her boot-faced expression.

'Oh, it's you.' Her cold gaze dismissed Jo instantly and she turned to Richard. 'When is this circus going to start? I'm not sure I can stand much more.'

'Not enjoying yourself?' Viola looked sympathetic.

'Not particularly. Weddings always give me a headache. I don't even know why we had to come.'

'We came because we were invited.' Richard's voice was low.

'So? I've lost count of the number of invitations we've turned down because *you* didn't feel like going.'

Jo and Viola exchanged glances. Sensing a row brewing, she decided it was time to beat a hasty retreat. 'I don't suppose anyone's seen Marcus around?'

Her question had an alarming effect. Kate and Richard forgot their bickering and both turned on her sharply.

'Why do you want him?' Richard demanded.

'He's supposed to be giving the bride away.'

Kate snorted. 'He's such an unreliable bastard he probably hasn't bothered to turn up.'

'Thanks. That's just what I wanted to hear.' As if Lara wasn't hysterical enough. She'd trash the hotel room if Marcus didn't show up.

Just to add to her panic, a man in black leather started playing a souped-up version of 'Here Comes The Bride' on a mandolin. 'Look, if you see him, tell him I'm looking for him, will you?' Gathering up her skirt she pushed her way through the crowd.

She finally found Marcus hunched on a low wall under a silvery eucalyptus tree in the courtyard, smoking a cigarette. From his crumpled clothes, three-day stubble and bloodshot eyes he looked as if he'd been burning the candle at both ends and in the middle too.

'Bloody hell, you look awful,' she said. 'What have you been doing to yourself?'

'Sleeping in the back of the truck.' He turned mournful turquoise eyes to hers. 'Louise kicked me out of her flat.'

'About time too,' Jo said briskly. 'You deserve it, after the rotten way you've treated her. You've taken advantage of that poor woman for far too long.'

'Don't you start. I've had enough ear-bending from women to last me a lifetime.'

His fingers shook as he inhaled deeply on his cigarette. Jo frowned. She'd never seen him like this. Marcus wasn't the type to let anything get him down. Louise must have given him a very hard time.

'Do you want to talk about it?' she ventured.

He smiled wryly. 'How long have you got?'

'Until Lara starts screaming again.' She sat down on the

wall and arranged her billowing skirts around her. 'So what's up?'

'You really don't want to know.' He took another drag of his cigarette. 'Let's just say I failed to come up to someone's expectations.'

'And this someone – I imagine it's a woman?'

'Of course.'

So it must be Louise. 'Let me see – she wanted commitment and loyalty and fidelity and you didn't?'

He smiled wearily. 'How did you guess?'

'Because it's always the same story with you.' Jo shook her head. 'Look, she's probably upset now. But I expect once she stops breaking her heart she'll realise what a lucky escape she's had.'

'I hope you're right. She could make my life pretty hellish if she doesn't.'

He was right there. As press officer, Louise was in a prime position to drop juicy snippets of gossip to the wrong people.

'I know someone else who could make your life hellish if you're not careful.' Jo plucked the cigarette out of his mouth and stubbed it out on the cobbles. 'The bride will be wanting your head on a pole if you don't get a move on.'

Marcus grinned. 'I love dominant women. Are you this bossy in bed?'

'You'll never know, will you?' At least he was back to his old self again. Weeks after their disastrous date, Marcus had finally realised he was wasting his time with Jo and they'd settled into an easy, flirtatious friendship. She didn't even feel a fleeting twinge of lust for him these days. She could see him for what he really was – gorgeous, sexy and charming, but feckless, self-centred and as faithful as a tom cat on the tiles. Men like Marcus should come with a government health warning. Preferably branded with a red hot iron somewhere painful

'Come on,' she said. 'We've got about thirty seconds to

get you upstairs and make you look presentable before the bride throws another tantrum.'

They were making their way back into the hotel when Marcus suddenly said, 'Thanks.'

'What for?'

'For talking to me. And for being the only woman in the world who isn't madly in love with me.'

Jo laughed. 'Bighead!'

'No, I mean it. You're a real friend.' Before she could react he stopped, pulled her into his arms and kissed her in a very unplatonic way.

'Excuse me.' They sprang apart at the sound of Richard's voice. He was standing in the doorway watching them, his face curiously blank. 'I just thought you ought to know, the bride's on her way downstairs.'

'Oh hell!' Jo grabbed Marcus's hand. 'Forget about making yourself presentable, we'll head them off in the lobby.'

They were all coming down the staircase when they arrived, breathless. Lara swished in front, followed by a brace of stylists, a photographer and her manager Bernie, gabbling into his mobile. Then came Jo and Marcus, and Lara's mother, now barely recognisable in a Vivienne Westwood bustier and black capri pants, teetering down the stairs on a pair of Prada mules.

Lara's father trailed behind, his dapper morning suit standing out among the colourful circus.

'But you're my only daughter!' he was saying.

'I know, but *Goss* wants Marcus to give me away, and they're paying for it, so there.'

'But Dawn, love –'

'I TOLD YOU NOT TO CALL ME THAT!' Lara's screech echoed up into the chandeliers. 'Look, you're lucky I even let you come. I fought long and hard to get you and Mum an invitation, so don't you try and spoil it for me!'

She flounced off, leaving him standing helplessly at the foot of the stairs.

'But I don't understand,' he said. 'We're her parents. Why shouldn't we come to her wedding?'

'She didn't let the rest of the family come, did she?' his wife sighed.

'And she won't even let us take any snapshots of her big day. Did you see the way that big security bloke took my camera off me when we arrived?'

Lara's mother patted his arm, and Jo heard her say, 'It could have been worse, Brian. Just be glad she didn't make you wear a sarong.'

Jo twirled a radicchio leaf idly between her fingers and decided she'd never been so bored in her entire life.

Beside her, Marcus had recovered from his earlier depression and was engaged in some serious flirtation with Toni Carlisle, the outrageous blonde ladette star of Talbot TV's youth show *All Talk*. From the moment she'd shimmied over to their table in a thigh-length Versace chain-mail tunic, leaned towards Marcus and announced, *sotto voce*, that she wasn't wearing any knickers, Jo realised she might as well be part of the flower arrangement for all the notice he was going to take of her.

Instead she got stuck between Brett Michaels and an overweight breakfast show presenter. Brett was sullen and furious that Toni Carlisle was ignoring him, and the TV presenter, who had convinced himself he had a way with the ladies, kept trying to practise his twinkling charm on her. All in all, the evening looked about as promising as a game of strip whist at the WI.

She gazed around the room and immediately caught the basilisk stare of Louise, Marcus's former girlfriend. She looked as if she wanted to rush across the room and staple Jo's head to the table.

Jo hastily glanced away – and found herself facing

Richard's equally hostile gaze. This was getting ridiculous. Louise she could just about understand, but what could he possibly have against her?

She stared at her plate. It was a wonder she didn't choke on a polenta fritter with all the hate vibes coming her way.

By ten o'clock, when the music started and Leon got behind his massive mixing desk to treat everyone to his latest mega-hype-club remix, she decided she'd had enough. Marcus and Toni Carlisle had long since disappeared. The tubby TV presenter's wife had hauled him on to the dance floor and Brett had managed to find a waitress starstruck enough to snog him. The pounding techno beat was so loud it made her fillings buzz. Every time she turned her head a *Goss* photographer was pointing a zoom lens up her nose. It was all very wearing.

Then, when she saw Richard get up from his seat and make a move towards her, she realised it was time to leave. He looked as if he had something on his mind, and she wasn't in the mood to hear it.

She went upstairs to the Bridal Suite to change. She just hoped there wouldn't be a photographer waiting to capture that on film too.

But there wasn't. Instead she found something much worse.

Marcus was sprawled naked across the king-sized bed, his sculpted muscles golden against the crisp white linen. Toni Carlisle, also naked, was stretched out beside him.

As Jo froze in the doorway, Marcus rolled over on to his stomach and grinned at her. 'Angel! Want to join the party?'

'Go on. Live a little.' Toni giggled. 'You know what they say. Two's company, three's a blast.'

'No thanks.' Jo forced herself into the room, carefully averting her eyes from Toni's silicone-pumped breasts. 'Does Lara know you're in here?'

'Where do you think we got the key?'

They both fell about giggling. They were obviously on

something but Jo didn't want to know what. She grabbed her clothes from the end of the bed and headed off to the bathroom, slamming the door behind her.

She was just buttoning her shirt over her bra and knickers when she heard a shout from outside, followed by a splintering crash. A second later, Toni screamed.

'What the hell –' Without thinking, she flung open the bathroom door – and found herself right in the middle of a nightmare.

Chapter 19

The room was full of people. Half a dozen tough-looking men and women swarmed around, throwing open wardrobes, pulling out drawers and emptying their contents on to the floor.

As Jo stood frozen in the doorway, one of them barged past her into the bathroom and started searching in there.

In the middle of it all, Toni sat on the edge of the bed wrapped in a sheet, whimpering. Jo looked at her ashen face and felt a rush of fear.

'Will someone please tell me what's going on?'

'These people are police officers, angel. They're searching the room.' Marcus looked as unconcerned as if they'd arrived to deliver room service.

'What?' She suddenly noticed the uniformed officer guarding the door. 'But why?'

'Apparently someone in the hotel tipped them off that we might have drugs in here.'

'But that's ridiculous, I don't know anything about – what are you doing with that?' She sprang forward as one of the police officers picked up her bag and emptied it out on the bed. Immediately a hand closed on her shoulder.

'Would you mind sitting down, madam?'

'But he can't do that! That's my property he's mauling.' She was more worried about everyone seeing the clutter of tatty tissues, old till receipts, unwrapped sweets and stray

Tampax than any incriminating evidence. She took a step forward but she was grabbed from behind and forced into a chair.

'Better do as she says, angel.' For once Marcus wasn't smiling. 'Wouldn't want to upset the nice policemen, would we?'

Jo sank into the chair. How could he be so calm? She'd done nothing, yet her heart was hammering a bongo beat of fear against her ribs. She'd always had a thing about policemen. Once she'd gone into her local police station to hand in a purse she'd found, and just the way the desk sergeant looked at her had made her want to confess to all the crimes within a five-mile radius.

She tried not to make eye contact with any of them as they searched the room, uncomfortably aware of the police-woman standing at her shoulder. Two others were watching over Marcus and Toni, she noticed. One of them kept looking at her. Jo glanced away then, thinking this might make her look guilty, risked a bold stare back. He immediately narrowed his eyes.

Oops, big mistake, she thought, looking away again. Hers was clearly the impudent stare of a hard-faced criminal. If she sat there much longer she would have implicated herself in most of the city's unsolved crimes.

Keep your head down and your mouth shut, she warned herself. This is all a terrible mistake. Someone's idea of a wedding night prank, probably. They won't find anything. They can't find anything. There's nothing to find . . .

'I've found something, Sarge.'

One of the policemen emerged from under the bed. Jo caught a glimpse of the battered old tin as he passed it to the man in uniform. She recognised it immediately as the one Marcus kept his gear in.

'Oh my God!' She tried to get up but a pair of hands came down, clamping her to the chair.

'Oh dear,' Marcus said. 'I wonder how that got there.'

192

'You tell me, sir.'

'I hope you're not saying it has anything to do with us?'

'I think we should discuss this down at the station, don't you?' The policeman's gaze swept the room. 'I am arresting all three of you for possessing an illegal substance. You do not have to say anything —'

'But you can't!' Jo shot to her feet. 'I'm innocent. I don't know anything about any drugs.'

'— but it may harm your defence if you do not mention when questioned —'

'I've never taken anything stronger than a paracetamol in my life. Ask him!' She pointed a shaking finger at Marcus. 'He'll tell you. Go on, tell them!' Her voice rose a panicky octave.

Marcus's face was expressionless. 'I'm saying nothing until I've spoken to my solicitor.'

She carried on protesting her innocence as she was hustled out of the back entrance to the waiting police cars. In the distance, she could hear music and voices from the wedding reception, making it all seem even more horribly surreal. She wanted to rush back in there and scream for help, but the policewoman was gripping her arm in a none too friendly way.

'This is all wrong. You're making a big mistake,' she kept saying to the back of their heads, as she huddled in the back of the car with the others. But no one listened. It was like a nightmare, where she was trapped in a bubble and no one could hear her.

This isn't really happening, she kept telling herself. They can't lock you up for something you didn't do. Any second now they'll realise what they've done and let you go.

She was still telling herself that as the Custody Officer read out the charges against her and took away her shoes, earrings, bag and even the belt from her jeans.

'But I haven't done anything!' Her throat was sore with fear and panic.

'Of course you haven't. Neither have most of the others in here.' He gave her a quick smile. 'Put her in number five,' he instructed the accompanying officer.

It was only when the heavy steel door clanged shut and she heard the jingle of keys that her indignation turned to panic. She stared at the chipped dark blue paintwork, her stomach churning.

'No good you staring at the door, love. You could be in here hours.'

She turned, slowly. The room had all the tiled ambience of a urinal. The air was hot and stank of stale sweat and disinfectant. The only furniture was a hard, narrow bench.

There were two other women there already. A thin girl with straggly dark hair and hunched shoulders stood in the corner, chewing her nails. A fierce-looking woman in a leather mini skirt sat on the bench. Her badly bleached hair had more black roots than a reggae singer. Jo didn't fancy her chances against either of them.

'First time, is it?' Roots eyed her sagely. 'Thought so. It's always the worst. Why don't you come and sit down?'

She patted the seat next to her. Jo perched on the edge, ready to flee if necessary. She hugged herself, trying not to breathe in the stale air. 'How long will they keep us here?'

'Well, I've been here since last Tuesday. Only joking,' Roots grinned, as Jo's face crumpled. 'They can only keep you twenty-four hours without charging you. But they usually like to get you sorted out within six hours, otherwise it means more paperwork and hassle.'

'Six hours!' It would be nearly morning by then. The girls would be wondering where she was. Roxanne would be panicking . . .

'Might be less, might be more. Depends how busy it is. Now, you come in on a Saturday night and you could be here bleedin' hours.' Roots shrugged. 'I just call it an occupational hazard. Makes a change from freezing your

194

backside off on the streets when there's not much trade about.'

All this time the dark-haired girl had been shuffling sideways along the wall towards her, her eyes piercing beneath her stringy fringe. Suddenly, she said, 'I know you!'

Jo edged away. 'I – I don't think so.'

'I'm sure I've seen you somewhere before.' Her voice was rasping, like a rusty saw. 'You don't work on that corner up near the Wakefield Road, do you?'

Jo shook her head, too terrified to be offended. With her tangled hair and her wild bloodshot eyes, she reminded her of the girl from *The Exorcist*. Any minute now she'd whip her head round 360 degrees and cover them all in green vomit. Jo could hardly wait.

An hour ticked by, slower than any she'd ever known. She was allowed to speak to the duty solicitor on the phone. He sounded as if she'd just dragged him from his bed. In a sleepy voice he'd assured her that she'd be out in no time.

'No point in me coming down if they're going to let you go,' he'd yawned. 'Don't worry about it, I'm sure your friends will vouch for you.'

'Yes, but what if they –' she asked, as the receiver went down.

'Don't tell me – duty solicitor?' Roots shook her head. 'Might have known. You want to get your own brief. It's amazing how they'll put themselves out once they know you're paying them.'

Jo stared at the phone, tears of frustration running down her face. What if the solicitor was wrong? What if Marcus and Toni didn't vouch for her? What if they let her take the blame? People had been locked up for much less. Visions of all the *Rough Justice* programmes she'd ever seen came into her mind. All those innocent people imprisoned for twenty years for crimes they'd never committed, victims of circumstance and an inept police system.

She spent another half an hour or so trying not to cry,

aware that the dark girl was watching her with the peculiar intensity that only the very mad could achieve. Jo might never get as far as a trial. How many people were killed in their cells, viciously beaten by a deranged fellow inmate? Probably not that many, but she'd seen enough episodes of *Prisoner Cell Block H* to know it was a definite possibility.

'So what are you in for?' Roots asked finally.

'It's all a terrible mistake. I didn't do anything.'

'I know that, love, but what did you do?'

'I didn't do anything.'

'None of us did, did we? Come on, you can tell us.'

Jo caught Roots's speculative stare. She reminded her of a tough girl at her old school who used to beat up the weedy kids in the toilets. The only way Jo had escaped was to act tough herself. 'I hit my husband. With a bottle,' she added for good measure.

It worked. Roots looked impressed. 'Good for you. I expect he deserved it. Do him much damage, did you?'

'What? Oh – er – yes. Blood everywhere. Lacerations all over the place. The police said I must be a complete maniac –'

Dark Hair suddenly let out a bark of laughter. Jo nearly wet herself in fright.

'I know who you are! You're Stacey. Out of *Westfield*.'

She was just about to deny it when Roots chimed in. 'Oh my God, so you are! I never miss an episode. I always tape them if I'm working.'

'R-really?' Jo smiled weakly.

'I suppose you found out about that slag from the minicab office?' Dark Hair was looking frighteningly intense again. 'Fucking bitch. I know where she lives, you know. I could go round there for you, if you like?'

Oh great. Trust her to get stuck with the Psycho Branch of the *Westfield* Fan Club.

'Thanks,' Jo tried to look grateful, 'but you see, it isn't really –'

'I could. I could sort her out for you. I've done it before.'
As she leaned forward, Jo caught the unhinged look in her
unnaturally dilated pupils. 'I've got a knife,' she confided.

Thank God, just then there was a rattling of keys outside
the door. A police officer called her name and Jo practically
threw herself into his arms. At that moment she would have
admitted to anything, even being involved in a plot to oust
the Queen and put Fergie on the throne, if only he'd get her
out of there.

As it was, she didn't have to. Less than an hour later she
was free. She walked dazed and shaking into the brightly-lit
reception area, clutching her belongings in a small plastic
bag.

The first person she saw, alone on a line of hard plastic
chairs on the other side of the counter, was Richard
Black.

'Jo!' He shot to his feet as soon as he saw her. She tried to
smile bravely, but somehow she couldn't manage it. Just
seeing him there, the first familiar face she'd seen since the
whole terrible nightmare began, was too much for her. All
her pent-up emotions came flooding out, and she burst into
tears.

'Oh God, Richard, it was so horrible!' She sobbed against
his shirt as he pulled her into his arms. 'They wouldn't listen
to me, they just locked me up in this awful place –'

'Shh, it's okay. You're safe now.' His breath was warm
against her hair. Just listening to his deep, calm voice she
could feel her panicky heartbeat slowing down. 'Come on,
let's get you out of here.'

It was raining as he led her out of the back door and down
some steps to where his Audi was parked in an alleyway
behind the dustbins. 'The front's swarming with press,' he
explained shortly. 'They'll be round here too, in a minute.'

Sure enough, they'd barely reached the car before
someone yelled her name. A moment later came the
pounding of many feet. Jo stared, transfixed with shock and

horror, as they rounded the corner. There were dozens of them, all shouting at her. Richard flung open the car door and shoved her inside. 'Hold tight and for God's sake keep your head down!'

Jo cowered on the back seat, flinching at the thunder of fists on the car, and the machine-gun whirr of cameras all around her. Then suddenly the engine roared into life, and the car shot forward, scattering the reporters like skittles.

She waited until she sensed they were safely away, then uncurled herself. She looked out at the dark night. It had started raining again. The lamps cast slashes of yellow light across the wet, empty streets.

'They're not going to go away, are they?' she murmured. 'We might have got rid of them this time, but they'll be back.' A thought struck her. 'Oh God, what if they go after the girls? Or my parents? You know how those bastards work, they won't rest until they've got their story –'

'Calm down. Louise will do what she can to squash it and by tomorrow morning they'll be chasing after some other poor sod. You'll see, it'll all blow over.'

Jo caught his eye in the rear-view mirror. He didn't look convinced and neither was she. The story was too juicy to disappear overnight.

They were both too preoccupied to talk as they drove back to York. Only the rain drumming on the roof and the occasional squeak of the windscreen wipers punctuated the heavy silence.

Jo huddled in the back of the car, going over and over her ordeal in her mind. The memories clung, just like the stale smell of the cell clung to her hair and clothes. She longed for a hot bath to wash away the awfulness of it all.

At last they turned off the A64 and headed towards the city's outer ring road. As they neared her home, Jo's heart started pounding faster. What would be waiting for her when she got there?

'I shouldn't think the story will have reached here yet,'

Richard answered her unspoken fears. 'They'll probably still be looking for you in Leeds.'

'I hope so. Right now I just want to get home and make sure the girls are okay.' She watched the rain streaming down the window. She'd know soon enough, anyway. They were heading down the leafy, tree-lined Shipton Road towards Clifton Green, just minutes away from where she lived. 'What do you think happened to Marcus? Will they let him go?'

'I'm sure he can look after himself.' His curt reply surprised her. He was probably just exhausted, she thought. He must have been waiting half the night in that police station.

'I haven't thanked you properly – for coming to rescue me,' she said humbly. 'I wouldn't have known what to do if you hadn't been there. I just want you to know I really appreciate it.'

She jerked back in her seat as Richard suddenly swung the car off the road and screeched to a halt. He swung round in his seat to face her. 'I don't want your appreciation,' he said. 'Just tell me one thing. Did you do it?'

For a split second her head reeled with shock. 'How could you even ask me that?'

'Because I need to know.' He took a deep breath. 'Look, I know how you feel about Marcus. I caught you kissing him earlier on, remember? It's hardly beyond belief that you might have done something stupid if he asked you to –'

'Is that really what you think of me? You really believe I'd be capable of something like that –' She swallowed hard, fighting for control. 'I didn't do anything. The police believed me, so why can't you?'

'Jo –' Hot tears blurred her eyes. She jerked her face away and fumbled for the door handle. 'Where are you going?'

'Home.' She flung the door open and scrambled out.

'Get back in, I'll drive you.'

'I can walk the rest of the way, thanks. I don't need your

help. Not now you've made it clear what you really think of me!'

He sighed. 'Look Jo, I didn't mean –'

She slammed the door on his protest and started to walk away. She half wanted him to follow, to tell her it had all been a huge mistake. But a moment later she heard the engine rev hard behind her and he roared past, sending up an arc of muddy spray.

Jo kept walking, although she was so overwhelmed by misery it was an effort of will to put one foot in front of the other. Nothing felt real any more. Even the street, with its little parade of post office, bakers and hardware shops, seemed unfamiliar to her.

Richard thought she was guilty! Hurt, shock and betrayal gnawed away at her, leaving a hollowed-out feeling in the pit of her stomach. Of everything she'd been through that night, this was the worst. Even being locked up for hours and not knowing what was going to happen to her hadn't hurt as badly as this. Seeing the look in his eyes, knowing that he doubted her . . .

She turned the corner and was confronted by a small crowd gathered around her gate. Some were perched on her low front wall, some were sitting in parked cars. And they were all waiting for her.

Jo looked desperately up the street, but Richard's car had long since disappeared. There was nothing else for it. Squaring her shoulders, head down, she ran through the rain towards her house.

'Jo! What have you got to say about your arrest?' They closed in on her like jackals on a carcass. Jo pushed through them, jostled off her feet with every step.

'Is it true you were having a threesome when the police came in?' Charlie Beasley's nasal whine rose above the rest. 'What's Toni Carlisle like in bed? Game for anything, so I've heard.'

'Just fuck off, will you?' She lifted her eyes for a fraction of a second. Just long enough for a flashbulb to explode in her face.

Charlie grinned. 'Thanks, darling. That'll look great in the late edition.'

Biting her lip to stop herself crying, Jo pushed her way through her gate and up to her front door. She fumbled in her bag for her key, but her vision was too blurred with tears to see anything. In the end she gave up and banged on the door.

'Piss off,' a small voice whimpered from the other side of the frosted glass.

'Roxanne? It's me, Jo. Let me in.'

'Jo?' The door opened cautiously and Roxanne's pale face peeped out through the narrow gap. 'Oh, thank God! Hang on, I'll take the chain off –' The door closed then opened again, just wide enough for Jo to squeeze through. They both threw themselves against it, slamming it on the reporters who instantly swarmed forward.

'I'm so glad you're back.' Roxanne's voice shook. 'It's been horrible. They've been shouting things through the letterbox –' She burst into tears.

'Shh, it's okay. I'm here now.' Jo hugged her. 'Are the girls all right?'

'I – I think so. I put a video on for them and told them to stay upstairs. I think they're asleep now. I didn't know what to tell them,' she sobbed. 'I wasn't even sure if you'd be back, after what they said out there.'

'It was a misunderstanding.' Jo held her closer. 'But it's all sorted out now. It's over.' Then she noticed the suitcases side by side at the foot of the stairs. 'Roxanne, what are your bags doing there?'

'I'm sorry.' Roxanne pulled away from her. 'I had to phone my mum and dad. I didn't know what else to do.' Her red-rimmed eyes pleaded for understanding. 'They told me to come home straight away. They said they didn't want me staying in the house with you. I tried to tell them it wasn't true, but they wouldn't listen. My dad wanted to come and pick me up straight away, but I told him I had to wait until you got back. I couldn't leave the girls.'

'Thanks.' Jo shuddered to think what would have happened if she'd walked out on them. But she couldn't blame Roxanne's parents. They were only trying to protect their child, just as she would Grace and Chloe.

'I don't want to go,' Roxanne whimpered.

'I know. But you've got to do what your mum and dad say.' Jo summoned up a smile. 'Do you want me to give you a lift? I'm sure if you waited until morning some of this lot would be gone.'

'I can't.' Roxanne couldn't meet her eye. 'Dad says I'm to get a cab and he'll pay at the other end.'

'No, I'll pay. It's the least I can do, after everything you've been through tonight.'

While Roxanne went off to call the taxi firm, Jo risked a glimpse through the crack in the living-room curtains. They were still out there, camped in her tiny front garden, trampling the shrubs and kicking over Chloe's lovingly-arranged miniature rockery. Jo held back a sob. They just didn't care, the bastards. Just like they didn't care if they ruined her life with their lies.

'Mummy?' Grace stood, pale-faced, in the doorway. 'What's going on? Why's Roxanne calling a taxi?'

'She's – um – going on a little holiday.'

'Is she coming back?'

Jo and Roxanne exchanged glances. 'I hope so, darling.'

'Why are all those people shouting?'

Jo briefly considered making up a story, then realised Grace would probably see straight through her. She might only be eleven years old, but she wasn't stupid.

'There was a mistake and I had to go to the police station,' she explained. 'But those reporters have got it all wrong and want to print a story about it in their newspapers. They'll be gone by tomorrow, you'll see.'

'And you're not going to prison?'

'I'm not going anywhere,' Jo assured her. 'But the next couple of days might be quite difficult and I need you to be brave for your sister's sake. You're old enough to understand, but Chloe isn't. She might get scared.'

Grace squared her shoulders. 'I'll look after her.' She looked so pathetically young in her Forever Friends pyjamas, Jo felt a choking lump in her throat.

The cab came and somehow Roxanne managed to manoeuvre herself and her suitcases through the clamouring reporters. Her departure set off another barrage of hammering and questions through the letterbox.

'Why's your nanny walked out, Jo? Didn't she want to share a house with a junkie?'

'Bet she could tell some stories!'

'Is it true you were all high on heroin when the police found you in bed together?'

Meanwhile, upstairs, Jo huddled with the girls under her double duvet, her throat aching from trying not to cry.

She stared into the darkness, listening to the rain and the voices outside and tried to work out her next move. She had to get the girls away until all this was over. Despite what Richard had said, she had a bad feeling it could go on for days. But where could she send them? Duncan was in the States, and her mother and father were on a wine-tasting mini break in the Languedoc. Hopefully by the time they returned all the fuss would have died down. But in the meantime she had a real problem on her hands. It came as a shock to realise that she had no one she could really trust or rely on.

She was still mentally going through her options when she heard the noise coming from downstairs. Below them, in the kitchen, came the slow creak of the back door opening.

Jo disentangled her cramped arms from around the girls and climbed out of bed. She crept on to the landing and strained her ears to listen. Someone was definitely moving about down there.

The bastards had got in! For a second she stood there, paralysed with shock and fear. Then the heat of outrage flooded through her veins, galvanising her into action. She crept downstairs, grabbed the first weapon she could find – which happened to be an old flat iron they used as a doorstop – and crept towards the kitchen door.

'Hold it, you bastard!' With a yell of fury, she flung open the door and hurled herself at the darkened shape of the mystery intruder.

She hadn't banked on him fighting back. She felt her wrists pinned in a powerful grip. Panicking, she dropped the flat iron. There was a howl of pain and the intruder lost his hold on her. Jo grabbed her chance and lunged for the light switch.

Chapter 20

'Christ, woman, what the hell do you think you're doing?' Richard clutched his foot and swore under his breath.

'What am *I* doing? What are *you* doing, prowling around my home in the middle of the night?'

'I came to help you.' His teeth clenched in pain. 'I think you've broken my bloody foot.'

Jo folded her arms across her chest. 'How did you get in?'

'You left your keys on the back seat.'

'And you decided to use them?'

'I told you, I came to help you.'

'What are you going to do, give me a lift to the Priory?'

He ignored her. 'We haven't got much time. I parked round the corner and sneaked in through the back to avoid the reporters. If we're quick we can get out before they realise what's going on.' He limped over to the kitchen window and peered out into the darkness. 'How long will it take you to pack a bag?'

'Now hang on a second –'

'Do you want to stay here and take your chances with that lot out there?'

Put like that, she didn't have much choice. 'I'll wake the girls up.'

Richard had told her to pack as little as possible. But he obviously wasn't familiar with the luggage requirements of three women. He groaned when Jo dragged the two suitcases into the kitchen. 'I thought I told you to travel light?'

'Believe me, this *is* light. You should see what I talked them out of packing.' She bit her lip. 'Grace is bringing the rest down in a minute.'

'The rest?' His words dripped with ice. 'What rest?'

'Chloe refused to leave without her Barbies. Sorry,' she shrugged. 'I'm afraid they have a rather extensive wardrobe.'

'So I see.' He eyed the holdall Grace was hauling through the door. 'Anything else?'

'Only the hamster,' Grace said. 'We've got to take Richard, haven't we Mum? He might not survive on his own.'

'Richard?'

'They insisted on naming him after you. Sorry.'

Richard's face didn't crack. 'You'd better bring him then, hadn't you? Only tell him he can carry his own flaming suitcase!' Grabbing a bag in each hand he headed for the back door, muttering darkly about 'wretched women' and 'only going away for a couple of days, not cruising around the bloody Bahamas'. Jo would have laughed if her stomach hadn't been in such a knot.

'You still haven't said where we're going,' she said as they turned off the outer ring road. It was the first time she'd been able to speak after the hair-raising start to their journey. A couple of reporters had spotted them piling their luggage into the car and rushed to give chase. Richard had had to put his foot down to lose them, which left Jo clinging by her fingernails to the dashboard and impressed Grace no end.

'To my cottage. It's in the dales, just outside Richmond.'

'I didn't know you had a cottage.'

'No one does. That's why you'll be safe there.'

Jo glanced at the girls sleeping on the back seat. 'It's very kind of you to let us stay there. We would have been in a real mess if you hadn't turned up.'

'I couldn't just leave you to cope on your own.' He stared

at the road ahead of him. 'So what happened to your nanny? I thought she'd be with you.'

'She went home.' She told him about Roxanne being summoned back to Thirsk.

'But that's appalling!' Richard looked horrified. 'You mean her parents just wanted her to drop everything and abandon the girls? My God, what must they be like?'

'You can't blame them for jumping to the wrong conclusions. They don't know what really happened in that hotel room. No one does.'

'Including me?' He glanced sideways at her.

'It seems to me you've already made your mind up, just like everyone else.'

'Look, I'm sorry if I upset you earlier, but I had to know the truth. You can't imagine the kind of things that were going through my head when I found out what had happened. I just didn't know what to think.'

'So you thought the worst?'

'Maybe. What the hell were you doing in that hotel room anyway?'

She told him. It was a relief to be able to give her side of the story to someone at last.

Richard listened in silence. 'So there's nothing going on between you and Marcus?' he said at last.

'I told you, he's just a friend. Or he was. After tonight I don't care if I never see him again.'

'Me neither. I'm beginning to think his days on *Westfield* are numbered.'

Jo bit her lip. 'You do believe me, don't you? About what went on tonight?'

'I've always believed you. I just needed to hear it from you.' He shot her a look. 'I know you'd never do anything to hurt those kids.'

Jo stared straight ahead at the swishing windscreen wipers, unable to speak for the lump that filled her throat. 'Can we change the subject? I just want to forget the whole thing, if I can.'

'Suits me. What do you want to talk about?'

'Anything, as long as it's nothing to do with drugs, or police, or Marcus bloody Finn!' She shuddered in spite of the warmth inside the car. 'Tell me about this cottage of yours.'

'It's nothing special, I'm afraid. I bought it as an investment to let out to holidaymakers. Luckily there aren't usually many bookings this time of year.'

'So you don't use it yourself?'

'I can't remember the last time I went there. I'm more of a city man.'

Jo smiled. Somehow she couldn't imagine Kate tramping over the fells in her Manolos, communing with nature.

'It's about half a mile from the nearest village, so you won't be bothered with neighbours,' Richard went on. 'There's a woman usually comes in to clean once a week, but I'll call her in the morning and tell her not to bother. The fewer people who know you're there, the better.'

'Fine.' Jo could feel her eyelids drooping. Her whole body ached for sleep. But she did her best to stay awake as they left the lights of the motorway behind and followed the winding roads deep into the dales. It was too dark to make out her surroundings, and she was too tired to care.

Richard turned off the road and headed down what felt like a narrow, rutted track. Bare tree branches scraped at the windows as they bumped along. Then he made a right turn and stopped.

'We're here,' he said.

She helped Richard haul the bags out of the car. At least it had stopped raining, although there was a bitter chill in the air.

She was just about to wake the girls when Richard stopped her. 'Don't disturb them,' he whispered. 'We'll carry them inside.'

Jo followed him into the cottage, Chloe in her arms. It

gave her a guilty pang to see him carrying Grace, her head lolling on his shoulder. Poor Richard, he must be wondering what he'd let himself in for.

'Sorry it's a bit basic.' He dumped Grace on the sofa. 'We usually just get birdwatchers and hikers staying here, and they spend more time outside than in.' He reached over and flicked on the lamp. 'I keep meaning to do it up a bit, but I never get round to it —'

'It's fine.' Jo took in the bare furnishings, the freezing cold and the strong smell of damp. It was far from perfect, but at least it was safe. And the way she was feeling, she could curl up and sleep on the runway at Leeds-Bradford Airport.

She laid Chloe down next to Grace on the battered old sofa and for a moment they stood and watched them sleeping peacefully, their heads together. Then Richard said gruffly, 'I'll go up and make the beds.'

'Let me.' Jo moved towards the stairs but he stopped her.

'I'll take care of everything. You need to rest.'

'But what about you? You've had a long night too.' It suddenly occurred to her he was still wearing his wedding suit. There was a five o'clock shadow on his chin and dark welts of weariness under his eyes.

'You're right.' He raked his hand through his dark hair. 'I hate to tell you this, but there were a couple of times when I nearly fell asleep at the wheel.' His eyes met hers uncertainly. 'I was going to ask if you minded me staying the night? I don't know if I could face making the drive home. You can say no if you're not happy about it —'

'Of course you can stay. It's your cottage, after all.' She didn't want to admit that she would feel much safer if he was around. 'But won't Kate be worrying where you are?'

'Kate doesn't worry about me.' Was it her imagination, or was there a hint of bitterness in his voice? 'But you're right, I'll call her on the mobile later. After I've sorted out those beds.'

He went upstairs and Jo settled herself on the sofa with the girls. The springs twanged and creaked protestingly, and the cushions felt as if they'd been stuffed with boulders, but she was too exhausted to care. She felt herself relax, listening to the thumps overhead. Richard was taking care of everything. After so many years on her own she'd forgotten how good that felt.

'Jo?' She woke up with a start. Richard was standing over her. Befuddled by sleep as she was, she imagined his expression looked almost tender in the lamplight. 'Shall we go upstairs?' he said softly.

She was instantly awake. 'What? Upstairs? You mean –'

'I mean I've finished making the beds, if you can help me carry the girls?'

'The girls. Of course. Yes.' The sofa springs groaned like a badly played violin as she struggled to her feet. Thank God Richard couldn't read her mind.

Together they hoisted the girls into their arms and carried them up the narrow staircase to the bedroom.

Jo stood for a moment, looking down on them huddled under the duvet in the double bed. Their sleeping faces looked so innocent. Poor little things, they didn't understand any of this.

'I've put you in the room next door. I'll take the sofa.' Richard's voice broke into her thoughts.

'Are you sure? It's not exactly comfortable.'

'What else do you suggest?' The quizzical look in his eyes threw her into instant confusion.

'I meant I'll sleep downstairs,' she said quickly. 'I wouldn't want to put you out at all.'

'Jo, it's four in the morning. It'll hardly matter where we sleep if we don't get to bed soon.'

She woke up to find bright sunshine streaming through the tiny dormer window.

She looked around, taking in her surroundings. It didn't take long. The room was only slightly larger than the single bed she occupied. When she stretched out she could touch the faded roses on the opposite wall with her fingertips. And if she sat up, her head brushed the sloping eaves. Talk about small. Chloe's Barbie collective lived in more commodious surroundings than this.

Her breath misted in the cold air. Tentatively she stretched a leg out of bed, then snatched it back under the quilt. It was freezing.

She was still trying to make herself get up when the girls came into the room, bundled up in several layers of jumpers.

'It's really cold.' Grace shivered. 'And there isn't a telly.'

'I don't suppose Richard needs one, if he never comes here.'

'*We* need one. What are we supposed to do without a telly?'

'You'll just have to make the best of it, won't you?'

'Why are we here, anyway?' Chloe demanded. 'Grace said it's because we're on the run from the police.'

'Did she indeed?' Jo shot her eldest daughter a warning look. 'Well, we're not. We're having a sort of holiday, that's all. That sounds like fun, doesn't it?'

'I'd rather go to Disney World.' Chloe went over to the window and looked out. 'It's got a really big garden,' she reported. 'Can we go and explore?'

'Wait until I'm up.' Jo extended a cautious toe out from under the covers. 'What time is it?'

'Nearly half past ten.'

'What?' Jo swung her legs out of bed and winced as her feet touched the cold, bare boards. She groped around for the clothes she'd abandoned the night before. 'Why didn't anyone wake me? Where's Richard?'

'He's gone.'

'Gone? When?'

'Dunno,' Grace shrugged. 'His car wasn't there when we got up.'

'Didn't he leave a note or anything?'

'Don't think so. What are you shouting at me for?'

'Was I? Sorry.' Why was she so disappointed? Surely she hadn't expected Richard to hang around the cottage with them all day? 'Oh well.' She forced a note of cheerfulness into her voice. 'We can't lie around in bed all day, can we? Better see what we can find for breakfast.'

Not very much, was the answer. Luckily the last occupants of the cottage had left a few basic provisions, although the girls curled their lips at the idea of Ryvitas and raspberry jam.

'I'm afraid that's all we've got.' Jo stuck her head in another empty cupboard. 'We'll sneak into the village and buy something decent later, I promise.'

She was determined to approach their situation with a positive frame of mind. But her optimism faded as she struggled to get to grips with her new surroundings. It wasn't just a TV the cottage was lacking. There was also gas central heating, a basic plumbing system and any kind of kitchen appliance that didn't come out of the Ark.

After she'd battled for over half an hour to get the ancient Aga to light, she became seriously depressed. 'Why can't he have an electric kettle like normal people?' she cursed, as yet another match burnt her fingers. Her hands were shaking from caffeine withdrawal.

'You'll just have to make the best of it, won't you?' Grace cheekily parroted her words back at her.

'I've changed my mind about that,' Jo growled. She changed her mind even more after she'd spent another twenty minutes watching cold brown sludge come out of the bath taps. She gave up on the idea of a bath, secretly relieved that at least she didn't have to take off her three layers of sweaters, the only thing between her and hypothermia.

Why hadn't Kate got to grips with this place? she wondered. If she had, Jo was sure there would be state-of-the-art showers and gleaming chrome appliances in place before you could say Philippe Starck juice extractor.

Determined not to die of hypothermia, she bundled the

girls into their coats and took them outside to collect wood for the fire. It was freezing cold and the biting wind whipped her hair around her face as she watched Chloe and Grace dart around the garden, in and out of the trees. At least they'd managed to forget about the previous night's trauma.

And so had she, she realised, as she hauled an armful of wood into the cottage. This place was exactly what she needed. It would be perfect, if only Richard were here . . .

She shook her head, dismissing the thought before it took hold. Richard was miles away, back with Kate in his *Westfield* office. Back where he belonged. Whatever adolescent fantasies she might be harbouring for him, she wouldn't do herself any good imagining that his kindness towards her was anything but that. The same kindness he would show Viola, or Lara, or anyone else in the same situation.

Or was it? Had she imagined that look in his eye the night before? What would he have done if she'd offered him the chance to share her bed?

Probably been halfway down the motorway before she'd finished brushing her teeth, she thought. Face it, Richard Black wasn't interested in her. If he was, why had he left without saying goodbye?

By the time they got back to the cottage they'd already missed lunch and the girls were complaining of starvation. Jo decided to abandon her plan to build a fire until later and trek off to find the village instead.

They followed the narrow winding lane, tramping between fields and stopping every so often so Chloe could talk to the quizzical-looking sheep. The sky was the same threatening grey as the looming limestone fells in the distance, and the cold wind whistled through their coats. It was a relief when they finally spotted the spire of the village church around the bend. Soon they were in a pretty little hamlet, like something out of a National Trust guidebook, full of quaint cottages in mellow, honeyed grey stone. They found a village shop-cum-post office, and Jo stocked up on groceries. She also bought a bottle of wine, as a thank you gift for Richard when she saw him again.

If she saw him again. She grew desolate at the thought.

'Can we have some sweets?' Chloe asked. Jo turned round to answer her – and then she saw it. Her own face, strained and blotchy with tears, on the front page of the *Globe*. Similar pictures stared back at her from the *Sun*, the *Mirror* and the *Sport*.

Her heart shot into her mouth like a high-speed lift as she dropped her shopping, scattering loo rolls, cereal boxes and bags of oven chips all over the floor.

'Mummy! Can we have some sweets?'

'What? Oh – yes, I suppose so. But hurry up.' She gathered up her shopping, her hands shaking. She had to pay for her things and get out fast. Suddenly it felt as if the walls were crowding in on her.

She paid for her purchases, keeping her head down and her scarf pulled up over her face. On impulse, she grabbed a handful of newspapers and paid for them too.

'That'll keep you busy.' Miraculously the woman behind the counter didn't seem to recognise her. 'I love a bit of gossip, don't you? See what all those celebs are getting up to.'

She almost ran all the way back up the lane to the cottage, the girls struggling breathlessly to keep up. Once safely inside the front door, she drew the bolt across and pulled the curtains.

'Why are you doing that?' Chloe asked. 'It's not night time.'

'It's – er – more cosy, don't you think?' She hurried around the kitchen, making sandwiches, her hands shaking. All she could think about were the newspapers she'd stuffed in the back of the cupboard. She was desperately torn between wanting to read them and not wanting to know.

Once the girls were settled in the sitting room with their sandwiches, sweets and comics, Jo shut herself in the kitchen. She took out the newspapers and spread them over the table.

It was worse than she could ever have imagined.

'*Westfield* Stars In Three In A Bed Sex And Drugs Romp', was the lurid headline on the *Globe*. The rest of the story was even less accurate. According to Charlie Beasley's version of events, she and her lover 'sexy stud' Marcus Finn had enticed 'outrageous blonde TV nymphet' Toni Carlisle into the bridal suite for an orgy. The *Sun* had them snorting coke, the *Mirror* had them all as crack addicts, while the *Sport* carried an interview with a teenage prostitute who swore she was there too.

Jo ripped up the papers and stuffed them into the bin. She wanted to scream with pain and fury, but she couldn't. She couldn't do anything. All she could do was sit helplessly by while the newspapers made up terrible, poisonous lies about her.

She sat on the kitchen floor beside the bin, her face buried in her hands, and sobbed. Once she started crying she couldn't stop. She heard the kitchen door creak open and Grace's voice whisper, 'Mum?'

'Go away.'

'But we —'

'Look, just go away and leave me alone, will you?'

The door banged shut. Jo tried to call them back, but all that emerged were more great, gulping sobs.

Chapter 21

Some time later the door opened again.

'Jo?' She knew Richard was standing over her but she couldn't look at him. 'Jo, what is it? What's going on?'

She couldn't answer him. She was crying so much she could hardly breathe. It was as if floodgates had been opened, and she couldn't close them again. Tears were flowing from everywhere – her whole face felt waterlogged.

He must have caught sight of the newspapers she'd stuffed in the bin. He sighed. 'You've seen them, then? I hoped you wouldn't.' He knelt beside her, and she felt his arm around her. 'Come on, it's not that bad.'

'N-not that bad?' She managed to gulp the words out. 'H-how much bloody worse could it be?' A torn fragment of headline caught her eye and she started sobbing again.

Richard's arm tightened around her shoulders. 'I told you, it'll all blow over by tomorrow. Besides, no one really believes all that rubbish.'

'So what? It doesn't m-matter if it's true or if they believe it. Mud sticks.' She wiped her face with her sleeve. 'It doesn't matter what I do or what I say. Those filthy lies will follow me around f-forever.'

'But the people who care about you know the truth. Who gives a damn what anyone else thinks?'

'That's easy for you to say!' She turned on him viciously. 'Your children don't have to face their friends at the school gates. They have a hard enough time as it is, without the other kids calling their mother a whore and a – a junkie!'

'Well, you're not making it any easier for them, are you?' His fingers bit into the flesh of her shoulder. 'Don't you realise they're out there terrified because they think you're having some kind of fucking breakdown? They need you to be strong, not fall apart on them.'

'I can't help it, can I? You don't know what it's like –'

'I know what it's like to have a mother who's so wrapped up in her own problems she can't see what she's putting everyone else through.' His eyes blazed with anger. 'If you really want to help those kids I suggest you stop feeling so fucking sorry for yourself and start thinking about them!'

He released her and slammed out of the room. A moment later she heard his car roar off.

Jo crouched on the kitchen floor, hugging herself. The cold had seeped right through to her bones. Bastard. What did he know? He wasn't the one who had to go out and face the world every day. And as for being wrapped up in her own problems . . .

Well, maybe she was. She hadn't handled this very well, she knew that much. Poor Chloe and Grace, she must have terrified them, losing it like that. Richard was right about that, too. They needed her to be strong for them. She was all they had, and she couldn't let them down.

She stood up, brushed down her jeans, and went to look for them. Darkness had fallen outside the cottage, and a bitterly cold wind was rustling the trees. There was no sign of Grace and Chloe. Just a note propped up on the mantelpiece, hastily scribbled in Grace's writing – 'GONE WITH RICHARD'.

God, he'd love that, wouldn't he? After a hard day at work, the last thing he'd want was to play babysitter. Especially when he didn't even like children that much. She just prayed her two wouldn't decide to play up.

She went up to the bathroom, splashed her face with cold

water and pulled a brush through her hair. Her swollen face looked back at her from the chipped bathroom mirror. She still looked as if she'd gone ten rounds with Lennox Lewis, but it was a slight improvement.

She was doing her best to build the fire with the wood she'd collected when she heard Richard's car outside and saw the flash of his headlights through the window.

'We've been to the fish and chip shop.' Chloe raced into the room ahead of the others.

'And Richard let me drive the car up the lane to the road,' Grace added proudly. 'He says I'm a natural.'

'Really? That's nice.' At least they didn't seem any the worse for seeing their mother reduced to a howling mess.

Then Richard came into the room. Jo ducked her head and concentrated on building up the fire. She could feel him watching her.

'Go into the kitchen and lay the table, would you, girls?' Amazingly, they went like lambs. Jo heard them clattering about in the kitchen drawers. She still didn't dare look up at Richard as he stood over her.

'That wood's too damp. It'll never light,' he said shortly.

Jo bit back a sharp retort. He was right to be angry with her. And if she didn't want them to spend the rest of the evening in sullen silence, it was up to her to make the peace.

'Look, I'm sorry.' She stared at the black, empty fireplace. 'I shouldn't have lost it like that. You're right, I was just feeling sorry for myself.'

There was a long silence. 'I'm sorry too,' he said at last. 'You had every right to be upset. I don't know what I'd do if my private life ended up all over the papers.' He crouched down beside her and gently took the lump of wood out of her hands. 'I just got so angry when I found the girls cowering like that. For a moment it just reminded me of my brother and me –' Jo risked a glance at him. His smoky eyes were full of sorrow. 'But then I realised, you're nothing like my mother was. You're strong.'

218

Jo smiled weakly. 'I don't feel very strong at the moment.'

'Maybe not. But you'll pull through this.' He reached up and pushed a stray lock of hair off her face. The gesture surprised them both and they froze, just as the door flew open and Chloe fell through it.

'Dinner's ready!' she yelled.

The moment was forgotten as they sat around the scrubbed kitchen table with the girls, tucking into their food. Richard showed Jo how to light the Aga and a pleasant warmth filled the room. With the low lamplight, it was positively cosy.

'Sorry it's not more imaginative,' Richard said. 'The village isn't exactly blessed with takeaways.'

'This is fine,' Jo assured him. 'Although somehow I never pictured you eating fish and chips.'

'Yes, well, it makes a change from the flesh of innocent virgins, doesn't it?'

'Is that really what you eat?' Chloe looked at him, wide-eyed.

'Only when I'm working.' He flashed a look at Jo. He seemed so different tonight. He even looked different. He'd abandoned his suit for black cords and a chunky grey sweater.

She looked around the table. The girls were giggling about something and despite all her problems, for the first time in a long time she felt truly at peace. Why couldn't it always be like this, she wondered, instead of her always worrying about the following day's scenes or next week's scripts? Wouldn't it be nice if she didn't always feel as if she was running to catch up?

And did Richard feature in this blissful domestic picture? Unfortunately he did. Quite largely, in fact. It was a bit pathetic really, Jo decided. Other women might have fantasies about tearing his clothes off with their teeth. Hers consisted of cooking his supper.

'Jo? Are you all right?' She came back to earth, a chip

poised midway to her mouth, to find Richard and the girls watching her. 'You were miles away.'

'Was I? Sorry.' She put down her chip, her appetite forgotten. 'I'll start on the washing up.'

'Leave it, we'll do it later.'

'Then I'll put the kettle on.' Anything to take her mind off what she'd been thinking.

'Looks like you've made a couple of fans,' she said, when they finally got around to clearing the plates away. The girls had gone to bed after a spirited game of Monopoly, during which Richard had done his best not to notice them cheating appallingly. Much to Jo's embarrassment, they'd insisted on him coming upstairs to say goodnight. 'I'm sorry if they've been a nuisance.'

'They've been fine.'

'All the same, it can be a bit much if you're not used to them.'

'Jo, I have seen a child before. I was one myself once, remember?' His eyes twinkled. 'Look, just because I'm not keen on having kids myself doesn't mean I hate them or anything. I just don't think I'd be that good a father, that's all.'

'But you're brilliant with children! Anyway, just because you've had a bad upbringing yourself doesn't mean you're going to repeat it with your own family. If anything, it might even make you better at bringing them up, because you wouldn't want to make the same mistakes.' She realised she'd gone too far and turned back to the sink in confusion. What was she doing, trying to talk him into family life?

'Maybe you're right,' Richard agreed. 'I must admit, sometimes I wonder what it would be like to have a family to come home to. A real home.'

'But you've got a home.'

Richard's smile faded. 'I've got a place to live. It's hardly the same thing.' He paused. 'Yours is a real home,' he said.

She laughed and slipped the plates into the hot, soapy water. 'Mine is a pigsty!'

'No, it isn't. It's warm, and it's kind, and it's full of laughter and love. Like you.'

Jo turned around, and suddenly they were facing each other, only inches apart. Her heart bounced like a turbo-charged yo-yo.

'Mum! Chloe's being a pain. Come up and tell her, will you?'

Grace's yell from upstairs was like a bucket of icy water. They moved apart. Jo didn't know whether to feel relieved or disappointed.

There must be something about country air, she decided, fumbling for her watch on the bedside table. It was almost ten o'clock again.

She lay in bed, listening to the voices from downstairs. She could hear Grace, and Chloe's high-pitched squeaks, and . . . Richard?

She hurried out of bed and into her clothes. As she threw open the curtains, she was amazed to find it had started snowing overnight. Soft flakes fell against her window and a deep blanket of white covered the ground. The whole world was muffled in stillness, as if life had been suspended. It was like a scene from a Christmas card. Any minute now Bing Crosby would come into the clearing, crooning away about treetops glistening and children listening and all that other nonsense. She felt quite festive, despite the fact that it was mid-February.

Then she heard Richard's voice again, bringing her back to earth. What was he still doing here? He should have left for work hours ago. In fact she'd been relying on it. She wasn't quite sure how to face him after last night.

Had he really meant what he said? He certainly looked as if he did at the time. She wondered what might have happened next, if Grace hadn't called out when she did.

But that was last night. This morning was a whole new day, and the moment, or whatever it was, had probably gone for ever.

She found them all in the kitchen. Richard and Chloe were at one end of the big scrubbed pine table, while Grace buttered her way through a heap of toast at the other.

'Mum!' She grinned. 'Have you seen outside? It's snowing! Real snow, not that grey slushy stuff we get in town.'

'I know, darling.' But Jo's eyes were fixed on Chloe, who had her entire Barbie collection spread in front of her. She was dressing them from their extensive shoebox wardrobe. Nothing unusual in that, except that Richard was helping her.

'No, no, you've got it wrong again!' Chloe snatched the half-dressed doll out of his hands. 'This is Aqua Dazzle Barbie, she has to wear the sparkly swimsuit. That goes on Snow Queen Barbie. See?' She held it under his nose.

'I'm not very good at choosing women's clothes.' Richard sighed. 'Couldn't I dress Ken instead?'

'I told you, the Barbies are going clubbing. Ken has to stay at home and clean the house.'

'How very politically correct of him. He doesn't look much like a new man to me.' He looked up at Jo and smiled. He was looking very dark and desirable in a black sweater and jeans. Her stomach lurched.

'Shouldn't you be at work?' she squeaked.

'I thought I'd work from here today.' He folded one of Barbie's minuscule cardigans. 'The roads will be a nightmare. It'll take me so long to get back to York I might as well not bother. If that's okay with you?' he added.

'Of course. Why shouldn't it be?' Jo tried to suppress her leaping excitement. She picked up the kettle and ran it under the tap. 'But won't they need you in the office?'

'I've got my laptop and my mobile if anyone wants to contact me. I've told Louise that you're off until further notice. And Kate's more than capable of running the office in my absence.'

I'm sure she is, Jo thought. Kate could probably run a small country without too much trouble. Whereas she couldn't even run a bath without having a nervous breakdown.

She put the kettle on the hob, and then she noticed that morning's *Globe* lying on the worktop. She stopped, every muscle in her body tensing.

'I walked into the village to get it earlier,' Richard said. 'It's okay, you can read it.'

There were no splashy headlines this morning. Gingerly she flipped the page. A summit conference somewhere in Europe, a supermarket price war – and there it was, on page five. A photo of Marcus, looking rumpled and furious, getting into a Bentley with Murphy under the headline 'Disgraced Soap Star Goes Home To Face The Music'.

Jo read on, her disbelief growing with every word. According to Charlie Beasley, Marcus's father was Lord Finnimoore of Wyston, and the Hon. Marcus was heir to several thousand prime acres of Gloucestershire.

'That can't be true!' she whispered.

'Apparently it is. Bit of a dark horse, isn't he?'

'You can say that again. I thought his family were a bunch of old hippies!'

'They are. Very rich and well-connected hippies, though. Which is probably how he manages to stay out of jail.' His voice was bitter.

Jo went on reading. There were a couple of paragraphs about Toni Carlisle being admitted into rehab, but nothing about her.

'It looks like they've forgotten all about you, doesn't it?' Richard said quietly. 'You could probably sue them if that's what you wanted, but I think it's probably better if we just let it die a natural death.'

Jo nodded. 'A court case could take months, and then it

would all get dragged up again. I just want to forget it ever happened.'

After breakfast the girls started clamouring to go outside and play in the snow. Jo was caught up in the rush to find boots and coats.

'Aren't you coming outside with us?' Chloe looked disappointed as Richard opened up his briefcase and took out his laptop.

'I'm afraid I can't. I have to work.'

'Can't you just forget about work for one day?'

'I'm sure Richard's got far too much to do,' Jo cut in quickly. 'Come on, we'll go outside and build a snowman.'

It would be easier for him to forget to breathe than to forget about work, she decided, as she followed the girls out into the garden, her boots plunging into the deep, crunchy snow. She could see him sitting at the window, his dark head bent over his computer screen.

She tried to keep the girls quiet, but it was impossible. They weren't used to real snow, and they couldn't help whooping and shrieking as they fell about in it, picking it up in their gloved hands and shaking it off the overhanging tree branches. Every so often Richard lifted his head to look out at them. Jo could feel his irritation at the constant interruptions.

Finally she got the girls organised into making a snowman, only to find she had no idea how to go about it. After half an hour they'd made nothing more than a small, unsatisfactory pyramid with a misshapen head that kept rolling off.

'It looks stupid.' Grace drop-kicked the head into the trees.

'Oh, I don't know.' Jo did her best to be encouraging. 'I think it looks like that snowman in the video. You know, "We're walking in the air −"' She flapped her arms and floated round the garden.

'MUM!' Chloe and Grace chorused.

'Could I make a suggestion?'

Jo turned, mid-float. Richard was standing in the door-way, looking rugged in a thick cord jacket, his hands plunged into the pockets. She was so hot with mortification she could almost feel herself melting a hole in the snow.

'Yes?'

'Perhaps you're going about it the wrong way?' He crunched through the snow towards them, his Timberland boots making deep holes beside the girls' smaller wellie tracks. 'If you want to make a real snowman, the best way is to start like this.' He crouched down and began gathering up snow.

Jo watched him, her arms folded. 'So you're an expert, are you?'

'I've obviously had more experience than you.'

'Why don't you put the kettle on, Mummy?' Chloe suggested patronisingly.

Jo stomped into the kitchen, shaking the snow off her boots. She knew where she wasn't wanted. Actually, it was quite a relief to be inside. The Aga spread a cosy warmth through the cottage. Jo peeled off her damp gloves and boots and pulled up a chair after she'd put the kettle on, propping her feet up on the oven door to watch the steam rise off her socks.

Outside, she could see the girls rushing around, gathering up armfuls of snow and bringing them back to Richard, who was constructing what looked to be an extremely impressive snowman. He really had them under his spell, she thought. Unlike her other boyfriends in the past, who'd tried to bribe them with treats and presents, he seemed to win them over just by being himself.

She nearly fell off her chair. *Unlike her other boyfriends . . .* what was she thinking of? Richard was very, very far from being a boyfriend. She wasn't his type, for one thing. You only had to look at the woman he was with to know that.

She finished making the coffee, took the mugs outside and set them on the windowsill.

'I've made the –' She didn't even get the words out before a snowball hit her square in the face, knocking her sideways and filling her mouth with snow. 'Right, who did that?' she spluttered, as the girls screamed with laughter.

'He did!'

Grace and Chloe pointed at Richard. 'Only because they told me to,' he protested. He held up his hands. 'Jo? What are you doing with that? It was just a joke, there's no need to – ow!'

Jo brushed the snow off her gloves. 'I may not be able to make a snowman, but I'm a deadly aim,' she said calmly. She turned away to pick up the mugs, and a snowball bounced off the back of her head. She looked back, and another caught her on the chin. The girls were almost hysterical by now. Richard was leaning against a tree, looking smug. 'That does it,' she muttered. She advanced towards him slowly. He watched her, his eyes narrowing.

'Truce?' he suggested.

'No chance,' she said sweetly. She reached up and shook the branch. There was a soft thump, and he was covered in snow.

It all happened very quickly after that. Jo saw the look of menace in his eyes and backed away. She turned to run, but Richard made a flying tackle, grabbing her legs and bringing her to the ground. As she screamed and wriggled and begged for mercy, he began stuffing handfuls of snow into her jacket and down her shirt.

'No! Please, don't, I'll do anything –'

She looked up into his laughing eyes, just inches away from hers, and suddenly attraction hit her like a blow in the solar plexus. She stopped squirming and lay there, his weight on top of her, pinning her down.

It seemed to hit him at the same time. His smile slipped and he froze, his eyes looking deep into hers.

Chloe's giggling broke the spell. Jo was suddenly conscious of them standing over them. Richard rolled off her

226

and sat up, brushing the snow off his shoulders. 'We'd better have that coffee before it gets cold,' he said.

They sat on a fallen log, watching the girls play. Jo wrapped her frozen fingers around her steaming mug. She could feel the sexual tension crackling in the air, and this time she knew she wasn't imagining it. The question was, what were they going to do about it?

Richard answered for her. He drained his cup and stood up. 'I'd better go and finish that work.'

They stayed a cautious distance from each other for the rest of the day. Richard spent the whole afternoon hunched over his computer while Jo entertained the girls and pottered around the kitchen preparing supper. It felt as if they were circling each other, each waiting for the other to make the first move.

This is mad, she told herself as she washed her hair in a half-filled, tepid bath. If she had to make a list of the men she might conceivably fall in love with, Richard wouldn't even be on it. Or if he were, he'd be down there at Number 103, right below Chris Evans and her ex-husband.

She'd always thought he was attractive. Even at his most arrogant, there was something deep and dark and sexy about him. He was a powerful man, and power was always irresistible.

But it wasn't just that. Not any more. In the past weeks she'd seen another side to him. He wasn't nearly as arrogant and aloof as he liked everyone to believe. It was just a defence mechanism to keep the rest of the world at bay. But she'd been allowed to glimpse the fascinating, complicated, warm and caring man beneath.

And she'd seen that smile. A smile that lit up his eyes and transformed the cynical hardness of his face. A smile that made her shiver whenever she thought about it.

Stop it, she told herself as she emptied another tooth mug of tepid water over her head. So you fancy him. A lot. So he might even fancy you. So what? He's also got a criminally chic girlfriend with hips like a Twiglet and shoes that cost more than your mortgage. This cannot be.

But that didn't stop her slapping on some Issy Miyake body lotion after her bath. Or putting on make-up. Thank God she hadn't packed a dress, she thought. Otherwise she would have put that on too and made a complete fool of herself.

It was a weird evening. Jo had never been so heart-stoppingly, nerve-twangingly aware of anyone in her whole life. All through the meal, she kept sneaking glances at him, noticing more and more things about him. His long, sensitive hands. His deep, sexy voice. Even the way he handled his fork sent her hormones into overdrive.

She couldn't tell what he was thinking, but she had the feeling he was as nervous as she was. There was no laughter, no easy conversation flowing between them. Every look, every word, every movement was laced with meaning.

She'd hoped the children might act as a kind of buffer between them. But somehow Grace had picked up on her nerves and realised Richard was the cause of them. She'd also decided to act as an unofficial matchmaker. As soon as supper was over and the plates were cleared away she declared in a loud voice that it was time for bed.

'But I thought we were going to play Monopoly again?' Chloe whined.

'Not tonight,' Grace said firmly. 'We're tired and we want to go to bed. Now.' She fastened her sister in an armlock and manhandled her towards the stairs. 'Don't worry, Mummy, I'll put her to bed,' she insisted, as Jo made a move to follow them. 'Then you can stay here and be alone with Richard.' She added a few eye rolls and encouraging semaphore hand movements, just in case neither of them had got the message loudly or embarrassingly enough.

The bedroom door closed overhead, plunging them into

awkward silence. 'Subtle as a sledgehammer,' Richard said wryly.

'I never thought I'd say it, but I think I preferred it when she was slamming doors and sulking every time a man came within ten miles.' She glanced sideways at him. 'At least it means she likes you.'

'I'm flattered.'

What happens now? Jo wondered. She felt sure something was going to happen. The air tingled with expectation. The lamps were low and the sitting room was lit by flickering firelight. Snow was falling outside, and the wind rattled the lattice panes, but inside everything was warm and bathed in a soft golden glow. The scene had 'seduction' written all over it.

For want of something constructive to do, she went into the kitchen and fetched the bottle of wine she'd bought the day before, and two glasses. When she got back to the sitting room Richard was standing at the window, staring out into the night.

'I bought this in the village yesterday. I don't know if it's any good or not –'

'Not for me, thanks. I've been thinking – they've probably managed to clear the main roads by now. Maybe I should be heading back?'

Disappointment hit her like a punch in the stomach. She nearly dropped the glasses. 'Why?'

He turned slowly to face her. 'I think we both know the answer to that one, don't you?'

'But the roads will still be treacherous –'

'I'll take my chances.'

I don't understand, she wanted to scream. One minute he was making it clear he fancied her, the next he was saying he'd rather die of frostbite on the hard shoulder than spend another minute alone with her.

Unless it was because of Kate? Perhaps he was having a guilt attack?

229

She looked down at the bottle in her hands. 'I suppose Kate will be wondering where you are.'

'Kate doesn't give a damn where I am!' His vehemence startled her. 'She wasn't at home when I called last night, and she isn't there now. Do you really think I'm rushing off because I can't wait to get home to an empty flat?'

'Then why are you going?'

'Because of what's happening with us. There is something happening, isn't there? I mean, I wasn't imagining what went on today?' Jo shook her head. There was no point in hiding her feelings any longer. 'And I guess I'm right in thinking that if I stayed here tonight we might do something we'd both regret?'

'Who says we'd regret it?'

'Oh come on!' Richard said gruffly. 'Surely you can see it wouldn't work?'

'Because of Kate?'

'Because of us. You don't need someone like me in your life.'

'What you mean is you don't need someone like me. That's what all this is about, isn't it?' Anger flared in her eyes. 'You're afraid I and the girls might mess up your oh-so-perfect lifestyle.'

'There's nothing perfect about my lifestyle. And maybe I'm afraid I'll end up needing you too much.' His eyes were dark with pain. 'Jo, I know what loving someone can do, remember? I grew up watching my mother falling in love with men, giving her heart to them and having it all blow up in her face. She put her trust in other people, and it destroyed all of us. I don't want the same thing to happen to me.'

'Who says it would? My God, do you think you're the only one who's ever been let down by the people you love? How do you think I felt when I found out Duncan was having an affair? It shattered everything I thought I could believe in. But I survived. And just because Duncan let me down doesn't mean every other man in the world is going to do the same.' She took a deep breath. 'Look, what happened to your family was terrible. But you mustn't let it stop you being happy.'

'I am happy.'

'No, you're not. Just because you're not miserable doesn't mean you're happy.'

'Spare me the self-help psychobabble! You don't know me well enough.'

'No, you're right. I don't.' She stalked into the kitchen and started on the washing up, crashing pots and pans around to ease her mounting frustration.

She was staring at the water running into the sink when he came into the room. 'I'm going now.' She didn't turn round. 'Jo?'

'What? What do you want me to say? Bon voyage? Have a safe trip? I'll see you in the office on Monday?'

'Don't do this, Jo –'

'Do what?' She swung round to face him, a frying pan in her hand. 'If you want to go, then go. I'm not stopping you.'

'You think I really want to go? You think I haven't dreamed about being alone with you like this? Christ, I've thought about nothing else for weeks.' His voice was husky. 'But it's not going to work, Jo. We can't start something we can't finish.'

'Then there's nothing more to say, is there?' She turned back to the sink and started scrubbing the pan as if her life depended on it. She was still scrubbing when she heard the front door close. Only then did she allow herself to break down.

He was right. She knew he was right. They both wanted and needed such different things in life, their relationship didn't stand a chance. But that didn't take away the terrible, searing pain.

'Jo?' The pan scourer fell from her hands. She turned

231

round. Richard was standing in the doorway, his dark hair dusted with melting snow.

'Who the fuck am I kidding?' he groaned. 'This thing started the day I first set eyes on you. And there's not a damn thing I can do about it.'

Chapter 22

He crossed the kitchen in a couple of strides. A moment later, she was in his arms and he was kissing her, passionate and fierce. Jo clung to him, kissing him back just as passionately. It was as if a dam had burst inside them, sweeping them both away in an emotional torrent.

Richard finally pulled away and looked down at her. 'You don't know how long I've been waiting to do that.'

Not as long as I have, Jo thought. 'So what happens now?'

'What do you mean?'

'Do we go upstairs now, or what?'

He looked shocked. 'Are you suggesting we go to bed together?'

'No!' A flash burn scalded from her face to her feet. 'I mean, I'm not sure –' Then she heard him chuckle and risked a glance at him. 'You bastard!'

'Sorry,' he grinned. 'I couldn't resist it.' He pulled her into his arms again. This time his kiss was less urgent but much, much sweeter. 'I think that would be a great idea. But perhaps we should start slowly – maybe with that bottle of wine?'

They curled up together on the rug in front of the flickering fire. Jo couldn't remember when she'd felt this happy, snuggled up next to Richard, feeling the roughness of his sweater against her cheek and the comforting beat of his heart under her hand. The weight of his arm around her shoulders felt so right somehow. They talked a little, laughed a lot, and listened to the whirr of the hamster's wheel as Richard the rodent did his nightly exercise routine.

'Doesn't that wretched animal ever shut up?' Richard muttered.

'Leave him alone, he's sweet. Besides, you bought him.'

'Only because I wanted an excuse to see you again.' He held her closer. 'And then I lost my nerve and nearly didn't bring it round. I spent most of Christmas Day wondering what to do. It was only the thought of being saddled with the bloody thing that made me come in the end. And then, once I got to your place, I realised what a mistake I'd made.'

'Charming.'

'You know what I mean. Seeing you totally confused me. I knew you were everything I'd spent my whole life trying to avoid, and yet I couldn't get you out of my mind.'

Jo pulled herself up to look at him. 'Thanks very much! I'm not that much of a disaster area, you know.'

'No, but I am.' He brushed a stray tendril of hair off her face. 'I didn't think I'd be that good for you, either. Why do you think I spent the last six weeks avoiding you? I'd just managed to convince myself I'd got you out of my mind when I turned up at that wedding and saw you with Marcus fucking Finn. I didn't know whether to be furious with him or with myself for letting you go when I had the chance.'

'I told you, Marcus is —'

'Just a friend. So you keep saying. But he's a good-looking bastard.'

'He's not my type.'

'Thank God for that. Otherwise I'd definitely have to fire him.'

Jo stared at him in disbelief. 'Of all the arrogant —' He leaned over and stopped her mouth with a kiss. Her pulses leapt in response but she pulled away, still uncertain.

'What about Kate?' She saw the light fade from his eyes and wished she hadn't said it.

'What about her?' he said abruptly.

'I mean, there's no love lost between us or anything, but I don't want to think of anyone getting hurt because of me —'

'Kate won't get hurt. She's not the type.' He sat upright. Jo felt cold and bereft as he pulled away from her. 'I suppose that's what attracted me to her in the first place. We were never a couple. Just two independent, ambitious people in a mutually satisfying arrangement.' His jaw was hard with tension. 'Although frankly, I don't think Kate's all that satisfied with it either. She's been acting strangely since before Christmas, taking herself off with friends every night and weekend. We're hardly what you'd call together any more.'

'And is that why you wanted me? As a replacement for Kate?'

Richard's eyes crinkled. 'Jo, if I'd been looking for a replacement for Kate do you seriously think I would have chosen someone like you?'

'God, you're such a creep!' Jo picked up a cushion and took a swipe at his head. Richard ducked at the last minute and lost his balance. Jo seized her advantage and threw herself on top of him, straddling his long, lean body between her thighs. 'Say you're sorry,' she demanded.

'Make me.' Before she could make a move his hands flashed out, pinning her wrists and pulling her towards him so their faces were just inches apart. She breathed in the clean, male smell of him, heard his breathing grow ragged. She could feel his erection pressing warm against her belly. She looked into his eyes, burning dark with longing.

'Make me,' he whispered again.

They stumbled up the stairs and barely made it inside the door before Richard pushed her against it. They pulled at each other's clothes, kissing deeply, their hands exploring, caressing bare skin, hard muscle and hair.

Jo heard herself crying out as he stroked her breasts, circling her nipples with his fingers, then his tongue before travelling down, down . . . She arched her body, a drumbeat of desire deep in her pelvis. She'd never experienced such passion or desperate physical longing. She reached out for him, feeling the thick silkiness of his hair as she pulled him up to her. She couldn't take any more of his questing tongue. Her mind was emptied of everything but the urgent feeling that she would explode if she didn't have him now.

They just made it to the bed.

'Sorry,' Richard groaned afterwards against her skin. 'That was a bit lacking in finesse, wasn't it?'

'I'm not complaining.' She couldn't have waited a moment longer either. 'Besides, we can do the finesse bit next time.'

'Next time?' He pulled away, his damp skin peeling from hers. 'You think I've got enough energy for a next time?'

Jo smiled. 'I'm counting on it.'

'You're an insatiable woman.' Richard bent his head and kissed her again. He folded her into his arms and collapsed backwards on to the bed, pulling her in a giggling heap on top of him.

They spent most of the night making love and talking. They talked about anything and everything, sharing their memories, their hopes, their dreams. Most of all they talked about their future.

'I'll talk to Kate as soon as I get back,' Richard promised. 'It's only fair to let her know what's going on, rather than let her read it in the newspapers.'

'Will she be very upset?' Jo ventured. 'I know you said the two of you were drifting apart, but –'

'The only thing that would upset Kate is the thought of losing her lifestyle.' Richard's profile was carved in moonlight. 'I'm sure that's the only thing keeping us together at the moment. But she can have the flat and anything else she wants. She's always liked that place more than me anyway.'

'But where will you live?'

He turned his face towards her. 'I was thinking, I might do

this place up and move in here. It'd be great to have somewhere to escape to, out of the city. And maybe I could stay over at your place sometimes? If you think the girls wouldn't mind —'

'Are you kidding? They'll be thrilled.' Jo grinned. 'Grace has already been dropping massive hints, just in case you hadn't noticed. But I think she's more interested in your car than you.'

Richard groaned in dismay. 'Just don't ask me to give her another driving lesson. I don't think my nerves or my gearbox could stand it.'

'Your nerves will have to take a lot more than that.' Jo snuggled up to him. 'Are you sure you're ready to take us on?'

His eyes gleamed in the silvery moonlight. 'I'm looking forward to it.'

She drifted into a contented sleep in Richard's arms and woke up to find pink dawn sunlight filling the room, birds twittering noisily outside, and the bed beside her empty.

Jo sat up, disorientated, wondering if last night had all been a blissful dream. Her body, aching as if it had been through a strenuous workout at the gym, told her it couldn't have been. Smiling to herself, she lay back against the pillows, luxuriating in the warm hollow of the bed where Richard's body had been. She didn't deserve to be this happy. Surely something had to come along to spoil it?

Then she heard the voices drifting up from downstairs and she realised that 'something' had already arrived.

She pulled on her dressing gown and hurried downstairs. They were in the kitchen. Richard was at the Aga, watching the kettle with scowling intensity. Kate was sitting at the table, her head in her hands. For once she didn't look immaculate. In fact, she looked awful. Her eyes were pink and swollen, her smudged mascara blended with the deep circles under her eyes, and her hair was hastily pulled back off her face in what looked like a tatty, non-designer rubber band.

In short, she looked like a woman who'd just been dumped. Jo, who'd been through the experience more often than she liked to remember, felt a pang of sympathy, swiftly followed by guilt and the urgent desire to be anywhere but there. The atmosphere was leaden with misery and recrimination.

Kate lifted her face from her hands and regarded her stonily. 'Oh, it's you.'

Who did you expect, Princess Caroline of Monaco? Jo resisted the urge to snipe back. After all, she had just stolen Kate's man. She could hardly expect her to clasp her to her bosom like a long-lost sister on *This Is Your Life*.

Richard pushed a mug in front of Kate. He also looked utterly miserable, Jo realised. His unshaven jaw was clenched, his dark eyes devoid of expression.

'Would you like a coffee?' he offered.

'Thanks.' Smiling, she made a move towards him. He physically recoiled. Don't come any closer, his stricken expression seemed to say.

Jo stopped in her tracks, bewildered. What was going on? Did he think she was going to drag him to the floor for a reprise of last night's performance? Give her some credit. She might fancy the boxers off him but even she could see it would be a touch insensitive to show it in front of his recently ex-girlfriend.

Unless she wasn't his ex yet? Jo glanced at Kate, then back at Richard. He frowned and gave the slightest shake of his head. So he hadn't told her yet. In which case, why was she so upset? And why, come to that, was she even here?

'Here, have mine.' Kate pushed her mug across the table towards her. 'The way I'm feeling I can't face coffee at the moment.'

Jo pulled out a chair opposite Kate's and sank into it. 'I didn't expect to see you?'

'Didn't you? Well, life's full of surprises, isn't it?' Kate's voice was edged with ice. Her nails, Jo noticed, were chewed ragged. What the hell was going on?

'Are you – er – okay?'

'Do I look okay? Would I drag myself up here and risk fucking suicide on those roads if everything was just tickety-sodding-boo?' Her red-rimmed eyes flashed.

Jo glanced at Richard. He was staring into space, oblivious to what was going on around him. He looked so unreachable it frightened her.

Suddenly he galvanised himself into action and emptied his untouched coffee down the sink. 'Let's just go, shall we?' he muttered.

Jo stared at him. 'Go where?'

'I'm taking Kate back to York. I'll send someone down to pick up her car later.' He turned to Kate. 'Ready?'

'I can't wait.' She stood up, pushing back her chair. 'The sooner we get home, the better.'

Home. Jo's head reeled. Whatever had happened, Kate still believed she and Richard were a couple.

Maybe Jo was the one who'd got it wrong? She watched Richard unhook his overcoat from the peg behind the door. He slid his laptop back into his case, checked his pockets for his keys. He didn't look at her. It was almost as if she'd ceased to exist for him.

'Richard?'

Finally he looked up at her, and she almost wished he hadn't. He didn't even look like the same man. She hardly recognised the dark, frowning face with the haunted eyes and rigidly set jaw.

'Are you coming?' Kate stood in the doorway, her arms folded.

'Wait in the car, Kate. I won't be a moment.'

'But if we want to miss the traffic –'

'I said wait in the car!' His eyes never left Jo's face. Kate sighed heavily and slammed the door.

'What the hell's going on? What's she doing here? Why didn't you tell her about us?' A million questions tumbled over themselves to be answered.

'I couldn't tell her, not yet. She's – had some bad news.' Richard raked his hand through his hair. 'Things have changed.'

A cold wave of fear rushed over her. 'What do you mean, changed?'

'I mean it's complicated.' He looked haggard. 'Look, I owe you an explanation but I can't give you one, not yet. Not until I've sorted things out.'

'Sorted what out? Richard?'

He started to speak, but Kate's voice interrupted them. 'Are you coming, or what? It's bloody freezing out here!'

'In a minute.' He glanced over his shoulder, then back at Jo. 'Look, I promise I'll talk to you later. When I know what's going on.' He picked up his case. 'It'll be all right, I promise,' he said. And then he was gone.

Jo watched them driving off together, making slow progress down the lane. In spite of the warmth from the Aga she hugged herself with cold. Richard hadn't even kissed her goodbye. In fact she'd got the impression he didn't even want to be in the same room as her.

Things have changed, he'd said. She only hoped his feelings for her hadn't changed too.

Chapter 23

'That's it, Jo. If you can just get a bit closer – go on, lean in together – lovely.' The photographer snapped a few more frames. 'Now, if we can have you a bit more cheek to cheek, that's it – blimey, you're meant to be in love, aren't you? I've seen more passion on a fishmonger's slab!'

'It's all right, angel, you can get a bit closer. I haven't got anything catching.' Marcus pulled her closer.

'How do I know that?' Jo's *What's On TV* cover smile was frozen in place. 'The amount of women you've slept with, you could have diseases medical science hasn't caught up with yet!'

He laughed. 'Are you mad at me or something?'

'Heavens no, why would I be mad at you? Just because you dragged my name through the mud and nearly got me jailed for life!'

'Don't be so melodramatic darling, they wouldn't have put you in jail. Look at me. I admitted possession and my solicitor reckons I'll get off with a fine. Besides, how was I to know the police were going to turn up? Although I'd like to know who tipped them off.' He gritted his teeth as the camera shutter clicked again. 'I wouldn't be surprised if it was the Grim Reaper.'

She pulled away from him. 'Why would he do that?'

'I wouldn't put anything past him. He's always hated me.'

'But he wouldn't risk *Westfield*'s reputation just out of spite.'

'Oh, so you're on his side now, are you? What's brought this on? Don't tell me you've fallen for his warmth and charisma?'

She could feel her face flaming. 'Fuck off, Marcus.'

'Ooh, have I touched a nerve? I noticed he was quick to jump on his white charger and rescue you. He left me hanging out to dry.'

'Only because you'd admitted you were guilty. Besides, you didn't exactly need his help, did you? You had Daddy and an army of barristers, remember?'

Marcus's face clouded. The news that he was the Hon. Marcus Finnimoore, heir to half a county, had seriously dented his street cred. Even when it was revealed that his father Lord Finnimoore was an eccentric sculptor who wore kaftans and enjoyed *droit de seigneur* with most of the women on his estate, people still kept referring to Marcus as 'Your Majesty'.

'Anyway, it's all over now,' he said.

Is it, Jo thought bleakly. A week after she and the girls had come out of hiding, her life was slowly getting back to normal. Roxanne was back, having defied her parents and turned up on Jo's doorstep at midnight. It had taken several phone calls and a hefty pay rise to persuade Mr and Mrs Morgan that she wasn't about to introduce their daughter to Class A drugs or sell her into the white slave trade.

'The stupid thing is, I could probably get my hands on more dope than you!' Roxanne giggled, which had somewhat shaken Jo's faith in her as a nanny.

Her own parents, thankfully, had been oblivious to the whole thing. By the time they returned from the Languedoc the scandal had blown over. Although Jo's father did ask her in a puzzled way why his fellow Rotarians kept mentioning 'Three in a bed sex romps' whenever he was in earshot.

Duncan had offered to act as a character witness – 'You

just send them to me, I'll tell them you're as sexually adventurous as an amoeba' – while the rest of the cast of *Westfield* had been sweetly supportive. Except Brett Michaels, of course, who found the whole thing a huge joke.

She could have put the entire miserable episode behind her, except for one thing. She still hadn't heard from Richard. She'd stayed at the cottage for two days after his hasty departure. Two days of watching through the window for his car to come up the drive. Two days of thinking, of turning everything over and over in her head until she thought she'd go mad. Finally she couldn't bear it any longer. She'd summoned a taxi, rounded up the girls and headed home. Fortunately by then the press had got bored of staking her out and moved on to pursue another scandal.

But still she didn't hear from Richard. According to the gossip, neither he nor Kate had been at work for days. Jo felt an icy drip of dread down her spine when she heard that. What if they'd had a heart to heart and Richard had realised Kate was the one for him after all? What if they'd gone off for a romantic reconciliation somewhere? The thought made her feel sick.

After another two days of waiting for news and snapping at Roxanne for tying up the phone every evening, Jo screwed up her courage to call him herself. His mobile was switched off and the answer machine was on at the flat. She didn't have the nerve to leave a message. What was the point, when she'd obviously become a dim and embarrassing memory to him?

After the photo shoot, she and Marcus had an interview with a journalist from a TV listings magazine. Jo sipped coffee and struggled to keep a smile on her face as she answered the usual inane questions about her character, and ignored all the intrusive ones about her private life.

The interview over-ran by several minutes. Afterwards, Jo grabbed her bag and dashed off to the studio building. It was a bright, crisp day, and the grassy verges were spattered with yellow and white crocuses. All around her the trees were bursting forth with early blossom. As she crossed the courtyard, she couldn't help looking back up at the top floor of the production building.

It didn't help that the girls never stopped talking about him. They kept asking when they were going to see him again. It was just her luck, Jo thought, that the first time they actually liked a man, it had to be Richard.

And it was just her luck that the moment she realised she loved him was the same moment he realised he didn't give a damn about her.

Her first scene that day was in the corner shop. According to the storyline, Stacey was due for yet another ding-dong with her mother-in-law. Ma Stagg had found out about her affair with Vic, and wanted to put a stop to it.

As she picked her way across the studio she heard uncontrollable screams coming from the brightly-lit set. Her heart sank. She'd forgotten Ma Stagg's grandchildren, Keifer and Keanu, were supposed to be in this scene. The small boys were cowering behind a tinned fruit display while their real-life mothers tried to console them.

'Here we go again.' Rob, who played their screen father Tony, raised his eyes heavenwards as Jo approached. 'I've begged the scriptwriters not to put them in a scene with Eva, but they never listen. And then they wonder why this happens!'

'What is it this time?'

'It was that line where she says she's going to take them to the park. They heard her say that and they just went hysterical.'

'I'm not surprised.' Jo glanced at Eva, who was hunched behind the shop counter, eyeing the children malevolently while her assistant Desmond fussed over her. She wouldn't want to go to the park with her either.

She took her script and went over to sit on the edge of the set behind the cameras. She put her hands over her ears to cover the noise as she tried to go over her lines. Usually she could tolerate the kids' tantrums, but her patience was at breaking point this morning.

And here was someone who could push her beyond the limit. Jo braced herself as Brett swaggered over.

'You're late, junkie,' he greeted her. 'Been round the back tooting charlie, have you?'

She forced a smile. 'Of course, Brett. How else could I get through a day with you?'

His brow furrowed. Jo could see his lips moving as he puzzled over her remark. Then, with the lightning speed of a tractor on the M1, he came back with, 'So what was it today, then? Dope? Crack? E?'

Jo ignored him and tried to concentrate on her script, but the sound of screaming filled her head, making it impossible for her to think straight. Everywhere she looked there was chaos. Children howling, Eva teetering dangerously close to a tantrum, the production crew muttering tensely among themselves.

And all the time there was Brett's face, looming into hers, so close she could smell the garlic on his breath.

'Do you know what I've heard?' he was saying. 'Coke gives you an even bigger buzz if you stick it up your backside.'

Jo raised her eyes slowly to meet his. 'Do you know,' she said. 'You took those last five words right out of my mouth?'

She thrust her script into his hands and stalked off, ignoring the chorus of astonished noises that followed her. Just before the studio door slammed behind her she heard Desmond cry plaintively, 'Where's she going? No one's allowed to walk off set except Miss Lawrence.'

Anger propelled her out of the building and across the courtyard to the canteen. Mercifully, it was empty.

'We're closed,' Joyce yelled immediately, but Jo took no notice. She sat down at a corner table and put her head in her hands.

She'd spent four years at *Westfield* and she'd never realised how much she hated it until now. Four years of playing the same dreary bimbo, doing interviews and photo shoots, living her life in a goldfish bowl. She was sick of never having any privacy, of having her dustbins raided and her every secret paraded on the front pages for the titillation of strangers. She was sick of people rudely demanding photos and autographs in the street and then getting angry when she said no. The whole business with her arrest had made her realise how public her life had become. The only thing the job had going for it was a regular income, but even that barely made up for what she had to go through day after day.

And yet, she couldn't give it up. She needed that security, no matter what the price. She was tired, bored and trapped.

She felt a warm, wet rasping on her cheek, as if she was being buffed with a piece of soggy sandpaper. She looked up and found herself staring into Murphy's friendly brown eyes. Marcus stood over her, a cup in one hand and a doughnut in the other.

'I've brought the tea, and Murph's brought the sympathy,' he grinned.

'Thanks.'

'I mean it. You listened to me when I needed a shoulder to cry on, it's only fair I return the favour.' He sat down opposite her. 'So what's the problem?'

'I don't know.' Jo picked up a spoon and absently added three sugars to her cup. 'Just the job getting to me, I suppose.' She wished she could tell him what was really on her mind, but she didn't dare share that with anyone. 'Maybe I'm just coming down with something? I haven't felt too good the past few days.'

'If I were you, I'd go straight home before the Grim Reaper catches you. He's seriously pissed off.'

Jo dropped her spoon with a clatter. 'You've seen Richard?'

'Unfortunately.' Marcus grimaced. 'All I did was say hello

to him in the corridor and he practically took my head off. I'm telling you, that man doesn't forgive or forget – where are you going?'

'To see Richard.' She pushed back her chair with a clatter.

'I wouldn't do that if I were you. He's not exactly feeling sociable.'

'I don't care.'

'In that case, can Murphy have your doughnut?' she heard him say, as she slammed out of the canteen.

At least she didn't have to face Kate standing guard outside his office. A temp sat in her place, filing her nails and reading Jonathan Cainer. She looked up, mildly surprised, as Jo stormed past her.

'You can't go in there. He's in a meet –' By the time she was on her feet Jo had already flung open the door.

Five heads turned to look at her. Jo barely took in the faces of the script editor and the storyline writers. All her attention was focused on the man behind the desk.

'Jo.' He stood up. His appearance shocked all the anger out of her. His face was gaunt and there were dark hollows under his eyes. He looked as if he hadn't eaten or slept for a week.

'I told her she couldn't come in,' the temp babbled over Jo's shoulder. 'I said you were in a meeting.'

'It's okay, Tammy.' Not taking his eyes off her, he said to the others, 'Perhaps we could continue this meeting later? Say, an hour or two?'

They all filed out of the office, leaving them alone. All the fury and frustration that had been building up on the way to his office seemed to melt away. 'What's happened to you?' she whispered.

'I'm sorry.' Richard sank back into his chair. 'I know I should have called you. I picked up the phone a few times, but I didn't know what to say.' He buried his face in his hands. 'It's all such a fucking mess.'

'What is?' Her whole body tensed. 'Richard, what's happened? Are you ill? For God's sake, tell me. It can't be any worse than what I've been imagining.'

'Can't it?' He looked over his fingers at her. His eyes were dark and haunted. 'Kate's pregnant.'

All the blood drained from her head, leaving her faint and weak. She sank down into a chair. 'No! It can't be true.'

'I wish it wasn't, but it is. I've seen the test results.'

'But how – when?'

'Sometime around Christmas, apparently. She's known for a couple of weeks but she couldn't bring herself to tell me. She wasn't sure how I'd react, as we haven't been getting on recently.' He sighed heavily. 'I hardly understand it myself. We've always been so careful. But apparently these things aren't one hundred per cent foolproof.'

'She certainly picked her time to give you the good news.' Jo stared towards the window until the bright sunlight hurt her eyes. No wonder Richard couldn't think straight when he left the cottage that morning.

'I'm sorry. I know you must have been wondering what the hell was going on. But the truth is, I didn't even know myself. Kate and I have spent the last few days and nights just talking, going over everything again and again, trying to make some sense of it. I've never seen her in such a state. She's completely gone to pieces over this.'

What about me? Jo wanted to scream. I've been going to pieces too, wondering what's going on. 'How is she now?'

'Still pretty shell-shocked, but coming to terms with it.' He paused. 'She's keeping the baby.'

Jo's head went back in shock. 'But I would have thought –'

'She'd want an abortion? I assumed that too. But she's had some kind of medical problems since she was a teenager and apparently the doctors have warned her that a termination would be a risky surgical procedure for her. She's got no

248

choice but to go ahead with the pregnancy.' And neither have I, his trapped expression said.

She swallowed hard. 'And how do you feel – about her keeping the baby?'

'It's her decision, obviously. I have to go along with whatever she wants. And I wouldn't be happy about getting rid of a baby just because it's not convenient. Especially if it means putting her health in danger.' He leaned back in his chair. 'It does make things bloody complicated, though.'

Complicated? From where she was standing, it made them totally impossible. 'Does she – know about me?' She couldn't bring herself to say 'us'. The whole idea of them being together seemed like a dim and distant memory now.

'Of course, I told her.' His voice was steely. 'I said I was going to, didn't I?'

'Yes, but that was before –'

'Kate's pregnancy doesn't change anything as far as I'm concerned. It's you I want to be with, not her.'

'How can you say that? This baby changes everything.'

'Why?'

'Because that's what babies do, whether you want them to or not!' Jo stared at him, exasperated. 'Look, this isn't some kind of gimmicky kitchen accessory you can stuff in a drawer when you get bored. It's a living, breathing human being. It's going to need both of you for support.'

'Of course I'm going to support it. I wouldn't dream of doing anything else.' Richard lifted his chin. 'I've already told Kate I'll pay for whatever she needs –'

'I'm not talking about money!' Anger flared in her eyes. 'Babies don't just need nappies and toys and private school fees. They need love and care and security. They need a loving home. And they need both their parents.'

'Your daughters don't have both their parents.'

'Yes, and it's bloody hard work, which is why I wouldn't want anyone else to go through it.' She leaned forward, desperate to get her point across. 'I didn't become a single parent by choice, you know. It just happened and I have to deal with it. But it isn't easy. It can be exhausting and confusing and pretty lonely a lot of the time. I manage because I have to. But that doesn't mean I wouldn't prefer it if I had someone to share it with.'

'You've got someone. You've got me now.'

'And soon you'll have a child of your own to worry about. Do you really think I could let you abandon it while you play happy families with me and the girls?'

He narrowed his eyes. 'So what are you saying?'

'I'm saying' – she took a deep breath – 'I'm saying you should try and make a go of it with Kate. She needs you,' she went on, as Richard opened his mouth to protest. 'Maybe not now, but when the baby arrives. Having a child is a massive step, more than you can imagine. You can't let her go through this by herself.'

'So you think I should stay with a woman I don't love just because she's pregnant? It's hardly the ideal way to bring up a child, is it? With two parents barely speaking to each other?'

'It doesn't have to be like that. You and Kate had a relationship once. You could do it again.'

'That was before I met you.'

His eyes met hers across the desk. Jo felt herself weaken and looked away. If she stopped now she might not be able to go on. 'Like I said, this baby will change both your lives for ever.'

'You think it will bring us closer together? Quite a tall order for a baby, isn't it? Especially when I want to be with someone else.'

'You might feel differently once the baby's born. It's the most wonderful feeling in the world, watching your child grow up, seeing it take its first steps, hearing its first word. You couldn't miss all those things.'

He looked down at the empty desk in front of him. Jo sensed he must have been having the same thoughts himself. 'But I want you, too,' he said hoarsely. He lifted his gaze to hers. 'I love you. Is it such a crime for me to want us to be together?'

She felt a lump rising in her throat. If she'd heard him say those words a week ago she would have been the happiest person alive. But now . . .

It would be the easiest thing in the world to tell him she felt the same. She knew if she did, he would leave Kate and never go back. All she had to do was say the word . . .

'We can't,' she whispered. 'I couldn't let you do it, and deep down you know you wouldn't want to. How long before you end up resenting me for keeping you away from your own flesh and blood?'

He stared at her in silence for a long time. 'So that's it, then?' he said finally. 'Even if I packed my bags and walked out on Kate tonight you still wouldn't have me?'

Of course I'd have you, she wanted to cry. Deep down her heart ached for him to do just that. But her head knew how wrong it would be for both of them.

She stood up. Her legs felt weak. 'I'd better go.'

He didn't try to stop her. He didn't even move until she reached the door, when he suddenly said, 'I'm sorry.'

'What for?'

'For letting you down so badly.'

'It's not me you should be worrying about now.'

She forced herself to keep walking down the softly carpeted corridor towards the lift. Her throat ached, and it was all she could do to stop herself crying and rushing back to him. But there was no point in going back. Their future had been resolved, and nothing could change it now.

Chapter 24

'At least the accommodation's nice,' Viola commented, as they pulled into the wide sweeping drive that led to the clifftop hotel.

Jo stopped the car and got out, the salty wind whipping at her hair. She was just relieved they'd all made it in one piece. It hadn't been an easy journey, with four of them and a travel-sick Irish wolfhound crammed into her Cinquecento, not to mention Lara's entire designer wardrobe. Viola had offered to read the map, and it was only after two hours of wrong motorway exits, twisting back lanes and ending up in deserted farmyards that she'd finally admitted she'd left her glasses at home. Jo's head ached from trying to concentrate against a background of Murphy retching, Marcus's tinny Discman and Lara screeching into her mobile phone.

'What do you mean, the record company isn't interested?' she snapped as they tumbled out of the car. 'You said they'd love my demo. You said they'd be desperate to sign me up. You *promised*, Leon. Yeah, well, I'm fed up with listening to you, too. Oh, go and get fucked!'

She shoved the phone in her pocket and stalked up the drive, her kitten heels crunching on the gravel, leaving the others to struggle with her luggage.

Viola sent Jo a meaningful look. 'I think the honeymoon's over.'

'And her pop career, by the sound of it – ow!' Jo banged

her head on the boot lid as Murphy rushed up and goosed her from behind. 'Don't just stand there.' She turned to Marcus, who was standing downwind trying to light a cigarette. 'Are you going to give me a hand with these cases?'

'Don't be too hard on him,' Viola said. 'I expect he has servants to do that at home, don't you, Trust Fund Boy?'

'Bog off, you old lezzie.'

'Charming! I suppose that's what they taught you at Eton?'

Jo listened to them trading insults, but for once she didn't have the energy to join in. She'd been very tired lately. And the idea of two days filming on location in sunny Robin Hood's Bay wasn't going to raise her spirits.

A month had passed since she'd had that heart to heart with Richard. Since then they'd tried to avoid each other. It was harder to keep away from Kate, whose pregnancy was now the talk of the *Westfield* studios. Soon she would be strutting around, proudly displaying her bump. Jo didn't know how she'd cope.

Or maybe she wouldn't have to? The week before, she'd called her agent and told her she was thinking of leaving *Westfield*. After a lot of squawking and swearing and bandying of words like 'career suicide', Julia had finally agreed to look around for other offers. 'But don't hold your breath,' she'd warned. 'You don't know what it's like out there these days.'

It can't be any worse than it is here, Jo thought miserably, as she trailed after the others towards the hotel. The way she was feeling, even a few cameo appearances at the dole office were beginning to seem attractive.

Just to make her feel even worse, the first person she saw when she walked into the hotel reception was Kate, signing in at the desk.

'Bloody hell, what's she doing here?' Marcus groaned.

'Come to keep an eye on you, I expect. Make sure you don't get up to anything in the bridal suite this time.' Viola squinted at them. 'I can't believe she's pregnant, can you?

She still looks as thin as a rake to me. Hello darling.' She switched to sweetness-and-light mode as Kate came towards them. 'I was just saying, pregnancy obviously suits you. You're positively blooming.'

'I don't feel blooming,' Kate snapped back. 'The sea air's making me feel sick.'

She stalked off to the lifts. 'Well, I never,' Viola declared.

Jo shrugged. 'It's probably her hormones.'

'Not her. Him.' Jo followed Viola's gaze towards the double doors. Richard had just walked in, carrying an overnight bag. 'Arriving separately, eh? And he doesn't look very happy. I wonder if they've had a bust-up?'

He glanced up at them and nodded briefly. Jo forced herself to smile back, dismayed at the lines of tiredness and strain etched around his eyes and mouth.

'Looks like they're in separate rooms, too. What's all that about, do you suppose?'

'It's none of our business.'

'Spoilsport!' Viola made a face. 'Since when has that stopped you enjoying a bit of gossip?'

'Ooh, look! It's Stacey, isn't it?' Jo was saved from answering by the shriek behind her. She turned round as a middle-aged woman in a headscarf thrust her face right up to hers. 'It *is* you! I knew it. I never miss an episode.'

Jo pasted a dutiful smile on her face as she listened to the woman reciting her all-time favourite moments. She was right, she hadn't missed a single episode in fifteen years. Unfortunately.

By the time she'd finished signing autographs and posing for photos, the others had drifted off to their rooms. Jo collected her keys and had her bags sent up to her room, and went outside to get some fresh air.

It was a cold, grey March day and the salty wind carried a spattering of rain as she followed the path over neat lawns to sit on a bench overlooking the sea. Jo hugged herself as she listened to the muted roar of the waves crashing against the rocks below her, mingling with the mewling seagulls overhead. The wind whipped at her, tangling her hair across her face.

Christ, this wasn't supposed to happen! How was she meant to cope with Richard here? She hadn't banked on that, on top of everything else.

The trill of her mobile phone broke into her thoughts. Jo plunged her hand into her bag to retrieve it. She hoped it wasn't one of the girls in trouble, or worse still, her mother ringing up to ask if there were any nice single men at the hotel.

'Are you sitting down?' Julia Gold never bothered to introduce herself. Her agent just assumed everyone was hanging on the end of the phone, waiting for her call.

'Actually I'm sitting on the edge of a cliff wondering if I should jump.'

'Oh my God, don't do that. I've just found you the most fantastic job and I'd hate to lose my commission.'

Jo straightened her shoulders, instantly alert. 'You've found me a job?'

'Well, as good as. You'd have to audition of course, but unless you make a monumental fuck-up the part's yours. The producer's desperate for you.'

As she described the role, Jo felt herself go light-headed. It was the kind of thing she'd always dreamed of. *Heartland*, a '60s period drama series set in a rural Yorkshire village, were bringing in some important new characters and they wanted her to play the new headteacher at the village primary. It meant more money, more prestige, and a chance to escape from the daily grind of soap life. It also meant she would never have to go near Stacey's sprayed-on jeans and fluffy jumpers ever again.

'You see, I've always said it was time you spread your wings,' Julia said. Jo widened her eyes, but didn't say anything. She knew Julia Gold's memory could be extremely selective.

She switched off the phone, still in a daze. This was brilliant news, better than she could ever have hoped. But even though she felt like jumping up and down and hugging everyone she met, there was still a tiny, hard lump of dread in the pit of her stomach.

She would have to leave *Westfield*. That meant never seeing Richard again.

But then, why was that such a bad thing? Surely seeing him every day and knowing they couldn't be together could only hurt her more? And it could only get worse, especially once Kate had the baby. Then Richard would realise how much his child meant to him and he'd forget all about her and anything they might have had together.

Still troubled, she went up to her room. As she put her key in, the door next to hers suddenly flew open and Murphy trotted out, followed by Marcus. He grinned when he saw her.

'I've been knocking on your door for hours. Where have you been?'

'Just walking and thinking.' She didn't tell him about the job offer. She was still getting used to the idea herself.

'At the same time? Ooh, clever girl. I can't quite get the hang of that myself.' He swept his flopping hair out of his eyes. 'I'm just taking Murphy out for a stroll along the cliffs while I try to work out a way of avoiding dinner tonight.'

'Why would you want to do that?'

'Haven't you heard? We've all been summoned to the restaurant by the Grim Reaper at eight. I think he wants a nice group huggy-bonding session or something. My bet is we'll all be aiming steak knives at each other's hearts by half past.'

'Oh God,' Jo groaned.

She retreated to her room to unpack and absorb this latest piece of bad news. Great. This evening was just what she needed. As if she didn't have enough to think about.

As she finished unpacking she came across the unopened

256

box of Tampax in the bottom of her suitcase and felt a fleeting moment of panic. She was late. She'd never been late in her life, except when —

Bile rose up, burning her throat. No, that would just be too monumentally unlucky. Even fate, never her best friend, couldn't be that cruel. Besides, there could be lots of other reasons. Stress, for one. She'd certainly had more than her fair share of that recently.

And tonight would be even more stressful. Jo considered her options as she showered and washed her hair. She could just refuse to go. They could hardly drag her kicking and screaming down to the restaurant, could they? Or she could develop a tactical migraine. Or food poisoning. The thought of spending the evening with Richard and Kate already made her feel queasy.

Or she could just go and get the damn thing over with. After all, she was leaving *Westfield*. In a few weeks they wouldn't be able to hurt her any more.

But in the meantime, she had the next few hours to get through. And it was no help when she walked into the bar at ten to eight and found to her horror that Richard was already there. On his own.

Panic assailed her. She started to creep away, but he turned and saw her.

Stay calm, she told herself as she walked towards him. But it wasn't easy when her ribs were closing like a fist around her heart and lungs.

'Drink?' he offered.

'Gin and tonic, please.' She sent him a sidelong look as he ordered their drinks. He was wearing a sharply-tailored black suit that made him look so sexy it almost hurt. His face was still gaunt and shadowed, but if anything it just made him look even more darkly attractive. She found herself staring at his fingers and imagining them stroking her body.

Her drink arrived and she downed it in a single gulp. Richard looked surprised. 'Another?'

'Please.' He was drinking whisky, she noticed. Was he drinking to dull the pain, like her?

'So – er – how are the girls?' he asked.

'They're fine.' Jo stared at the optics as if her life depended on memorising their contents.

'Is Grace still obsessed with cars?'

'She's more obsessed with getting me to part with a great deal of cash for some state-of-the-art trainers.'

'Expensive, are they?'

'Obscenely. The money they cost would probably cancel the Third World Debt.' She took a steadying gulp of her drink. 'So – um – how's Kate?'

'Okay, I suppose. When she's not throwing up or throwing a tantrum.' He slammed his glass down, making her jump. 'Look, I can't do this. I can't just behave like we're polite strangers. I miss you like hell. I spend every waking moment thinking about you. It's driving me out of my mind.' She flinched at the raw despair in his eyes. 'Why do you think I came down here? I'm not needed on this shoot. It was just a pathetic excuse to see you again.'

'But you brought Kate?'

'I didn't bring Kate. She came by herself, although God knows why. We might still be living under the same roof but we're not having any kind of relationship, if that's what you're thinking. Anything she and I had died the day I met you.' He slid his hand across the bar and covered hers, his long fingers curling around her wrist. 'God, I want you so much,' he groaned.

'I want you too.' There was no point in denying it. Just the way he caressed the soft skin of her wrist was sending electric pulses of sensation up her arm and straight into every erogenous zone in her body, including some she didn't know she had.

'So what are we doing? Why can't we just be together?'

'You know why.'

'So we've just got to go through the hell of seeing each other every day, is that it?'

'Maybe not.' She took a deep breath. 'Richard, I've been offered another job.'

'What kind of job?' His fingers tightened around her wrist.

'A very good one, actually.' She told him about *Heartland*. 'It would be a great career move, and it would mean I could still be based at home –'

'And you wouldn't have to see me again?' Richard's eyes narrowed. 'That's why you're doing this, isn't it?'

'What if I am? What good is it doing either of us at the moment? And it'll only get worse when Kate has the baby –'

'Someone talking about me?' They sprang apart. Kate stood behind them, looking chic and superior in a narrow-fitting cream cashmere sheath that showed off her jutting hipbones and still enviably flat stomach. Jo, poured into her little black dress, looked more pregnant than her.

Kate sidled between them and waved to the barman. 'I'll have a vodka and tonic, no ice.'

'Is that wise?' Richard bit out.

'Probably not, but who cares? On second thoughts, make that a large one.' She smiled bitterly at Richard. 'Don't tell me you're worried about the baby, darling? Bit ironic, isn't it, considering you'd rather it wasn't born at all.'

'That's not true!' Jo gasped.

'Isn't it?' Kate's eyes glittered with malice. 'Let's face it, this pregnancy has been a bit of an inconvenience all round, hasn't it? But at least you two don't have the misery of carrying the fucking thing for nine months.' Her drink arrived and she took a massive slug. 'I don't see why I should let this little bastard stop me from having a good time.'

'Why are you having it, if you feel like that?' Richard muttered into his glass.

'Because I have to, don't I? My insides are fucked-up enough as it is. I'm not going to risk killing myself just so you can rush off into the sunset with your girlfriend.'

Just at that moment Viola and Lara arrived with the rest of the crew. Jo was so relieved she nearly hugged them.

'Sorry we're late,' Viola greeted them cheerfully. 'Lara had a few calls to make. No sign of Marcus?' She looked around the bar.

'Last time I saw him he was taking Murphy for a walk along the clifftop.'

'Let's hope he falls off,' Kate muttered.

Richard glanced at his watch. 'We can't wait for him. He can join us later.'

By the time Marcus finally appeared, it was half past eight and they were already halfway through their starters. Jo eyed him with dismay as he weaved his way across the restaurant. He'd obviously been doing some serious damage to the mini bar.

'You're late,' Kate snapped. 'We've started without you.'

'Now how often has a woman said those words to me?' He flung himself into the empty seat next to Jo and reached for the wine bottle. Jo caught Richard's steely look and longed for the evening to end.

Unfortunately there was a long way to go before then. She pushed her fork around her plate, her stomach too taut with nerves and unhappiness to eat more than a couple of mouthfuls. Her wine glass sat untouched in front of her while Marcus kept helping himself from the bottle, growing louder and more lively every minute. Jo squirmed as he idly fondled the back of her neck, and toyed with the idea of sticking a fork in his leg to make him stop. Meanwhile, everyone's smiles were growing more and more fixed.

Thankfully the meal finally ended and they all drifted into the lounge for coffee. Jo's heart sank when she saw Marcus weaving in behind her clutching a bottle of brandy.

'Thought we might need a chaser.' He collapsed in an armchair and beamed around the table. 'Well, this is nice, isn't it? Reminds me of my old prep school, with the headmaster keeping an eye on us all.' He topped up his glass and lifted it mockingly at Richard. 'Why are you here, by the way? Come to make sure we all behave ourselves?'

Richard said nothing, but a muscle pounded in his rigid cheek.

'You're drunk,' Kate accused.

'And you, my darling, are a bitch. But at least I'll be sober in the morning.'

Everyone stared at their coffee cups. Jo felt her insides turn to water. 'Leave it, Marcus, please,' she begged. But Marcus was in self-destruct mode, and nothing was going to stop him.

'So why are you here? You still haven't told us.' He squinted drunkenly at Richard. 'Is this some kind of power kick for you, having us all bowing and scraping? Do you get off on it, or something?'

'Not as much as you get off on behaving like an arsehole, obviously,' Richard snapped. Even Marcus looked wary. Oh God, they're going to fight, Jo thought.

'What's all this? Looks like I arrived just in time.'

Never in a million years would Jo ever imagine she would be pleased to see Charlie Beasley. But as he stood there, smiling like an insurance salesman, she could have kissed him. With him was a squat, bearded man, a Hasselblad slung around his neck.

'Carry on, don't let me stop you,' he beamed. 'But let me know if you're going to punch him, won't you? Tony would hate to miss the shot.'

Richard didn't take his eyes off Marcus. 'What do you want?'

'Just a couple of words with Marcus here.'

'A couple of words? Certainly.' Marcus drained his glass. 'How about "fuck off"?'

'I wondered if you had any comment to make on this.' Ignoring the remark, Charlie pulled a photo out of his pocket and handed it to Marcus. 'Recognise her?'

Marcus stared at it for a moment. Then, slowly, he tore it in two.

Charlie's smile didn't waver. 'I'll take that as a yes then, shall I?'

Marcus reached out for the brandy bottle and refilled his glass. He wasn't laughing any more, Jo noticed. In fact the whole place had fallen ominously silent.

'Would someone please tell me what's going on?' Richard asked the question for all of them.

Charlie turned to Marcus. 'Well? Are you going to tell them, or shall I?'

Chapter 25

'I wish someone would tell us something.' Richard's voice was icy.

But Charlie Beasley was enjoying the moment too much to rush it. 'I'm amazed you managed to keep it quiet for so long,' he said to Marcus. 'You covered your tracks well, I'll give you that.'

'Not well enough, obviously.' Marcus's smile didn't reach his eyes.

'Oh God, what's he done now?' Lara giggled. 'Robbed a bank? Been caught dealing heroin?'

'He's married.'

Cups clattered into saucers all round the table.

'Bloody hell!' Viola gasped.

'You're kidding?' Lara laughed.

'B-but I don't understand,' Jo stammered. 'When –?'

'Seven years ago. It was seven years, wasn't it Marcus?' Charlie said.

'You tell me. I was stoned at the time.'

'She was the reason you were kicked out of your posh boarding school.' Charlie recited the facts gleefully. 'Little Samantha Frost. The caretaker's daughter. She was sweet sixteen.' He looked proudly around the table, like a conjuror who'd just produced a rabbit from a hat.

'Is this true?' Jo gasped.

'Probably.' Marcus stifled a yawn with the back of his

hand. 'Like I said, I was stoned at the time. I vaguely remember rushing off to the register office or something.'

'But why?'

He shrugged. 'I suppose it would have taken too long to book a church.'

'No, I mean why did you get married?'

'God knows. I think it had something to do with her not sleeping with me unless she had a ring on her finger.' He refilled his glass. 'Although as I recall it was all a bit of a wasted effort. She was fairly abysmal in the sack.'

'Or maybe you were just too stoned?' Richard muttered nastily.

'So why haven't you divorced her?' Kate wanted to know.

'Never got round to it. To be quite honest, I'd forgotten all about the silly little cow. We're not exactly on Christmas card-exchanging terms.'

'She could have divorced you, couldn't she? If you've been separated all these years –'

'That's just it, you see,' Charlie interrupted. 'They're not quite as separated as Marcus here likes to make out. Isn't that right, mate?'

'If you say so – *mate*.' Marcus's eyes narrowed dangerously.

'You see, Marcus likes to pay a visit to the marital home every so often. Just to claim his conjugals, so to speak.' Charlie beamed around at his audience. He had a hot story and he was enjoying every sordid moment. 'She lives somewhere on your dad's estate, doesn't she? Very handy, that. And of course Daddy picks up all the bills as usual. He's very good at sorting out your little problems, isn't he?'

'That's enough.' Richard suddenly stepped in. 'You've got your story. I think you'd better go now.'

'But I just wanted –'

'Are you going to leave, or do I have to throw you out myself?'

'With a photographer here? You wouldn't dare,' Charlie grinned.

'Wouldn't I?' Richard rose from his seat. He looked so angry even Charlie wasn't going to take any chances.

'Okay, okay, I'm going. Like you said, I got what I came for.' He turned to Marcus. 'Thanks for your help. This will make a great human-interest story for the late editions.'

There was a long, uncomfortable silence after he'd gone.

'Well, I don't know about you, but I could do with a drink.' Marcus reached for the bottle, but Richard stopped him.

'I think we've all had enough,' he said.

'But the party's just getting started —'

'Then I suggest you continue it in the privacy of your own room.' His voice was like a steel blade. 'I think we've all had just about enough of you for one day.'

They faced each other across the table. For a frightening moment Jo thought Marcus was going to argue, then he backed down.

'Fine.' He stood up. 'I don't much like the company here, anyway.' Grabbing the bottle, he stumbled towards the door.

The party broke up soon afterwards. Richard went up to his room and Kate announced she needed to go outside for some fresh air. Jo, Lara and Viola stayed in the bar to gossip about the evening's events.

'Can you imagine?' Viola said. 'I had no idea, did you?'

'I think he's an absolute bastard,' Lara declared, then ruined it by adding, 'Fancy having a juicy secret like that and not telling anyone. He could have shared.'

'I'm amazed no one found out sooner. I expect they've been trying to dig up some dirt on him ever since he started on *Westfield*.'

'They didn't have to dig very deep, did they?' Viola shook her head, her red curls tumbling. 'My God, Charlie Beasley must have thought all his birthdays had come at once.'

'He's a bloody reptile,' Jo said.

'Oh come on, darling, that's hardly fair.' Viola looked pained. 'Some reptiles can be quite sweet.'

'Actually, when he first turned up I thought he'd come for me.'

They both turned to look at Lara. 'You? Why?'

'I'm getting a divorce.'

'Oh my God, how awful for you. What does Leon say about it?'

'He doesn't know yet. I've just been on the phone to my solicitor to sort it out.' She stuck out her chin. 'He says we've got irreconcilable differences.'

'How can you tell? You've only been married five minutes.'

'Shut up, Vi.' Jo turned to Lara. 'What kind of irreconcilable differences?'

'I dunno, do I?' she shrugged. 'That's just what my solicitor reckons. I think it's 'cos I want a record contract and he hasn't got me one.'

'Oh well, in that case I'm not surprised you want to get rid of the bastard.' Viola drained her glass. 'That's positively mental cruelty.'

Two gin and tonics later, Jo left them still mulling over Marcus's revelations and Lara's divorce plans, and went up to her room. It was only ten thirty but she was so weary she felt just about ready to drop.

Then, as she passed Marcus's room, she heard voices coming from inside that galvanised her and made her forget all thoughts of bed.

'I think we should talk, don't you?' There was no mistaking that voice. Jo stopped to listen.

'I hate it when a woman says that,' she heard Marcus drawl.

'You really are a bastard, aren't you? Why didn't you tell me you were married?'

'You never asked.'

'You could have mentioned it. Or did it slip your mind?'

'I didn't think it was that important.'

'Not important? Marcus, I'm carrying your child. Don't you think that gives me a right to know?'

Jo froze. Her blood turned to ice in her veins.

Kate.

'My child? I thought it was Richard's?'

'Don't play games with me, Marcus. You know as well as I do that you're the father. I've checked my dates. It had to be Christmas.'

The Christmas she was supposed to be spending with her family. Jo felt sick.

She crouched down, her nose to the keyhole. She could see Marcus's long legs as he sprawled on the bed, Murphy stretched out beside him. Kate was pacing the room agitatedly. Jo caught a tell-tale flash of cream cashmere every time she passed.

'So maybe it is mine. So what? We've been through all this.' Marcus sounded bored. 'I told you to have an abortion. I've even offered to pay for it, for Christ's sake. What more do you want?'

'I want you to be with me. I want us to bring this baby up together. I love you.' Kate's voice was so pleading Jo might have felt sorry for her if she hadn't had the overwhelming urge to kill them both.

'And what about Richard?'

'I don't give a damn about Richard and you know it.'

'So why did you tell him he was the baby's father?' There was a long silence. 'Don't tell me, you were trying to make me jealous? Hoping I'd come forward and lay claim to my rightful heir?'

'It's not fucking funny!' A sob caught in her throat. 'I thought you might at least do the decent thing. But that's not like you, is it? You don't mind someone else sorting out your mistakes for you.'

Marcus sighed. 'Look, I don't know what you're worried

about. You'll get your big white wedding, won't you? I'm sure Richard will oblige eventually.'

'I don't want to marry Richard. I want to marry you.'

'Sorry, no can do. As Mr Beasley pointed out earlier, I'm already married.'

'You can unmarry, can't you? Other people do it.'

'What if I don't want to?'

'Then I'll go public. I'll tell the whole world you're the baby's father. I'll get DNA tests —'

'You can get certificates from the Kennel Club and I still wouldn't want to know.' Marcus's voice went from bored to icy in seconds. 'And neither would your precious Richard. You'd lose your meal ticket. You wouldn't want that, would you?'

'Maybe I'll get your father to support me?' Kate wasn't beaten yet. 'He looks after his other bastards, surely one more wouldn't make any difference?'

'You can try, but I don't fancy your chances. He's having to sell off the family silver as it is. But if you want to take that chance, I could let you have his number?'

Jo pushed closer to the door. Next moment there was a *basso profundo* bark from inside and Murphy suddenly leapt from the bed and hurled himself at the door. Jo toppled backwards with a yelp of alarm as he began scratching at the woodwork from the other side, trying to tunnel his way through the carpet.

'What's wrong with that sodding dog?' she heard Kate say impatiently.

'He's probably sick of listening to you, like I am.'

Kate ignored the jibe. 'I think there's someone out there,' she whispered.

'Now you're being paranoid.'

'I know what I heard. Just look, will you?'

Jo didn't wait to hear any more. She scrambled to her feet and searched for her key. Sod it, it wasn't there. She heard the door handle rattle as she frantically pulled out handfuls of used tissues, make-up and old biros.

The door opened and Murphy flung himself at her, trapping her against the wall. Marcus stood in the doorway.

'Hi! I'm – er – just looking for my key,' she said feebly.

'Well, if you don't find it you can always sleep in my room.' He winked at her, whistled Murphy back inside and closed the door. Jo made a face at it. What a creep, flirting with one woman while he was breaking another's heart. Even if that woman was Kate, who frankly deserved everything she got.

She slept very little that night, tortured by dreams of Marcus, Kate and Richard. But oddly, once her alarm call came at 6 a.m. she suddenly felt as if she could sleep all day. She dragged herself, heavy-limbed, out of bed. She had a brewing headache and her eyelids itched as if they were lined with sandpaper. The last thing she felt like doing was facing the others. It took a sheer effort of will to drag herself into the shower and then into her clothes.

'Blimey, what have you been doing with yourself? I don't know if I'll have enough panstick to cover those shadows,' Madge the make-up artist greeted her cheerfully as she staggered into the caravan half an hour later. 'Hangover, is it?'

'Something like that.' Jo took her seat at the mirror, wincing at the bright lights.

As Madge arranged a blue plastic cape around her shoulders and got to work backcombing and spraying her hair, Jo closed her eyes and tried to make sense of what she'd heard the previous night.

Kate and Marcus. It just didn't add up. They barely even liked each other, let alone anything else. Jo couldn't remember a time when they'd been in the same room without getting into a bitching session. Unless that was just a cover-up for what was really going on? If it was, it was a pretty elaborate one.

Or maybe Kate was just one of those women who were attracted to unreachable men? After all, she'd stayed with Richard long enough. Maybe she saw Marcus as a new challenge? The ultimate unattainable bastard, a man so monumentally unfaithful he'd make a stud stallion look monogamous.

A bit too unattainable, as it turned out. Kate had gambled everything in one last desperate bid to win him – and she'd failed. Now she was pregnant and in a total panic. Which was obviously where Richard came in.

'Could you not screw your face up like that, lovey? You're cracking your foundation.'

'Sorry.' Jo tried to relax, but inside she was still burning with anger. How could Kate be so utterly selfish? She'd lost the man she wanted, so she'd looked around for the next best thing. Never mind that she was condemning Richard to a life of unhappiness bringing up another man's child. And as for Jo's feelings, they simply didn't come into it. Kate needed a father for her baby, and she'd got herself one. She'd behaved like a complete bitch, and she wasn't going to get away with it.

'Morning, everyone.' Marcus sauntered in, grinning all over his face as usual. It made Jo sick to look at him. 'Hi, angel.' He leaned over to kiss her, but she flinched away. 'Ooh, what's up with you? Wrong time of the month, is it?'

'Fuck off, Marcus.' How dare he joke around as if he didn't have a worry in the world?

'Was it something I said?' He flopped into the chair next to hers and put his feet up on the work surface. 'Thanks, darling.' He smiled appreciatively as one of the other make-up artists handed him a cup of coffee. 'God, I need this.'

'Tired, are you?' Jo looked sideways at him as Madge applied sweeps of pink blusher to her cheeks.

'Not especially. Why?'

'I just thought you might not have slept too well last night. Maybe your conscience was playing you up?'

His smile slipped a fraction. 'Any reason why it should?'

'You tell me.'

His hand, she noticed, shook slightly as he put his cup down. 'I slept like a log, since you ask. I always do.'

'Well, I suppose you can, can't you? I mean, you've got no worries. Not like other people.' She wanted to say more but Madge silenced her by applying a slick of Stacey's trademark fuchsia lipstick.

'You are in a bad mood, aren't you?' Marcus did his best to sound light-hearted. 'What is this, Pick On Marcus Day or something?'

'Possibly. You see, unlike you I didn't sleep too well last night. I had a lot on my mind.'

'Anything in particular?' His eyes were wary.

'Just something I overheard.'

'There you are, lovey. All done.' Madge removed the plastic cape with a flourish.

'Thanks.' As she slid out of the chair Jo's eyes met Marcus's in the mirror. His face, where the make-up artist hadn't sponged a thick layer of foundation, was satisfyingly pale.

So he knew she knew. Now it was time for his lying bitch of a girlfriend to find out too.

She found Kate on a lounger beside the heated indoor pool, wrapped in a white towelling dressing gown and flipping through *Hello!*.

'If you're looking for Richard, I think he's talking to the director.' She didn't bother to look up as Jo approached.

'It's you I wanted to see. Can I have a word?'

'Can't you see I'm busy?'

Jo grabbed the magazine out of her hands and threw it, pages flapping, into the pool. It landed with a splash. 'A word. Now.'

A look of fear crossed Kate's face, quickly masked by her

usual sangfroid. 'And I thought I was the one with the raging hormones?'

'You'll have more than raging hormones to worry about by the time I've finished with you!'

Kate stifled a yawn. 'So what is it you want, exactly?'

'The truth would be a start. Is this really Richard's baby you're carrying?'

Panic flared in her eyes. 'Of course it's Richard's. What a ridiculous question.'

'Then I must have got it wrong. You see, Marcus swore to me it was his.'

'He told you that? But I thought –' Then she saw Jo's face. 'Very fucking clever,' she hissed. 'Well, so what? What difference does it make if it is Marcus's baby?'

'What difference does it make?' Jo stared at her, appalled. 'How could you do it? How could you lie to Richard like that?'

'Because I don't like the alternative.' Kate's voice was sharp. 'Who's going to support me if Richard doesn't? Marcus won't, he's already made that very clear. And I've no intention of becoming some pathetic single parent, scratching around to make ends meet.'

'You could support yourself –'

'What, me and a kid on a glorified secretary's wages? Do you really think it would buy us all this?' Kate uncurled herself from the lounger and stood up. 'It's all right for you. You're an actress, a celebrity. You don't have to live in the real world. Well, I do. I know what it's like to have to get by on sod all. It's humiliating and demeaning.' Jo watched in amazement as Kate transformed before her eyes. Her face took on a narrow, mean look, and her cut-glass accent slipped into flat Yorkshire vowels that were more Hull than Home Counties. 'I'm not going back to that for anyone. And if it means telling a few lies, well so fucking what?'

'But you're ruining Richard's life –'

'Says who? He was happy with me before you came

along.' She stopped. 'That's what all this is about, isn't it? You want him for yourself? You're in love with him!'

'Of course I'm not.' It hurt to deny it but she couldn't bear to admit her weakness to Kate. 'Richard and I were over before we'd even begun. I just don't want to see him hurt, that's all.'

'Oh yeah? And what can you do about it? Tell him?' Kate's eyes flashed with malice. 'That would be nice for him, wouldn't it? The whole world would know he'd been taken for a fool. That I'd had an affair with another man right under his nose and then duped him into thinking it was his baby. He'd really thank you for letting that little cat out of the bag, wouldn't he?'

'No one else need know –'

'Oh yes, they would. Because I'd tell them.' Kate's chin lifted in triumph. 'If you breathe a word of this to Richard I swear I'll go straight to every tabloid in town. I can probably get a few grand for my story, don't you think? I can just see the headlines now – 'How I bedded *Westfield* star behind the boss's back.' I wouldn't need either of them then, would I? I'd be set up for life.'

'You wouldn't dare!'

'Try me.'

Jo stared at her in frustration. Kate had won, and she knew it. 'You really are an absolute bitch, aren't you?'

'You have to be if you want to get anywhere in this life. Now, if you don't mind, I need my rest. All this stress is very bad for baby.' She'd barely sat down before she was on her feet again. 'What was that? Did you hear someone moving about outside?'

Jo crossed over to the window and looked out. 'I can't see anyone.'

'What if there was someone out there?' Kate looked panic-stricken. 'They might have heard the whole thing.'

'Why should that bother you? Five minutes ago you were ready to sell your story to the highest bidder.'

'Exactly. And if it gets out I won't get a penny!'

Jo swung round, a red mist rising behind her eyes. Before she knew what she was doing, her pressure-cooker anger took over and she struck out at Kate. It wasn't a hard shove, but it caught her off balance. Jo watched in horrified fascination as Kate staggered backwards and then, arms flailing and eyes bulging, toppled in slow motion into the swimming pool.

'Bitch!' she screeched, when she finally surfaced, splashing and floundering. 'Of all the fucking stupid –' Jo could still hear her screams and curses halfway to the set.

Chapter 26

'So it now gives me great pleasure to declare – er –'

'Wisebuys of Wigginton,' a voice hissed in her ear.

'Wisebuys of Wigginton officially open.' Jo cut the yellow ribbon stretched across the doorway. A smattering of applause broke out, most enthusiastically from the manager at her side. He was a dapper little man in his fifties, with a boot-brush moustache and hair that was suspiciously black for his age.

Jo acknowledged the applause with a weak smile. After a tense two days filming in Robin Hood's Bay she was supposed to be taking some time off. She was so tired and out of sorts the last thing she'd wanted to do was drag herself out of bed on a Friday morning to open a supermarket. But she'd promised to do it weeks ago, and she didn't want to let anyone down.

Although she had a feeling she'd already done that. As the small, straggling crowd pressed forward with their autograph books and cameras, she heard a woman in a polyester raincoat say loudly to her friend, 'She doesn't look much like a celebrity, does she? I mean, you'd have thought with all the money they're paying her she could have done something to her hair.'

'I know what you mean,' her friend agreed. 'Now that Barbara Windsor, she always looks so well turned out –'

Jo wanted to turn around and tell them exactly why she

looked so awful, but she fixed a steely smile on her face and went on signing the autograph books being thrust at her. Just be nice, she told herself. In another ten minutes you can collect your cheque and go home to bed . . .

'If you'd like to come this way, we're ready for the trolley dash.'

'I'm sorry?' Jo frowned at the manager.

'The trolley dash. The competition winners?' He tutted impatiently. 'We ran a promotional competition in the *Evening Press*. The winners get to keep whatever they can bung in their trolleys in two minutes.'

'Oh, I see. And you want me to start them off, do you? Wave a flag or something?'

'No, I want you to take part. Your agent agreed it weeks ago,' he hurried on, sensing opposition.

I bet she did, Jo thought. Weeks ago she might have gone along with it too. But now . . .

'Look, I'm terribly sorry, but I don't think –'

'But I've got it in writing.' The manager bristled. 'And I've got customers in there looking forward to it. I don't want to let them down.'

Then why don't you do it? Jo looked longingly at her Cinquecento on the other side of the car park. The crowd was growing restive. If she made a break for it, they'd probably lynch her. 'Okay,' she sighed.

'Oh, and there's just one more thing. We want you to wear this.' With a flourish, he produced something red, flaccid and rubbery from behind his back. Jo stared at it in dismay. It looked just like a –

'A Willy,' the manager explained. 'That's what we call them – Willies. After Wisebuys Willy, our mascot? He's a cock.'

He probably is if he wears one of those. Jo went on staring.

'It's a novelty hat, see. You put it on your head, like this.'

He stretched it over his hands. It was like a swimming hat with a flabby cock's comb on top. 'The kids love 'em.'

'I'll bet.' Oh God, what did it matter anyway? As long as it got her out of this hellhole. And the sooner the better.

The trolley dash contestants, two women and a man in a Fair Isle cardigan, were already lined up, empty trolleys poised. They spared Jo the briefest glance as she took her place at the end of the row. Their eyes were already fixed on the shelves ahead, working out their strategy. One of the women had drawn a sketch map, Jo noticed. The other kept giving her mean, sideways glances. She already felt faint from the tight grip of the rubber Willy squeezed on her head. The aisles ahead swam in and out of focus, and the smell of food made her stomach churn.

'Ready, everyone. On your marks, get set – GO!'

It was like the chariot race from *Ben Hur*. She was barely halfway up the Canned Goods aisle before the man in the cardigan veered across her path, sending her crashing into a display of tinned peaches. As she rounded the next corner, the two women closed in on her from either side, smashing into her ankles. Jo stopped, screaming with pain – and then she spotted the newspaper stand.

'Watch it!' Cardie Man cannoned into the back of her as she stood, gripping her trolley handle to support herself, her eyes fixed on the front page of the *Globe*.

'*Exclusive! MY SECRET NIGHTS WITH MARCUS FINN – Woman at centre of Westfield love triangle speaks out.*' Then, in smaller letters, '*See tomorrow's Globe for full story.*'

'Where do you think you're going?' The manager stepped into her path as Jo headed for the door. 'You can't go yet.'

'Watch me.' Jo ripped off the rubber Willy hat and thrust it into his hands.

'You won't get your cheque.'

'I don't care.'

His voice followed her as she ran across the car park. 'I

knew we should have paid the extra grand and got Dale Winton!'

It was a miracle she made it to the *Westfield* studio in one piece. She was so agitated she could barely see the road in front of her, let alone any other cars on it. She screeched into the car park, abandoned the Cinquecento at a careless angle, and made her way straight up to the top floor of the production centre.

A small crowd of script editors, directors and location managers had gathered around what had been Kate's desk. Tammy the temp was vainly trying to fight them off.

'I told you, I don't know anything,' she kept saying. 'Yes, I know you've got a meeting scheduled but I can't do anything about it if he's not here, can I?'

Jo glanced past her. The door to Richard's office was open, and he plainly wasn't in it. So he hadn't turned up to work. She didn't blame him.

She took the lift back down to the ground floor. The temp didn't know where Richard was, but Louise might. It was the press officer's job to know everything, just so they could stop anyone else finding out.

'No, I don't know where he is, or when he's coming back.' Louise was hidden behind a toppling mound of newspapers and press cuttings, a phone clamped to each ear. 'No, there's no comment to make. As far as *Westfield* is concerned, this is a personal matter between the individuals concerned. I've nothing further to add. Thank you.' She slammed both the phones down and looked up at Jo with murderous eyes. 'I suppose you're looking for Marcus fucking Finn too?'

'Well no, I –'

'I don't know where he is. I hope the lying little bastard's burning in hell.' The phone rang again. 'Oh fuck off!' She buried her face in her hands. 'Fuck off, the lot of you!'

'Sounds like you need a break.' Jo came round to her side of the desk and slid her arm around Louise's plump, heaving shoulders. 'Come on, let's go to the canteen and see if we can bribe a coffee out of Joyce.'

They were lucky enough to get to the canteen during the ten-minute slot Joyce had decreed for serving beverages. The place was heaving with other grateful customers, but Jo found them a quiet table in the corner and parked Louise there. 'So what's the problem? This isn't just pressure of work, is it?'

As Jo primed her with cappuccinos, Louise poured out her troubles. How she was still in love with Marcus, how deep down she'd always hoped he might come back to her. She was so naïve Jo wondered how she'd managed to function on the same planet for so long.

'And all this time he and Kate were — together.' Louise blew her nose noisily on a scrappy tissue. 'I just can't believe it. I really thought it was you he liked. I was so jealous of you. That's why —' She broke off.

''That's why?' Jo prompted her gently.

She lifted large, swimming grey eyes to meet hers. 'That's why I — did what I did.'

The skin at the back of Jo's neck began to prickle. 'What exactly did you do?'

'I tipped off the police that night at the hotel.'

'You did what?' Jo crashed her cup down, missing the saucer. 'You mean it was you who told them we were taking drugs in that hotel room?'

'I didn't actually say it was you —'

'No, but I still got arrested! Do you know the trouble you caused? I nearly got jailed because of you!'

'I know, and I'm sorry. As soon as I'd done it I knew it was vindictive and stupid, but I just couldn't help myself. I'm so, so sorry,' she sobbed. 'I was so angry and upset — I just wasn't thinking.' She blotted her face with what was left of the tissue and squared her shoulders. 'You'll be glad to know I've decided to resign.'

Jo looked at her puffy red face. A few weeks ago she might

have been howling for her blood, but that nightmare seemed a long way behind her now. Poor Louise. She was as much a victim as the rest of them. 'You don't have to do that.'

'But after what happened —'

'Look, Marcus Finn made us all look pretty stupid, one way or another. He's certainly not worth losing your job over. Let's just keep it our secret, shall we?'

'Are you sure? Oh, Jo!' Louise started sobbing all over again. 'I promise I'll never make you do another photo shoot as long as I live! I'll make up quotes for your interviews so you never have to speak to another journalist, I'll —'

'You could help me find Richard.'

'Richard?' Louise sniffed back her tears. 'But why do you want — oh!' The truth dawned in her clear grey eyes. 'You don't mean you and he are —?'

'I don't know what we are.' Jo sipped her coffee. 'I just want to make sure he's okay, that's all.' She had another reason to see him, but she'd pushed that to the back of her mind.

Louise looked regretful. 'I wish I could help you but I don't know where he is. I went straight round to his flat this morning myself but there was no answer.'

'Maybe he just wasn't answering the door?'

'I thought that too, but then the concierge downstairs said he'd seen him putting some cases in his car two days ago. He hasn't seen Kate either. You don't think she and Marcus have run off together, do you?'

'I doubt it. Marcus was willing to leave her high and dry when he found out about the baby, so I doubt if he'd come rushing to her rescue on his white charger now — That's it!' She put down her cup and leapt to her feet.

'What is?'

'Something Marcus said once about Richard coming to rescue me on his white charger. God, I've been such an idiot. Why didn't I think of it before? He's bound to be there.'

'Where? I don't follow you –'

'That's okay. Just make sure the press don't either.'

It was an effort of will and memory to work out where the cottage was. Thank God she'd taken more notice of the road signs on the way home than she had on the way there. But it took several wrong turnings before she recognised the chocolate box-pretty village with its local store where she'd bought the newspapers that fateful day.

She followed the twisting lane, straining her eyes for the half-hidden turning that led to the cottage. Then she spotted a flash of metallic dark green through the trees to her right. Richard's Audi.

As Jo manoeuvred in beside it, the adrenaline rush that had kept her going all the way over the moors suddenly deserted her, and doubts began to set in. What if he didn't want to see her? What if he didn't want to see anyone? What if – the horrible thought slowly dawned on her – he was more heartbroken and humiliated than she'd imagined, and had come down here to end it all?

'Richard!' Her trainers crunched across the gravel as she ran to the front door and hammered on it with both fists. 'Richard, it's me. Are you in there?' There was no answer. 'Richard, open this door!'

She ran to the window and peered in, shading her eyes with her hand. His bags had been dumped on the sofa, but there was no sign of him. Surely if someone were contemplating suicide they wouldn't bother to bring a change of clothes with them?

'Looking for me?' Jo nearly collapsed with relief as Richard emerged from around the side of the house, wearing an old workshirt, paint-spattered jeans and carrying a brush.

'Richard! Thank God you're all right.' She ran to hug him, but he backed away.

'I'm covered in paint,' he said tersely. 'Any reason why I shouldn't be all right?'

'I was worried. I thought you might have done something stupid –'

'Bit late for that, isn't it? It seems to me I've already made an idiot of myself.' His eyes were hard and cynical. 'Well, as you can see, I'm all in one piece. So you can stop worrying about me, can't you?'

He turned and strode off. Bewildered, Jo followed him round to the back of the house. He was already halfway up a ladder, slapping paint on the wall in angry, untidy strokes. The smell of the emulsion made her feel sick.

'Richard, why are you so angry with me? What have I done?'

'It's what you didn't do.' He dropped his brush back into the tin and twisted round to face her. 'You knew, didn't you? About Kate and Marcus? Why didn't you tell me I was being taken for a fool?'

Jo paled. 'How did you find out?'

'I heard you and Kate talking by the swimming pool a few days ago. Very illuminating it was too. I learned a few things about both of you, I can tell you.' He snatched up his brush and started slapping on more paint, not caring that most of it was spattering the window.

'Richard,' Jo pleaded with his turned back. 'I wanted to tell you about Kate, but I couldn't. She threatened to go to the papers if I said anything. She said she'd make sure you were publicly humiliated –'

'And you really think I would have been that worried? Can you seriously imagine that I'd rather spend the rest of my life being duped than risk a day of people pointing and staring at me? Christ, I've lived through worse than that. I'm the Grim Reaper, remember? The man the tabloids love to hate?'

A lump rose in her throat. 'I – I'm sorry. I didn't think –'

'Or didn't care?'

'What's that supposed to mean?'

'Oh come on, I heard what you said to Kate. You told her

you didn't love me, that we'd never really started. Do you know how it felt, hearing you say that?' He splashed more paint carelessly on the wall. 'No wonder you were so keen for me to stay with her. It saved you the hassle of dumping me.'

'That's not true!' She strode across the garden towards the ladder, ignoring her stomach's heave of protest. 'Why do you think I came here today if I didn't care about you?' Her eyes were level with his scuffed Timberland boots. 'I meant all the things I said about you staying with Kate for the baby's sake. I meant them even though it broke my heart to say them.' The hand holding the brush slowed down a fraction. 'I admit I should have told you about Kate. But you've got to believe me, I only did it to protect you. I thought you'd want your personal life kept quiet. Remember just after Christmas, when you were worried about the press getting hold of the story about your family?'

'That was different,' he said gruffly. 'I had to protect my brother. I don't give a damn about myself.'

'Yes, well, I didn't know that, did I? I made a mistake. I wish I had told you, then maybe we'd be facing all this together.' The smell of paint hit her stomach, which responded with a Mexican wave of nausea. A familiar clammy sweat broke out on her upper lip. 'Richard, do you think you could come down? I can't go on talking to your boot like this, and if I stay here much longer I really think I'm going to be —'

Too late. Jo clamped her hand over her mouth and dashed off.

Thank God it was a false alarm this time. By the time Richard caught up with her she was on her hands and knees in the rose bushes.

'Sorry.' She sat back on her heels and disentangled her hair from the thorny branches. 'I seem to be making a bit of a habit of this lately.'

'Meaning?'

'What?' She squinted uncertainly at him.

'You said you've been making a habit of this. Maybe it's the fact that I've been living with someone who throws up on a regular basis, but is there something I should know?'

She looked up at him. There was no point in putting it off any longer. 'You'll probably find out eventually. I think I'm pregnant. No, actually, I know I'm pregnant. I haven't done a test yet, but all the signs are there. And before you insult me by asking – yes, you're the father,' she went on, as Richard started to interrupt. 'I know, I'm an idiot, I should have told you I wasn't on the pill. But we were a bit too carried away at the time, if you remember?' She could feel herself blushing. This wasn't quite the way she'd envisaged breaking the news, both of them hunched down on the gravel path among the ornamental roses.

She wished he'd say something. Anything to stop him staring at her like that. 'Ironic, isn't it?' She forced some lightness into her voice. 'But don't worry, I'm not like Kate. I won't be slapping a paternity suit on you and demanding maintenance. I've been in this situation before, I can cope.'

His stood up, towering over her. 'So I'm allowed to take responsibility for a child that isn't mine, but not for one who is, is that it?' His voice was harsh.

'No, I'm just saying it's my mistake and I'll take full responsibility.'

'A mistake? Is that how you see it?'

'Don't you?'

'No, I don't. But then I love you, and you obviously don't give a damn about me.'

'Of course I love you! Why do you think I'm here?' Tears filled her eyes and spilled down her cheeks. 'I'm sorry, I can't help getting emotional. I seem to do that a lot lately too.'

'You're not the only one.' As he crouched down and folded her into his arms, for once the smell of paint on his shirt didn't bother her in the slightest. 'Christ, you don't know how wretched I've been,' he muttered into her hair.

284

'When I found out that baby wasn't mine my first feeling was relief, because it meant we could be together. And then when I heard you tell Kate you didn't love me –'

'I only said it because I didn't want her to feel she'd got the upper hand.' She buried her face in the rough flannel fabric, feeling the hard warmth of his body underneath. 'I didn't know you were listening.'

'Thank God I was, or we'd still be in the same bloody mess now.' They held each other tightly. Jo felt as if she never wanted to let him go.

'What did Kate say when you confronted her?'

'Just what she'd threatened. I told her I was moving out and that if she wanted a man in her life she should talk to the baby's real father. At first she tried to say it could be mine, which we both knew wasn't really true. She's always been scrupulous about taking precautions. It was only with Marcus that she allowed herself to – how did you put it? – get carried away.' Jo groaned and hid her face further in his shirt. 'Then when she realised I wasn't buying her lies, she went ballistic. She said she wasn't leaving the flat and if I wanted to earn myself a few more juicy headlines by turning a pregnant woman out on the street, I was welcome to try.'

'The bitch! What did you say?'

'Nothing. I told her I didn't care where she lived, as long as I didn't have to share a roof with her. Then I packed my bags and walked out. I presume she must have gone straight to Charlie Beasley, because the next thing I knew were the headlines in this morning's paper.'

'Ah, so you've seen those, have you?' They looked round. Charlie himself was fighting his way through the overgrown rose bushes towards them, his shiny grey suit snagging on the thorns. 'Good, aren't they? Should shift a few copies.'

Jo felt Richard's muscles tense through his shirt. 'What the fuck are you doing here?'

'More to the point, what are you?' Charlie's eyes gleamed behind his spectacles. 'I had no idea you and Jo had such a close – working relationship. I don't suppose I could have a piccie for the paper?'

Richard looked down at her, and she saw the unspoken question in his eyes. She smiled and nodded. At least their news might knock Kate off the front page.

'I think we can do better than that,' he grinned at Charlie Beasley. 'How would your paper like a *Westfield* exclusive?'

Epilogue

'And . . . cut.'

Everyone on set relaxed. The sound man lowered his boom mike, and the chargehands moved in to gather up the cables as the cameramen moved into position for the next shot. Jo eased her bulk carefully out of her car seat. Pregnant women and Mini Travellers didn't go together. Neither did a thick 1960s angora coat and the hottest July day for thirty-odd years.

She smiled gratefully as a make-up girl descended with an ice-cold Diet Coke and a cool sponge for her hot, perspiring face. At least they were working outside. Aberthwaite, the picture-book village where *Heartland* was filmed, was looking particularly glorious today, with rampant roses, clematis and honeysuckle spilling around every cottage doorway. Across the square, the rest of the cast were already gathering for lunch outside the Fox and Rabbit. Trays laden with cold beer and the Fox's famous crusty sandwiches were emerging, as the actors mingled with the locals at the outside tables in the sunshine. Jo sighed longingly, wishing she could join them.

Working on *Heartland* couldn't have been more different to *Westfield*. She missed Viola, of course, but the cast and crew had made her feel really welcome. Everyone was friendly and professional, there were no petty jealousies, no monumental egos to avoid. And best of all, as this was the last episode of the current series, she had a lovely long holiday to look forward to.

Not that she'd have much time for relaxing, she thought ruefully, rubbing her bump. It was like sharing a stomach with a Thai kick boxer.

'Looks like you've got visitors.' The make-up girl nodded towards the other side of the square, where Chloe and Grace were running towards her. Richard was sauntering behind, looking relaxed and sexy in aviator sunglasses, black cords and a white t-shirt that showed off his newly acquired tan. He'd grown his hair slightly longer, which suited him.

'Not bunking off work again?' She squinted up at him teasingly.

'It seemed a shame to waste the day, especially with the girls being on school holidays. We thought we'd come and watch you work instead.' He lowered his shades so she could see the warm smoky grey of his eyes. 'We wondered if you fancied some lunch at the pub?'

'Please. You go over and order. I'll be with you when we've finished the next scene.'

Half an hour later they were sharing a plate of huge ham salad sandwiches under the overflowing hanging baskets. The air was fragrant with honeysuckle and old-fashioned roses. It was all sheer bliss.

'We've been shopping for the baby,' Grace announced excitedly.

'Again? It's not due for another three months and it's already spoilt rotten.'

'But you should see what we've got him. Some tiny little jeans from Baby Gap. They've got fly buttons and everything.'

'How very practical,' Jo said wryly. 'You're sure it's going to be a boy, then?'

'It'd better be.' Grace pulled a face. 'I don't want another sister.'

'Can we watch it being born?' Chloe asked. 'Matthew

288

Watson in my class saw his little brother being born and he said it was better than a horror film.'

'We'll see.' Jo pushed the plate away, her appetite suddenly lost. 'Why don't you two go and play on the swings if you've finished eating?' As they rushed off, she 'They'll be selling tickets to their mates next.'

'Maybe we could organise a photo shoot with *Goss* magazine?'

Jo grinned. 'That reminds me. Did you see that piece in *Hello!*?'

'The four-page spread on Lara Lamont's life after divorce, you mean?' Richard shook his head wryly. 'You've got to hand it to the girl, she never misses an opportunity. Photo or otherwise.'

Jo leaned back, enjoying the warm sun on her face. 'So what else is new on *Westfield*? Is Ma Stagg still in her coma?'

''Fraid so. Doesn't look like she's coming out, either. Not unless Eva Lawrence agrees to her new contract.'

'I still can't believe you did that,' Jo giggled. No one had ever stood up to Eva the Diva before.

'Neither can she. But unless she agrees to toe the line like everyone else I'm afraid we might have another *Westfield* funeral coming up.'

'They don't call you the Grim Reaper for nothing, do they?'

They sat in silence for a moment. Then Richard said, 'I saw Kate today.'

'Oh?' Jo's smile faded. 'How is she?'

'Hardly blooming. The baby's due in a few weeks and she's still chasing Marcus for money.'

Jo quelled the unworthy thought that Kate deserved everything she got – or didn't get, in the case of Marcus's maintenance payments. 'Hasn't she tracked him down yet?'

'No one's seen him since he walked out of *Westfield*. One thing we do know, he certainly hasn't run home to Daddy this time.'

'I still can't believe his father disinherited him like that.'

'I suppose even the loopy lord has his limits. He can't keep bailing him out.' Richard sipped his beer. 'Kate seems to think Marcus might be bumming his way round the States.'

Jo nibbled thoughtfully on a cucumber slice. 'That sounds like him. He's probably a rich woman's plaything over in Beverly Hills or something.'

'Leaving Kate to pick up the pieces,' Richard said. 'I know I shouldn't after what she did, but I can't help feeling sorry for her. That's why I agreed to let her stay on at the flat. I hope you don't mind?'

'Why should I?' Apart from the misery she'd briefly caused both of them, Jo had no reason to resent Kate. After all, she had everything she really wanted.

She gazed at Chloe, laughing and shrieking on the swings while Grace pushed her higher and higher, and smiled. She had Richard, and she had her family. Kate would never know that kind of happiness, because she didn't understand the value of it. 'I think she's been punished enough,' she said.

Charlie Beasley had seen to that. When Kate went to him with her story, she'd expected him to write about her as some kind of doomed romantic heroine, with Richard as the villain of the piece. Instead, Charlie had done a bit of digging and come up with the story of Kathy Gilbert, the wannabe word-processor operator from Doncaster who'd shed her past, acquired a fake finishing-school accent and a designer wardrobe, and reinvented herself as the daughter of a wealthy Sussex family. To have her past exposed so cruelly was just about the worst fate Kate could have suffered. Like Richard, Jo even managed to feel sorry for her.

'We're ready for your next scene, Miss Porter – sorry, Mrs Black.' The PA blushed at Richard. He had that effect on women, Jo realised. But strangely, he never seemed to notice.

She lumbered to her feet. Thanks heavens they'd managed to shoot around her massive bulk with clever camera angles.

She'd never had so many close-ups in her life. 'Well, I suppose I'd better be going. Are you going back to work later?'

He shook his head. 'As it was such a nice day I thought they could manage without me.'

'They're having to do that quite a lot lately, aren't they?'

'And they'll have to do it a lot more in a few months' time. Didn't you know I was a New Man?'

'I sort of liked the old one.'

He grinned. Marriage hadn't changed the way it made her heart skip.